The cloak fell back. I saw his face.

It was not a face I knew, and I had never seen its like before: but simply put, it was the most beautiful face I had ever seen, or hope to see again. Not beautiful as a man's face is, not like Raoul's with its faint scars, its blood running beneath the skin, but beautiful as a statue carved in stone, such as since I have seen, with thick curled hair, smooth marble skin, dark eyes that too seemed shaped of stone.

My first reaction was sheer panic. I felt my breath come in gasps, as if I had run a great distance. *Men will ride into your dreams*, the old woman had said. That was how he rode into mine, to be my bane...

Critical acclaim for Mary Lide's previous book, *Ann of Cambray*

GIFTS

OF THE QUEEN

MARY LIDE

WARNER BOOKS

A WARNER COMMUNICATIONS COMPANY

WARNER BOOKS EDITION

Artwork and map © 1985 by Fran Gazze Nimeck
Cover art by Max Ginsburg

Warner Books, Inc.
666 Fifth Avenue
New York, N.Y. 10103

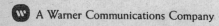 A Warner Communications Company

Printed in the United States of America

First Printing: October, 1985

10 9 8 7 6 5 4 3 2 1

To My Dearest Aunt, Ruth Lomer.
In her house I spent a happy childhood;
In her house I wrote this book.

Acknowledgments

As a background to *Gifts of the Queen* I used contemporary chronicles wherever possible, although not many exist for the early years of Henry II's reign. The following writers were useful: Roger of Howden, Walter Map, William of Newburgh, Robert of Torigny and Gerald of Wales. Recommended books on general history of the period include: *From Doomsday Book to Magna Carta* by A.L. Poole and *Henry II* by W.L. Warren. Specialized books which were useful were *A History of Wales* by J.E. Lloyd, *Norman Castles in Britain* by D.F. Renn, and *The English Medieval House* by Margaret Wood. I would also like to suggest reading contemporary poets; two useful anthologies were *Lyrics of the Middle Ages* by Hubert Greekmore and *The Earliest Welsh Poetry* by Joseph P. Clancy.

I should also like to take this opportunity to thank my family for their tolerance, my neighbors, Nonie Gorey and Lee Tyree for their support and my many friends for their encouragement. In particular my thanks go to Linda Martz for her help, to Francesca Moorse for her journey with me to Poitiers, to the Corfmat family for their hospitality at Fontevrault, and to Carmella and Peter Harris without whose kindness in Cornwall this book might never have been finished. Finally, my gratitude to Elise Goodman, my agent, and Fredda Isaacson, Vice President of Warner Books, whose advice and help have been invaluable.

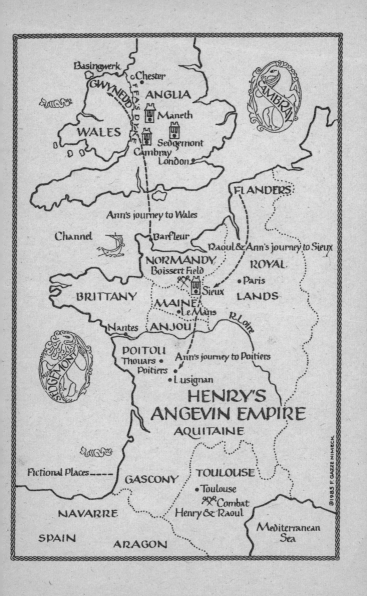

GIFTS OF THE QUEEN

PROLOGUE

URIEN OF WALES, BARD TO THE Celts, high poet of the old people, record these things. Out of long silence do I write them, not in my own tongue but in priestly fashion of the Norman courts, that men who came hereafter should read and remember. It is for the Lady Ann of Cambray I speak, wife now to Lord Raoul, Earl of Sedgemont, Count of Sieux in France. At her bidding I write. And although there will be many who question my right to act as scribe, I would have them know that I have heard of the Lady Ann and her kin since childhood, that, like her, I was born at Cambray, and like her, of Norman father and Celtic dam, and that, of all men else, she chose me to speak for her.

I was a child, half-grown, when first I saw her and her husband, Lord Raoul, who was so great a lord. And the story of her upbringing here at Cambray and then at Sedgemont where she was ward to that Raoul—it is known to every child. But how she was wed to him who was overlord, and how they left Cambray and Sedgemont far behind and withdrew to France, I was grown before I heard tell of that.

"I was happy at last," she used to say, "whom happiness before had passed by. Can it not suffice that I had long waited for Lord Raoul, hoped that he would wed me, had feared for his life and safety in those bitter wars that tore our island kingdom when I was young. But nothing is that constant is. As we grow older, it seems to me the circle of events grows larger, ripples from a stone thrown in a mountain lake. In ever widening arcs do they stretch out, beyond our sight, out of our past into a future we cannot guess at; as Lord Raoul of

Sedgement once said, 'Anything that the great do has effect upon everyone.' I would amend his words. I believe that there is nothing done that does not have effect at last, that does not come back upon some distant shore. Happiness, like sorrow, must happen."

And so it is, that I, who am poet, high bard to the Celtic folk, write, that what they were and what was done should be known. It is a story of love, hate, loyalty, ambition, and conspiracy, that many-tangled snare which traps all men. And a story, too, of revenge, a two-edged sword whose blade cuts both him who deals the blow and him who bears it. We are come to the year of Christendom, 1155. At the Yuletide season before, Stephen, who was King of England died, and in his place was the young Henry the Angevin, who was known as Henry of Anjou, crowned King, second of that name and his wife, Eleanor of Aquitaine, made Queen. In the early spring of that year came Lord Raoul to Henry's court, to claim his land and titles and his bride. Within the month were they wed and gone from England to France to Lord Raoul's estates there, to find what happiness held for them.

Ora pro nobis.

1

THUS FROM THE LADY ANN:
Long ago, when I was a child and lived still at
Cambray, I used to come up on the moors with my
father's men when they went hunting. The lands
around the castle at Cambray were full of game, and sometimes
when the guards had time to spare, or were in a good mood,
perhaps because they had eaten or drunk well the day before,
or had found a woman to please them at night, I could coax
them into taking me with them when they rode out. They
always gave some excuse for these expeditions: that they should
exercise the horses, those great gray stallions of my father's
herd, or that they should patrol the border for some Celtic
band trying to slip across unseen; but mainly I knew the younger
men often humored me out of kindness because I was a lonely
child with no playmates of my own age, no mother to care for
me, and my father and brother were often gone from home
about border affairs. As a child, I did not miss such company,
having never known it, and the young knights made up the
lack. They were a cheerful group of men, short and sturdy
built as I remember them, plain spoken, rough-tongued yet
good-hearted. They wore plain armor, too, and carried weapons that were old when they inherited them; all about them
was plain and serviceable, such as more fancy men might scoff
at. The only things of worth they had were the gray horses of
Cambray and they were famous in my father's time. I had a
small moorland pony of my own, so nimble footed that when
it reached a stone outcrop or tree stump a larger horse could
clear, it would scramble over like a cat. Not that there were
many trees upon the moors, a wild open countryside it is,

covered with heather and gorse patches, and granite boulders
that jut in jagged clusters on the crest of rolling hills.

We had been coursing mainly for hares that day and had
ridden far inland, where the foothills begin to rise, ever sloping
upward to the north where the high mountains lie. We had
come to the end of our sport, and I had been amusing myself
with setting my pony at the gorse bushes still in flower or
leaping the boulders that cropped out of the coarse grass. The
men rode more sedately behind, talking of the wars, the civil
wars that had beset the land, although we here at Cambray
had as yet scant news of them. Suddenly, without warning,
the mists came as they are often wont upon the higher lands,
the sudden sea mists that roll inland in waves so that within
moments, you cannot see your hand before your face. We are
used to such mists at Cambray, which sits above the sea cliffs,
but that day, they were thicker than usual and we were far from
home. I wiped my long hair, which had twisted and curled
with the damp into a mass of red snarls, pulled a woolen cloak
from my saddlebow, and settled down to a slow wet ride back.
I rode astride like a boy, with skirts hitched about my knees
and sleeves cut off short like a tunic so I now felt the cold.
The men shouted to each other in their soft border voices for
fear we should be separated. It is easy to lose your way in a
fog, and you must keep close watch where you are. The paths
are not marked, and run faintly through the moors at the best
of times, and if you stray, there are patches of hill marsh and
bog, deep enough to swallow horse and rider both. We moved
forward slowly in a line, I in the middle with someone to watch
me on either side. I could hear the creak of saddle, the scrape
of spurs, and from time to time sense rather than see the
shadowy forms of men and beasts. One of the men was whistling through his teeth, and occasionally a horse tossed its head
with a rattle of bit and bridle chain. Suddenly, the captain of
the guard who rode ahead reined back his horse so violently
that those behind rammed into him.

"Jesu," he whispered, and I saw him cross himself. The other
men peered past him in the mist, I saw another make the sign

of horns with which to ward off evil and all of them crowded close together as if taking comfort in one another. I nudged my pony past them, for they had knotted in a mass, their horses snorting and stamping with fright, not yet stampeded but on the verge of it. Ducking under the captain's outstretched hand, for on my pony's back I came barely to his waist, I pushed to the front. I knew at once where we were. High on the moors above Cambray, the highest place in all that southern part, there is a spot which all men shun. Even in bright daylight, I would have avoided it myself. It is a large mound of earth or "barrow" as we call it in the Celtic tongue, thrown up by men centuries long gone. A circle of gray stones sags there, once set upright, now leaning this way and that, but still a circle clearly marked. What manner of men had put it there or for what purpose I cannot tell. The priest at Cambray claimed they were evil men who used the stones for purpose vile, but I do not know. In truth though, the place had a taint of evil, as water has a taint or taste, so that even horses would not graze within the circle, and the very sheep and goats avoided it.

The mist had blown clear somewhat in this high place, and wisps floated and ebbed about the crooked stones. Against one of these, a figure knelt or leaned perhaps, so wrapped up it was hard to tell; but I felt a rush, I cannot say of fear, but of some emotion else that at once made my blood run chill, yet set the hair at the nape of my neck starting up.

"Turn away, turn away," the captain of the guard mouthed at me. He was usually a cheerful man with a joke for everyone, taller than the rest and broad-shouldered, my favorite when my brother was gone. I thought him the bravest man I knew, yet his face had paled with fear. He made vague gestures to haul me back yet did not dare come closer to the stones. The figure stirred and raised her head, the many wraps and shawls fell wide, and I saw her face. I do not remember if she were young or old, or what she was, it was her eyes that held my gaze. Deep, dark they were, dark-lashed, and full of strange things. Behind me now I heard the men hiss for dread, and again the captain tried to spur his horse between me and the stones. It would not budge and reared, almost falling back upon itself.

"Nay, come you on, little mistress," the woman said, and her voice, although soft, was clear and strong. She stretched out her hand, and I saw her arms were shapely and white as a young woman's might have been. But her hair was gray and blew in long strands across her face.

I was ever forward as a child. Being left so much on my own had given me a sort of assurance, outspokenness if you will, that well-reared maidens would not dare to show. Ignoring the whispers and the cries, I heeled my pony toward her. It says something for the little creature's courage too that I could hold him to my will, for I felt him tremble with the strain and his head hung low.

"Now, mistress," she said, when I approached her, "you do not fear me?"

"I am not afraid," I told her stoutly, lied, "not with six men of my father's guard to back me."

She nodded her head to where they milled about the gap in the stones. "Not one, I think," she said, "would have the heart to pull a sword in this place." And I thought she smiled. Then she rose up and stood by my horse's side. I felt him tremble again as she stroked his rough mane, then presently grow still as her white hand smoothed and smoothed between his ears and down his soft flanks.

"And so, Ann of Cambray," she said to me, "you have been hunting on the moors. What is it that you hunt so freely without asking leave of me?"

"It is my father's land," I said, "but I will show you all the same."

"And before your Norman father, Falk," she said, "who owned the land then?" She took the little hunting pouch that I had tied in proper fashion behind on the saddle and pulled open the strings. Inside were two hares that I had brought down with my sling, and a bird, a partridge, that had flown up from the heather beneath our feet. She smoothed its ruffled feathers with her long slender fingers, and as I watched, I thought I had never seen fingers so long, so smooth, nor yet feathers so clearly mottled, green and brown. And as each feather fell back into place, I felt a comfort steal over me, a sense of ease, as if I had known her for a long time.

"Who are you?" I asked her then, curious and excited at once, as if at something I knew but could not place. "Are you one of the Saxon vagabonds?" (For so I had heard my father name those who, since the Normans had taken their lands, roamed homeless, finding shelter where they could.)

"Do I look like a Saxon?" she said. "Or still more a vagabond? This is my home, before ever Saxon or Norman came ravaging." She moved slightly as she spoke and beneath her outer wraps, I caught the glimpse of some fine silk, dark and glittering, like the sky on a cloudy night when the ragged storm clouds part and let moonlight through. And it came to me that, although at first she had spoken in the Norman-French we all use now, her last words were in Celt, the language that I spoke in preference to any other tongue.

"Then you are Celt," I said. "Are you one of their wise women, a Celtic witch, to tell the future from the past?"

"One day, Ann of Cambray," she said, "men will put that name on you, call you witch. Tell me then if you like to be so called. But if I am Celt, then we are kin. Your mother was Efa, high lady of that race, who died when you were born. As to the future, is it not made out of the past, out of the present now, that all men could foretell it if they would? But you have used that word 'future,' not I. If you would know what it is, what will you give me to tell it you?"

"It takes no wisdom," I said in my blunt way, "to know who I am. With me are the men of my father, Lord Falk; and for all your claims, this is his land, and he is a Norman lord to own it. As for what I have been doing, why I have just shown what I have hunted. And tonight, no doubt that is what we will eat."

She almost smiled once more.

"You speak as freely as a boy," she said. "Ann of Cambray you will rue your tongue one day. But you also speak as a child.

A long life lies ahead of you. Many and many are the paths and byways you must pick and choose. Are you not curious to know where they lead or what the end may hold for you?"

Put like that, her questions intrigued me. Nor did I like to be called a child, thinking myself already old enough to know my own mind.

"What else can you tell me?" I bargained.

"What will you give me?" she countered. "Something to tempt the brightness forth."

I leaned forward on the saddle prow, crossed my arms as I had seen my father do and considered her. There was a power in those large dark eyes, a look on that white oval face framed in gray hair, that fascinated me.

"I have a cross of gold," I said at last, "hung on a thick chain of gold. My godparent gave it me upon my birth..."

She made a sign of disagreement when I spoke of the cross, but nodded at mention of the chain.

"Although your birth was a sad one," she said, "yet give me now the chain, that something good will come from it."

I almost laughed back at her. Anyone would know that such a gift was not for everyday wear.

"It is locked in a chest at Cambray," I told her, "but I will get the key and bring it you tomorrow if you will tell me where."

"No, no," she said, her voice sunk low again, "tomorrow will be too late."

She stayed motionless so long that I thought she had forgotten me. Then, at last, she moved more abruptly than before, startling the little horse which had almost fallen asleep where he stood.

"So be it," she said. "But I will tell you what I can. A long life will you have, Ann of Cambray, but not a safe one. Far from us and far again, over the distant sea shall you go. But however far you wander, you will come back to Cambray at last and do us a service greater than you know." Again, she was silent.

"That is not so much," I said to hide my discomfort, for her words made strange impression upon me, although I might not then have understood all they hinted at, "to be worth a golden chain. Even the peddlers in the village tell more than that."

"What do they tell?" she asked, quick to test my lie.

I flushed a little, for in truth, I had never spoken to them, only heard the castle servants talk.

"Well," I said hesitatingly, "who to wed, what he will be like, if he will be a great lord."

"Aye," she said almost absentmindedly, "a great lord indeed. High above you shall you look for a husband. But landless, landless, he shall before you wed."

"And will he love me?" I said, not liking the sound of landless, which was disgrace, remembering other things the castle wenches spoke of carelessly before me, so that I gleaned parts of it, "will he love me true?"

"Love," she said. "If you will speak of love, why then, many men will you have in your life to ride into your dreams. Some will love you, some will desire you, and some will use love to do you harm. And one you will love but fear he does not love you. And because of the hatred of three men you shall do us a service so great, we shall throw off the Norman yoke. But what follows after will not depend on you."

Her list of—prophecies, I suppose I should now call them, daunted me. I would not let her know it. I threw back my head and squared my shoulders under the woolen cloak. The mist had condensed upon it in great drops, even the reins were black and slippery with wet and the rain had beaded upon her hair.

"And is there no more than this?" I asked, although my voice trembled despite myself.

"Only this," she said, and for the first time, there was anger, cold and stern, in her voice. "Death and grief are within your power. Use your hold on them carefully. Beware the malice of womenfolk."

"And is there no hope anywhere?" I cried, afraid of something I could not see, but glimpsed at darkly, far-off.

She said, "Men will lay down their lives for you. Be comforted. They will do so willingly. Trust the impulse of your own heart. And one day, you shall come safely home."

The men at the entrance to the stone cried out, or perhaps now I was suddenly able to hear them.

"Come back, Lady Ann, come back," I heard their captain shout.

"That one," she said and she pointed to him on his gray horse. "Come back, he says. Long will he wish it for himself."

"And shall I bring you the golden chain?" I said, nudging my pony away from her, for the coldness in her voice was like ice. "Tomorrow, if you will tell me where."

"No," she said, "you will not bring it to me although one day I shall claim it. But not tomorrow nor tomorrow's morrow will you come up here again."

The captain had forced his horse through the gap at last, and lashing it, reached over the side to grasp my bridle with his other hand. With whip and spur, he forced the frightened beast, almost dragging me underfoot.

"This is no place for you," he cried, his Norman voice a trumpet blast. "Away from this ring of death."

"It is you who have spoken the word," she said, standing up very tall. "And on your lips is death recorded, not on mine."

As she spoke, the animals stopped their struggle, turned meekly to one side. We jostled through the gap in the stones; the other men, as if freed from whatever had held them there, swung round, roweling their horses down the narrow path, moving into a gallop on the level ground.

I shouted the words, "Tomorrow then?" over my shoulder, but the mist had come down, the circle of stones was hidden, everything blurred and faded away.

We came to the open fields, the village beneath the castle walls, in a thunder of hooves, fear driving at our heels. Well, she spoke the truth in this. I never went up there the next day. On the morrow's morning was my brother dead, murdered, if the correct name be given; and within two days my father, Falk of Cambray, had followed him; of grief and loss he died.

I left Cambray of sea and moors and came to the castle of Sedgemont, as ward to my overlord, Lord Raoul, who but a boy himself, had recently inherited those lands from his grandfather. The handsome captain of the guard was lost in one of those many battles far away and never ever came back to Cambray. And many weary years passed until I returned.

And it was true that since that meeting my life had not been an easy one. My brother and father had died, even my castle of Cambray had been lost when a Celtic force had taken it, and other enemies had coveted it too and tried to kill me for my little lands. And true it was that many men had died for me. That they did so willingly had not made their deaths easier for me to bear. And although I had never thought to marry with an earl, Lord Raoul was indeed a great lord, lord of many lands and titles when I knew him first, but landless when finally we were wed, a month ago at the English court. For after my father's death, those wars, those civil wars I have spoken of, had fallen on us in all their fury. Not one part of England had been free of them, not my lands at Cambray, nor Raoul's at Sedgemont. And Raoul, who had sworn to support one claimant to the throne, who had fought loyally to the end for King Stephen, not even Raoul had escaped the enmity of that other claimant, Henry of Anjou, who on Stephen's death, had at last gained his heart's desire and been crowned king himself.

What put it in my mind this last day of our journey south, the thirty-eighth day (I know, I had kept count, scratching each morning a fresh mark on the saddle flap), what made me think now of the lady of the moors? More than ten years had passed since she had appeared to me, and I had hidden memory of her as a dream is hidden, so deeply buried I had never thought of her again, as if grief and death had supplanted her. And yet I had never forgotten her either, and on remembering I must remember the occasion complete, the cold wind, the smell of peat, the chink of bridle chain, the rivulets of mist. Who knows what God puts into our minds to make us recall this thing, then that. We are but part of a vast plan whose beginning and end are never known. I can tell you only that

now we were riding along the river's bank toward Sieux and
all the mist of the spring evening curled about our horses' feet.
We splashed through the reed beds, startling flocks of geese
and ducks that broke away across the wide expanse of open
water where the river had widened into a lake. A month or
more had we been already on our journey here, a long hard
month since we had set sail from the little southern English
port and crossed the sea and come to France, more than a
month since I had been wed at the court of this new English
king, Henry, second of his name. More than a month since
my new husband, Lord Raoul, Earl of Sedgemont, Count of
Sieux, had brought me here to France, to his own lands now
restored to him.

I looked ahead of me where Lord Raoul rode. Only a few
knights accompanied us, on this our last day's journey south
to Sieux. From time to time, Raoul turned painfully, for riding
was not easy for him these days, and looked back where I, my
two squires, and a rear guard rode in single file. He was simply
dressed, this great lord, no sign of rank, a leather jerkin, no
rich rings, no golden chains, no furs. His hair, silver-gold,
grown longer on our journey here, tossed freely in the wind.
And his right arm, sword arm, wounded arm, was still strapped
tightly to his side. But when he smiled as he now did, his eyes
of Norman gray turned blue-green like the sea, and the laugh
lines fanned out. God knows that he was tired and thin, but
he did not look so fine-drawn, if I can use that expression for
a man so full of energy, as on his wedding day when he had
outfaced King Henry in his court. You would not know, on
looking at him today, what cruel wrongs had been done to
him.

For Henry hated Raoul, a hatred that went back even to
their forefathers' time, a hatred so strong that even before
Henry had been crowned king, he had seized Raoul's lands in
France and occupied that castle of Sieux, toward which we
now were riding. Worse, on succeeding to the throne, Henry
had seized Raoul's English lands as well, had openly proclaimed
Raoul an outlaw, and had named him a traitor whose lands and

titles and life were forfeit. The story of that time has been already told. Wounded in a last great fight with one of Henry's men, Raoul had been rescued and hidden by the Sedgemont guard who, for love of their overlord, went willing into exile with him. These same men rode with us today. Well did they deserve to rest this night. And the story too has been told how I, as Lord Raoul's ward, had come to London to find the king and plead with him for Raoul's life, and how, alone, friendless, I had been befriended by Queen Eleanor. She it was who in the end had persuaded Henry to pardon Raoul and his men, give them the kiss of peace, and restore to Raoul his lands and titles, all that had been lost.

Perhaps it was the mists that reminded me, the mists that curled and eddied with each step, or perhaps the creaking of the saddles or the clink of armor as a man turned to talk or laugh, or the jingle of a bridle piece when a horse tossed its head. Or was it the way our shadows loomed and wavered, sometimes large and distorted, against the wall of fog? Or was it simply my listening to one of my squires, Walter the elder, who loved a tune, and was whistling one between his teeth, a song learned of a kitchen wench the night before? Or perhaps the glint and shimmer of the water where the lake opened up between the matted reeds reminded me of the sheen of the lady's gown beneath her rags. I do not know, but will tell you only this: back the memory came, fresh as yesterday, and her words chimed like bells within my head. And all that had happened since my meeting her echoed and echoed in my mind. I thought as I had thought often this past month, What is done is done. God have it so, that all bitterness be finished and enmity and death. And that we come home safe to Sieux.

But perhaps it was none of these things, only the day itself, unlike any of those other days, a month of them drowned in rain and cold, which, since the start of our journey here, seemed to have dogged us with storms, as if even the weather wished us ill. Today, despite the wet, there had been a feeling in the air, an excitement so intense as almost to give substance to mood, to things intangible, to sounds, waking me from an

uneasy sleep. For often now I had the same dream, except it
was no dream; it was the true past relived. We were still in
Henry's court, and Henry had pardoned Raoul. *Take your lands
and titles back*, Henry had said. *I grant you the title of Earl as in your
grandfather's time. I restore to you willingly your lands and castle at
Sieux—if you take Ann of Cambray as wife*. I still heard Henry's
laugh; I still saw the open hot looks he cast at me, the hope,
perhaps, to bed me first himself. I still felt his tinge of scorn,
to make me a jest, a pawn, for a king to play with. But more
than that, I still felt the scorn he put on Raoul. Henry could
not have made his jest more plain. "If you would have your
lands back, Raoul," he should have said, and sometimes in my
dreams he did, "marry beneath you, you who could marry
where you choose, marry Ann. At my command."

It was an order no man of pride or rank could or would
obey. But Raoul had. Sometimes I had wondered what would
have happened had Raoul refused, Raoul, who when I first
knew him, was already betrothed to a French lady of high
degree. That Isobelle de Boissert, as she was called, had been
heiress of many lands. Why would Earl Raoul marry with Ann
of Cambray, whose small castle at the end of the Norman world
had no value, was already part of Raoul's own estates, and he
already my overlord? But there was one other reason for Raoul
to marry me, one Henry did not know, and that, too, a cause
to make me start awake. Had Henry known, he would have
rather kept us apart and revelled in a greater jest. What he did
not know was this (although the Queen who had helped me
did): that Raoul had already bedded me, and I was already
with child, conceived when Raoul left me, as he thought, to
go to his death. This then was another reason for our haste,
why since our coming to France we had avoided any place
where Henry might have news of us, and why in the dark I
relived again and again our wedding night when Raoul had lain
with his unsheathed sword in his hand. And why in nightmares,
I heard Henry and his men break into our room, to prove for
themselves that I was no maid, and this my new husband had
already lain with me and given me a child. So, when at today's

dawn I started awake, you know what I thought. But it was only the noise of Lord Raoul's black stallion that had wakened me. We had spent last night in a simple country hostelry, less villanous than most although that does not praise it highly, no doubt a haven for local travelers, although it had neither beds nor space for us. We were but a small group even so, a score of mounted men whom my lord had brought from his lands in England, from Sedgemont, half as many again of foot, a baggage train, and my womenfolk, whom I willingly would have abandoned after the first day. This morning, hearing the sounds below the granary where we had been lodged, these selfsame ladies, in various state of undress, had fluttered to the openings in the mud walls, hung with sacking still straw filled which gave at least some protection from the bitter wind.

The day was damp and dreary, as I have said; spring had not come to us as I thought it must have come to all parts else. The rains which had followed us from the coast still dripped and blew about the roof thatch and gathered in black puddles in the cobbled yard. The knights of Lord Raoul's retinue were mounting up for the day's ride. They had slept no doubt even worse than we, with saddles for pillows and their cloaks for beds, but I never heard them complain. They were old friends, had served Lord Raoul long and faithfully; discomforts were but pinpricks for them. I noted at once how today they rode their battle horses, their destriers, which normally their squires led at their right side, with gear slung at the saddle pommel ready at hand for instant use. Today they wore their chainmail coats, had had them burnished with care, and over them flung the surcoats of red and gold which they wore usually to mark them as men of Sedgemont and which they had kept hidden on our march south. Already some were in the saddle, others were still buckling on their sword belts while squires knelt to strap on their spurs. Lord Raoul's horse, a great huge beast, famed for its strength and its temper both, had taken fright at something or dislike of one of the stableboys. Or perhaps it too scented excitement in the air, for it had already kicked its way through part of a stable wall, a flimsy partition of plaster and wattle. Now with a toss of its head, it sent the Sedgemont grooms tumbling among the mud and straw. Across the crowded yard it plunged, a broken strap dangling dangerously between its hooves. Those knights already mounted fought their own horses to keep them under control, those men on foot dived for cover as best they could. The black horse, enjoying freedom, reared, and flayed with its forefeet, shaking its head with all teeth bared. Then down it jarred, crashing against the bales of straw that were piled beside the courtyard gate. My ladies screamed, their hands before their mouths, and whispered excitedly to one another as they let the men below see them in their shifts. Not that there was time to enjoy their charms so displayed, the men were more intent to escape those deadly hooves. The stableboys shouted at each other in their strange harsh French, the landlord wrung his hands and cursed, the Sedgemont grooms, picking themselves up gingerly, began to move toward the gate to bar escape.

Into this confusion strode Lord Raoul. He was dressed for riding as were his guard, but was not able to wear his mail coat yet. Brushing between his men, he came forward, my young Lord, who once had been as quick as a cat, moving more slowly today, his squire behind, tugging at his good arm in vain to make him stop. In the center of the yard, Raoul and his horse came face-to-face. The horse was not yet saddled and now I could see clearly the strap that dragged between its feet. I knew Lord Raoul could not use his right arm, I knew his broken shoulder blade was hardly knit, I knew his right side was still unhealed, and yet, although he scarce could mount a saddled horse on his own, he would ride this one unsaddled. I left my womenfolk to their screams, threw a woolen cloak about my shoulders, ran to the wooden steps outside and barefooted came down into the yard.

He still faced his horse, left hand on hip, until the horse slowly backed into the position he was hoping for, against the fallen bales of straw where he would have leverage when he needed it. Suddenly he bent and grasped at the broken strap between forefeet which I had once seen tear a man to shreds.

Then, with one laborious movement, he pulled at the horse's head, until it faced away from the mass of men framed in the gateway. The bales of straw served him as a mounting block; he clambered up, each step a strain upon his ribs, and with greater effort, flung himself upon the horse's back. I had seen him before leap into a saddle with all his armor on, not needing rein nor stirrup iron. This move was clumsy, so unlike his usual self that I felt my heart contract—I cannot use the words "with pity" (that would be an expression he would have spat back) but "with pride," perhaps—that for pride he drove himself. The abrupt movement startled the horse again; it plunged and reared and thrashed away. But Raoul hung on, his left arm wrapped about the horse's neck, hand knotted in its mane, and slowly began to gather up the broken straps to bring pressure on the curbed bit. Back and forth they fought, the horse's sides lathered, gouts of foam flying from its mouth. Raoul still clung with hand and knee, until at last the horse obeyed him once more, and its rage died out. It hung its head quiet as a lamb. There was a gasp of breath expelled; the women's wailing died upon a sigh.

Raoul's squires ran to take the reins; he let himself slide over the horse's back, limped to a bale of straw and leaned upon it, struggling for breath. I longed to go to him but did not dare, and waited instead by the wooden steps, my feet curling against the cold. His men would tend him if he needed help. Never since our wedding day had he let me tend to his wounds, although I knew of salves and potions that make flesh heal quickly and help bones knit. I think now he thought to spare me the sight of those scars, perhaps he even feared they might sicken me, yet they were wounds nobly borne, and nobly had he endured them for my sake, too. But seldom had I chance to see him at all these days; since our marriage we had tarried nowhere long, and since we had come to France, as I have explained, each day at dawn, with his men, he led the way and kept guard, with patrols to scout for danger on all sides. I, my squires and the foot soldiers, traveled more slowly in company with the womenfolk and baggage carts. And at night, so weary he could scarce stand, he slept where he could, not even taking time to unpack or use the gear we brought with us. But today, the dawning was long past. Perhaps today he would ride with us.

When his breathing had slackened, and his squires had left him, I approached cautiously. A new wife, I thought, must learn her husband's ways. I did not want to intrude. He turned his head slowly as I came up.

"Good morrow indeed, Lady Ann," he croaked, "to have you run barefooted in the rain to greet your wedded lord. Judas, I shall think you dote on me to hang about my neck half-clothed."

He had spotted that beneath the cloak, I, too, was dressed only in my shift. He spoke softly enough, but I blushed. He smiled then, the strange smile he had, part rueful, as if he mocked at himself; but ever since we had first met, his teasing voice had put me on my guard.

"I thought you'd stay up there and scream." He jerked his head to the room above where my ladies still lingered and called down wantonly to the men below.

"God's wounds," I said, the oath slipping out before I could give it mind, "I'd as sooner bed with a herd of swine."

He laughed then, an infectious laugh that made you want to laugh with him. Someone had brought him water for washing, but I noted how his shirt was still stained red. His hair was curled about his neck with heat and sweat, and his efforts had left him pale; but even then, I sensed the ripple of expectation running beneath the surface. And when he turned his head again to speak to me, I saw the thin scar that cut across one high cheekbone, a reminder of a coward's blow he had taken for my sake.

I replied carefully, for his quick looks, his mocking voice, had always made me ill at ease. I was still not comfortable, you see, with his teasing ways, although I should have been; he had used them with good effect since I had first known him. "We sleep," I said, "as best we can . . ."

He pounced upon those prim words.

"As best we can," he repeated them. "Why, Lady, you must tell me what that is. For a soldier, one piece of ground seems like the rest. And I think I saw more of my wife when I had to woo her into bed. Since now you are here, climb up, unless you think to freeze your bare feet in the ground."

He patted the straw beside him, and when, with an effort, he had helped me clamber up, he wrapped the cloak ends about me.

"You are a great lady now," he mocked at me, for, in truth, I had not stopped to think how it would look to run abroad half-naked in the rain, "with cares upon your mind, your household cares, your womenfolk..."

I bit my tongue. It does not suit a wedded wife to berate her husband openly for flaws in his arrangement for her comfort. But he had chosen these ladies to tend me, or rather bade me which ones I should choose, as was fitting to his position, from among the many who came clamoring about us at King Henry's court. He must be responsible for naming them, but I would have liked to tell him how I disliked them.

I said, in a stiff way I had adopted to make me seem more suited to my new rank, "I trust they are on their knees by now, giving thanks to God that you are not trampled underfoot. As do I."

He had ignored the words, concentrated rather on my way of speaking them. He had ever been quick to catch hypocrisy.

"Now, by the Mass," said he, "that is a fair speech, as fair as any courtier at Henry's court. Well said indeed. Is that how your honey tongue sweetened Henry's plan for me and persuaded him to give you as my bride? Henry had not a wedding in mind before I came to London. Was it your Celtic charms, your long red hair, or your smile, which you have yet to show me today, that made him decide to give me the fairest maid in the land? Was that why the queen loaded our baggage train with gifts for you, so my men and I must lug them along?"

As he spoke, his left arm was already stealing about my waist, under cover of the cloak. It embarrassed me that here, with all eyes watching us, he should show such familiarities.

And yet, too, I thought how his men had named him long ago—Two-Handed Raoul, not only because he could fight with left hand as well as right, but also because he could hold a woman in either arm. He had wed me, it was true, because King Henry had bade him to, and for that other reason still hid from the world. But I did not like to hear him jest of these things, and I had hid my pregnancy for so long for fear of Henry's rage that I could not even now bring myself easily to speak of it. When I did not answer, he shrugged, a habitual gesture that must have caused him pain.

"Come, come, your answers used to give me better sport," was all he said. "Do not pretend to have turned prude like those maids of yours. If maids they be, which I doubt, being Norman ladies at a king's court. What shall I do to make you smile? What if I tell you that we are close to Sieux?"

I caught my breath. Here then was the explanation for the excitement I had sensed. Perhaps he took my silence for concern. Although I had tried never to let word of distress fall in his hearing, yet in truth this month had not been easy for me.

He fumbled with his left hand beneath his tunic and pulled out a roll of parchment which he spread between us on the straw. It was some kind of chart. I had never seen its like, with thin blue lines for rivers, green for forests, small rounded hills whose names were written in fine cramped letters of red. I cannot read, but he could show me where our journey led.

"Past these hills, marked so, along the river where it widens into a lake, then round the cliff point. Here stand the towers of Sieux." He marked the spot with his nail, midway down the page.

My first thought was that the chart looked so small, my whole hand could cover it. He may have sensed what I thought, for he put his hand over mine and, for a moment, I felt the roughness of his palm, the long strong fingers that could be gentle when he wished. The strength of that left hand was warm and comforting.

"Not so small," he said, and his eyes were gray, his head close to my own, "that this does not show all the kingdom of

France. Here be the lands of the French king, Louis himself, which we have skirted round, and here are those of King Henry of England, his lands in Normandy, Anjou and Maine, which he inherited when his father died. And here is Aquitaine which he acquired when he married with its duchess, Eleanor, who now is England's queen. And here is Sieux set betwixt and between. A gateway are we, like that gate behind my back, to let men through from north or south."

But I scarce heard his words, looked where his thumbnail rested. Suddenly, it was only Sieux that looked small, a nail's breadth, surrounded on all sides by enemies.

He must have sensed my shudder of dismay.

"No danger now," he said. "They would have attacked before this. They will not dare march against me on my own lands within sight and sound of my own castle guard at Sieux. But a few more days and our journey will be done. Unless," he was rolling up the parchment as he spoke, "unless you think to ride on alone with me and some of my men. Without the burden of the slower foot soldiers, the baggage carts, and your womenfolk, we could reach Sieux tonight. You would not miss your womenfolk this once? God's wounds, they wail like waterspouts upon the hour, with every day a fresh downpour." He smiled again. "I cannot say a bath would come amiss, nor yet a dry bed, nor yet a wife to share it with."

He rubbed his sound hand across his face. He usually wore no beard, but water and time for shaving had become luxuries. His jerkin and woolen cloak, like mine, were mud-stained and travel-worn. But when he smiled, a glint shone beneath the weariness.

I said with some asperity, to hide the thoughts that leapt in me, "I am used, as you know, to care for myself. I have no need of women servants."

"I know well," he said with a grin, "how you manage on your own. But you will not mind?"

His second asking unnerved me. I was not yet used to such courtesies. It was not until he repeated it a third time that I understood what prompted his concern.

"We shall ride over rough paths. You will promise me," and again his hand was back about my waist, "that you will not come to harm. I would not have your son dropped untimely on his head. But one day more and you shall come safely home."

His arm had tightened about my waist. It was not so thick yet, nor so slender as he would have remembered it. I stiffened at his words and against my will, the blushes flared. I did not want that knowledge aired abroad, certainly not to my ladies for their gossiping. Besides I could have laughed at him. He should know the child was not due yet.

When I did not answer, he shrugged in his way, bid his pages spread a path of straw for me to walk on, and turned to his men to give command: this one was to ride with him, this one to stay, the baggage carts, those cumbersome, great wooden carts that bogged to their axles in mud at every turn, were to go another route, longer but easier. I left him bareheaded in the drizzle and hurried up the stairs to the hostile little room. My ladies were in sour mood, nothing new for them, and their spokeswoman, Mistress Alyse de Vergay, to give her full name as she preferred, an older, ill-satisfied woman, ill-favored, ill-tongued, was already advancing. Flaxen plaits a-swing, mouth screwed up tight, her beringed fingers were outstretched to tick off grievances as she numbered them.

"Last night," she said, as she had said each day; I scurried into my clothes by myself, knowing her words by heart, grateful for distraction which would prevent her helping me. "Last night we slept on straw flea-ridden."

She rolled up her silk sleeve to show me the marks on her plump white skin. "And made do with stale bread and mutton, rank enough for villein's fare. We are used to our own feather beds, carried before us and aired each day. Bolsters of goose-down we need, and fur wraps against this cold. I did not think to travel like vagabonds without a stitch to our backs."

"Ermine fur," breathed one of the others, peeping over her shoulder. But even I knew that to be a sign of nobility.

"Why cannot the baggage train be unstrapped for us each night? Why cannot we find place to stay as our rank demands?

Why cannot..." and so forth and so on, Alyse de Vergay's voice shrilled. When my squire brought word that Lord Raoul awaited me, a new outbreak of her yapping sent me running for the yard.

"We are not used to such unseemly haste," she screamed behind me and the others muttered it, like chorus, to echo her words. "It is not fitting for a lady to ride alone. We are not used to such country ways. And you, you are not used to lady's wants. You are new-wed and should be advised by us; you are not Norman born and do not know our customs nor our needs."

I waited grimly in the stable yard while my squires brought up my mount, a palfry, quiet enough for a woman more than five months gone with child. Such chaperons as the Norman ladies would drive me wild, and certainly make me regret such resolutions for discretion and obedience to my lord's wishes, as I had vowed on our wedding day. Out of the corner of my eye, I saw the squires heave Mistress Alyse upon her horse. She was plump with long fair hair and cornflower blue eyes that stared out in a round white face. I had seen such eyes once before, the stare if not the color, in a wall-eyed horse that my father had killed for madness sake. Her fat buttocks swathed in blue silk caught the saddle rim with a jolt. I glimpsed the flicker of a grin run through the men. They had felt the rough edge of her tongue often enough. They disliked her, I knew, as much as I did. I edged my horse out of her sight to avoid a further deluge of distress. Neither she nor any of the other women would willingly keep up with us. You would think it was hardship enough for them to ride at all—litters they wanted, and men to haul them over the roughest parts, although I think in general Alyse de Vergay complained for effect. I had seen her ride fast when there was need. However, I was not even sure I could endure a hard ride myself. But to reach Sieux safely would be worth the pain. And for Lord Raoul to return there, restored to lands and castle and titles, that would be a satisfaction for him. I did not intend to hinder him. Today I knit up my skirts about my knees and rode astride as troopers do, for all my women's clacking at the sight.

"Mount, man, mount," Lord Raoul roared at one knight who had misfortune to have got off his horse for some private last minute talk with a local wench.

The standard-bearer unfurled the flag, the gold hawks floated behind on their field of red. We thundered out of the gateway, the last man still scrambling into his high-backed saddle as we went. My squires and I were swept up in the midst. The local women sighed and waved their kerchiefs at us, the most noble group ever to have graced their little world, although we did not look so fine for all our titles and rank. (Most lusty, too, I suspect. Our men were not so weary that they would not have sought out some companionship at the day's end.) My own women glowered, but I was free of them, could ride as once, long ago, I had ridden with men.

So that is how I came to be riding alone with Lord Raoul and a few chosen knights, and that is how we came in the evening mists to the river at Sieux. The paths had been rough, but not too difficult, even for me who was with child, for I had been used to horses since I could walk and today I had good cause for pleasure in such a ride. We had come through those hills that he had shown me on the chart, unnamed hills that only a man bred among them could have known, and although he rode fast (the baggage train could never have lumbered up and down those rocks), yet often today he paused to point out some narrow stream or stand of trees that served as landmarks on the way. Never before had he time for that. And seeing him now, suddenly eager as a boy, with a boy's enthusiasm for where he was, I realized the strain he had been living with, long before our marriage day, long before King Stephen's death. For although Raoul had served King Stephen well, fought for him loyally, King Stephen had not always kept faith with Raoul, and at the end, had betrayed Raoul to Henry's revenge. Once I had asked Raoul what he would do if the civil wars should cease, thinking that he would say he hoped they would never end, for he was young then and had been chosen as King Stephen's champion, an honor to which all young knights might aspire. I had surprised him into revealing what was in his mind. "Why, I should go back to France," he had said, "back to my home at Sieux." Today, many times, perhaps unconsciously, he had revealed his same desire. And when he reined back the black stallion into step with my palfry to explain where we were, to show me how he had once climbed a cliff, and, caught by a landslide, been trapped on a ledge, or retell how, under that large stand of beech trees, he had flushed his first deer, I caught again that sense of anticipation and excitement which had set this day apart.

When we paused for a hasty meal of bread and wine, "Praise God," I heard one man say, "tonight we drink the wines of Sieux. This tastes like horse's piss." And he spat more in sorrow than anger—well, as I have explained, if any men deserved tonight to rest at ease, these men did.

While they ate, Raoul took me by the hand and led me to another outcrop of rock. From its top, I could see clearly what that chart had showed, the rounded hills behind us, the valley below, the distant thread of a river, silver-blue among the green.

"There is the river of Sieux," Raoul said. "Westward, it flows to the Atlantic Sea; eastward, it widens into a lake. And beyond the lake stands the castle of Sieux. The land before you is all Sieux land."

Those words had a strange impact upon me. I almost closed my eyes. He betrayed such unconscious pride when he spoke. And suddenly what had been a nail's breadth on the chart widened out into reality; real river, real meadows, real trees, a real castle where I must learn to live and conduct myself as its fitting mistress. That thought was a frightening one and for the first time my ladies' jeers hit hard. I was not used to such land or such wealth. I did not know how to be countess of so much. Perhaps Raoul guessed something of my thoughts; he was a generous man, loyal to his friends, more so than any man that I have ever known. Surely he would remember that, although I might not be used to Norman ways, nor be an heiress like that lady he could have wed, yet I had stood by him when he was outlawed by the king; I had gone to plead for his life; I had not failed him as a friend.

"The castle of Sieux is old," he was explaining, "strong-built. Its towers are famous, like two tall masts on a pointed prow above the cliff face. Its main hall is all of fifty feet, of stone, but its rafters are of oak, dark and old. They say the timbers came from a Viking boat. When my ancestors rowed here, upriver from the open sea, they made their first fort where they had beached their long ship. And when they built a stone keep to take the place of their wooden fort they used those same wood beams to roof their hall. Those Viking lords were thrifty men, wasting nothing, taking all."

His words conjured up a day when that quiet landscape below had been rent by war and death. So might yet Henry's men come after us. He clasped his good hand on my shoulder.

"That was centuries ago," he said, comforting. "And Henry's men too are long since gone. You must not fear Henry, Ann. There is a rhyme that all know here. Remember it when you feel afraid."

He pursed his lips, whistled the tune as Walter, my squire, might have done, then sang:

> No love ever has been due
> Betwixt the Counts of Sieux
> And bastards of Anjou.

Except the word he used for "love" was a soldier's phrase. And he had an even coarser term for "bastard." I had to laugh.

"There," he said, "I have made you smile after all. Your father, Falk, taught me that tune."

He hesitated. I think he searched for words. To bring a wife back to Sieux was a new experience for him. *I have not yet had wife or children to my bed*, once he had told me, *but if you will, I shall lie with you until it is you who cries cease*. But that was lust, not love. Two-Handed Raoul, who could have any woman in the land, also had to learn that paramour and wife are not quite the same; he too had to become used to me.

He said, "I have told you, Lady Ann, of all my grandfather's friends, the man he trusted most was your father, Falk. When I was sent for safety to Sieux as a child, Falk brought me here.

Falk took me hunting for the first time. We rode together on his gray Cambray horse. And he cuffed me soundly afterward for spoiling his aim. He taught me the value of keeping quiet; he taught me how to use my eyes and ears. He taught me too how to fight."

He said, almost formally, "Sieux was Falk's home for many years. He loved it well. So may it be his daughter's home, safe for her and her child."

Well, long ago, ten years ago, when I had lost all that I loved at one time, brother, father, friends, Cambray, I had never thought to have love given back to me. Yet so it was, and Raoul the man that God had given me to love. Out of all hope had Raoul escaped from certain death and been restored to lands and titles. Out of all hope had he married me. Yet I was a bride he had been forced to take; a wife he had not looked to have. A king had ordered him to wed. Out of loyalty to me who had been loyal to him, he had married me to give my child a name. A courteous man, he would show me courtesy. *You will never know if he loves you*—so had the lady of the moors warned. Perhaps she was right. Love in marriage is much to hope for. But where love is, it is a gift that is freely bestowed. It cannot demand a similar love in return. Scarce three months ago I did not know if Raoul still lived. If God had given us each other back, if God had made us man and wife, surely, I thought, that too was for a cause? What I looked for at Sieux was not rank or fame. All I wanted was an interlude, a time of peace, a respite from other men's wars, and a chance to show Raoul my love. I did not think then, nor do I now, that was overmuch of happiness to ask.

Perhaps Raoul hoped as much himself. Releasing me, he picked up an old horn beaker and filled it full. Behind us, his men raised their goblets in silent toast. In silence we drank the bitter wine. Safely home. Was not that also something the lady of the moors had promised?

Pray God, I thought as we mounted for the last ride down to the river plains. Pray God for safety for my noble lord; pray God for safety for my child.

2

SUPPOSE, AS I RODE ALONG THOSE
last miles, thinking on these things, my pace had
slackened. But when I noticed, it did not matter,
for Lord Raoul was not so far ahead that I could
not sometimes hear the laughter of his men. Besides, he deserved to have first look at his castle on his own. If it were
Cambray to which we now returned, I should have liked to
see it for myself, and savor it alone.

My two squires and I ambled more slowly, letting our horses
mouth the peaty water. Presently, as Raoul had explained, the
lake began to narrow again at its eastern end, where the river
funneled from a channel running swifter there with a rush and
clatter over pebble shoals. There would be good fishing among
these rocks where the water plunged from a gorge, and by the
lakeside where the meadows had opened wide, good pasture
for the spring herds, good hunting in autumn for flocks of
geese and ducks. The path had begun to rise above the water's
edge once more; and as we rose, we left the mists below us
like some gray cloak spread, and moved into clearer air. You
could see dimly ahead the great cut the river made to our right,
around the cliff edge like indeed to a ship's prow. And so in
this way, idly, without haste, we came to the start of the cliff
climb, where Raoul was waiting with his men. They did not
speak as we came up; there was no sound, save the tired horses'
stamping against the flies, the distant water's chatter. There
were no trees on the cliff, bare rock it was with a few stunted
bushes and sparse grass. You had to tilt your head as you looked
up to where the day was already ending in a rack of clouds.

And there, above us at the cliff's height, where should have stood the towers of Sieux, there was nothing, a blankness against the sky. At last Raoul spoke.

"Now, before God," he said, "I had not thought Henry to have done so much."

And after a long time, he moved up the path. I remember thinking, I should have known. And my heart grew heavy with what we would find at the gates of Sieux, and what he would do when he got there.

The cliff was steep. We had to strain for footing on the flinty ground. The horses in front sent out showers of dirt and grit and, before we were halfway up, a hail of arrows came rattling down, like dead leaves falling. Had I had better knowledge, I would have known it for a flight too soon loosened, too ragged to be dangerous, but it made the horses shy, and a man cried out where a bolt took his upper arm. Some of the men tugged at their shields, which they had slung for comfort behind their saddles, others freed their swords, snatched for their helmets.

Raoul spurred forward, without pause, without armor, bare-headed in shirt and jerkin. He threw the reins loose across the horse's neck, with his left hand plucked forth his sword. Its blade glinted as he drew; I heard his cry, that terrible battle cry that I had heard but once before, that made my blood run cold. His men took it up, the battle cry of the Normans, men of the north, the old berserkers calling down their gods of havoc and war. They rode like furies up the path, and far off, I heard that thin shriek of fear I never hoped to hear. And I thought, covering my face with my hand while my belly heaved, Not again.

Then, without thought, without will, I too went lumbering up the path, the squires shouting at me to hold, trying to force their skittish horses round mine to bring me to a halt. Without thought I rode, but whether it was in my mind to stop the slaughter or to help it, I cannot tell. I only know that when reason came back, it was already done. As indeed I might have known from the start. No disciplined band would have given

themselves away so soon, or shot down on armed men to lose
the advantage of surprise.

Lord Raoul had already paused where two men had fallen
in a welter of blood. Others were scrambling over the cliff's
edge; the rest, with some of Raoul's men in pursuit on foot,
went backing down the further side of the path. Even as I
looked, another fell. Miserable curs they were, dressed all in
rags. We had caught them at their food, for their cooking fires
still smoldered in the outer bailey beside the gates.

Gates did I say? There were no gates, no walls, only two
twisted piles of wood and iron that had once held the drawbridge chains, from which the great beam sagged now too low
for man on horseback to pass underneath. The towers that had
stood on either side scarcely reached waist high, black with
soot and smoke, and all the walls that had stretched beyond
were tumbled down into the courtyard, filling it with stone.
And on the cliff side, the fallen blocks fanned out, like to a
giant scree.

But there was worse. Where the walls, or what was left of
them had stood at the steepest side, things were still hanging.
I averted my eyes, but not before I had seen the rusting chains,
the stains they left, the foul and rotting things they held. I
turned and heaved my heart upon the ground. And fear and
grief, and something darker I cannot name, blew like a great
cold wind upon the distant moors.

When I looked up, the work was done. For what revenge
was worth against those wretched creatures, squatters all, within
the castle ruins? Lord Raoul had known it, yet had not, could
not, prevent it. All were victims here, of revenge, of cruelty,
of blood. Already Raoul had summoned his own men back.
They picked their way carefully among the fallen rubble, no
easy work to run and fight in boots and spurs with all your
harness on.

I had not thought Henry to have done so much.

That said it all. Henry the King. This was his answer then,
his safe passage promised, his kiss of peace. It must have been
a bitter thought. And I could help remembering how, through

all of my childhood dreams, dark and hideous, I had seen
Cambray and Sedgemont, sacked and destroyed. No nightmare
had ever been as real as this, these broken towers.

Still sitting on his horse, which pawed the ground as if it
scented blood, Raoul was withdrawn and silent. His eyes were
their darkest gray, almost without focus in their intent. He had
sheathed his sword and his ungloved hand beat nervously upon
the saddle rim. I had seen him thus once before, when battle's
heat or rage or despair so took him that it numbed him to all
else. But there could be no battle here, with only dead men
left. Those whom he should fight were already gone, marched
safely home when their butcher work was done. He fought
today against shadows.

And, against my will, the thought came again how, once
as a child, Raoul had seen an army attack his castle here. Count
Geoffrey, Henry's father, it had been at that time, whose troops
had milled about the walls.

*They fired the vines. For spite. Because they could not get in they
destroyed all they could*, Raoul had told me. Like beasts then, that
tear and ravage for sport. And now, having this time by luck
or skill got in, they still must despoil, still must ravage.

I cannot say how long Raoul sat upon his horse, hunched
forward as if in thought. Perhaps it was no longer than a
moment, and it was I who saw that moment stretched out as
if it would have no end. Or perhaps for him time moved as
slowly, and before his eyes passed all that he must remember
of Sieux. He had last seen it as a boy when, come to the age
of sixteen on his grandfather's death, he had returned to England to take up arms for Stephen. He had known before the
last campaign, before King Stephen's death, that Henry had
seized Sieux. But seized only, not sacked. This devastation
must have a later date.

You could see grass already green among the stone, some
pale yellow flowers grew at the cliff top, and there were paths
beaten down among the boulders. How much later then had
Henry sent more men to destroy Sieux? And how much later,
or was it at the same time, had he ordered the castle guard

dragged from the dungeons below and hanged on the shattered walls? The household guard, friends of Raoul's childhood, his companions, men he had hoped to see again, he would be remembering them, their lives, their shameful deaths. And in their memory would he find the ghosts of his own childhood, his hopes, his own dreams. Had Henry's men laughed and whistled about their work? Had they marched away with their banners flying? Or had they crept silently, in the dark, stained with murder? No king, I thought again, no Christian king, anointed of God with holy oil, would show such cruelty to men unarmed, helpless prisoners, without just cause. And I remembered what I had heard of Henry, whose mother let him see men die that he might become used to death, whose ancestors had come with their long ships to wrack the world, for the glory of the conquest, the joy of war, who in his rage, men say, would roll upon the ground and tear his own flesh. The boy Henry I had known in London, the young king, cherishing his wife and her desires, now had he showed the terror of his claws. And the thought came clearly, deadly clear, that even here, we were not safe from him.

Raoul's squires were already running to his side, helping him climb down from the saddle (for he needs must have someone hold the stirrup iron), were unstrapping his spurs, his sword belt. One by one, the mounted men swung off their horses as stiffly, as if too tired to move. Most of them had had comrades here, others would know of them by repute. How was their jesting this last day turned to dust.

Yet there was much to be done, no place for brooding. None of us had time to grieve. Space must be made for men and animals; covering secured against the weather; defense of sorts established so that, by nightfall, we could know some security. The squatters had done us this much service, for where their fires were still burning, they had partially cleared the stones away by tipping them over the ravine. There would be room enough there to spread a canopy against the wall, unstrap the saddles, spread them out. Only when this was done did Raoul turn to face me.

There was no shade in this bare and broken place, just white stones streaked with gray and black, no shadows, nowhere to hide. His face was blank, his voice expressionless as he helped me over the rubble, and for a moment, all the world swung dark.

The moment passed. Lord Raoul was speaking, formally. "Lady," he was saying, "this is not the welcome I would have you have, but you are welcome all the same to Sieux."

I took his hand, sensing its light tremble as it closed upon my own. Across the palm I could feel the calluses from rein and sword and the open cuts where he had grasped the hilt so tightly. I smiled at him as I picked my way with care. "Why, my Lord," I said as brightly as I could, "it is no hard thing to camp out. We can bivouac in France as well as along the Celtic border. And look," for I would not have him bear the weight of my distress, "at least the weather may clear tonight." I wished to do him courtesy for courtesy, and no doubt he thanked me for it, although he made no open sign. But like a drum, the words beat in my mind: *I had not thought Henry could do so much.*

The twilight here was short, not as lingering as I was used to in more northern parts. Water had to be fetched in leather buckets from the river, a tiresome business, for the wells, two of them, a rarity in castles as I knew, had been so choked with stone, packed down and rammed in tight, to be rendered useless until we could clear them. For ease, we tethered the horses down by the river's edge where there was some grazing, too far away for comfort if we should be attacked, but then, if attack came, we were all dead; we had no defense, and we were too few to do more than sell life dearly.

Raoul had sent some men upon the walls to tear down the chains and carry away the things that hung within until a priest could be found to give them decent burial; a sad slow business that, that made us all in pity or in anger cross ourselves. Others rode back to the villages we had passed earlier in the day and returned with food and provisions, and best of all, with some of the villagers from Sieux itself.

They had not fled as lesser folk might have done, but locked themselves stoutly in their homes to see what manner of men we were. Their spokesman, a burly, bearded fellow with a limp, was swift to welcome Lord Raoul's return, loud in his condemnation of King Henry's men, those Angevins, whose attacks he had endured before. For they had not spared the village either, had looted and burned what they could, had rioted as soldiers will when there is no real work for them to do, had taken the village girls for their sport.

As for the castle, there had survived at least one man from the attack. He had crawled into the river reaches to die and been rescued and hidden by the villagers, to their credit and greater peril. They brought him in a litter, still not recovered from the spear thrusts that had laid him low, and he wept, tears rolling slowly down his cracked cheeks, when he told how Henry and his men had breached the wall. He made no attempt to wipe away his grief, but explained in slow, painful words how the Angevins had come upon them, surrounded them a whole long month. Inside the castle were thirty or so men, trained and ready, veterans all, who, although not discounting the danger, had expected to survive it, for the Angevins had several times tried to capture Sieux and had never before succeeded. These guards then, having food and water in plenty, were not unduly alarmed. All they had to do was keep watch and wait.

But perhaps there were too few of them, or perhaps, having come to know the castle, the Angevin army had had time to reassess its strengths and weaknesses. They had mined one of the walls by night, stealthily, under cover of noise and singing from their camp. They could not work by day, there being no natural way to shield their digging, but had taken pains to hide all their workings underground. The place was a blind angle not easily overseen from the castle walls. With sappers then the Angevins had uncovered the foundations, lit fires to heat the rock to bursting and, thus blowing away part of the surrounding wall, had made a gap large enough for them to pour through.

"We could not hold them, my lord," the wounded man said—more than once he repeated it as if the saying gave him comfort. "What can thirty do against a hundred? With Henry at their head, they overran us even before we could gain the keep. Most of us died then, praise God. Better to die with sword in hand than strung up like beef."

He was silent after that, face turned away, eyes closed, and Lord Raoul sat by his side for a long time. It was the village spokesman who finished the tale, explaining how, having won the castle he had long coveted, Henry left for England, and how, having passed a year within the keep, the remaining Angevin soldiers suddenly, this past autumn, had begun to tear down the walls. They summoned up all manner of lawless men, vagrants, outlaws, to do the work, the remnants of whom we had just surprised. The villagers had refused, or rather, since peasants have no say in what they will or will not do if they have no just lord to speak for them, had worked so slowly, so bungled the task, that the Angevins had despaired of finishing it. And then, when the walls were almost down, they had dragged out the castle guard.

"A deed most foul," the villager said, "most foul to slaughter men who had done no wrong, save fight for what was their sworn lord's right. Those murderers got no cry for mercy though." He sighed and spat. "Defiance at the end. Our priest stood there at the furthest part where all could see him." He indicated a place with his thumb, on the far side of the ravine. "He read the prayers for the dead and shrived each one, until he was silenced too with an arrow in his throat. Traitors, they named our men, traitors to Henry of Anjou, who now is Henry of Normandy, and King of England." He spat again. "One man called out before they threw him over that there was no lord here but he who was rightly Count of Sieux. And so, my lord, we are glad to have you back where you belong. Although they killed some of us for their pleasure and stole what they could find, they did not get all the harvest grain. We keep it hidden, as well you know, each year, we store some in a secret place for such emergency as this. We have tilled what we could.

There will be a harvest, not much, but enough. As for the vines," he shrugged, the gesture so like the one his lord often made that I almost remarked upon it, "it will take time for them to grow back. But with you here, you'll give us time."

This then was better news than could be hoped. When Cambray had been taken by the Celts, the villagers had run away, everything had become overgrown, farmland turned to waste. On the other hand, at Cambray we had had shelter and defense, and we had not the thought of dead comrades, hanged for spite.

It was a subdued meal we made, no jests, no songs, each man deep in his own thoughts. Soon there was silence, except for the customary sounds of camp and watch. Raoul and I shared a small space against an inner pile of stone. The grass that grew there was dry and the stone still held some heat. We had spread cloaks about us as much for privacy as warmth and lay there sleepless. Raoul said little. Now he was stretched upon his back, his shoulder against his saddle, one hand clasped behind his head. The weather had cleared as I hoped, a moon had come up, bigger and clearer than any I had seen. In its light, his face had taken on a shuttered look, remote, closed off. It was a look I remembered—it hid his thoughts from all the world. And I remembered too how, in these past years, he had given lands and youth, all he had, in loyalty to a king who had not kept faith with him. He was twenty-six years old, not old but not so young as he had been when first he served King Stephen. In the course of the years between, he had suffered exile, beggary, imprisonment, and had risked death. The only thing left to him untouched was honor. And loyalty, which, having pledged its word, he would not go back on. I thought, in all things else, his wife should at least be a consolation to him. Yet there are men who do not welcome help from women and he was such a one. And he had been forced to marry me. It would be difficult to break through his guard. Yet it must be tried.

I said, "My lord, this is a grief to you."

He gritted out, through clenched teeth as if the words stung, "I did not bring you here for this."

I could understand that. What man cares to seem helpless, unable to defend his family, friends? He had suffered great loss before. Could not I fill the void for him?

"At least we have each other," I ventured. "For me, it is not as before, not knowing where you were, whether you were still alive."

He did not answer. I thought that I must goad him into speech, else this silence would drown us.

"Sieux can be rebuilt," I said.

Silence.

"It must be rebuilt," I cried. "Castles have been taken and destroyed. And rebuilt. Friends have died and been avenged."

Then he did turn to me, the moonlight glinting in his eyes.

"And how," he said, his voice ominously low, "shall we do it? 'Must' is a hard word, lady wife."

"There are ways." Yet his expression frightened me. If he did not think it could be done, no man could. But he had at least replied. That gave me hope.

I said, "I do not think it will be easy. Who ever thought a castle could be built overnight?"

"It can be overthrown in one," he said.

"There must be men to build it up once more."

"Again, that 'must,'" he said. "There are no 'musts' here, lady. You prate as if a child. Soldiers, peasants, cannot build up walls. Men are paid to do it, stoneworkers, masons, skilled about their craft. Or your siege masters—there are your best builders of all."

"Where are there such builders?" I interrupted him.

"In the towns," he said, "there you would find them."

"Then go to the towns," I said. "Bid them take work here. Are there not quarries among the cliffs where stone can be found?"

At that, he did laugh, a sharp, short sound, as if mocking at himself. "Aye," he said, "there are quarries here no doubt,

although overgrown. We have not had need of stone at Sieux
these many years. And masons in the town, also no doubt,
who, if they will spare the time from their chapel building,
could build a castle for me here. But you did not heed me.
There are men to do it, but they must be paid."

"Paid?" I said, the idea new to me. "How paid?"

"With coin," he said, almost impatiently, "gold or silver,
they care not which. They are townfolk," he said, as if that
said it all. When still I did not understand, he added, "Men
who have their own laws and customs, who live outside the
feudal ones. They need no overlord to act for them, they have
their own guilds to protect them and select a master to speak
for them. And they hire themselves out for pay, having no
duties else, no overlord. To 'bid' them come here as you suggest,
to order it, stands outside possibility. Even if I brought them
here as prisoners, I could not get them to work. And to hire
them . . . have you forgot how little I have left?"

At that, I was silent in my turn. I had known of it, of course,
have I not just said he had been beggared by these wars. But
knowing does not always mean understanding. I had come from
a small fief, but even I had felt the lack of revenues when
Cambray had been captured early on.

I tried to remember how the accounts of Cambray were
kept. Dylan, the seneschal, would have them in his charge.
Upon a certain day in the autumn months, at his command,
a man who could read and number would unroll the great scroll
where the records were kept, would read out each serf's name,
have him pay his dues, work and goods in return for protection.
That is the feudal law, the feudal way. So many sacks of grain,
of flour already milled, so many heads of sheep or cattle, so
many hours of work in field or barn or castle guard, in return
for a lord's watch and ward. But when peasants cannot work
the fields, when the harvest is not planted or reaped, when
the cattle is lost or stolen, what revenues should a lord get?
The wars that had stripped my little estate of all its wealth had
stripped Sedgemont likewise. Moreover, Raoul had freed many
of his men at Sedgemont. Knowing that Henry would brand

him as traitor, he had wished to spare his men the same fate. It must rub deeply that he could not have spared his men at Sieux. But, in any case, most of his worldly goods had gone to provide for those who would have been destitute without him. The rest Henry had taken or had demanded as relief or tax when he had restored Raoul to his lands and given him title of earl. A relief unfairly levied, the tax having been paid already when Raoul had first inherited upon his grandfather's death.

"How little I have left," he said. I had not really known what that meant. I was used to so little myself, I had not thought that a lord might feel the need so keenly. What lord, however low, who does not carry his purse openly to scatter alms to the poor? What lord, however low, who does not like to ride out with his men well equipped, his horses sound and matching, his armor blazing with his colors? Some lords would squeeze more from the peasants, force their payments, but Raoul was not the man, nor I the woman, to steal more than our rightful share. And, I thought, my Norman ladies were at least right in this, and I the fool not to have minded for him, that we rode like outcasts and lodged like paupers. And I thought as well, But even so, there must be some way.

Perhaps he was thinking it, too. For at last he said, slowly, "There is one hope."

He turned toward me on his sound side. The moon caught his eyes again, how they gleamed, and a new timbre was in his voice. I felt resolution flooding through him. He said, "The baggage train. Tomorrow, or the day after it will come. There's our gold."

I must have stared at him, because he laughed, amusement creeping back as he spoke.

He said, "In the town, there are men who would barter for coin what I could sell: saddles, spare armor, horses." He smiled. "Iron spurs serve as well as gold, plain saddles as well as fancy ones. What we can sell at their fair we will."

"But Raoul," I almost hesitated to say it, what knight is there who does not wear his golden spurs, what squire so humble that he does not hope to keep his second horse? But I would not mention that, rather I hoped to keep him talking to raise his spirits and so raise mine.

"And those builders, which ones are best?" I asked.

He said, "It is true about the siege masters. I meant it for a jest, but it is true the best castle builders in Normandy have been the men who knew how best to tear them down. Geoffrey of Anjou, this Henry's father, was one; my grandfather, Raymond, who built Sedgemont, another. And your father, Falk, who built Cambray. Think, how was Cambray built?"

Again I stared at him. "Of stone," I said at last.

"Yes, yes," he said almost impatiently, "but in what manner?"

He pulled himself to his feet, clumsily, limped to the fire and thrust a torch into the embers to make them flare up, bright as day. The men who had been on watch turned to look at us, black silhouettes against the silver sky, then moved on, recognizing who we were. But what Raoul had to say was for all his men.

"Look here," he was saying, "here and here."

With a sweep of the torch that illuminated the litter of stones, he went to where the larger ones had been tumbled down and stuck the torch between the cracks.

"And where," he said, "Hell's teeth, think, where did Falk get the stones along that benighted borderland? Where could he find men to quarry stone or shape and fit it?"

"He found the stones," I said, almost stupidly, "there was a fortress built before, he took the stones from that."

"Yes," he said, "so he used stones that had been used before. Roman stones a thousand years old. Now look here, and here."

The rest of his men, who had been sleeping, or lying as we had been, brooding and remembering, were stirring now, coming toward us. Like us, they had bedded where they could, stripped down to shirt or tunic for comfort's sake. Their tired faces with the stubble of beards showed suddenly intent and watchful in the harsh light.

"He who would destroy a castle," Raoul said, "must grind it

to dust. Henry's men did their work well, but not well enough. Had Geoffrey of Anjou been alive to see to it, we had not been so fortunate."

He was rubbing his hand over the stone as he spoke. I passed my hand over another, as did his men, at first hesitatingly, and then with growing comprehension. Beneath my fingers, the beveled edges ran cool and straight. There were many such stones, piled upon each other, pried out of place, levered out perhaps. Some had shattered as they fell, some had been smashed with hammers, but for the most part, they lay where they had been pushed, intact, ready to be used again.

"And see here."

On his knees, with a dagger in his left hand, he was already scoring lines across the patch of earth; each time he spoke, he etched the lines in deeper as if to make an imprint that would last. "Henry's men left us another hint on how to rebuild Sieux," he was saying. "Henry himself is a good siege master, as are all the Angevins. Here," a slash, "he breeched the wall. Well, it was a weakness as we all knew. From the battlements, there was no view down, a blind angle then that must have been remedied some time. When we rebuild, we'll throw out a skirting wall, a curtain wall, thus and thus."

Again a decisive stroke. His men were already hunkering around him, drawing lines of their own, arguing, agreeing. One summed it all. "By the Mass," he said, straightening himself and scratching, "I cannot cut stones, nor yet lay a wall to order, but, by God's breath, I'd haul those stones with my teeth to best that bastard yet."

"You may have to," said Raoul. He smiled at us, the scar on his cheek suddenly very clear. "Used stones will spare us time and expense. We needs must save both . . . They have given us the stones of Sieux. We shall use them to advantage."

There speaks my hawk, I thought, well-satisfied, and left them to their talk. Presently, they went back to the fire, opening a wine cask, one the villagers had brought, settling down to their drinking, their storytelling. Thus did they honor their dead companions, after all, that they should not be forgotten. And for the first time since our sad homecoming were the men of Sieux mourned and comforted in soldier fashion.

I lay by myself, content to have it so, and thought too of my father Falk, and of his dear friend who had been Raoul's grandfather, and of all the men they had known who would have remembered them. And I thought too, almost defiantly, that when my child, my son, was born, he should have memories of Sieux's towers... standing strong again.

When Raoul returned to his place beside me on the inner wall, he was more cheerful, or rather, overlying grief were plans, things that could be done. Yet, as he eased his long legs in beside my own, I could feel the tautness of his body like whipcord.

"You are over-reached, my lord," I told him softly, "rest now."

He sighed and stretched himself painfully. "Others have said as much," he admitted. "King Stephen, when the mood was on him, would swear I'd carry his kingdom on my back. Well, it is my way. I am too old to change."

He leaned upon his saddle. For a moment, with his eyes closed, the lashes against his cheeks, he gave the lie to his own words. He looked almost as he used to do, the laughing, mocking boy who had plagued me when we first met. A great wave of sympathy coursed through me that this, his happy day, had ended so bitterly. To hide my thoughts, I went on resolutely.

"Is there no one nearby to help us, no friend?"

He sighed, answering as if to a child. "When I was in England last year, there were not many men then to give me help. Still fewer here. I would not alarm you, Ann, who, God knows, has suffered harm enough, but I have shown you where Sieux lies to the south of Normandy, between it and Anjou and Maine. Now that Sieux is destroyed, the Norman barons would like well enough to take my lands. If we can but keep secret our plan to rebuild, that will give us a breathing space. Henry cannot leave England now. The Angevins have slunk back to their dens and will not stir without him, let's hope the Normans will bide their opportunity to deal with us."

"Cannot the king help you," I said, quailing at his words although his voice was calm. "King Louis of France?"

"He did not think to do so before." And Raoul's voice was still level when he spoke. "Louis may live to regret his lack of foresight. But he is a shifty man, never letting his right hand know the left. He should be quicker to our defense a second time, not liking Henry to have gained so much land as to own three-quarters of France. Nor does he like it that Henry also owns his queen, Eleanor of Aquitaine who once was Queen of France. Louis does not take kindly that she left him to marry Henry within two months. I should not like it myself. I'd not let my wife leave me to take another man." He smiled at me. "So it is to Louis's gain to keep Sieux as barrier between Henry's lands south and north, but I would not rely on Louis to act as he ought."

He shifted awkwardly to find resting place, burst out, "God's breath, but it is no jest to be trussed up thus, like to barnyard fowl, not able to belt my own sword on. Devil fry me, I had not thought these wounds would take so long to heal that I am like to die of boredom first." He was silent for a while until again, the words broke out. I had never heard him speak so unguardedly. "Ann, I am caught here in a trap. I must endure it best I can, but it will be hard on you. If we go back to England, then are we truly in Henry's grasp. If we bide here, the wait will be long and dangerous. We shall have to shift to defend ourselves. Will you mind that? Will you mind to be so far from friends and home at such a time? By the Holy Rood, I did not bring you here for this."

I tried to tell him what was in my heart, if only he would be safe, then could we all be safe from Henry's reach.

He said, almost unexpectedly, "Long have I known Henry of Anjou, since we were both lads here in France. And ever since that boyhood, he has pitted himself against me. Ambition gnaws at him that he must be first, and he has inherited the

Angevin rage along with their lands. That rage will choke him yet; it twists him from man to beast. He is a good soldier, that I grant, but rage destroys his reason, turns him mad. It is his greatest enemy." He smiled his rueful smile, "And to think I showed him once how to hold a lance. Got rot me, that he should ride as I do. Or did."

He was silent for a while after, shifting and turning on his hard pillow.

"It is not easy to fight with your left hand," he said, as if admitting to a weakness. "I can do it if I must. It is the strangeness that takes your opponent off his guard. Although, after the first surprise, he has your weaker side exposed to his counter thrust."

Again, silence. At last, he said what I believe was truly in his heart. "I thought to bring you here to keep you safe until your child was born. By my knightly oath, no less than that."

When he spoke me fair, I wanted to put my finger to his lips to stay his words. Hard was it for me to tell him openly how I felt for him. But God had given us each other back; we were man and wife by God's grace; an archbishop had seen us wed; surely, by God's mercy, we should live to know each other's worth. Yet he had been forced to marry. Without Henry's threat, might he have still thought on his past loves, and remembered his old betrothal, his former pledge to the Lady Isobelle? Would he resent marrying me?

He had lived long alone, trusting no one's counsel but his own; since boyhood had he fended for himself, pitting his wits against the intrigues of Stephen's court, I think it was hard for him to trust anyone, or to put his naked thoughts before the world. I know his pride was cut to the quick that his physical weakness left us so exposed. Once the most active and brave of men, he saw weakness as failure, and failure was more painful than those unhealed wounds. When he spoke of such things, simple as his words were and often hidden beneath a jest, they seemed forced from him as if he confessed to some crime. Beneath them, I sensed the hurt of a vulnerable man, sensitive to the needs of all he felt his duty to protect. And what he said was simple indeed.

"Nor hold it against me," he said, "that I make so poor a show of protection for you."

"And you," I whispered back, my confession to match his own, "you will not mind, who could have married a great lady, to take me of so little worth?"

"Mind," he said, "and what is worth more than one who would have died for me."

He stretched out his hand and took mine in his own. "You have been great comfort to me these past months," he said. "Without you, I would be dead. What other friend stood by me in Henry's court? What other woman have I known who would have endured today with such grace? It was to have been other than this, our homecoming. But lady, this day is done. Passed, if not forgot. Since we cannot go back, we must go on. We have scarce had any time to ourselves since our marriage day, so long since first I took you to my arms on such another day when we won Cambray for you." He smiled, that rueful smile. "I thought to have had you to myself this night," he said, "unless, lady, you would shrink from me, a crippled man who gives you a bed of stone." He jested, but underneath there ran a hint of truth.

I turned to him, where his hand was slipping around my waist beneath his cloak, his clever fingers already feeling for the laces of my shift. I tried to tell him he was all that I desired, but shyness held me back. I could not speak for fear that I should weep. And then his mouth was covering mine and there was no time for words. I tried to say, It is not meet, but those words did not come either.

Now I think that he was right, now I believe that it is both right and just that life should be born of death, that after sadness, pleasure comes; grief is not forgotten because it is put aside for its place. We lay beside each other on the ground. Everything was still, only the beating of my heart like a drum. Nothing mattered then, Henry's revenge, our present danger, the loss of Sieux. It was the first time since our marriage we had been alone, cut off from the rest of the world.

"And now I have you, *ma mie*," he said, his hand about my breast. I felt his thumb brushing against the tip; I felt myself arch up, felt him trace down between parting thighs. "What more meet than Norman pleasure his lady to her heart's desire." Mouth to mouth, body fitted shaft and cleft, his fingers moved upon a feathered tide. And when I met each thrust, I heard myself cry out like a bird, high and exultant. He wound my hair about my throat and stopped the sound with his own mouth.

"Ann," he said, "who has bedeviled me since first we met, so you are now bid welcome to your castle keep. If all is lost, we have had this."

Well, this was the homecoming we had. I cannot distinguish now, nor could not then, pain from pleasure; bittersweet it was and like all the rest foretold, both true and false, so intermixed you could not tell which was which. Well again, grief there was, and happiness, and if no safety yet a homecoming of sorts. And if nothing else, we had had this.

3

RESENTLY HE SLEPT, AN UNEASY sleep, and I noticed how often his left hand stretched, tensed, toward his sword hilt. So at Sedgemont had he lain, after his wounding, when his men had placed an unsheathed blade within his grasp to let him have the feel of it. Athwart the moon, new rain clouds were already gathering, casting shadows across his face. What thoughts, what fears, lay behind those dark-fringed eyes, to make him start and turn? Who here was hunter, who the hunted, what the snare? One thing was certain: there was nowhere else left for us to go; his other lands in France, Auterre, Chatille, were too scattered, too small, unfortified. Nor should we look for friends; Sieux was ringed with enemies. And suppose that Sieux could not be rebuilt, suppose Henry's army came back, suppose Raoul's right arm did not heal . . . you see how my thoughts went turn and turn about, to make me twist as restlessly. Not for the first time, I took comfort in the memory of my mother, Efa of the Celts, that lady whom I had never known, how she had left her kin, married a Norman who had been her father's enemy. Her marriage had not been easy at the start, yet in the end, it had turned to love. They say my father, Falk, saw her first on the walls of a mountain fort which he and his men had taken under siege. On seeing her, a soldier in battle's heat, he had desired to possess her, made a bid to take her as a hostage for his orderly retreat. Thus a truce was signed between him and the Celts; an ill-omened start for marriage, you would think, yet so strong was the bond between them, my father and this Celtic bride, that in losing her, part of him had died, that in losing her son, his own heart and life had ceased. Should not I hope as much from my marriage to a Norman lord? But then, I thought too what the lady of the moors had hinted at. Once in our Celtic world, there were many women who possessed such ability to foretell the future as she had done, *awenyddion* were these soothsayers called in our tongue, who spoke as if in trance and, waking, claimed it was the will of God speaking through their voices. I do not know if their claim was true, but this I do believe: if God, as I think, put it into my mind to remember the lady of the moors on such a day, which of itself must be engraved in memory, there must be reason that, in time, would be revealed. And I should know it too if only I had the skill to make it out. Double-tongued she had been, but not for malice or pride, almost sorrowing had she spoken. *On your lips be it recorded, not on mine.* Now for the first time, the thought ran cold, suppose what she had said was yet to come, the truth or untruth of it not yet proved, and all that had gone before was only prologue to the rest. I tell you, it was that realization most of all that haunted me. We were not safe then, not home, the prophesy had not yet begun to be fulfilled the worst still lay ahead. And I also thought this. Three times in my life so far has it been given me as gift (if gift it is) to see time out of place, and never have I wished to know what it had shown. Dear God, I would not want to have that power to foretell what happens to poor souls. Poet, long were the prayers I made to preserve us all from harm. And, most of all, I prayed that out of this morass my noble lord could find a safe way through.

When in the morning I awoke, for at some point even I had slept, it was to camp's misery. The day had dawned to rain, turning the ground to mud, our clothes to sodden rags. Lying on stones cricks your neck, your legs grow stiff, your back stiffer again; fires, banked overnight, blow bitter smoke into your eyes. The men were hungry, bleary, foul-mouthed, not like to give comfort nor yet to look for it. I have spent time in a border camp, as you know, although none might say so to my face; there are days, as old soldiers are aware, it is best to keep out of the way, no hope of courtesies on such a

morning as this. Before it was an hour old, Lord Raoul and his
men had ridden out, and so they did each day henceforth, to
scour the countryside for fodder and food, to keep watch for
enemies and to look for help, although I suspected we could
whistle for that. It was true I had not found many friends in
Henry's court who were willing to risk themselves when Raoul's
luck had run low last year. Those of us left behind began to
shift the piles of stone—a thankless task, yet one we did each
day, even the village women and I, sitting on the ground,
sorting through the shards as if gleaners in a harvest field.
Remembering us now, as we were then, bent double in the
rain, I am overwhelmed by the enormity of our task. Yet I
recall thinking, my legs outstretched, a wicker basket set between my knees, my fingernails scrabbling through the dirt,
how in ancient times along the border, men had raised up those
gray henges of stone, those circles on the Cambray moors,
without any help or benefit of tools. If they could, so could
we, I thought. And, although at each day's end it seemed as
if scarcely a stone had been moved, yet gradually a sort of wall
was built between the base of the gate towers. A battering ram,
nay, a tree stump with six strong men, could have rammed it
through, yet it gave illusion of defense, and behind it, we set
up tents, established our camp with military routines. Watch
was maintained along the river banks; even village lads were
trained to mount guard and peasants in the outlying parts bribed
to act as spies. So we lived, each day a gift from God, each
night of rest a favor deserving of thanks.

When, by the week's end, the rest of the baggage train came
stumbling in, we might have been settled there all our lives.
But for those of you who see romance in every hour of outdoor
life, I tell you it is no jest to be hungry, wet and cold, and
even today I cannot bear the thought of eels. For such was our
food—fish and eels and fowl, but mainly eels—with handfuls
of green stuffs pulled from the peasant's plots, washed down
with river water, bare mouthfuls to satisfy men with appetites.
Nor is it easy to fend for yourself in a camp of men. As I did.
For when in company of the baggage train, the ladies of my

retinue came tottering along, poor ruffled souls, more like bedraggled birds in their ruined silks, all but speechless with shock at the state of Sieux, I determined to send them away. I made this decision on my own, and on my own I ordered it. And for the most part, they went willingly, all save the youngest, that is, and the eldest one, to voice protest, not at what they saw but rather at the ruin of their own hopes.

"They told me when we left England," the youngest whined, not much more than a child so much could be forgiven her, "that as part of an earl's entourage, I should have a white pony of my own, with bridle of crimson leather, fringed with bells, and I should bide here at Sieux, be taught the ways of wife, until a noble lord should claim me as a bride."

The other women hushed her with murmurs of common sense. "There be no horses," one blurted out, "neither black nor white, nor food to eat. We do well to leave."

But the Mistress Alyse de Vergay was not so easily got rid of. "By the Mass," she said, her anger loud enough for all to hear, "I did not look to be thrust out like a kitchen wench. How dare we be treated so. The counts of Sieux were proud men once. They did not think to live like tramps nor have their offspring dropped like tinker's pups. I am no trollop to be abused although I know there is a trollop here. My *virtu* is not questionable to bear a bastard child."

Her voice, stripped of all polite pretence, raged without cease. I have said before that she was tall, overripe and plump in her pale gown, but for the first time I sensed the determination that lay behind those billowing silks. Her face had flushed, her blue eyes burned. I could not understand the reasons for such malice and certainly would not debate *virtu* or bastardy with her. I turned my back and stalked away.

But her words angered and distressed me, the more I suspected she voiced what the other ladies dared not say. We had housed them, these Norman ladies who thought themselves so fine, at the village edge in a half-ruined barn which Henry's men had stripped bare. It smelled of mice and rats but scarce contained a wisp of straw to harbor fleas. I resolved I would not have them there, not for one more hour than was necessary, and so went at once to bid our men prepare an escort without delay. I would have those ladies hence before the day was done. The men were tired, but listened to my orders patiently. Now, as chance would have it, Lord Raoul and his guard had just ridden in and were down in the horselines, sorting through the saddles and accoutrements to determine which could be spared for sale. Lord Raoul looked up quickly on hearing me; his ears were sharp and my voice was perhaps too loud. He eyed me thoughtfully. Then, as I flared past, he threw another strap on the pile and caught at the hem of my cloak with his good hand.

"Hoity-toity, lady," he said. "What brings you here?"

Still too angry to speak coherently, I bit my lip. He must have known why.

"Accompany me," he suggested in a courteous way, but his hand was firm on mine so I could not escape. He drew me out of earshot. I glimpsed a flicker of mirth run through his men. They thought, no doubt, their lord led me apart to chastise a wife who took too much upon herself. Their mirth fanned my rage.

I shook myself free and faced Lord Raoul, no wifely precepts left in me today; forgotten were all those demure ways I had tried to adopt. Oh, I know my faults. I can be as blunt as any man and certainly think what often would make a man's ears burn. I know what marriage vows and Holy Writ and all men's Holy Sacraments enforce: that womenfolk must be controlled by men, and wives must obey their husbands. I know, too, that no man likes a harpy as his wife, but there are some things that no one, man or woman, should endure.

"I'll not have them here," I blurted out. "Off they go. I'll see their backs; they'll give me space . . ."

"Certainly Alyse de Vergay could," he broke in dryly, "more than twice your size." Which showed he knew exactly who had stirred my wrath and why, but he waited graciously for me to finish my complaints. Cunning in my way (for what man likes to hear women complain?), I pointed out these ladies were so many useless mouths to feed and their needs were such, their demands so great, we could in no way satisfy them.

"How else will you be served?" he asked. He spoke abruptly, to the point, but still courteously. "Who will attend you when your time is come?"

"I shall manage," I repeated stubbornly.

He sighed, set me down firmly on a stone, stood back, legs apart. "Lady," he said at last. "I have no time to play at games. God's wounds, 'tis hard enough to find food and keep a shelter over our heads. I cannot act as wet nurse to a babe." He caught back the end of his speech, but not before I guessed what he would have said, Bad enough even to have a babe at all.

"I know," he went on trying to be reasonable, I grant him that, "you find our Norman ways difficult; I know you dislike these ladies. But, in truth, I'd rather them than their menfolk about our ears like bluebottles on a side of beef. I'd rather Norman women here as spies than their men."

"Spies?" I cried. I know my voice rose a notch. "I'll have no spies in my household. What are those men, Alyse de Vergay's father for one—if she be not too old to have a father left— and who is she, that I am loaded with her for convenience sake?"

He said, still in that controlled, patient way, although I could tell his temper too was rising, "Lady Ann, you need those women for women's work. But think. I have showed you where Sieux is set, between Normandy and the lands of Anjou. We think of ourselves as Normans, we men of Sieux, but we are not bound to a Norman overlord. I hold my lands direct from the King of France. What I have not explained is that Henry has not been long Duke of Normandy, which his father took. The Norman barons have little liking for Henry, and while he is away in England, will take the chance to stir up trouble if they can. Nor did I explain that the Normans have small liking for Sieux, either, and have long been jealous of our independence. The more they know of our plight, the more like are they to take advantage of us. I'd rather their womenfolk as hostages for peace than have Jean de Vergay, since you have named him, roll up his siege machines before our gates. Although, in truth, he is more like weasel than a man, burrowing at his overlord's heels. That overlord is the Sire de Boissert. If Jean de Vergay's fighting days are done, for he suffers, so they say, from a weakness in the breast that causes him fainting spells, de Boissert's fighting days are not. There's little mischief in Normandy that does not have his mark on it."

There was a tone of contempt in his voice when he spoke that name. I remembered how, when Sieux had been lost, it was the Sire de Boissert who had repudiated his daughter's betrothal to Raoul. I could tell there was still no love lost between Raoul and him.

"Send Alyse de Vergay off in a rage," Raoul was continuing, "and her father will support her in all her wrongs. In private he cowers before her, but in public he boasts she is worth twice his sons, and should have been a man herself. The more he bleats for peace, the more he longs for war, although he cannot fight himself. Off he'll trot to complain to his overlord, with enough gossip to whip de Boissert in a fret."

"They'll get no gossip from me," I began, when he interrupted me.

"Aye so. Comes a thought in your head and all the world knows." Which comment did not endear him to me. "But before you open your pretty mouth, Lady Ann, to talk me down, think. And as a start, control those Norman ladies as you should."

"It is too late," I said. "I have already ordered them to go."

"Ordered!" he choked on the word. "Ordered. No one orders my men but me. That is man's work. Keep you to yours."

"No," I repeated stubbornly. Well, it is not fit for a wife to contradict her married lord, and I know it is part of the marriage vow that women should let men control them. But God knows men are not always wise and God, I think, does not really favor fools. "No," I said. "*You* order them be gone. I'll be better served by peasant folk."

I saw how the muscle twitched in his cheek as he ground his teeth. "I shall not quarrel with you, lady," he gritted out, "to upset you now, but it is not fit for your rank and state."

I saw how the scar on his face stood out, that scar a coward had given him. It had paled and faded these past months, but I think he minded it more than any other wound he had, caused by a blow that he could not even return, bound and imprisoned as he had been. On seeing that scar and remembering how that blow had been given, my own anger died. I stifled the hot reply I had planned, What rank or estate, when we live like tramps? Those words belonged to Alyse de Vergay and her like. Instead, what I said was to mollify.

"If my ladies leave, my lord, there will be no one to tell the queen how we use the gifts she gave us," I said. "And we can live simply, without luxuries, as those spoilt creatures cannot. I have never even looked but I am sure the queen gave me many rare and costly things which make up a large part of the baggage train. With your other gear you can barter with them at the fair. There will be your mason's hire."

He hesitated, still frowning. "The gifts of the queen were made to you," he said at last. "How should she feel if we used them to rebuild what her husband has destroyed?"

"She was, is, my friend," I maintained stoutly, on securer ground when I spoke of the queen. "She rewarded me out of love. And out of fairness too, I think, knowing that Henry had been unfair. She alone persuaded Henry to make peace with you. She persuaded him somehow, let no man ask how or why, to let us be wed. She and her kinsmen, her southern courtiers, alone befriended me in Henry's court."

I could see how he mulled over my words and made sense of them despite his first rejection of them.

"Royal gifts," he said, "usually come with a price. And the great are ever fickle in their friendship. But I cannot deny we could make use of them."

"The queen helped me," I argued next, "because she claimed I befriended her first. I helped her when her second child was born. She has often told me she counts me as having brought her good luck so that she was delivered of a healthy son, especially since her older son is weakly and sick. She wished such fortune for me. Of all people else, she would approve that I put what she gave me to such good use." I looked at him sideways. "Besides," I said, "you would not deny it was women's work that prompted her to show me favor in the first place."

He almost laughed. "Christ's bones," he said, "you have not lost the knack of twisting words after all. Well, lady, if we follow your plan there goes my hope of keeping secret what I do at Sieux. Even if your ladies depart, all of France soon will know who gave those gifts to us and what we use them for. But that's a risk I'll take. No sense then to keep those ladies. Let them go and gossip to their heart's content. But, lady," and now his voice was stern, "leave the ordering of men's affairs to me. Concentrate on women's work, and give me, in turn, a healthy son."

"And suppose," I said meanly, for I love to have the last word, "it is not a son I bear? Suppose, after all, it is a girl child? What then?"

Then he did laugh. "A second Ann of Cambray!" he mocked me, with his sudden grin that lit up his face. "By the Mass, I'd run. One of you is enough for any man." And so my lord had the last word himself.

He drew me up, clamped his left hand about my waist, and led me forward toward the tent where we were camped.

"And now," he said solemnly, although his eyes still smiled, "we will walk on if you please, lady wife. I seldom have the chance to speak with you alone, and there is other women's work we should discuss, work a man might well find interesting." He smiled again in a way I could not resist. Well, are not man and wife bid make love to create more children for this world? Do not the Holy Sacraments, no doubt written by men, endorse that claim? And should not women have the right to twist dull argument to fit their own needs? And, since it is also true that women love to have the last word after all, is not our loving as pleasurable to us as to men?

So I put Mistress Alyse de Vergay's words and Raoul's warnings out of my thoughts. I should not have done. The men who rode escort on her to her father's lands (for we gave her fitting departure so no one should realize how few men we had), on their return, those men warned me, too.

"Lady," they said, cautious how they phrased themselves, it not being fit for squire or knight to speak harshly against womankind, "it is said she looked to catch a man herself whilst in your household, having three times force led a man to the altar and at the last moment he escaped, who can blame him, wedding such. They say, thwarted of husband, she dotes upon Isobelle de Boissert, helps her with her *affaires*, and lacking lovers of her own, enjoys as voyeur those of Isobelle's." They fidgeted then, as well they might, to speak such slander; but it was concern that made them continue, "Lady Ann, they say she hoped to rule you, you being young, and act as spy in your household for the Lady Isobelle, who, had she been wed here as was hoped, had promised Alyse the post of chateleine, to keep the keys and be mistress of the household. Robbed, as she now insists in some strange, twisted way, of husband, position and rank, Mistress Alyse turns her spite against you and Lord Raoul and contends that, knowing as you must the condition of Sieux, you wronged her to bring her here, and such wrongs must be avenged."

More than that they would not say, although more no doubt was told to Lord Raoul. I heard their words but let them slide by, too many other preoccupations at the time; nor did I welcome news of that Lady Isobelle. I should have paid more heed. As an older woman with pretensions to grandeur above her place, with bitter hopes of being wed, with malice that some cunning steel-honed, Alyse de Vergay was not likely to let that malice go unfed. But how could I, or even Lord Raoul, who was more used to such intrigue, how could we guess what women's work would one day do? For the while I forgot Mistress Alyse, sought, perforce, for help among the village women of Sieux in their straggle of huts on the further side of the castle walls; I'd rather be served by them than Norman ladies swollen with rank and pride. And, in truth, more kindly and honest souls I've yet to meet. So I lived among them, shared their daily bread, black and moldy for the most part, such as knights would scorn to eat, watched them with their own children, and so learned from them. What time I could, I spent with my noble lord, who drove himself and his men so hard that their task seemed harder, more like to landless man than belted earl or count. For is it not also told by women as we sit alone, around a fire or at our spinning wheels, that of all times else, women lust for men when we are already great with child? And do not men feel greatest tenderness for their wives when they hope to have an heir? I cannot claim the truth of these things. I say only I gave what comfort I could and took back eagerly what was returned. And if I was not lady of a great and noble hall, if all about me lay in ruins, yet was I mistress still of my lord's bed. And that too seemed most natural.

So, as each day burned to its close and the summer began to ripen now around us like a flowering vine, even the ruins of Sieux brought some happiness. We sorted through the queen's gifts, rich furs, tapestries, and jewels wrapped in leather bags, blues and greens and flashing reds more than even I had dreams of; a lord's ransom had she given us. The men picked through their gear; we waited for the fair day in the nearest town, at which time Raoul hoped to buy the masons for their fee. Nothing threatened us, praise God, north or south; but all was poised and waiting like a morning without breath of wind.

Yet, if sometimes in the dark hours of the night when thoughts run darkest, I wondered if I should have consented to become Raoul's wife, perhaps that fear was natural also. We put a double burden on him, the child and I. Without us, unencumbered, he could have managed differently and would have been free to act as he wished. And sometimes, when I saw his weariness— he never seemed to rest, one difficulty solved, another took its place—sometimes I wondered if, despite himself, he resented what the king had made him do. And suppose that in giving birth, I should die, as my mother had with me, would he take the child then to his heart, build his hopes and dreams on him as had my father on his son? Or, not acknowledging him, set him aside, make disdain and dislike his lot as my father had done with me? These thoughts were for the lonely dark hours, I say; I was too proud to voice them aloud, but it would have been a comfort to have had someone of my sex and rank to share them with.

The nearest town was but a few hour's ride away, outside Lord Raoul's lands, yet having close ties to it, named, as was the church that crowned its hill, for the patron saint of these parts, Saint Purnace. The day of the fair dawned bright and clear, a feast day in early June with a hint of heat beneath the morning's cool, with a hint too of something else, like the faint scent of woodsmoke to give the alarm of fire. The day before, we had labored mightily to get all things arranged and packaged; now the time was come, expectations rose. We splashed through the river shallows at first light, sending the silver water showering into mists. I say we because I rode along too. Wrapped into the best clothes I could squeeze into, an old gray cloak about my shoulders, I might have been any woman with any bunch of men mounting escort one last time on a baggage train. There are those who even now sneer that I did so, but there was no other choice. And cruel choice it was for Lord Raoul to make, since riding or staying was equally unsafe, with only a skeleton guard left at Sieux, more for show than strength, the rest of his men needed with him and nowhere else for me to hide. It was like Raoul, of course, to give no sign of what he felt. Expecting danger, he did not shrink from it. He acted in his decisive way, deployed his men to their best advantage, trusted to God and his own strength to win us through.

Yet, despite his calm, there was a strange mood to that day that set the senses flaring, uneasiness pulling like an undertow in the way men moved and spoke, a current beneath the things they left unsaid. They all rode armed, with helmets on, lances drawn, yet no mark of rank, not even a flag to show who they were. Raoul himself rode at their head, his black horse already pawing dust, churning the ground white beneath its feet.

Turn by turn about, Raoul and the captain of his guard cantered back and forth along the line, joking with the men, urging the villagers who drove the carts behind us to whip them up. Sometimes as he passed, he smiled at me. I should have remembered that smile. I had seen it before when things looked dark. But, "Cheerily, cheerily," he said as he went on, and the dust eddied beneath those great hooves, "we'll be free of this in another hour." Free, but of what, dust or danger, he did not say. I noted how he still could not wear his hauberk, had his sword belted for left hand use, and how the sun caught at the thin scar on his face. His men were in strange mood, too; they laughed and jested as they went. So they used to ride out from their border camp when they knew trouble waited ahead. In truth, there was no way we could have hidden our progress across those woodlands. "Woodlands" is not the name for them, more like to grassy fields with large clumps of trees in between. The woods around Sedgemont are so thick you must force your way through the underbrush. Here, if I looked back, I could see the winding train of carts and men, hear the straining oxen plodding through the dirt, hear the creak of leather and rumble of wheels as we moved from one stand of trees to the next. And I could mark, as any watcher might, the white trail of dust that streamed in our wake.

But perhaps I was in a strange mood myself. For despite those prickles of unrest and unease, I felt in better spirits, full of hope. So they say it often is for fighting men, that when the moment comes, their blood runs faster, their courage mounts, they seem impervious to fear or threat, might even welcome danger with open arms. So it was too for my squires, who clung like limpets to either side of me; they chattered on to hide their thoughts, but apprehension and excitement glowed about them like a sheen.

I liked to hear my squires speak, especially Walter, the older one. His west country burr reminded me of home and he had that sweet tongue of a border man, hung in the middle to clack both ways. His peat-brown eyes were west country, too, and sparkled with delight at a good tale. It was he who explained how the queen's gifts would be exchanged for gold inside the town where there were rich merchants who would make a bid.

"Or rather," he said, warming to his yarn although, as I knew, he had never been to Saint Purnace before and spoke from hearsay, full of scraps of knowledge as a stable is with straw and husks, "rather they will look and covet, but the Jewish traders will be the ones to buy. They say these Jews are the richest men in France. They live in hovels in the worst parts of town, yet behind their broken doors are strongrooms full of gold and such, lendings for many a noble lord. But of all things I shall best like to watch, it is the masons of Saint Purnace. They say they are a quarrelsome lot who love to bargain for a higher wage and are more zealous for their rights than any lord about his rank. They'll take their time, depend on it, to wring as much from us as they can, each man of them speaking his mind as freely as a belted knight. They say they are hot tempered too, free with their fists. They like to fight and often taunt their fellow townsfolk into open dispute with knives and daggers instead of swords. I'll wager we'll have our fill of townsfolk before this day is through."

Thus he lured us on the hot road with snippets of fact and fantasy, although, on the whole, what he said was right. And his wager too came true, although not quite as he had expected it. And so we edged our way along, sweating by now in the hot sun, expecting attack perhaps at every turn. None came. It occurred to me afterwards that if our progress was so clearly seen, so would that of any other horsemen, and an ambush relies on secrecy. The place for attack was not on these dusty plains. And so in safety we came to Saint Purnace.

The town was not large, but was surrounded by walls, pierced north and south by great iron-studded gates of which the townspeople were justly proud. Outside the northern gates, under the walls, the fair of Saint Purnace had been set up. It was the kind of fair you find in country parts for selling of pigs, sheep, and goats. Their rank smell, combined with the heat and dust, made one's senses reel. Many traders were there, shouting, haggling, and arguing over price. They quieted, though, on seeing us, and watched almost in silence while the peasants unharnessed the oxen and unloaded the carts. Some of our men carried our bundles wrapped in their plain canvas bags (those with the queen's cypher seeming too obvious for use) inside the town, under the supervision of Raoul's seneschal, a youngish man, hastily summoned back to Sieux from one of the other estates, it not being proper work for a lord to negotiate price. The other knights had their pages and squires untether the horses that were for sale and trot them up and down. If the men were distressed to see their chargers sold, they never showed it; but it must have been so, especially for squires like Walter and young Matt. A squire needs a horse to become a knight; without these, their knighting must be that much further postponed. It struck me as I watched them ring the horse pens round, that, like their master, our young men made sacrifices also for loyalty. But they showed no sign of resentment or despair, jutted out their hips as men do when they want the world to see their swords, swaggered in good imitation of fighting men, and made sage comments on each horse's good points as it went round and round, with boys hauling on the leading straps to keep it under control.

At first I wondered that country knights would be so eager to bid for battle steeds, but then I noted that, among the local men, there were men-at-arms and bailiffs from many different regions, as I could tell from their speech. Raoul's knights noted that, too. Without fuss they began to move toward the town gates, too many armed men about to take a chance, too many outsiders to be safe. They left their village spokesman, that stolid cautious man, to make arrangements for the final sales. Together with all Raoul's other men, we should take shelter inside the city walls.

The city of Saint Purnace, as I have explained, was not large, and two main streets, stretching from each of the gates, came together in the central square. In between, the town was a maze, honeycombed with smaller lanes, passageways, crammed tight and intermeshed. Even the houses were laced against each other so that the upper stories almost met, a fire hazard at worst, at best a weakness to the town's defense, for there were spots where the buildings were carved into the outer walls. At first, the town seemed cool and empty as we passed the gates. The guards in the towers lounged carelessly, not exactly friendly, not hostile either, impassive in their leather jerkins and steel caps. They let us through without constraint, although I saw how other travelers, perhaps not having our air of fierce resolve, were stopped and questioned. I suppose on fair days it was hard to keep track of everyone, but there seemed many strangers about. Once inside the town, the impression of coolness was soon dispelled. A country midden in summer heat could not be worse. At least my squires, who followed at my heels like shadows, wore boots to keep themselves above the filth. The main street, if I may term it thus, was not clearly marked, and on passing beyond the gates, veered to the left. Not knowing this, Walter took a middle road that seemed to offer the most direct route toward the square, whose position we could judge by the stone steeple that crowned its church. This central road quickly narrowed to a lane, wound in and out, and we were soon separated from the rest of our men. In ordinary times, I would have enjoyed walking through the town, despite the smells and heat, for these smaller streets were full of women and children about the daily business of their lives; and beneath the overhanging eaves were stalls, loaded with goods of many kinds. Yet, as soon as they saw us, the women and children seemed to disappear, to shrink back behind their wooden doors; and whenever we stooped to examine the contents of the stalls, their owners clapped great shutters down and hammered home the iron bars. I even saw one man make a sign behind our backs to turn away the evil eye. At first I thought it was the presence of my squires—soldiers and townsfolk do not mix—that made the people start with fright. But since they never looked at us, kept their eyes fixed around or above us as if we did not exist, the feeling grew on me it was not we that they feared.

Walter noticed their manner, too. He tried to hurry me

along, although it was difficult to walk faster through the piles of dirt. But presently, rounding another bend, we caught a glimpse of the main square and some of our guard, pacing to and fro. We were not far from them, perhaps two hundred yards or less, and the closeness of those familiar figures made us feel more at ease. So, when I stopped in a patch of sun to buy a cup of ale from an old woman selling it, Walter let me drink, leaning on his scabbard.

"I drink your health, Countess of Sieux," Matt said shyly. Younger, he was not free of speech and his fair skin blushed easily when he spoke, but his blue eyes shone. He saluted with the old horn beaker as if with a silver cup. "Success and long life at Sieux."

He set the beaker carefully down on a wooden bench. The old woman muttered and snatched it back before melting away into the shade. I smiled at him kindly, for I liked him well, he was not more than a lad, fresh out from home.

"I'll drink to that," I said, "when we return and the first stones are laid."

Walter took my arm, helped me to my feet. "And I too, Lady Ann," he said, eyes narrowed against the sun, his face stern. "Pray God the masons' fee not be too high." He settled his sword. "They say their master mason is a shrewd but honest man. That's more than can be said for most town people. They claim that we countrymen be full of whims. But I think these city folk are mindless as a gust of wind. Blow them up like bellows, they spew out hot air. I'll be glad when we get back to Sieux. I'd rather broken walls than these rabbit warrens."

Behind us another shutter clattered close, a tile fell to the ground almost at our feet. It made us aware suddenly where we were, and then, too, how far off seemed the square and the men in it, too far away, distorted by a trick of light, yet only two hundred yards, as I have said. It speaks much for the scorn our enemies had for us that, within sight and sound of Lord Raoul and his guard, they should strike as they did.

That sense of distance, that distorted light, sent a chill, a

tingling to the fingers, like touching ice. I paused to fuss with
skirt and gown, pulling the hood closer about my face, as if
to hide. That pause saved us. From out of the shadow of a
wooden gate, which stood half-open to a passage thread, something stirred, a movement perhaps, an extra depth to the darkness there. The squire on my right, young Matt, must have
sensed it when I did, or my hesitation warned him. With one
hand, he knocked me back, so that I fell and slithered on the
stones. His other arm flew up to take the blow. Along the
length of his mail sleeve, a line of red jetted out, where a knife
caught and ripped, and clattered to the ground. Even as he
clutched his arm and gave a shout, a group of men plunged at
us with drawn swords. Walter already had wrenched his own
blade free, swung up at them, straddling me until Matt behind
could drag me up. We crashed against the house wall, both
squires now together thrusting out. Our attackers, some half
dozen or so, hampered for a moment by the narrowness of the
passage where they had issued forth, startled perhaps by the
clearer space, paused, bunched together still, not having the
sense to fan out. Their hesitation gave Walter time to shout
again, lunge through them, driving with his sword point.

One of them reeled back, cursing as his own arm was sliced.
In the square, our men spun round. Some, seeing our plight,
began to run, but slowly it seemed, in their heavy skirted mail
and spurs. Others leapt to their horses' heads. I could hear
Raoul's voice thunder command even as he spurred his stallion
down the lane, bent low over its neck to avoid the overhanging
gables and walls. Our assassins held their breaths, drove on.
My squires had been well-trained; they knew how to back each
other, and how to thrust and slash, yet they were two to five—
no, less, for another of their number had taken a gash in the
throat. But Matt by now had begun to falter, his sword hilt
sticky with blood, knees buckling as he moved. One to four,
and a woman to defend. There was a great clatter in the lane,
sparks flying where steel hooves struck stone, even as the fourth
man, masked with coif and helmet drawn low, grabbed me

round the waist and began to drag me toward the passageway. I saw Walter stumble and go down. Raoul's sword smashed through his attackers' guard. Over one went, crumbled like chaff; a second fell, backed into that left-handed sweep, a third, turning to run, was trampled under those heavy hooves. And before the horse had ceased to snort and rear, Raoul had wrenched his feet free of the stirrup irons and dived over its side, running as he hit the ground. Only his own quickness prevented his cutting me through as he lunged after me into the passageway. The fourth man who held me had thrust me to the front, so he could retreat, using me as shield.

"Stand off, Raoul of Sieux," he said. "I use your woman as buckler to test your skill." And he laughed. Step-by-step he drew me back, his words echoing in this dark and narrow place, more like to tunnel than to lane, with walls that jutted out in damp, sharp points. I remember this distinctly now, although then I remembered nothing, only the hard cruel grip which moved to stop my mouth, the sword blade against my ribs, the panting whisper at my ear. The passage was some sort of forgotten way, I suppose, ancient, with houses built around and over it. It led directly to the city wall, where once perhaps there had been a main gateway. It was blocked now, or partly so, for suddenly, at the tunnel's end, a gap of light appeared where a heavy iron grill, recently forced out of place, was propped open with an iron bar. And on the other side of it was sunlight, open space, the sound of many men and horses moving freely about.

"A few steps more," my captor breathed, confidence rising as he neared escape. His wine-hot breath scorched my cheek. "We'll take you and him. And your gold to line our purse." He snatched a look to judge how close. That look was his last. Even as I bit at the hand that held my mouth, Raoul leaped. Thrusting up with his wounded shoulder, he plunged his sword, left-handed, beneath my arm. I felt its passing on a rush of wind, felt it force through flesh and bone, heard the gasp, almost of surprise. The fellow tried one more time to get his

own sword up, a gush of blood flooding us both. Yet even as
he loosed his grip, even before he sagged to one side, Raoul
leaped again, over him and over me, toward the open grille.
There was a spate of shouts and yells as he began to drag it
shut. A sword came snaking from the outside, raking along his
leather coat; a shower of arrows hissed through the gap and
fell upon the overhanging walls.

"Fools," I heard a voice rasp out, as now both Raoul and I
struggled with the bars, "I gave no such command." The voice
was sharp like flint; it made me shiver to hear it.

Another man shouted, "They are both here," and we heard
the rattle of swords unsheathed.

But the passage which had been too narrow for a group of
men was an advantage to one. Raoul beat their swords back
as he tried to wrestle the grille closed. It was too heavy for
him to manage alone, too heavy for me to strain and heave.
One of his men, bursting after him, drew it shut; together then
he and Raoul could ram the beam across and notch it into
place. On the other side, men thrust against it to force it loose,
cursing viciously when it held firm. We heard them mutter and
whisper outside the wall, then the creak of leather, the jingle
of spurs, men mounting and galloping off, silence.

"Back, back," Raoul now shouted to his men, pouring behind
him into the alleyway. "They are too many, our hope is the
square else we be all trapped like a denned fox. Ann, can you
walk, are you harmed? God's breath, I did not think them yet
so close." He tried to wipe the blood from my hands and face,
a helpless gesture from a one-armed man, his own face lined
with anger and concern.

I mouthed denial, too stunned to speak, my lips bruised
from that merciless grip. And, to tell the truth, I was not even
sure. Where I had fallen, been dragged, a soreness grew about
my ribs and my breastbone ached. I was splattered with blood
from head to foot. I felt I would never move again.

Aware of impending danger, still shouting orders for my
comfort, Raoul thudded into the wider lane, snatched at the

stallion's reins, and heaved himself up awkwardly, sleeving blood. Down he galloped toward the square. Another trooper, slower, took me up behind. I saw two more haul up Matt and Walter, both white-faced, half-conscious, scarce able to hang on. We clattered back, the bodies of those others rolling beneath our feet. Already the church bell was tolling its warning note.

In the square, confusion swirled, alarms, shouts. Our men left there had made a tight shield ring, facing out from the church steps. The merchants whose houses stood around the church had already flapped indoors; iron gates shot home. Wise citizens escaped when there was chance. A group of soberly dressed men in long cloaks began to bundle up their purchases, drifted off, melted into the small streets, and were gone. Overhead, the clapper of the bell swung to and fro as if it would break from its hold.

"Silence me that bell," Raoul cried. He pivoted his black horse round, looking for bowmen, spearmen, on rooftop or church tower. "Or hang me the man who pulls it."

His seneschal, already mounted, came spurring up, still tying big leather bags to his saddle bow. Clutching him round the waist, the village spokesman tried to grin. "At least they failed to get this," he said, and shook the one he held so that it jangled merrily.

"They may yet." Raoul was grim. "That was what they have been waiting for. Only someone sprang the trap too soon. Lady Ann, your squires were mad to walk that way, and yet, thank God, although I would not have used you as decoy, no lasting harm is done. Stay close where I can watch you myself. That trap is sprung, but they've still the means to set it again. More than we by threes and fours."

He pivoted round. Above him, the bell clanged twice, then was silent. "They'll wait," he said, "by the northern gate as we issue forth. Best place to catch us, pick us off with their cross-bows. We'll go by the southern gates. That route will be longer for us, but it will take them off their stride. Let them find us at the river ford or the woodland road, more space for us to form ranks. A group of Normans looking for easy wealth. But undisciplined. They broke their cover without command. Thank God, their slowness gave us speed. They'll not attack a group of trained knights." I do not mean to say he said all this at once; round he pivoted to each man until all were mounted again, giving encouragement, advice, command, each to each so that everyone knew what was to be done, what expected, what feared. He had even time to smile encouragement at me. I thought, Trained men, yes, but few. There had been many men outside the wall. That flint-like voice would not brook another disobedience, and the longer we waited, the more time for another ambush.

"My lord, my lord." One of his men came spurring back from the northern gate. "The gates are closed but they are waiting outside the walls."

I had a sudden vision, like a cold wave, of the line of black-horsed men bearing down among the cattle pens as we rode out.

There was another cry and we all swung round. On the southern side of the square, a group of men stood forth, not men-at-arms or knights, but townsfolk, and as we watched, more came to join their ranks. They stood in such a way, athwart the southern street, as to block all exit from the square. They were surly men, armed with staves of wood and knives, but resolute. Even as Raoul jarred up his arm to call a halt, their leaders moved to confront him.

"Who breaks the peace of our town," they shouted, "who rides through it to bloody our streets? Restitution must first be made. Leave by the nearest gate, to the north. Our streets are closed."

"Christ," I heard my trooper swear. "By the bones of Christ, they look to drive us forth."

The muttering grew. More men stepped out, legs apart, swinging their wooden staves, stout enough to break a man's head, strong enough to hurl and trip a horse. Even mounted men might be wary of them.

"Out, out," some cried, "out from our town. We'll not be party to your private quarrels." And others, more loudly, "The Count of Sieux has been gone too long and never given thought of us. We've no need of him," while others, voicing perhaps their real hopes, "Give us back our gold before you leave." Raoul's face had paled beneath the brown, the white scar stood out like a cord. I heard our men suck in their breath. A shutter swung open overhead. "Bad luck to you, sod you," a woman screamed, and another tile or rock narrowly missed Raoul's back. Any moment now, violence would erupt.

"Where got you that word?" Raoul's voice was low, but not so low it did not carry through the square. "Restitution, is it, that you want? Before God, you shall have full payment yet. Gold is it? You can have your bellyful." Now he was a just man as you know. I have never heard him do or say an unfair thing, and a massacre of townsfolk would have never entered his mind, especially those whom he had long considered as his friends. But I saw the order form upon his lips. They had trapped him in, no way out but to cut through them. I saw his men settle down to a charge, their lances grated on their saddle bows, behind him, his flag bearer broke his standard out, red and gold glinted the hawks with their cruel beaks and claws. Few foot soldiers can withstand a mounted charge, certainly not untrained men even as resolute and sturdy as these citizens. There could be no doubt in the end, we would ride them down. But the end for us would be as bitter as for them. For they had an advantage which they would use, the narrow streets down which a horseman could not pass. They would retreat and force us to fight through, step-by-step, we would have to hew and thrust. And even if we won to the southern gate, unless we went quickly, it would be too late. All those thoughts flashed through Raoul's mind. I read them as clearly as if they were my own. But again he had no choice. And the consequences also burst clear, like pain, red-hot and burning, before my eyes. I felt the flesh spill open to bone and blood, I felt the fierce grab of those steel spikes. And at the southern gate, waiting, waiting there for us, the dark mass of men and horses in unbroken line.

Men will die for you. But not this way, not now. "No," I think I said, "Raoul, stop. There has been enough bloodshed as it is."

He looked through me, a stranger who does not understand, battle lust so fierce in him that he was numb to all things else. Well, that too is the way of fighting men.

I thrust myself free from my trooper's arms until he let me down. I pushed my way outside the shield wall, advancing into the center of the square. Even the townsfolk quieted on seeing me. I had not thought how I must look, stained with other men's blood, drenched with it.

"Let God provide," I think I said. "I will have no death upon my head. If they want me, here I am."

And even as I spoke, I felt another thrust of pain, like to a spearpoint thrusting through. It weakened and tore. I felt myself bow to it, unknowingly. "Let God provide," I think I said. "Here is your church behind our backs. I claim the right of sanctuary in the name of your saint, who is patron to all things lost and found. Let those who built your church and those who worship there honor its pledge."

And a second wave, a new gush of blood, forced me to my knees, no weapon this to cause such pain, save only that which God uses against all womenkind when their time is come. Except I knew it untimely come, too soon, and fear gripped my vitals in a vice.

God, I think, put the thought and words into my brain, as he has done before, to save us. The right of sanctuary is as old as men, and few are so impious as to disdain its claim. Certainly not the townsfolk of Saint Purnace. As Walter had pointed out, they were no less superstitious than other men and they were proud of their saint and his miracles. To invoke his name was to touch upon their honor, too. And then, to condemn men to certain death was one thing; they might have watched Raoul and his men hacked down without remorse. To

condemn a woman, great with child, is grievous sin; to cut off
an unborn soul from grace is an offence to God; but to kill a
woman at her birthing is an affront to God and man. When
they realized what was happening to me, there, before their
eyes, they might think again. All these ideas then, although
perhaps without form, without name, made them hesitate. But
there was one thing else that made them pause. As for its
worth, count it more or less than these other reasons as your
own tastes dictate. For, since in townspeople's affairs there are
always factions, sides, old enmities waiting a chance, old quarrels rising afresh, a town quarrel was to rescue us.

A second group of men burst through the first, as resolute,
as armed as the others were. "Stand back, masters," their
spokesman cried. A tall, broad-shouldered man he was, with
calm face, short-cropped black beard, small, sharp eyes. His
voice had air of authority. He spoke out words as if they were
made of stone, to be hewn in shape and made to last. "You do
yourselves harm," he said, turning to face the mob, "and those
who urge you on are fools."

The effect was like cold water flung. Those who before had
cried the loudest now began to shout his name. "Master Edward,"
they cried, "Master Edward, our guild master. Hear him." But
others shouted, "He and his stone workers have most to gain.
Pay no heed but thrust Count Raoul out." He held up his hand,
imposing in his short fur-lined gown, not as long as a knight's,
better made than a serf's, silver-belted about his broad waist.
His men stood their ground behind him. I have seen Raoul's
men stand thus to back their lord; these men would be as hard
to budge.

"My lord Count," he turned now to face Lord Raoul, "My
lord, although I think you have greater English titles that come
not now to mind, many have been the prayers said in our
church for your safe return. Saint Purnace is a free town; we
are not part of your lord's domain, yet your forefathers since
time began have been benefactors of our church and town.
Disgrace it would be for us to betray you and your lady wife.

The greater disgrace since we have had nothing but good from
you."

He swung back to face the townsfolk who listened to him,
openmouthed. "And greater disgrace," he roared at them, "if
we deny our patron saint. This church was of my father's make.
I know every stone that houses the holy relics beneath the
high altar. I helped cut and shape its tower. Now, by Saint
Purnace, whom we all love and revere, shall we deny help to
men sore pressed? You have all heard of the sack of Sieux.
Those Angevin soldiers had no pity on the men they hanged.
Shall we look for pity when we need it? I tell you plain, unless
we are beasts, not men, we must help this lord and lady home.
And I also tell you this. Unless we see Sieux rebuilt, we'll not
rest easy in our fine, free town. Murder we'll have, and robbery,
and knavery, creeping in to lure citizens to devil's work. On
your knees, yourselves, that Count Raoul not thrust the truth
of what I say through your spines. Peace brings prosperity to
all of us, not more to one group than another one. It is the
castle of Sieux that guards our peace."

The whispers grew, ebbed away, one last attempt. "We'll
have no bastards born within our holy church."

Now, during this talk, I had somehow managed to creep
aside and found myself seated, I know not how, on the broad
steps of the church. Someone had opened the doors and the
cool air, dark and stale with incense, flowed about me where
I sat. I had the impression of many tall pillars crowned with
leaves, and long dim aisles, and at one end, a window that
glowed with rose and gold.

Master Edward stretched out his hand. "Bastard is it?" he
questioned, suddenly sharp. "The great Duke William was bastard born, yet he lived and died a king. I'd not throw that word
for crows to eat."

I think that he smiled. "Come, lady," he said, "we'll bear
you home." His smile was gentle, his small eyes shrewd. I saw
how his men ran to throw him a cloak, a boy led up his horse,
leading it as if Master Edward was a knight, although he scram-

bled upon it as ungainly as a sack of wheat. I thought he turned and smiled again, showing yellow teeth.

"My lord Count," he said, "we had a meeting planned, you and I. Now, since our place of rendezvous has been disturbed and time is pressing for the lady here, perhaps we have your leave to take advantage of your protection back to Sieux."

The look on Raoul's face changed, he almost laughed. "Now by the Mass, Master Edward," he said, "you are a cunning man and wise. Protection is it that you seek? Rather I think you will protect us." And he smiled. That rueful laugh, that smile, made others join in. Some men ran to fetch their own mounts, ponies for the most part and donkeys, others, still armed, came with us on foot. There was even a churchman or two issuing down the steps, carrying the blue banner of their saint, and a *pax* with a bone or so for extra help.

I sat in the cool shade, unable to move nor think, not even when Raoul himself rode up to the steps and looked down at me.

"What more's amiss?" he began. I almost laughed at him then for his blindness.

"Hurry, my lord," Master Edward trotted past, "if you would have your son born at Sieux."

I looked at Raoul and he at me. His face had paled, all laughter gone. "Is that so?" he almost whispered. "I had not thought. Ann, I had not known. Dear God, forgive me. It is too soon . . ."

And I thought he said, almost too low for me to hear, "Forgive me, Ann, that I take such poor care of you."

And I, I thought I said, "Raoul, acknowledge him, and love him well." Another wave of pain from the belly burst up, drowned me in its aftermath so I cannot be sure we said anything at all.

Well, that is how we returned to Sieux, how we escaped despite all expectation of our loss. And that is how my son was born. All of France has heard the scandal of that birth. No hope then to hide an eight-month child after three months of marriage. Even a patron saint cannot claim such a miracle! Sometimes I think that much that was said and done that day took on a dreamlike feel, as if it happened to someone else. And sometimes too parts of it stand out so clear I can reach and touch them after so many years. There are two memories more that I will share with you, because they show how real, unreal, all things then became.

I thought we were still onboard ship for France. The sailors hoisted upon the ropes, the white sails dipped. The coast heaved like some humped sea beast, the deck boards tilted and leaned.

"Shall we go to France, my lord?" I thought I asked.

"Not so," said Lord Raoul. He leaned against the ship's side, the wind blew his hair back from his face, his eyes were blue-green like the sea. "First to Flanders, longer by twice the distance. I'll not have my son born on Norman soil."

"It is too far," I thought I said. "If we do not hurry, we'll not reach Sieux in time. They will call me peasant slut, to bear my child like a beast in the fields."

Lord Raoul laughed, a laugh that went echoing underground, down a long tunnel with points that pierced and ripped.

"Upon the ground then," he said, "no better place. So did my Viking ancestors see their sons born, upon the rocky shores at the world's rim. If that be his fate, let him seek no better one, and no more gracious lady to grant him it."

The second image is clearer still, death cold, ice cold, etched white and black. I thought I was again at Sedgemont the last Yuletide. It was the day of Christ's birth; all men rejoiced, but there was no joy for us. We thought Raoul near death in the woodcutter's hut where he was hid. I crept out at night from the castle gates, through the storm. Raoul's men stood round the hut, cold as ice, pinched with grief, their faces pale. Snow fell on their cheeks like tears. I thought this pain that nagged and tore was his, that he had suffered it for my sake. I thought their grief was mine that he might die. I stretched out my hands to comfort them, hope, despair, contending which was which, and felt Raoul's own hand, as firm and steady as his courage, take mine.

"He shall live," I said, "I promise it."

But whether it was of Raoul I spoke, or Raoul's son, I do not know. The snow fell in great gouts of white, the cold buried us. All else sank to darkness and was lost.

4

SO DARKNESS THEN, ASK ME NOT how long. Imagine if you will a sleep so profound, that when you emerge from it you do not know at first if that dark place where you have been is sleep or death. I suppose there must have been a time when I knew I could think, could breathe, when perhaps I moved or knew I lived, and later still, when I could begin to have a memory. But it was the noise, a continuing throbbing noise, a tap-tap-tapping, irritating as a water drip, that made me concentrate.

"What is it?" I cried, pulling myself up.

The woman beside my bed rose to her feet, called to the others clustered round the peat fire, crossed herself for fear or relief. "The lady speaks," she cried in her rough dialect, more strange a language than any French I'd ever heard. "She speaks and recognizes us. God be praised. Why, lady, as you know, it is the masons at their work. They build up Sieux, God praise that, too."

I wanted to ask her what should I know of them, but found the question would not form, as if my tongue had forgotten what sense to make of words. I did not even recognize where I was, smoke-grimed walls, earthen floor, a small dark room. For a moment almost I imagined I was still back at Saint Purnace and would have cried out my fear. The women gathered round sensed terror's hold on me and told me many times until I accepted the fact at last (that day, another day perhaps?) that I was in the village at Sieux, I and my child, in the village midwife's hut, and she had saved us both. They pushed her forwards then, a wizened old dame, her brown face like an apple kept too long, its soft wrinkles splitting for pride. Although she wrapped her fingers in her apron strings, and wiped them for embarrassment, she was nothing loath in the end to have the other women sing her virtues, praise her skill. The story of how she had been summoned to the castle for the birthing of my son, she was not shy about telling that. It would warm her memories for a score of years, if she lived so long, although she had come too late for his birth. He had already been born, yet barely lived.

"Why, lady," she told me many times, as if with each telling she would improve upon the last, "we had heard the town bell of Saint Purnace ring out alarm, as we do when the wind is right. And I heard the horse hooves beating up the village street. Well, there I was, sitting by my own hearth stone as now, warming my feet, never dreaming what it meant, or how they'd come for me. Three men from Sieux they were, clattering in, all in their mail coats, battle-stained. I thought they'd draw their swords to prick my heels. 'Run?' said I, 'I'm old. I've not run to a birthing in a score of years. I could have known your fathers and your mothers both as babes. Get someone else if it's running you want.' But when I heard the way of it, then run I did, picking up the skirts of my gown, and they, letting their horses fend for themselves, they ran behind, never caring that those great beasts trampled down my own meadow grass. Well, well, grass will grow again. First babies take their time, but not our darling boy, our little lord. Twice we thought he'd ceased to breathe. But I blew air into his lungs so, so, and dipped a cloth in wine to make him suck."

The women showed me the child then, unwrapping the swaddling clothes they had bound him in, that I might see him for myself.

"Look how long his legs," the midwife said, as proud as if she'd given him them, "and his narrow feet. Proof of noble birth although he came too soon. And his cockstub for a man, a Norman lord in every part. See his eyes, how gray, and his hair, as silver fair as any Viking's, like to his father and his father's father, whom I saw both come out upon such a summer day, long ago."

Her voice flowed on, as soothing as the lapping of the lake. I let it pass, lay with the child crooked in my arms, and knew happiness. Oh, I know other children are born and are beloved, but this one had many reasons to be cherished: the first child and a son, conceived out of darkness and despair; a bid for life when his father's life hung by a thread, and out of fear and death to be so snatched back to life. And I remembered, almost marveling, how when Queen Eleanor brought forth her son, in view of all her courtiers, amid the greatest luxury, I had wondered what it would be like when my turn was come. How like, how unlike. And yet, some have claimed my son was a peasant, born in a peasant's hut. Not so.

"Upon the very stones were you delivered," the midwife told me and laughed in triumph at the memory. "Lord Raoul brought you in a litter from the town. It was tied between two horses, a rough way to travel at best, and he had to ride fast to avoid attack, which he feared still might come. It was too fast for your needs. At the castle gates, his men spread their cloaks and laid you down. But you could not wait. The master mason, Edward his name, being the only older married man, he pulled forth the child. Well, children will be born; those soldiers have seen their hounds in whelp, their mares in foal, but round they stood like amazed sheep.

"'Out of my way,' says I to them, 'let me to my work; you've done harm enough.' Lord Raoul sat upon the ground and held the baby on his knees. Quiet he was, his face all streaked with blood and sweat. He sat there like one amazed himself. Aye, that's the way of men. They can hack themselves to bits with their sharp swords and never feel the bite of it. But let them see a companion's wounds, a lady's distress, they flinch away like children fearing pain. So it was for your noble lord. I know he is no coward, yet I saw him weep for you. But to the other men there I said, 'No need to look as if the world's end has come.' I scolded them when I had the chance. 'See what you

do, you great lumpish knights, that women should bear the
fruits of lust. There are two maids yet in the village, maids say
I, well so they were once, who will give birth, too, within the
year, and who's the father there, I'd like to know.'

"'Go to, you old besom,' mutters one. 'We be knights bachelor.'

"'More shame you,' says I, 'best marry then to get a son.'

"'Married am I,' Master Edwards says, the stone master,
standing up. He flexes his strong arms. A goodly man he is if
I say so, well bestowed. He smiles and smoothes his short black
beard. 'Six daughters have I had and at each of my home-
comings, my wife hangs about my neck that I should have
another chance at a son. But a son have we given you today,
my lord Count, a son to be count here in his time. And when
he has grown to half his height, God willing, his castle shall
have grown to its full one.'"

She smiled at the thought, showing toothless gums, took
the baby and rocked him on her ample lap.

"Now there's a tide," she said, "in the blood of men as in
the sea. When it ebbs out, out flow men's souls. Catch it at
full flood, it will drown death. By nightfall, I knew the child
would live. You, my lady, were another case. I thought the
priest they'd brought from Saint Purnace Church would baptize
your son and bury you.

"'How do you name this child?' he croaks out, expecting
death to rain down on him from the skies as it had done for
our priest here, poor blessed soul, shot arrow-full for comforting the men of Sieux. Well, God's will be done. They
christened the child in haste, in the place where he was born.
No ceremony, more's the disgrace; no great lords to support
him, two knights to hold his little arms and legs, your squires
propped up themselves at his head, unshriven, hot with battle
rage, not even chance to wash off all the blood, a flick of holy
water and it was done.

"'But how do you name him?' moans the priest a second
time, eyes closed for fright.

"'Robert of Sieux,' says Count Raoul. Up he heaved himself upon his feet. For the first time, he smiled. 'Son of my flesh, heir of my house. So I name him before all men.'

"So is he called, our darling boy, our little man. For all of his hard birthing, it is a just and fitting name." Robert of Sieux, so had Raoul acknowledged him. I lay and savored it, for hours, perhaps days. I lost count of time. Thus is joy numbered, like golden beads upon a knotted chain, to run your fingers through one by one. I learned to tend my child as seldom ladies of rank do; I suckled him, saw to his wants. It pleased me. I felt we should not meet as strangers, he and I, whose lives had so been entwined. The least I could do was help him thrive, whose first breaths had been such bitter ones, whose feeble movements of arm and leg were a fight for handhold, foothold, upon this earth. And the second Robert of Sieux grew and prospered. Although sometimes seeing how he stared with his blue-gray eyes, I wondered if those months of secrecy had bred a caution into him, that he should hide what he truly thought. He seldom cried, but watched silently. Yet even in this peasant's hut, no princeling at a royal court could have been better served. The village children hung over him, a toy to play with, marvel at. Their mothers would have driven them off, but I bid them stay. At Cambray, I had been too much alone; I would not have my child want for friends, and every day one of them, an urchin not yet grown, round of eyes and face, mounted guard with wooden stick to chase off pigs and hens. The villagers too came freely in and out, with village gifts such as I remembered from Cambray; fruits still warm from the vine, green duck eggs, goat's cheese. And Lord Raoul himself came to visit us.

I had not realized how tall he was. His head seemed to brush the rafters and his shoulders rubbed against the cobwebs on the wall. He stood looking down at us for a long while. The baby stirred and mewed in its sleep, the sort of sounds babies make. A look of alarm crossed Raoul's face. I have seen such a look on a wolfhound eyeing its young, and my women, noticing him, hid their smiles behind their hands. I motioned to them to leave us alone. Yet even then, he did not speak for a long while, his eyes dark and full of thought. When he did, his voice was low, as it is when he reveals something that he holds deep within him, some private thought that it almost pains him to give it voice.

"My father's name was Robert," he said. "He died young, my mother and he within one night. I never knew him, poor soul, to die of fever far away from home before his life had begun. They say he spoke of Sieux in his last hours and remembered it amid the cold of that English winter in Sedgemont. Now a second Robert gives him a second chance to live. And you, you gave him that chance. You saved us. Without you, we would be dead. How shall I thank you for my life and for my son?"

I said, to make him smile, for his words touched me painfully, I almost wept for them, "You see, my lord, it was not a girl child after all. You have not given me thanks for that."

But he could not jest that day. Yet from that time he began often to come, joining us at the day's end when his work was done, sitting like any man on the hearthstone or, as the evenings continued warm, at the threshold, listening to my women's homely chat. But I could never get him to approach closer to his son, as if he feared in truth the child might break apart, until one day he brought a gift, too. I had gone to the cradle to straighten the coverlets and was startled to find a handful of nuts dropped at its foot, chestnuts they were, round and ripe.

"Mercy," I said aloud. "Who put these there?"

After a pause, "I did," said Raoul. He was leaning, in his way, against the doorjamb, looking in at us. I had not known he had come inside. "For the child," he added after another pause.

I had to laugh. "But my lord, he has no teeth." My women tittered in their way, behind their hands.

"I know that," he began stiffly at first, "I know a baby sucks at milk." Then, relenting, "For a plaything. All boys play with chestnuts, tie them on a string . . ." His voice trailed off.

I began to say, In another year, but stopped myself, put the nuts aside thoughtfully, came up to him and pulled his sleeve.

"You have never watched your baby fed," I said to him softly. "Why not stay."

I sat down on the step in a natural way, had my women unwrap the baby and bring him. I put him to my breast, where, contentedly, he began to suck. Raoul looked at him for a while, then slowly, gently, reached a finger out to measure it against the baby's foot.

"How long it is," he said, almost echoing the midwife. "If his legs stretch as much he'll top me by a head." And he smiled himself.

Yet, although this first barricade was down, I still sensed a constraint in Raoul, a reserve that held him back. I began to notice how these days he had his right arm unstrapped and as he sat he stretched and flexed it, working the fingers open and shut, dropping and picking more of these same nuts which he kept in his sleeve for such a purpose.

I fight left-handed because I must. It is the strangeness that takes your opponent off his guard.

But what if this time that strangeness had not sufficed? Then should we all have been dead, too. Suppose soon, suppose next time, Raoul must meet his enemies in open fight and, suppose next time, he should falter in his stroke or not strike hard enough? And suppose, gauging his weakness, his enemies would know how to attack? Yet never a word spoke my lord of those enemies, and I had not the heart to question him. He came to us; he had named his son. There would be a time, I thought, for me to know what was in his mind even though now he hid it from me.

So the warm summer days continued, the harvest ripened, we were left in peace. And the tapping noise? When I was strong enough, I crept to the door, the old woman clucking behind me like one of her hens. Her hut stood central to the village of Sieux. Beyond it rose the castle mound, which that day hummed with activity. Workmen were busy everywhere, clattering up and down, their small horses dragging up white limestone from new-opened quarries in the cliff. Timber scaffolding edged the gate towers; there was a smell of raw sawdust. And everywhere the tap-tap-tapping upon wood and stone.

The masons were quiet men when they worked; I mean they seldom spoke, nor were they given to chat or song as many workmen are, presumably because they could not be heard above the noise their hammers made. Despite their reputation for being troublesome, they are noted for their seriousness, pay close attention to their work, and seldom stop once it is begun. As I came to know them, I liked to watch how they took the stones and measured them, fitted them to their secret design, hit and shaped with their square strong hands. I did not learn all this about them, of course, from that first look, and it was my squires who told me much about them afterwards. But the noise . . . As long as we remained at Sieux, we looked for it. That tapping became our talisman, heard first thing at dawn, last thing at dusk. It became a part of our life at Sieux, and while it lasted, we could feel secure.

I have spoken of my squires—it was a long while before I saw either of them, and had almost not dared ask news of them. The evening they arrived at the hut door was one to praise God for, another of His gifts.

"I thought you dead." My greeting to them was too blunt to be gracious, yet a fact. Any memory of how we had parted was not a happy one. Shyness made them as blunt at first.

"So thought we you," they said.

They sat and played with the tawny fur of a hound puppy they had brought for my son's christening, admired the wooden horse Walter had carved while his gashed ribs healed. What thanks could be given to either of them, their wounds still stiff, Matt's arm still festering. The cuts should have been stitched, but no one had had time for that. So we sat on the lintel step, silently for a long while, the village women behind us busy with their weaving looms, the stone workers laboring in the last shreds of light, the knights on patrol soon to come riding in. *Men will die for you.* Praise God, not yet. Perhaps they had the same thoughts, for when Walter spoke, he reached across to touch my baby's cheek. The little Robert stirred but did not wake.

"So, my young lord," Walter said. At a nod from me, he took up the child, wrapped in his shawls and linen cloths. A gentle way he had, my squire, wounded in our defense, a knighting promised him in the spring, almost a man, although he was perhaps two years my junior. Yet a third son of a small holding, as he now told us, in a family with many sons; a passel of younger brothers growing up behind, he had no hope of advancement in his father's lands. His western voice grew wistful when he spoke of home; he missed those little brothers more than he had even let be known and his hands were skilled, as if he were used to holding them. But the words he spoke were men's words, although he said them part in jest. "So, Robert of Sieux," he said, "imagine now. When you are grown to my height, or more, your father being a tall man, my son perhaps shall serve you. Thus was my father vassal to your father's grandfather in his day. There's a thought worth thinking on. From father to son, to son, is our allegiance sworn. I saw you born, Robert of Sieux. I remember well the day of your birth. I shall be glad to honor you and swear to be your man."

He put the child back in my arms. His voice was light, the voice of a young man whom death has passed by, whose future has brightened at last, who dares look ahead to fame and loyalty. The words had an older ring to them. They made me cold. Perhaps he sensed that, too; he was always quick to feel another's thoughts. He began to talk of this and that, as was his way to bridge an awkwardness.

Not so young Matt. A wounding had given him leave to speak where before, for modesty, he might have held his tongue. "We thought you dead, Lady Ann," he repeated. "We thought you captured for certain sure." His blue eyes shone. The look he gave Walter was one old comrades share, remembering a danger overcome.

But when I pressed them, "What danger, what men?" (for it occurred to me they might tell me what Lord Raoul had not), they eyed each other, at first mute. I knew that look too, the one men use to keep their womenfolk in ignorance.

"Danger must be thought on," I insisted, although instinctively I suppose I held the baby closer to my breast to shield him from more harm. Noting that gesture, Walter answered cautiously. He had pulled a scrap of wood from an inside pocket and had settled down with his whittling knife. Each flick of the knife on the wood made a point. I suddenly had the sense of what he might have been had fate not set him in the path of a knight; in other worlds there should have been a place for him, at once so practical and curious.

"First, Lady Ann," he told me, "those men were mercenaries hired by Norman lords. Secondly, they knew enough of our plans to surround Saint Purnace and bribe citizens to work for them before we reached the town. Thirdly, they wanted to retrieve the queen's gifts, or failing that, the gold those gifts would bring. The attack on you was an afterthought, although they would have harmed you if they could. And fourthly, their leader was well-known, a *routier* of the vilest kind who hires himself to many lords in Normandy, as pleases him."

Walter went on with his wood working in his calm, thoughtful way, but Matt in his eagerness broke in and said too much, revealing all those rumors which since the fair must have been sweeping through our camp, all those dangers that Lord Raoul had foreseen.

"The last master that *routier* served," Matt cried, "was Jean de Vergay." He spat. "His daughter, Alyse, threatened to reveal our plans. And if de Vergay and de Boissert are involved in conspiracy, as is said, why, conspirators need wealth more than most men. Ready gold they need, to buy themselves friends and win support and..."

The glance Walter gave him silenced him. But thus I learned how my child and I had become the first victims of that plot, that conspiracy, which in the end was to entwine us all.

Well, I was still young to the twistings of the world. I could not believe a woman would wish another harm; I did not think sworn vassals would plot against their lord; I did not think men could be hired to kill. My squires, more knowledgeable, told me I was wrong. But I ask you, what is justice, or where is it? The lot of a peasant is hard enough. All day long he toils that his lord may live. Left in peace, he has at least right to simple joys, to see his children, grandchildren, grow and thrive, to know his hut and crops are secure. Without just lord, his life is naught. Above him sits his lord who owns the land, orders him, creates the laws. His lord has power to make or mar his life. But above that lord sit other, greater lords, counts and dukes, princes, kings and queens, whose every word, whose every whim, can topple in an instant the hopes of lord and serf. *Anything that the great do has effect on everyone.* The attack on us was indeed not an isolated thing, although a woman's spite may have started it, but part of a larger scheme whose consequences began now to unfold. Those consequences reached far away and long afterward, beyond us here at Sieux to a wider world. And so the following day was to prove. It is seldom any of us, in this life, can withdraw in safety from great men's plans. I could not rest safe at Cambray; still less so here at Sieux, a holding of much more importance. So, although what happened next would seem simple on the surface, an event not worth being recalled, it was neither simple nor confined to us. For the man who brought the message came from the royal court.

Now, in normal times, the visit of a messenger is common-place and should bring pleasure to a household. But these were not normal times, and to have a guest at all at Sieux was strange. Back and forth I had pages running, and serviteurs, when Raoul sent me word of this unexpected visit. We had no place for dining save out-of-doors, no food except what the day's catch would bring. My womenfolk went scurrying to pick sweet smelling herbs, and carpenters knocked down scaffolding for table tops... All in vain, as it turned out. In haste, I rummaged through the remnants of my clothes to find what was still left, when down the rutted village street a man came slowly along, almost stumbling for weariness. Behind him at the castle gate his men held his weary horse, weary themselves, unarmed, streaked with sweat and dirt. My women were still trying to tie my overtunic of green silk, one the queen had given me on my wedding day (they stood in awe of such finery, having never seen it at Sieux in their lifetime) and started back in alarm. But the voice that hailed me was one I knew, a southern voice, sweeter than this harsher Norman-French, although the man who spoke was neither sweet nor soft. His name was Sir Renier, and last year in the English court I had known him well. He was one of the queen's most favored courtiers, her kinsman from the south who had helped me win audience with her. But he had also served as messenger for the king. He had helped me, but to Raoul he must be an enemy, one of those men Henry had sent last year to take Sedgemont and proclaim Raoul a prisoner. Last year he had called Raoul a traitor to the crown and would have had him executed for treachery. My women's alarm rekindled in me. For what reason was he come to Sieux, who for pleasure visits an armed camp? Surely he had heard of our plight by now.

"And have you seen my noble lord?" My greetings to Sir Renier forgot, I snapped the question out.

He smiled at me in his southern way, but his dark eyes were narrowed and he ran his hands through his dark curly hair to dry it, for it was still dripping wet.

"Aye, we met," he said succinctly. "The river's a fine place for fish and frogs. I did not think to stand there in my skin to give my message to the Count of Sieux. And he more gracious than when last we met."

"The more fool he," I said, "or the more fool you. He has reason enough to hate you. As do his men."

"I know that." For once Sir Renier was blunt. "Why do you think they threw me in, like to drown me in the reeds? But I do not think your lord would have me harmed, and as I bear a royal message he at least listened to it. He even offered me as good as what you have, cold water to drink, a bed of straw, a mess of fish bones. But I'll not stay. I must ride on." He leaned for a moment against the wall, overcome with fatigue. I had my pages run to bring him wine which he took and drank eagerly. "Ah," he said after a long draught, "Henry serves us sludge from the Thames if not from its sewers. This is more like the wine I knew as a boy. Well, Lady Ann, I have brought your noble lord a message from the king. Do not be distressed. As messages go it was courteous, although I would have preferred to have tendered it in more fitting place." He suddenly laughed, and beneath the laughter I sensed other stress and strain.

"I have given royal messages before," he went on, "welcome or not, but never naked, up to my knees in mud, while the lord of a castle takes a bath. 'I am but a mouthpiece,' I told the count, 'the king's voice speaks through me.' Never a reply Count Raoul made to that, just stripped off his shirt and had his squires pour water over his head; I saw his scars. Jesu, Lady Ann, I wonder he took that wound and lived. I watched him fight with Guy of Maneth as you know. I believed him dead. But never a thought he gives to the scars he bears, as much at ease as in his chamber's privacy. Well, if that is all the revenge he allows, to have me shiver while he bathes, he is well served. His men had gathered all about me on the banks, a villainous crew to grace a noble hall, although I should not say so aloud. I am no soldier as you know; I am a courtier who duels with words. I'd not like to answer to their sword points. Yet the loyalty of his men is proverbial. I saw how they rescued him beneath my nose.

"Well then, the king's message, which to set your mind at rest I shall repeat: King Henry of England, by the Grace of God, sends greetings to Count Raoul of Sieux, Earl of Sedgemont. I am bid tell the count that the king will soon come to France to settle his affairs. And 'warn,' (although that is my choice of word, not Henry's own) and warn the count that the Norman barons are 'treason-ripe.'

"'Treason,' Lord Raoul replied, and his men growled. 'That is a harsh word to use to us who have too often heard it misused.'

"I did not dispute with him; he spoke the truth. But, 'Treason is as the king shall find,' I repeated. 'There can be no rebellion in Normandy that does not touch you, whether you will or no. What shall the Count of Sieux do?'"

"Raoul would not stoop to common plots," I cried, "rather those Norman barons plot against us."

Sir Renier sighed at my frank response. Yet, "I believe you," he said. "And so should the king. But Henry also can be blunt. 'Tell my noble Earl,' he said, 'as he values his English lands which give him that name, that he must help me here in France.'"

The injustice of it took away my breath. "Henry should not try to threaten Lord Raoul," I said.

Again, Sir Renier sighed. "That too is well known," he said. "The king should not be surprised at the answer Lord Raoul sends back. Naked he stood. I believe he cared not where he was. I do him injustice to think he hoped to see me freeze. 'Here is my word,' he said. 'Bear it to Henry your King when you see him next. In England, I am his sworn man and so will attend him there. In France, I owe him nothing, and he shall nothing have. And tell him also this. He will never claim another inch, another life, upon my lands. We shall not reach for revenge, nor seek it out, although justly we could do so, nor do we plot behind men's backs; but make one move, we'll smite him body and soul to Hell.'"

Sir Renier took another long gulp of wine. "Thus the answer from the count. Not an unexpected one, but no more easy in telling for that. Yet the count might know that Henry has changed much from that boy who inherited. Henry may regret, although I am not bid to mention it, what was done at Sieux. Tell your noble lord, Count of Sieux, Earl of Sedgemont, *that*, if you will."

I noted how he rolled all the titles out, although there had been a time when he would have stripped Raoul of every one.

"And tell your noble lord, too, that after this affair in France, Henry has his eyes upon the western borders of his English lands. Matters stand as restless there as ever here in Normandy. I do not know if Henry has the force, or even wish, to take Lord Raoul's English lands away, for all his threats, but in

England, he has the right to command him. If the count will not help Henry here in France, he must in England one day soon."

"I cannot answer to that," I said.

"You should," he replied, his voice suddenly sharp. Here came the whiplash that I had looked for. "You should. They are *your* lands. It is against the Celts that Henry will move." He paused. His voice became soft again. "But it grieves me, Lady Ann, to see discord grow between the king and count. I would have peace."

When I looked at him, he hurried on, "Did I say Normandy was 'treason-ripe'? More like a vat of their cider, brewed to frothing point. De Vergay and de Boissert could well have mounted the attack against you, but even they would not dare such a thing openly unless someone encourages them."

He paused, looked round him, and suddenly stooped to pick up a skein of wool that my women had dropped. "Conspiracy is like this skein," he said, pulling at it as he spoke, "who knows where the ends start or how they ravel out. There are many strands to conspiracy and I, for one, do not wish to know how they interweave. But since, in the past, you and I have been friends, I would warn you. I come as the messenger of the king, but I also serve the queen. It is not easy to serve a master and a mistress both, but in private I will tell you that the queen does not always act as the king would wish. She has many friends here in northern France, made when she was queen of all of it, and among them in the past she has numbered the Sire de Boissert. And his daughter, the Lady Isobelle, who served as her lady-in-waiting for a while. She may not view this conspiracy so great a danger as the king does. After all, it does not affect her or her lands, only his."

"She would not turn against her own husband," I cried.

Sir Renier angrily threw down the wool he had been picking at. "You speak aloud what may ruin a man," he said. "Have a care. Lady Ann, perhaps you are in your husband's confidence and know all he does. If so, I congratulate you. Not all wives have such power. I have a wife myself; I keep her in southern

Poitou and there she'll bide. A courtier's life is best lived alone, she occupies herself with my three sons. So perhaps it should be in all men's homes, even in royal courts. I cannot speak of that. So simply this: I have a message for you from the queen. She has not forgotten you, although you seem to have forgotten her. She would still wish you well for the good you once did."

"I have not forgotten," I said. "Her generosity to me was great."

"Enough," he said, "to threaten all of Normandy by building up Sieux with it? No," he went on, though I tried to explain, "it is not my intent to quarrel with you. What you have done cannot be undone, although it was not wise. Lady Ann, the queen bids me tell you how she would have you gone from France to join her in England. She expects another child and craves your presence at the birth. She peaks and pines, as does her firstborn, that Prince William, who has always been a sickly child. It is only the second son, the little Henry you saw born, who thrives. She asks you to return to keep her company, help her with her children. She would have you see her through her next confinement. It would be a better place for you than this. What shall you do for shelter here when the winter comes, how eat, how be served? You cannot stay in this serf's hut. The queen does not wish more harm on you."

There was real affection in these last words, to make me smile. He put his cup down with a thud so that it overturned. "God's my life," he said, "when you look thus, what should I say? Ann, the danger is very real. Your friends still wish *you* well. Come back to Cambray before it is too late."

I heard the message, more like threat, an order on the queen's part. I did not know how to answer it, nor what she wanted of me. "And should Lord Raoul come too?" I asked. "I have a husband and a son, whom I cannot leave. Nor should I like to follow your recipe for wives, to serve as mares when you men return to breed you up more sons."

He did not laugh. Nor did he comment on my having had a son, although he must have known. I suppose all men knew. Nor did he explain further the queen's part, nor what was his mission for her in France. Neither did he try to persuade me again.

"The choice of phrase," was all he said, "is yours alone. But notwithstanding, I think such arrangement is more natural. God did not make women to wear our clothes. However, if you have influence with your noble lord, bid him beware. That Henry will not win Raoul's support with threats, is something Henry has not realized himself. Nor will the queen be gainsaid. It is a lonely path to defy both king and queen. Courage I admire in any man, the more he shouts it from a shattered wall, the more in truth I lack such defiance myself. Yet Lady Ann, since first and foremost I serve the queen, one more thing: be careful whom you offend. Her friends are powerful and she uses them. So, in the end, as her last resort, she bid me give you this." He fumbled beneath his cloak, brought out a small velvet bag, and closed my hand over it in a fist. The rest of his sentence hung unsaid, like words that float in air. *In the end, if all else fails.*

"Take it as pledge of her good will," he said, "keep it as pledge of yours to her. And the message with it, for your mutual good, keep your husband safe at home." Again he paused, as if debating what else to add.

"God have you in his keeping, Ann," he said finally, "although you will not accept my help. But think well of me."

He bent to kiss my other hand. Then, rising to dust off his cloak, its Angevin crimsons and blues sadly stained and water splotched, he shook himself patiently as does a hound.

"Farewell, Lady Ann," he said, and strode back to his horse. His men, who all this age had been waiting patiently, forced themselves awake, fell in step behind. I sat at the door for a long while watching the way he had gone, and pondered all that he had said, and left unsaid.

When I opened the little bag he had brought, a strange heavy ring lay in the velvet folds, too large for me, more like a man's signet ring, with a strange carved stone shot through with light. A gift then, after so many others bestowed. Why should she resent the use I made of them? A piece of parchment was wrapped around the ring. I puzzled over its lettering, the black flowing script too difficult for my faint understanding. No salutation, no name, just one line which, as I cannot read, would have defied my deciphering had not Sir Renier already told me it: *Keep your husband safe at home.*

I cannot tell you if the writing was hers. (It might have been. There was a slant to the black letters that could have suited her flamboyant style, and I knew she could both read and write.) But the message itself seemed to echo the same thoughts that since our coming to Sieux had ever been my chief concern. Surely it meant well for me, a simple message then, not a threat? But two things I also knew. One was that the queen had not a thought in her head that could be called simple, so what was said or written by her was but the surface of her mind. Beneath were many secrets and divers schemes which I, for one, had never had any inkling of. The second was, that despite Sir Renier's claim, I had little knowledge either of what my husband meant to do. You have seen how Raoul kept counsel with himself and how, even now, he hid himself and his thoughts. And I remembered too what had been my first impression of Raoul when we met, when, as a child, I was brought to Sedgemont on my father's death. Conflict there had been between us from the start, flaring hot, that he should have plans for my little estate, for Cambray, and never tell me what they were, that he should arrange a marriage, between me, as his ward, and the man I knew to be our most bitter foe. What now should be afoot, and I not know the truth? Too long I had led a sheltered life, I told myself, too long been immersed in my woman's world. I sat and stared at ring and message until darkness fell and all men slept. I did not sleep, but watched my child in his cradle beside the fire, my women in their straw beds, the wolfhound puppy that scratched and snorted as if chasing sheep. Where Lord Raoul was that night, where he went each day, what were *his* intentions, I had no idea. I did not know where Sir Renier rode and what he did. Nor who these conspirators were who gathered to wreck our hopes. Thus were we drawn into the world of the great, that their plots and schemes should rob us of our peace. I resolved, come morning's light, to hunt down the truth.

At daybreak then, the child bathed and fed, I kilted on my old gray skirt and went out to search for Lord Raoul. Privy to his secrets I was not. Today I meant to change that. Early as I was, the patrols had already gone. Lord Raoul had gone, too; my squires, mounting up, would have stopped for speech but their captain, bawling at them for tardiness, bid them ride on. Within the shelter of the great castle towers a fire was burning to keep the workmen warm as they struggled into their clothes. I had not come up to the castle since their work had begun and, at first, I was appalled at the litter they had made. Even those carefully heaped piles of stone that had caused us so many hours' work were scattered abroad. There was not one place that seemed free of refuse and dirt. Between the scaffolding, apprentices leaped and swung as if they had been born in trees with tails. It has never failed to amaze me that, out of such chaos, they could build their clear and uncluttered designs.

"Save you, Lady Ann. You look for something, someone?" It was the master mason, riding up on his small white horse. He clambered off it as if climbing down a stair. Today he was dressed in his workman's clothes, a tunic cut off short to reveal his brawny arms and a kind of apron around his waist, into which were stuck his long-handled hammers and other tools. I had not seen him since he saved my life. I did not know what to say to him, but he was a kindly man as you know; he took the time to talk with me.

"If you would search for someone," he said at last, "climb up." He gestured toward the scaffolding that edged the towers and gave me his hand, not gracefully as do knights, barely letting their fingers touch, but firmly, so to draw me on. As we moved from plank to plank, he paused to run his palm along the layers of stone, as if to feel they were true to line, as if to search out hidden flaws. I had a strange sensation as we climbed. For the first time, I think I realized what strength lay in those walls, so that, on brushing past, you sensed, like some great sleeping beast, the power that was crouched in them. Like some sleeping beast, they waited for a touch to send them rearing, flaring up. And as we rose higher, we could see the faint lines of the outer walls, not apparent from the ground, hugging the contours of the cliff, curling along its crest. When they were completed, they would enclose two courtyards, an outer and inner bailey, both with their own gate towers, and where the cliff stood steepest, the foundations of the new keep were already being dug. There was even a water diviner with his hazel rods, testing for water in the inner courtyard. I watched how the twigs twisted and leaped as he held them before him, walking to and fro.

"Aye," Master Edward said, noticing my interest, "there's water in plenty beneath this rock. And so I told Sir Renier."

"You told him that?" I asked, dismayed.

"I only told him what he could see for himself," he said evenly. "We are not fools. I also told him that I once had heard in England such a castle cost more than six hundred pounds to build. Pounds English, that is," he added, as if that made the figure more reasonable. "I did not tell him, you understand, that within two years the castle was inhabitable. Let him think we lack for wells, that the two that were here were too fouled for use. And let him think we go as slowly as we can, so as not to spread alarm among those Norman lords. But remember yourself that the building season this summer has been long. We'll easily top our record of twelve feet of stone a year. And, since the foundations of the gate towers were not destroyed and we can use old stone at the topmost layer, we'll have you in them before the autumn rains fill our new wells."

He paused for breath, went on more slowly, outlining his plans. Already you could see the difference where the new white stones stopped, the old gray ones had been added on. And when we reached the topmost layer, where masons were busy with plumb line and rule, I saw for the first time the true strength of Sieux. Although not built to a part of its height, on a clear day like this, it had command of the whole countryside. When it was complete, no army, no column of men, no single traveler, could move unseen across those grassy plains, from the distant hills to the river's sweep. A gateway then between north and south, and Sieux guarded it.

As if guessing my thoughts, the master mason said, "Sieux was once the strongest castle in these parts. And this is a region known for castle building. The cost is great, but the work will be sound. I know my trade. I have worked in stone, both church and keep, from childhood, and what I learned, my father taught. And he, in turn, studied with the engineers, as they are called, who went from Anjou to the Holy Land when its Count, Fulk, fought on crusade. There were many secrets in Outremer, and castle building is but one of them. My father taught me how to build for strength, but from church records I have learned how to add comfort, too. Yet, Lady Ann, I dare say this: no castle is strong, however high its walls or deep its wells or thick its keep, unless the man who is lord of it makes of it what he should. This has been a hard homecoming for you. And a hard childbearing, God knows. And for Count Raoul bitter enough to have daunted a lesser man. You and your son will be a joy to him. He will need your comfort in the months ahead. Sir Renier is but the first to come visiting. They'll all be curious to see our work, those Norman lords, they'll soon come snooping around." And he spat in contempt. "But I, I and my men, we live to do you service, now and at your need."

A kind man, Master Edward, and wise, diplomatic in his way as Sir Renier. But he too seemed to echo my fears. And the queen's warning ran in my head, so I could not ignore it. *Keep your husband safe.* How I longed too for that. But to keep Sieux safe, and us safe, Raoul would not wait for safety to come to him. If danger threatened, he would seek it out, not hide and trust it would pass him by as another man might. I knew him well, too well to hope he could change. And even Queen Eleanor had warned me once that such men cannot be tamed. He had sent an answer back to a king who would crush him if he could, and I to a queen who did not like to be disobeyed.

Neither of us then had given ground, but danger certainly lay ahead.

"Well," Master Edward said, as if I had spoken my thoughts aloud, "lately I have seen Count Raoul with one of his men. They ride at dawn along the river banks..."

There was warning also in his voice. It too said clearly, Leave well alone.

I paid no heed. Barely stopping to bid him farewell, I hastened to the stable yards, had them saddle me a horse, although they cavilled at it, I being alone. I made them help me mount, then, spurring hard, I rode along the cliff to track Raoul down.

5

T HAD BEEN SO LONG SINCE I HAD
been out that the beauty of the day almost blinded
me. Beneath the sun was an autumn chill that made
you want to breathe in great gulps of air. At first
there were plenty of people for company: workmen hurrying
up and down the cliff, villagers gathering in reeds for thatch,
cutting grass for one last foddering, and squires practicing in
the tilting fields. I watched these for a while, not letting them
see me for fear they would question me. Both Matt and Walter
had improved, but especially Matt. Not once today did the
weighted bag of sand swing round to unseat him as he rode at
it. At another end of the great meadow, knights were exercising
their chargers. Out they galloped, turned, and wheeled. These
too are tricks you must learn if you mount a charge. But all
for war and the glory of it, nothing suited for so fair a day.

I urged my own horse on. The river path wound in and out,
the going slower where it was blocked with summer growth.
Presently we left the familiar tracks and moved on alone, following the twists and bends of the lake. We brushed past a
grove of withy bush, mounted a rise, and looked down upon
the placid waters spread below. Soon, when cold weather came,
the skies would darken with wild fowl, heading south, as Lord
Raoul had once described. Here also today nothing stirred,
only my horse and I, breasting through the undergrowth.

The noise was one, once heard, never forgot. It blinds the
eyes, deafens ears, pounds in the blood, the sound of steel on
steel, singing like a lash. Two men were fighting at the water's
edge. On foot alone, in the full sunlight they fought, the sandy
verge about them scuffed and torn. One of the men I knew at

once. Stripped to the waist, his flesh dripped sweat, shone gold, except where a great scar was curled like a whiplash itself from shoulder to waist along his right side. I knew his style of fighting too, the backhanded slash, the way he lunged with sword point (not many Normans like to stab) and the speed with which he turned and leaped. His opponent I did not know, then I thought I did. Dressed all in black with his back to me, he reminded me of another man, another time, and for a moment all went dark. I thought I stood in the great courtyard at Sedgemont, a year ago, and heard behind me, as I had heard it then, the mutter of watching men. I felt the cold wind blow, ice cold to bone, and saw again Lord Raoul fighting Guy of Maneth for my sake. I saw them drive themselves, two men met to be judged by God which told the truth.

If I but open my eyes, I thought . . . But my eyes were open and all was colorless, white like ice or snow or sand. The black figure of Maneth reared up, his sword blade glistening in the sun. Down it sliced. The snow covered ground at Raoul's feet splashed red. I thrust my hand into my mouth to stifle cry. Then sight and color and shape came back, and I knew where I was. True, it was Raoul who fought, but Guy of Maneth was dead, buried these many months, and the other man was one of Raoul's knights, Dillon by name, an old friend. They fought for exercise as companions do. All else was peaceful, their horses tethered in the shade, a hound or two sniffing in the reeds, Raoul's shirt slung upon a bush. And as I watched, he flung down his shield, that long triangular one a man can duck behind, and took up his sword in his right hand. Dillon did the same and, at a sign, both began to fight in earnest now. I had not heard of men fighting so, but I saw Raoul's intent. He set the pace, and being quick on his feet could often outreach his comrade. And once indeed I saw him hold back, as he had done for Maneth, to his own loss. But Dillon was as quick and there was one thing he could do which Raoul could not. And now I saw how Raoul forced himself to it, to raise his right arm above his head, to parry a stroke or sweep down from one. At each pass, I saw him urge Dillon to make the move that he in turn must make the counter one. Each time, defeated, he ducked under the blow or, at best, returned it awkwardly. And once, when he turned round, I saw his face. That look made my spirit quail. He willed himself; it was his own weakness he fought. *I may be crippled, Ann. I do not know if this arm will heal.* This then was his defiance hurled against his enemies, this part of his hidden secrets. He stooped a moment, splashed a handful of water to his mouth. I remember how he used to move, to fight, a cat that leaped with muscled grace. He straightened, wiped his hands upon his sides, tensed, gave his war cry, that Viking shout, and launched himself once more with all his strength. Dillon's face was equally taut. He knew his lord's weakness like his own, must play to it, yet control his stroke. But now Raoul forced him to fight to defend himself. Unaware, I bit my underlip until the blood ran upon my chin. What if Raoul slipped or buckled beneath the blow, what if Dillon tired and could not turn the blade? Then Raoul leapt forward again. In my mind, I have seen him make that move a hundred times. Up came his right arm. "Strike down," he shouted. The other backed, swung up his black-covered arm. Down whistled Dillon's sword. Raoul caught it full upon his own; this time he did not duck or parry, but caught it full and thrust up, using all his shoulder's force, held it above his head, locked into place. You could see the veins stand out, the muscles tense. Then his arm bent. Dillon's sword continued its downward sweep; I saw the line of red start out.

Not knowing what I did, I hurled myself from my horse, went slithering down the hill, briars catching at my face and arms, pebbles and dirt showering beneath my feet. They did not hear me, still intent about their work, nor did they see me, backs toward the land. I caught Dillon about the waist, hauled at his arm with all my weight, dug in my teeth wherever I could reach, clawed with my nails. He gave a great cry of alarm, back-handled me, clutched me to him so we both fell together into the lake. Head over heels I went, my skirts billowing out else I would have sunk up to my neck. Beside me Dillon floundered to his knees, mouthed and sputtered, flailed for his sword. On the bank, Raoul, still staggering from surprise, himself plastered with mud and wet, watched as if struck dumb; a fine sight, his companion and wife wallowing in the reed bed.

The oath he let out I'll not repeat. It scorched my ears. Nothing worse than the ones Dillon let fall. I felt myself flame with disgrace, every womanly precept broke at once. To come between lord and man is bad enough; to dispute him at sword point folly beyond belief. Poor Dillon. Spitting out mouthfuls of sand, liberally festooned with duckweed, he dragged himself out upon the bank, where he sat down heavily, feet still in the water, not having the sense to drag me after him. Spent for breath, he leaned upon his sword and observed me. The hounds, thinking to join in the sport, were already paddling about. It was Raoul at last who hauled me out. I wiped my eyes on the wet corner of my gown, tried to wring out my skirts, tried to make coherent speech. All that came forth was simply this: "I thought he had killed you."

"Mother of God," it was Dillon who replied. "I thought rather you who would kill me."

He looked at Raoul, opened his mouth to speak, closed it, and took up his sword, still dripping with weed, to clean it. Raoul too reached behind him, pulled free his shirt, began to mop the cut running down his arm, not much more than a scratch, no more than those which the thorns had left on me. Neither man looked at me, nor at each other, but I felt a ripple pass between them, gone upon the thought. Unnerved by it, I began to scold.

"I thought this oaf," for so I called poor Dillon to his face, "I thought this lout would tear you apart. I thought you spitted like a piece of meat. How could you let him use you thus?"

At a jerk from Raoul's head, Dillon clambered upright. "I tell you what I think . . ." he began, then swallowed hard, took up his shield and leather coat, called off the dogs. Dragging on his horse's rein, he went wearily up the hill. After a while we heard him catch my horse and, leading it, ride off toward the castle grounds. I was left alone with my noble lord.

The start was quiet enough. "So, lady," he says, not looking at me, staring straight ahead, legs apart, wiping at his arm, "you think to become an expert with a sword, when to thrust perhaps, how to use a shield. Now correct me if I'm wrong, but I remember when you were but a child, you tried to hack my heart out and nearly took your own. A swordsman now is it I have as wife, as no doubt last night you played at courtier."

I knew the sound of that voice very well, low, almost pleasant. He might have smiled. Beneath, the calm was ominous. I said not a word, sat still, wringing out my clothes.

"Well, well," he said, pulling his shirt over his head, his voice muffled by its folds, "a brand new weapon for our use, your head, with about as much sense in it as a mangonel."

I pursed my lips, began to drag off my boots to empty them. They squeaked at every move, my skirts sagged above my knees. "So let us count the ways," he said, numbering them upon his fingers, one by one, "that, in six months of marriage is it yet?, you have been so free with your advice, to toss my men upon their backs, challenge my command, spread scandal throughout Normandy . . ."

"And give you a son," I said.

"Aye, that too," he said, "I have not forgotten that. Else should I have pushed you back to drown, fit ending for such a scold. Count that debt well paid. God's wounds, girl, are you not abashed? Look at you, even your face is streaked with blood."

I had forgotten my bitten lip, and tested it gingerly with my tongue.

"Your Sir Renier would not know you."

"He is not *my* anything," I replied waspishly, angered at the injustice. "He merely gave me advice once again when I needed it. As I have reason to suspect he offered it to you."

"Which I refused. Then is he well paid to whisper secrets with my wife."

"No secrets," I said, "except those which you hide. The queen's message to me was simply put, to keep you safe. Which all of Sieux would wish save you yourself."

He stared. "God's wounds," he said again, "you would believe what she says? You are more simple than I thought. I doubt if she has my interest at heart these days. And what else?"

"That I hie home to Cambray," I said. "I am not so simple that I would not welcome it. Better than here. Although for foolishness what place more apt. You will kill yourself before you've done or have Dillon do it for you. Cannot you find other ways to pass time profitably?"

"I am a soldier," he said, belting on his sword to prove his point. He snapped the buckle close. "What else should I do with a right arm? Dig weeds, plough oxen with my peasants in their fields? Write script in a monastery, pray there that my enemies run away? But since you would spy out men's affairs," he reached out with his right arm, caught the slack folds of my gown, pulled me on my feet, "feel that," he said. "Almost as good as new. Were you a man, you'd not wish to come within reach of it."

I thrust my own right arm out, tried to break his grasp. "And were I a man," I said, breathless, "you'd not threaten me. I stand to my word. I thought you hurt, no more, no less. But since you speak of Sir Renier, what do you plot behind my back for Cambray, what for Sieux, that I should learn it from other men? What will Henry do in France that we must protect ourselves from him?"

"God's teeth," he sword, "lady, will you never give up? Your audacity would make a strong man blanch. Should I cower behind your skirts? If you want a mannequin, look to your son. These be men's affairs." He towered above me, a full head taller, broad of shoulder, his wet shirt plastered to his skin, his eyes their darkest gray, narrowed like a cat's. I could see his fingers itched to box my ears. But I had never let him see that I was afraid.

"Should not I have some knowledge of your plans?" I asked. "You mock me that I am no wife to you..."

"Wife," he said. "Of late I've had but little evidence of that. Look at your sad face, like widow at a burying. This is a day to rejoice in, you turn it to my funeral. Not that as widow you'd make a man's heart leap, more like to half-drowned sheep than wife."

"Not much better yourself," I cried, scorn completing what his anger could not do. "One of your serfs picking reeds." I would have kicked at him had I my boots on. "Go romp with them if you lack for sport. No doubt you've had your fill of village maids these past months."

He eyed me, not smiling exactly, as always perverse. When he had prodded me to rage, his own was gone.

He said, "Had *your* Sir Renier come one day late, you could have blurted all the truth out. This is a day to celebrate. At least you could wish me joy. I have been wounded before; I know when a wound will heal. If I can use my right arm once, I can again."

"I could wish anything as long as it not be here," I said. "I wish he *were* my Sir Renier. He treats me with courtesy."

"Courtesy is as it is found," he said. "Kind words do not always mean kind friends. 'Go romp with the peasant maids,' you said. Perhaps I shall."

He spun on his heel, whistled to his horse. It came trotting up on its tethering rope, a workaday horse, yet it answered to his call. He caught at its bridle, loosened the rope, vaulted on its back.

"Perhaps I shall," he repeated, "likely to afford me better game."

He kicked his horse with his soft boots; it cantered off. At the cove's edge, he wheeled, leapt off, then on again, came galloping back. I stood and watched him, tugging at the knots in my hair. In England once last year, Henry had mocked at him. *At my knighting,* Henry had said, *I could leap upon my horse, full-armed. Raoul, can you?* Raoul, scarcely able to walk, had not replied. Today he wore but shirt, braies and soft boots, was not armed except for sword and belt; one day again in full mail, I was sure he would show the king that he could equal him. He veered to my right, splattering sand. I felt the rush of his passing brush me, as once more he leapt and wheeled, putting all his weight on his right side. His long hair blew back, he smiled, dropped the bridle, stretched out both hands, thus balanced, rode as if with wings. I thought suddenly, Dear God, even anger today is but a show. This is his pleasure welling up from his heart core, that he must display it to the world. I looked at him, a man turned into boy, or a boy who feels himself a man, his strength restored and, with it, his hopes, his pride. Once more he swept round to gallop past.

Now, he could not know, nor anyone, that as a child, my dearest wish had been to see my brother ride like this, to have him leap upon his horse, set me before him, ride across the sands at Cambray. And, as suddenly too, it seemed to me that the years had rolled back, there was no time, and I was as young, as happy then. My brother, Talisin, still lived, my father lived, and all my life was centered here. Almost without thought I stepped full into his path, raised my hands. The woolen gown slid about my feet in a sodden heap; in kirtle only, I waited for him. Back he came at a gallop straight for me. I never flinched. At the last second he reined back, bringing his horse to its haunches, snorting and panting. I stretched my foot for the stirrup iron, too high, until he bent to pull me up. I sat in front of him, his other hand clamped about my waist. He flicked his horse's sides; we galloped off through the rush beds, water spilling beneath our heels. I clung to the pommel and let the wind carry us away. There was no time, I say, carefree we rode, Sieux and its dangers gone from thought, count and countess lost somewhere else. And after a while I leaned against him, felt his body's heat through the damp linen on my back, felt his exuberance mounting like sap in a tree, felt the thudding of his heart.

Gradually, we dropped back to walk, came to another sandy stretch. Without speech, he swung me off, dismounted himself, stripped off belt and shirt, his hose, his boots, let them fall where they dropped. He took me by the hand and drew me into the lake; when its creamy depths swirled about my waist, my cuts and scratches burned.

"Jesu, Ann," he said, "you have been missed." He smoothed the hair back on either side of my face. "Ann," he whispered,

"I would not hurt you again or do you more harm. I thought to see you die that day. Not remember how my son was born? Each day I have thought of it."

The sun fell on us, gold-flecked, the levels of the lake stretched into a heat mist. I smiled up at him. He reached down, tore off my shift, it floated away. He put his hand upon my neck where the pulse beat. "I hoped," he said, "to prove that you had not forgotten me."

I smiled again, and stretched out my hand to touch his face. The line of the scar ran faint beneath my fingertips. He swallowed hard, "Dear God," he said, almost to himself, "what should a man do and still be man?" He slid into the water in front of me; with his long legs, he parted mine, dived beneath, brushing between with all his body's length. Up he came, slowly along the spine, breathing warm against each bone, tracing out each knot until he came to the shoulder blade. The water fell in great drops on my breast; he bent and kissed each drop as if drinking it. Then beneath the water he went once more; I felt his mouth brush each thigh, felt it travel from cleft to waist and down, running like fire. His hands tightened along my back, fingers parting at the crack, thrusting, as he reared up; my legs caught high above his, he leaned me on the pillow of the lake, bent over as he thrust within.

Sun and fire, the water's cool, his flesh like silk, I wore him as a second skin, buried in, no space for breath, only light that fell in golden showers. Before even that time was done, he had carried me to the grass bank, stretched me out, parted me, slid in again. The air blew up the wild scents of mint and thyme; against my ear he breathed, running with a fingertip along each arm, each breast, each inner thigh, a circle cupped with but one liquid core. And when he rolled upon his back, he fitted me to his body, a coverlet to keep him warm, a sheath into which to plunge himself. I arched back to his desire. "Take me," I cried, my heart cried, "a hundred different ways." And at my neck bone he mouthed the same. *"Embrasse moi, touche moi, ma mie."* Impaled, imprisoned, imprisoning, we came to peace; nothing but sun and sand, the water lapping far away.

It seemed a lifetime before the world spun round. Perhaps it was. One can live a lifetime in a few hours. The day had grown chill when we thought of time. Within his saddlebag, he found a cloak to cover my nakedness, for my kirtle had drifted off somewhere and my gown lay waterlogged upon a bank. I helped him strap on sword belt, and sword, and, by and by, gather his other gear where he had left it. It was these things, men's gear, war gear, that brought the present back. And with it came those questions which had burned in my brain all night.

"Why should those Normans plot and plan? What does Sir Renier seek for the queen? Why does King Henry come to France?"

He reached round to clamp his hand across my mouth.

"Mother of God," he said, "like to swamp me, more questions than this lake has floods. Be patient. They will be dealt with in due course."

I wriggled free of his grip, exasperated that he still would not answer me. "And you," I cried, "what will you do at Sieux, what of your English lands?" He tried to silence me again. When I resisted, he slid back on the saddle to give me room.

"Careful," he said, for the horse had begun to start and skiddle about, "like to toss us on our backs—although I could become used to it." And he grinned, that lopsided grin that made my blood run warm.

"No secrets then, only what I know or guess. I have told you many times that the Norman barons are bred for war; they crave war as a starving man craves meat. Now Henry's lordship over them has been too harsh for their taste. For one thing, if they do not jump to his commands, he is more than capable of pulling their castles about their heads, which does not please them you can be sure. They like to fight only if they win. To topple Henry from his Norman dukedom would more than satisfy them, and Henry's brother gives them the excuse they have been looking for. Henry's brother is younger and suffers from a common younger brother's complaint, the lack of land. So now he lays claim to all of Henry's French lands that Henry inherited, and the Norman barons will support him in his rebellion. Both Henry and the rebels will seek my help (why else should Sir Renier come here on Henry's behalf?). But both sides, to be blunt, would prefer I be unable to fight at all. And no one wants Sieux rebuilt; much better for them if we are finished as a power in central France. When the truth be learned that Sieux is already partway restored, and I sufficiently recovered of my wounds to be more than capable of defending it, why, both sides may have to pause and reconsider what they will do next.

"As for Sieux, my intention for it is simple, too. It is an idea I have come late to understand, but my grandfather, Raymond, maintained that, just as Sieux was situated between north and south, so in policy it should act as a balance between contending sides. Raymond was considered a wise man in his day, noted for his diplomatic skill. At the start of the English civil wars, he tried to keep a neutrality between King Stephen and the Angevins. It was I who, for my pains, broke his rule by siding with King Stephen. For my pains, say I. Dearly have I paid for them, that Henry should have thought to have revenge on me. But if I can, I'll hold the balance in France again, maintain Earl Raymond's neutrality. Ann, I know these Norman lords; they fight to serve themselves. Let Henry's brother take note of that."

"Who is this brother," I asked, "how called?"

"You may well ask. Soon all of us will know him. Geoffrey Plantagenet, his father's name, whom they say in all things else he is like. Geoffrey *le Bel* was his father called, the fairest man in all of France, and of all men the most treacherous. Now Geoffrey, the son, claims the right to his brother's lands, and to Henry's titles, even those of Count of Anjou and Maine. The way of that is strange, too. Count Geoffrey, on returning from a successful expedition to the French court, full of triumph then, still in his prime and young to be father to these sons, he plunged into the river Seine. The sun was hot, he took a chill." Raoul grinned again. "We know the consequences of bathing in a lake," he said. "Count Geoffrey's were not so pleasant for him. He died. But before his death he wrote a will, or rather, not knowing how to write, had the monks where he lay pen it for him. In this will, he left to Henry, his oldest son, as is just, the paternal lands of Anjou and Maine. But if Henry were to inherit England, which seemed most like, then the second son, this Geoffrey Plantagenet, was to get them instead. The nub of the whole affair lies here. For when Count Geoffrey died, Henry was away hunting, a dutiful son, in faith, to follow the deer while his father dies, but then hunting is his most cherished pursuit. He returned to find the will was writ and the monks clamoring for him to agree to its terms. For Count Geoffrey had made them swear never to lay him underground until Henry had accepted it."

I shivered.

"Yes," he agreed, "a cruel wish, made and sealed by cruel men. Myself, I think it strange that the Count of Anjou would sign away lands from an eldest son. William of Normandy, first of the line, left Normandy to his eldest son; it was the second son who got England, for England was counted the lesser of his possessions. Nor, to be frank, should Henry give up Maine and Anjou. Lacking them, his other lands in France are two halves of an eggshell, without the meat. But Henry made a mistake as well. Out of grief, or under threat of force, he agreed to accept the will. On the putrefying corpse he so swore, placed his hands on it in most holy oath. Henry has lived to regret that oath, but the younger Geoffrey holds him to it. Well, Geoffrey Plantagenet inherited three castles as a younger brother's share; in spite of Henry's solemn oath, Geoffrey might wait forever for the rest.

"And what is more, he'll lose those three castles too if he threatens Henry over them. But I will tell you two other things which Sir Renier, not knowing well either Normans or English, may not understand. One is that, even if Henry and his brother tear themselves to shreds, not a single English lord will help Henry in France. In England we have had war's reality; the man who would seek a pretext for it is nature's fool. That is my opinion, although you would accuse me of wanting war.

And second, those Norman lords will never make a move again until the spring. They prefer to keep the winter months for their other loves such as hunt and feast. Too wet, too much mud, too cold for fighting, no profit for them until then. And, before the spring, Henry will have come back to France..."

"How can you be so sure?" I blurted out. "Mewed up as we are, how can you know that? And what of the attack on us?"

My first question touched him on the raw. Beneath his faint sunburn, I think he flushed. His answer was steady, without rancor.

"I may live the part of a wandering knight," he said. "How did you call it, like a serf, but at King Louis's court I am a count. Word comes to me. My scouts bring news; sometimes even Louis sends it. We do not live so isolated as you think. As for the attack at Saint Purnace, it was neither well planned nor well placed. It had all the signs of a Norman plot, brute force and not much skill. Those Norman barons would have liked our gold. They need gold to pay rebellion's costs but, being greedy, thought to take you, too. Thank God they failed. So your squires, I think, already have explained. But remember that those Normans never make a move unless some great power backs them to give success. And this is something Sir Renier himself must have told you." A reprimand this, if gently given.

"And now I will tell you why Henry will come to France, the truth—to do homage for all the lands he holds of King Louis; to be acknowledged by Louis as the overlord of all those lands and men and to show the world what is his. Such an open display of power is a challenge to Geoffrey Plantagenet, and will not please the barons who hope to support Geoffrey's claims. And there is one other person it will not please—Queen Eleanor. For Henry will also do homage to the French king for her lands in Aquitaine, and *those* the queen had hoped to keep for herself. She will protect her lands as fiercely as any vixen with her cubs.

"Now, what the queen and Sir Renier plan, I but guess at and Sir Renier may be simply gathering news. Yet I suspect the queen may regret having given us the means to rebuild Sieux, as much as Henry regrets having given us the cause. What her intentions are, better I think you do not know. And since kings and queens seldom keep faith long, unless at spearpoint, better too, I think, to follow my grandfather's advice and steer clear of them."

We had been riding forward all this while and were come almost to the castle gates. He turned his horse's head toward the village and paused. I bit a last question back, Suppose they force you to chose a side? Perhaps he guessed what was in my mind.

"Ann, trust me," he said. "If not this season's end, another one, or another, will see the building of Sieux complete. I'll not leave my French lands until that's fairly done. Nor for pride, if you will call it such, shall I go back to England because Henry commands. Let him beg for that. There's my revenge. I'll go when it pleases me. But do not you put your trust either in royal messages or royal gifts." He hesitated. "They say," he said at last, "that when Queen Eleanor left the French court, her marriage to Louis annulled and she hotfoot to reach the safety of her own city of Poitiers, she was ambushed on the way south by this Geoffrey Plantagenet. Ambushed or met by design, who knows. He claims she promised to marry him, and slept with him to seal her vow. He was only a boy, rash, reckless with ambition. She may have been as reckless herself." He shrugged. "Sir Renier would not have spoken of that either I am sure, yet it is commonly believed the queen became Geoffrey's lover as she had been his father's but weeks before and, on parting, promised him her hand. A second oath then, that has been broken to his great loss. But they say too that the queen feels she owes Geoffrey some recompense. They say she supports him."

Raoul mused a while as if to let his words sink in. Perhaps they did, although, since the queen was my friend, I was not the one to harbor gossip against her. Nor Raoul the man to speak evil without cause. That at least I could have remembered. When I did, it was too late.

At last he roused himself. "But while we wait until the spring," he told me in his decisive way, "I've no intent to become their plaything for them to bat between their paws. Neutrality does not mean sleeping in the sun. The more our enemies seek to use us, we'll use them." He paused again to throw one last question out himself. "You'd not return to Cambray without me then?" There was a new urgency in his voice, as if he had been debating with himself. Perhaps it was a point he was not easy on; perhaps he too had not slept last night.

"Ann," he said, almost to himself, "this has been a special day. No man can feel a man who is not fit to guard his family or his friends. No," as I tried to interrupt, "it is so. How shall I forget the way my men were used, my companions betrayed, my wife seized? God has given me back my strength. I pray to make good use of it. But there is no other answer to Henry than what I gave. And one day shall Saint Purnace be repaid."

He framed my face between his hands. "Nor have I forgot my son's birth. It is branded on my mind, white hot. By the Mass, I thought you gone, he gone, and all my hopes turned to ash. I've not thought much on sons," he said, almost shyly now, "a man does not unless they come. Then it is another sort of bond."

He paused one last time, almost broodingly he spoke, "Nor would I want another such memory to my charge. The old she-wife spoke true if that is all the payment there is for lust."

"Not so," I cried, "do not think of it. It is God's will, the lot of womenfolk. I have put it aside, so must you."

He roused himself, looked musingly at me. "I should grow used to wife and child," he said, "they bring new thoughts as well as cares. Well then, let there be a *pax* between us, you to your cares, I mine." He kissed me full upon the lips, the kiss of peace. A generous man he was in many ways. But proud, stubborn as steel. Such men will not bend, must break and tear. "One day soon, I swear," he said, "you shall play the role of Countess of Sieux and I alone to savor it. Meanwhile, if those Norman lords come trotting along, clamoring at our gates, with the Sire de Boissert at their head, just smile at them.

You'll send them stumbling back to their fat wives, too full of fantasies to think of plots. Let them eat out their hearts for envy's greed. I'd rather they covet me my lands than my wife."

He let go the end of the cloak; I dropped to the ground, as easily as he let fall those names, those tales, of the men who were to walk into our lives and make such havoc of them. And as easily, you see, he gave teeth to what Sir Renier had said, so easily did I defer to him; a woman's world is small, a man rules his own. What matter if it be for love or profit or expediency, we be but pawns to men's plans.

He turned and cantered off. I saw him give his half-salute as he clattered through the ruined gates; his men clashed to arms as he went past. One free day then was all we had. But one to be remembered, a golden bead on its knotted chain; now was the weight of watch and ward returned. Sometimes since I have thought, In another place, another time, there should have been a different life for us; that if fate had not pulled us on, and if we could have turned aside from it, from our appointed path, this story would have shown us in a new light. He might have told me all he hoped and feared; he might have found words to explain what those new thoughts and new ideas meant to him. He might even have voiced aloud his plans as I longed to hear. And, had I been less uncertain, less craving for love, less ill at ease in this strange world where I found myself, I might have known without his telling. But we cannot change. From birth, the chart is set. And, as a stone is cast into a lake, so do the ripples spread.

I should hasten on through the winter months. They were not easy ones, although, before their doldrums closed us round, like a nest of ants we feverishly gathered in the harvesting, stored it in the lower levels of the towers. No need to have an army to root us out; starvation could kill us as readily. And before Master Edward and his men returned to Saint Purnace, he had carpenters shore up flooring at ground level and frame a sort of roof over each of those same towers. Thatched with reeds, they were a fire threat, but at least they gave us floor and roof. In one of the towers we posted the castle guard, foot soldiers, menials. In the second tower the child and I, Lord Raoul, his household knights, and my village maids all cramped together like peas in pod. That's a drawback to castle life: its lack of privacy. I had been spoiled. Even at Cambray we had been accustomed to our own chamber place, and it was not one third the size of Sieux; and Sedgemont had had its own women's bower. Still, at least we had a bed of sorts, hung with sacks since the curtains were lost. The village women set up their looms at one side, there was a central hearth with smoke hole in the thatch, and we used the scaffolding for benches and tables.

The little Robert came to enjoy castle life and to know his father as he ought. He learned to crawl on those rush covered floors; his first laugh, the first full-throated he ever gave, was when his father set him on his wolfhound's back. He buried his face in its tawny neck, drummed his red stocking heels into its sides. Many were the hours my squires spent with him, but when his father passed, his face lit up. And so did Raoul's. Little by little, cautiously, as if still awed by a strange and delicate thing, Raoul began to make friends with his son.

Yet still no other knights of note, no vassals, sent their sons to act as pages, nor ladies sent daughters to grace our hall. Instead some visitors of other kinds, such as Master Edward had spoken of. Soon, scarce a day went by but that some local lord did not come "trotting along" to see what he could make of us. At first they came with some excuse: a hound had strayed, the deer they chased had foundered in the swamps, a horse had cast a shoe—all those neighbors who could have offered help and comfort nine months before when we needed it. In normal times, as I have said, such visits would be welcome; it is part of castle life to offer hospitality and, on winter days when it is too wet to ride or hunt, what else should men do but sit with friends, talk over old times, play at chess or dice? More like the last, although the Church has forbidden it. I have played at dice myself, and think it apt for a soldier's game; so are our lives arranged, turned on a single throw. But sometimes I could have resented these visitors. They were, for the most part older, stout-faced men, with hearty appetites for food and drink, their hunger and thirst were a drain upon our meager resources. Many of these lords reminded me of my father in his age, running a little to fat across belly and thighs, but strong-armed and lusty. And amorous. I kept my servant women out of their way, easy prey if caught alone, and these Norman knights never brought their women folk with them. Their talk, when I was by, was usually restrained, the talk of country men, of harvest, of the dry summer, whether it would have spoiled the wine. They seemed fonder of stable and hounds than polite company. But when they did speak of news, of King Henry and how he fared, and how they hoped he would stay abroad, there was something in their turn of phrase, their harsh stubbornness, that reminded me of Falk too, so that I often lingered to listen to them. Most of all, it was their talk of war that reminded me of my father. God's bones, I thought, rebellious one day when for the tenth time we heard how one was bloodied, and another won his spurs, do they never tire of it? I remembered how my father and his companions used to sit, reliving old campaigns along the borderlands, and how my brother and I would hang on their words.

One day, there was a commotion in the inner yard. By now we had come to the worst time of year, dank February, with all its attendant frosts and hail. It was a dreary day at best, the wind blew the rain in gusts and the cobblestones were slippery with a thin coating of mud and ice. I had been busy in the dairy shed, not that there was much to do since the autumn slaughtering, but we kept a goat, and I had been helping the village maids to milk. Two of us now came together into the yard, carrying a heavy pail. I had on my woolen gown, a shawl flung about my head; as ever in the wet, my hair had flared into wisps and snarls, and the cold had whipped color into my cheeks. Heads bent against the wind, feet thrust into wooden clogs, we were trying to run with the bucket and never noticed how many men there were, a dozen or so, newly arrived, the retinue of two greater lords. I had not heard the guard sing out or the great gate unbarred to let them in, and it was too late to turn aside. One of the older lords, loud-voiced with complaint about the storm which had driven them out of their way, angered at our lack of stable space, backed into us. I did not like his looks when he swung round on me with a curse. Tall he was, upright under his heavy cloak of squirrel fur, his hair scant locked but worn in the old Norman style, and a face so seamed with scars that one eye, on the left, seemed pulled into a sort of wink. Among my women, I heard later that that eye never closed; he slept, they said, with it agape, and so he appeared to have fixed it upon us now. The village girl let out a squeak of fear, dropped her hold upon the pail so the milk slopped out, and tried to run. It irritated me sometimes that these village girls were so in awe of greater folk. I was always urging them to stand and speak their minds, but they seldom would. They were free with me, as friends are, but never at ease with someone they did not know; an air of authority made them as wary as a bird and one command would turn them into stone. It did not occur to me that the girl showed such alarm exactly because she did know this lord and may have had good cause. I caught her skirts with my free hand to restrain her, made to pass on in a normal way. He thrust out his boot to bar our path.

"So Raoul keeps pretty milkmaids at least," he said. "I thought perforce he led a eunuch's life these days. Such red hair would warm a man's bed. What say he lend me you for an hour or more? I'm cold enough."

His voice was loud, the louder that our men, who had come to hold his horse's head, were stunned to silence. The village maid gave another squawk. I swung the pail with all my might. It was heavy, made of wood, iron-flanged, and it caught him about the shins to make him jump with a howl, half-stumbling on the slippery stones. I let the pail drop so that milk sloshed all over his feet and would have turned to run myself, dragging the girl, had she not perversely now hung back. And had not one of his men, as rough-voiced as his master was, grabbed my arm and twisted it.

"Stand," he said, as if to a horse, "when my lord speaks."

And grinned. I opened my mouth to say what I thought. Before I could answer him as I should and he deserved, Walter, followed by Matt, broke through the crowd, hands to their dagger hilts. The rest of our men muttered and scowled. Another movement, another word, and weapons would be out; then there would be vengeance to pay. A brawl in our court, knives drawn, was a serious offense, a hanging affair. Even the man who held me let go, unnerved by the suddenness of the attack. The older lord straightened himself, brushing aside the droplets of milk that had cascaded down his squirrel fur. His face had darkened, his lips drew tight. His men, half-dismounted, felt for their sword belts.

"Insolent varlets," he hissed, "and insolent maids. A lesson is needed to tame them all. Take the men, I'll see to the girl."

"If lesson is needed, my lords," Raoul's voice was cool, "we can give it in our own time."

They made space for him as he came to the tower door.

"Well, lad," the older man spoke in a familiar way to give offense, "a whip would do it and I've one at hand." He nodded to the fellow who had held me and grinned again.

Since Raoul's answer would have been equally terse, another man scurried between, the second lord, his face gray with alarm. A slight, gray-haired man, he was, with long gray face, and longer nose, his chest caved in as if he had no innards to hold it in place. His voice was breathless as he bleated out, "My lords, my lords, no need for quarrel over a serving wench. Save you, Count Raoul. We have ridden through this storm, having but recently heard of your return. A cup of wine would not be so amiss in this wet and cold. You'll not refuse old friends now we are here."

He babbled on, all his lies cunning in their way. The other lord stopped in his tracks, made a gesture to quiet him. Walter and Matt hastily removed their hands from their knives; the village maid had already gone, slipped aside in the way of her kind. I picked up the bucket, angry at the waste of good milk, moved back myself. The men made passage for me, closed ranks behind. With luck, I thought, it will be forgot.

"Save you Raoul," the older man said in a softer tone, hitching up his cloak, "but you've a wretched litter of curs in your yard. They've raised a rumpus about how the horses were to be bestowed. And now..."

"And now we shall forget it," the gray-faced man squeezed his arm, "and drink a toast for old time's sake. It is long since you were here, lord Count. We would pay our respects." Well, his lies were at least courteous. He made great show of unbuckling his sword belt, propping his sword against the steps out of the rain. Those of the men who were his reluctantly followed him.

The older lord and Raoul never took their eyes off each other; Raoul, simply dressed in tunic and shirt, but with his household guard at his back, two of his squires who already had shown how quick they could be; the first lord, full-armed as were his men, as I now could distinguish them. Black and white surcoats they wore beneath their cloaks, ragged and damp, and beneath again, their mail hauberks. I thought it strange that they should ride abroad on such a day; certainly not to hunt. And to ride so armed, not by chance. Yet, for a war party, they were few and, once inside our castle gates, had no hope of retreat if they attacked on our home ground. The older lord must have come to the same conclusion himself. Perhaps he had hoped, not knowing how many we were, or how bestowed, to catch us off guard, to have us at his mercy if he got in. Or perhaps, not knowing the state of Sieux, he had come with no fixed plan, prepared for any chance. Or perhaps, as had many other lords before, he came but to spy. Whatever his thoughts had been, he relinquished them, dropped his gaze.

"Well, Raoul," he said, pretending dismay, "this is sad change from what you were. What, no walls, no keep?"

Raoul said evenly, to hold his anger tight curbed. "The keep will come, as will the walls. We've better than that, two towers at least to serve in good stead as a double keep. But you remember, my lord, the tale I'm sure of how the Prior of Justin would build a tower. A belltower it was, as I recall, and two great bronze bells to hang therein. Every day that tower was higher built so the prior could boast that his bells would ring for thirty miles. Well, the tower was finished, the bells were hung. For a month, he rang them in his pride. The first autumn storm, down tumbled tower and bells and all. When I build, I build to last."

There was a guffaw, hastily suppressed. Someone whispered to me behind his hand, "The Priory of Justin belonged to him," and nodded toward the older man, who had grown mottled red.

"But wine we have for those who are here as friends," Raoul's voice became brisk. "As such, you are welcome then to come within."

Uncertain what to do, the gray-faced lord rocked back and forth upon his heels, almost gnawing his lips. The older one, half angry, half resigned, thrust back his cloak. His squire came running, knelt there in the mud to unbuckle him, and held the sword belt and sword, although his master, venting spleen, smote him for some fault. Both lords then followed Raoul slowly inside. Their men, disarming themselves, for the most part trailed behind them, although some, left without, no room for all, were forced to shelter in the stables built of wood along the cliff (where, for courtesy, to keep them quiet, we gave them food and ale).

Inside the tower, I slipped among the men, unnoticed I hoped, and gained my place with the other women on the far side of the fire. They kept their eyes downcast as is their style, but listened intently as did I, making great show to work their looms, although little work we did. The men stood now about the hearth, the wet from their clothes dripped and spat and their heavy boots caked mud upon the floor. Our serviteurs came with mulled wine, served decently on bended knee. The older lord took a cup, but at first did not drink, eyeing the room. For a gateroom, guardroom, it was strongly made; one great massive door, a winding stair, only part built to upper stories still planned, more stairs, covered with a trapdoor, leading to our supplies below, no window space, mere slits, that would serve for defense to shoot arrows through. Even half-finished, a few men could have held such a place against a siege. He nodded to himself, as if satisfied on that score, turned back to Raoul.

"And you, my lord," more polite, once in his hall, "I marvel to see you on your feet. We heard that you were hacked apart."

Raoul said, "Rumors are often exaggerated, or misspoke. It is a mistake to rely on them."

"We shall see that, come the spring," said the older man. "Without the art of war, we live in dream. Your reputation was once well known, but reputations, like castles can fall fast."

His companion, ever peacemaker it seemed, rushed in. "They say, my lords, that with the spring Henry will return to France, what say you to that?"

"He is already here." Raoul's voice was taut.

"Aye," the older lord spat. "And has met with Louis, weak-livered knave for king who turned his back on Geoffrey's claim and welcomed Henry with open arms. And Henry, too, ten days ago, on the fifth of this month, at Rouen, met with Geoffrey and denied him. A proper man, to swear and break such holy oath to keep his father's will! If indeed it is a father's will he breaks."

"What else?" Raoul's tone meant, "What the devil is it to you?

"There is a story," the gray-faced lord took up the tale; he pushed back his long gray hair, opened wide his pale blue eyes, and his voice grew warm as men's do when they gossip among themselves. He reminded me of someone, but I could not be sure. "They say that when Count Geoffrey of Anjou was first wed to the Empress Matilda, a marriage made for gain if ever there was for she was older, ugly, and a shrew, Geoffrey *le Bel* could not abide her. He sent her away and they lived apart. She came back to Anjou only when she was with child. Not his. So another man's. And if this Henry is not his son, then he is certainly not the older one."

"I heard otherwise," Raoul said. "That had she been a man, she would have been as great a king as her father was. Not that I have much liking for her, cold and ruthless and arrogant.

But beautiful and chaste. Which is much to look for in a wife."

The older lord smiled, a twisted smile he had. "Perhaps," he said, "perhaps too much. Myself, I'd not expect even that. Except no man would wish a bastard for heir if there were hope of legitimate get."

"Bastardy is as the word is used," Raoul said, still evenly, "and for sure only wives can tell. Or daughters for that matter, too. A whore as daughter can ruin a father's plans."

There was a pause at that, a heavy one, weighted with many things unsaid. Raoul broke it. "And men," he added almost pleasantly, "who are the cause of both, the last to know."

The gray-faced lord tittered nervously. The other drank his wine, dark-faced. The jugs went round, the tensions eased. Presently, their talk veered to generalities of war, of Henry and his plans, of how Count Geoffrey had fought to win him Normandy and how another Henry, his grandfather, earlier still, had fought to keep it. A bloodstained patch of ground this Normandy. But nothing was said of Geoffrey Plantagenet and his claims. The gray-faced lord, who had been drinking steadily to calm his nerves, called for a lute. Someone gave him the one Walter used and he began to sing. A stronger voice he had than I would have thought for one so frail, the more so after they said he liked better to speak of war than fight himself; a battle song then that soon had all of them thumping out the chorus lines. He gave us but part of it, adaptation of a more famous song that a southern poet had written. It was like him, I think, to suggest it was his own:

> I love to see
> Meadows, with pavilions spread
> Knights, horses, in battle red,
> Maces and swords and helms all rent,
> Shields riven apart and bent.
> I tell you I find no such pride,
> In food or wine or gentle sleep,
> As hearing the battle cry "On, on, ride,"
> The battle cry, the horse's leap...

Verse after verse in this fashion until they had lathered themselves into a fret; the knight's dream of war, enough to send the hounds slinking away and startle young Robert into howls. I saw at once where the older man had coined his phrase: *Without the art thereof, war is but a dream.*

Myself, I would have preferred a drinking song, and certainly they had drowned enough wine to come up with a bawdy one, such as often had sent us women scurrying (not so much, I might add, to cover our ears but our mouths, that our laughter be not heard). But with its end, there was another pause. I had the feeling that we were now come to the point of what their visit meant, all else but prelude to that.

The older lord turned again to Raoul. His words came out like arrow shots. "Shall we not try the truth of it? A tourney, in the old style, to welcome you? Where else got you your practice in your youth, to serve you as King Stephen's champion? Too long have we been sitting on our arses waiting for the spring. We'll call up each lord from here to the coast, let everyone bring as many knights, as many men, as he needs. We'll celebrate your return, boy, as we used; a mêlée in the old style, two sides as in real war, in open fight, each lord accompanied by eight knights, until one side cry hold. Let all who are engaged do battle. And God preserve all men who are unhorsed. But as sop to those younger, weaker men who prefer the pretence of war rather than a mêlée, which is war, just better planned, we'll offer a day of joust, men riding with a lance against each other, one by one. And he who is judged most successful in the joust or fight, we'll give him as prize the horse and gear of every knight he knocks from the lists."

Excitement filled the hall at his words. And even Raoul, although he still kept silent, his eyes too had brightened for a second. I was appalled. I had heard of mêlées of course, who has not; my father had fought in many a one in his youth to win his fortune with his sword. But at such a time, in such a land, so threatened with war, to seek the excuse for its pretense was, as Raoul had said, to be nature's fool. I could not believe he would take part, or that he would be tempted by what was promised. For the older man was going on, "And we'll let the champion choose a lady as his queen. We'll put all our women-folk on display. The jest of it, they'll fight among themselves as fiercely as ever on the battlefield to ensure their place as the chosen one. Their squabbles will afford us better sport. And I'll offer the tourney in a lady's name: my daughter, Lady Isobelle, whom you remember well. And you, my lord, have a new wife, whom I have not yet met I think. Roll her out. I hear she is no prude. We would know her charms, considerable as I have heard by all reports."

It was not the words themselves but their tone that was meant to offend, and even the words themselves held a threat, as if he might yet risk offending more. Yet, in truth, I paid them less heed, and much of what he intimated slid over my head; it was the name of Isobelle that rang its warning note. Now Isobelle is a common name in France, princesses and queens are so called. I knew of but one, and I had hated her since I had heard of her; first, because she had been Lord Raoul's bethrothed, second, because she had so readily thrown him aside, that Lady Isobelle de Boissert, whose father had forbidden the match when the capture of Sieux had left Lord Raoul disinherited. I looked at him, the Sire de Boissert, then, with even more dislike. And the slight, gray-faced man, jump-ing up to come between him and Raoul, I thought I had rec-ognized his gossiping, his pale blue eyes, his weasel face, thin where his daughter was fat and fair. No man seemed less like to arrange an ambush by himself. But his overlord would be more than capable of it, aye, and of conspiracy, too.

"My lords, my lords," Jean de Vergay flapped back and forth, "we'll look to the ladies at the joust; we'll have an Easter feast to drive away all cares; we'll set up tents; we'll . . ."

Ralph de Boissert held up his hand deprecatingly. "Gently, gently," he said. "I did but ask in courtesy, Raoul. Your lady is as welcome as the buds in May. My daughter yearns to make her acquaintance known. Alas, I have no wife, but the Lady de Vergay, my loyal vassal's wife, she will act the part, and equally will welcome yours, one so young, as we have heard, so unused to Norman ways. We'll greet her fairly in most gracious style."

Oh, it was cleverly done. He baited, withdrew, came back with wicked barb. As I had guessed from the start, a dangerous man. Yet Raoul was dangerous, too. He would not dare bait Raoul too far. And this time, Raoul was ready for him.

"Spring," said Raoul, "is treacherous. And what promises fair can turn to foul."

"My lord Count," Sir Jean was still rattling on, a peacemaker by profession he, perforce, if all his womenfolk were venom-tongued, "you'll not fail us. We depend on you. What greater champion than King Stephen's man?"

"He'll not fail us." Ralph de Boissert stood up abruptly, pulling on his gloves, tying the straps of his cloak. "It is too long since we saw him joust. He stands as much to lose, so more to gain. He needs to show us how he fights now."

He stamped out, and the others followed him. We heard them mounting up, the clash of salute, the grinding of the heavy gates drawn into place. I waited until they were gone, rounded on Raoul before he had chance to question me.

"How dare he show his face here?" I said. "How dare Jean de Vergay poke in his snout? How dare they wind us in their plans?"

"Less so," Raoul said, "than when de Boissert thought to have me as son-in-law. What caused the disturbance in the yard, which servant wench?"

I said, reluctantly you may be sure, "I poured a pail of milk onto his boots when he mistook me for a serving maid."

He stared at me as if I were mad. I felt my women shrink, those men still within the hall scrambled out-of-doors. For now, his rage did break out, the more I think he had kept it pent up so long, and endured in silence, as patiently as he had his wounds, all the checks and hinderances that his weakness had caused. The anger was not directed at me, but since I was there I felt the force of it. That too is natural between men and their wives. But I was nervous, over anxious, too. I make no excuse for myself except that. My response to his anger was not likely to mollify him.

"Damn him then to Hell," Raoul roared. He paced about. "Impudent cur. And you, God's bones, what possessed you to roam so dressed, so employed? God's my life, we'll have ladies to serve you yet, even if I drag them here myself. You'll not disgrace yourself again. But while you've got your village folk at your command, busy them to equip us for this Eastertide. We'll not ride out as beggars again. Ralph de Boissert thinks to make a mock of me. He has bitten off too much. He'll have a bellyful of us before he's done. Set a trap for me. I shall trap him."

"You'll not be such fool to go?" I asked.

Raoul took hold of my arm, in stronger grip than any of de Boissert's men had used, and propelled me to the door. It was not much for privacy, and the wind blew cold, but he propped it half ajar against his shoulder and kept me there.

"You'll not go," I said again, alarm making me too sharp, "into a snare that he has set? Who knows what deviltry he has in mind, but even a simpleton could see he plots against the king. And if he tried to kill us once, why not again? As for his daughter, that Lady Isobelle, why should you wish to see her? She never showed you much care. Why attend a joust in her honor who never honored you?"

"He wants to see if I can fight," said Raoul. "When I have knocked him head over cock, then let him spew out for help."

"And when you are knocked from the lists yourself," I said, "what then?"

"You'll make a nice little widow," his voice was sarcastic, "a plump little widow for a Norman lordling. Has it occurred to you I might not fall? And, unless my men get practice, how are we to fight together again?"

"You'll not risk your men, too," I blurted out. "Leave Sieux unguarded, all for pride?"

"Christ's balls," he bellowed out, "am I a child that you order my life and my men? You'd not expect me to ride in a mêlée

alone? And not to go is impossible. They'll not put coward's
curse on me because of you. I'll not live in fear of them. Nor
shall I boast of what I've done and can do. Watch me. And
watch you shall. I'll have you along if I have to haul you by
the hair. Put scorn on me because of you! Remember your
place: you are a countess, no peasant's wife."

"And what of my son?" I made one last attempt. "What of
him when I am gone?"

"That too is a thing," he said. "My son." When he lowered
his voice in that way, the worst was to come. "I'll not have him
bred up a monk, a gelding for your women's bower. I'll have
him from your charge, back to Sedgemont, yet..."

"You would not dare," I cried.

"By the Living Cross," he said, "dare me not. I bring you as
accoutrement, not encumbrance, to me and my men. I'll not
have you weep duckweed round my neck. God's wounds, a
bachelor have I lived all these years and never thought to have
a wife who talked me down as no man has. Henry did me a
service when he had me marry you."

"And he ordered me so well," I cried, "yoked to a man who
cares more for revenge than sense. You'll grow like those other
Norman lords you pretend to despise, gross with wine and
blood, squint-eyed, peering for battle praise, knock-kneed,
leaning over a broken lance." So I whipped my anger to curdling
point. Well, that was my way of looking at things. It was not
his. *I speak*, he had told me once, *of state affairs. No woman lives
who cannot help muddling them with domestic ones.*

"Rage all you please," he said, "but keep it for my private
ears. No need to spill out worse for all the world. You've not
done so badly as it is. Long has your tongue become. I'll tie
it in a knot to keep it quiet."

He suddenly looked at me and, in his way, almost laughed.

"Dear God," he said, "we make a fine pair, you and I, squab-
bling like two children in the rain, while our murderers go
unharmed. But we ride when I say ride. You'll attend me there."

So are vows of peace made to be broken soon. It was not
an easy start to our most difficult threat so far. Nor was it easy

to keep a quarrel hid when it has been shouted, blared forth. Nor easy to keep domestic quarrel alive when you share one room, one plate, one bed. I would not hold my tongue for all that he had mocked at it. And then, the words he used to describe Empress Matilda rankled also. *Beautiful and chaste*, as if they explained a woman's worth, nothing more, all for a man's pleasure, none of her own self. I felt a wife, a woman, could be a comfort to a man so that he might share, if not his troubles, at least his spirit with her, that she be more than a statue set for the world to admire. But most of all I felt my fears should be considered. For it was fear as well as anger that I felt.

6

NOW I WOULD NOT HAVE
it thought everything was so simple as I have made
out, nor so dark. There were many reasons for the
decision Lord Raoul made, and even I, reluctantly
you may be sure, came to accept them in time. For if you could
have seen the way Sieux prepared, how Raoul and his men
exercised when the weather cleared, how provisions and fodder
were somehow procurred, armorers brought from Saint Purnace, we having none left of our own, surcoats hastily patched,
you too would have thought an army's march was under way;
and how paid for, how maintained, any man's guess. And seeing
how those blacksmiths hammered and hit—I passed the forge
at midday once, when the fire's heat was enough to make you
cringe, and the smith, with arms bare, and chest, like some
demon sent from Purgatory. He took the spear he was hammering and plunged it into a water pail where it hissed and
steamed until he drew it out. He held it up, testing its sharpness
with his blackened thumb.

"How's that for strength and point," he said to all the world
passing by. "Lord love us, but that will split a gut, even a de
Boissert one," and he lunged into the air as if testing it against
a living man. The sun glinted on the arc it made. Perhaps it
was the fire's heat that made me pale, perhaps the swish of the
spear.

"Lady Ann," said Matt, to comfort me, "they use a wooden
lance at joust, not one to maim and kill. The skill lies in how
you turn it, inward at the very last, to thrust your opponent
from his seat." He mimed the action for me with a fallen branch,
small comfort indeed, for if a wooden lance at a joust, certainly

one steel-barbed in the open mêlée. In the mêlée, men fight as fiercely as on a real battlefield. A combatant there might readily be killed or wounded or maimed by such a spear. And even if he lived, defeated, he would forfeit all his gear, his horse, and certainly his sword and shield. But my squires would not speak of that, for they were anxious that I should feel at ease. And knowing, as they must, how things stood between me and their lord, they tried to put them to rights, no simple task that, either, a thankless one to come between man and wife.

But, as Walter finally pointed out (and these were reasons I did accept), "There are not many ways a knight can hope to acquire land or wealth. A tourney gives us who have no family inheritance a chance. Long may it be before I can earn a hauberk and a horse of my own, and since only knighted men may fight, the other knights of Sieux might earn one for me, too. And if we win enough and well enough—and we will— we could pay the mason's fee this spring."

He looked at me with his dark eyes, sideways, and smiled in a fashion he had taken up to make the village maids run after him. "You'd not expect us to *lose*," he said, and almost gave a half-wink. No, not lose to prove me right. And counting carefully, as I now did, the number of men Master Edward had brought back (for as soon as the weather allowed, he had returned), I realized how observant Walter was. There were fewer workmen this year, they went slower, not because the masons themselves were slow but because they lacked carpenters, ditchdiggers, quarrymen, each with his special skill, whose services had helped them in the past. A tourney then was needed to bring new wealth for Sieux. As for leaving the castle unguarded, that never had been Raoul's intent; he would take but a part of his cavalry; the rest, foot soldiers, swordsmen, under Dillion's command, would remain. And on that point, too, Walter dispelled any lingering fears.

"For," he was quick to note, "who will there be to attack us? They'll all be at the tourney, those Norman lords, all, that is, who can creep and crawl. They'll straddle horse even if we have to hoist them up, the prospect of a joust will so please them. Out from their holes they'll come creeping, like weasels, sniffing out for glory's crown. We'll knock them back in soon enough."

The word "weasel" made me think of Jean de Vergay, and I wondered aloud if he and his family would be there. "Bound to be," Walter maintained. "If de Boissert leads one side in the mêlée as he claims, Sir Jean will act as marshal of the field. His voice is loud enough when he sings; but, mark my words, he'll put his sons to fight in his stead, not liking to venture out himself. In any case, all these preoccupations will keep their attention away from Sieux."

Nor did Raoul mention again his promise, or threat, I give you leave to judge which it was, to take me along with him. I suppose I could have argued I should not leave my son, and in truth had little liking for that, but he was weaned, the village women loved him as their own, the guard at Sieux would have died for him; to give him as excuse was to make but a flimsy one. And I was proud. I would not have it said that for fear of those Norman lords I hid at home. Nor would I have Isobelle de Boissert and her friends have reason to put scorn on me. And when one day I heard Walter and his companions discussing that lady, their comments made me determined not to lag behind.

Walter had been strumming on his lute, idly plucking at its strings, a love song such as filled his thoughts these days, better than a Norman war chant at least.

"Those French ladies," he was saying in the manner of one who has made a pleasing discovery, "that Lady of Boissert is generous in her love, or so 'tis said, the higher born, the more she has to give." He struck a chord. "They say she and her women pick out lovers as freely as a man might choose a maid. Myself, I think that strange, unnatural, for a lady to be so bold."

"But one you'll profit from if you can," Matt put in, not having reached that stage himself.

Walter pulled Matt's hair affectionately, "Be patient," he told his friend, "your time will come. Myself, I would most prefer to visit in those courts in southern France, in Poitiers. They say that there ladies hold a gathering, whereby they dictate the laws of love, what it is, how bestowed, by whom, and afterwards rate performances and keep a list. But they are discreet, as this Lady Isobelle is not, and never brag, so husbands and fathers are not forced to vengeance, seldom having proof and being too lazy to search for lovers under their beds."

I almost smiled to myself as I passed on. But I remembered what Walter said. And when ladies arrived to wait on me, not unexpectedly of course, since Lord Raoul had promised them, I watched them carefully. They were young for the most part, kin to Lord Raoul's vassals here in France, a half dozen or so, if not exactly dragged to Sieux at least come with no great show of enthusiasm, lured, I am sure, with promises of the tourney. I eyed them as they eyed me, set them to embroidering of the finer work, and since they too had come with but one intent, and in their quiet way were determined on it, I had little choice but to go along with them.

The day we set out, early, before Matins, was a-drizzle, like that day a year ago when with high hopes we had first returned to Sieux. At the last moment I ran back to my villagers with whom I had left my son. They stood beside the castle gates and held him in their arms to watch us pass. He did not smile or cry, but stared intently with his blue-gray eyes, as if he wished to take in everything, as if he wished to understand all that we did. To turn his gaze, I dangled a bauble I had strung about my neck, no bauble but the great ring the queen had given me, too large for me to wear on any finger, so I had hung it on a chain. "See here, my love," I said to make him look at me, but he kept his gaze fixed over his nurse's shoulder at the men. I smoothed his hair, his face, his hands, marveling as I always did at their delicacy, seeing, as if with new intent, how fast he grew.

"And if there be need, or word to send," I cried in one last fit of anxiety, "trust anyone who bears this ring, no one else. It carries message from me alone." They repeated word for word among themselves, these village women I had come to love, no thought of treachery, no suspicion of falsehood in hearts so clear. Who defends such innocents against the burden of their innocence? They nodded at a thought their minds could not conceive. Robert bounced in their arms as the riders went by. I loosened my grip on him, walked slowly back to where my ladies, mounted, were waiting me. Another year, Raoul had promised Robert a horse; he should ride and walk at the same time. And another year, another time, it would be I who stood here and watched him go, and should never know when he would return . . .

At the top of the cliff path, Raoul leaned forward in his saddle impatiently. I had forgotten how he never liked to stand, but when mounted was prepared to ride out upon the instant. Well, today he must wait. He had already bidden his son good-bye, so should I. Out of the corner of my eye, I saw him come up, his black horse skittish, as if scenting battle on the wind; it shied, pawed, tossed its head. My ladies, so-called mine, these Norman chaperons, shrank back, unable to hold their own horses still until the squires ran up to help. I saw Raoul's scowl.

"We await your pleasure," he said, wheeling past, "your ladies attend you this half hour. We linger but to give the signal at your need." I sensed the satire beneath the words. They put me on my mettle as he meant.

"Give it," I said. I scrambled up in a flurry of skirts, a sidesaddle which I seldom use hindering me; half in the saddle, I kicked my horse forward even as he raised his hand. He cantered on, no more courtesy then from him. But I rode a step behind, grim mouthed, hair flaring wild. My ladies, in the rear, bumped along helplessly. Let them tumble off, I thought, let them see how it is to be unhorsed; that is the sport they anticipate. But he'll not outpace me. Down we went in uneven line, Raoul, his guard, myself, fast; Walter and Matt hotfooted after us; the ladies and their escort complaining loudly in our dust. Let them ride as best they can, I thought again, they came here of their own free will to serve me, let them work for it. But when at last we did slow down, they were left too far away to be of service even if they would.

"God's wounds," I thought I heard Lord Raoul say, as if to air, "she'd lead a charge if she had the mind."

I shook the rain from my cloak and pinned back my braids.

"Women have done as much," I retorted to his back, "a Celtic army once was so led. And the men those women defeated were Norman men."

His guard turned aside to hide their grins and we rode on. But when we came to the borders of de Boissert land, in good time although not so gently as we might, and stopped to let the stragglers catch up, "We joust well, lady wife," he said, and this time there was no trace of smile, "but here we tread carefully, you and I. Make no move out of line, for all our sakes. It is not against Sieux alone they sharpen their spears. Be warned."

God pardon me, I closed my ears. I was not in a mood to listen to anyone. His hand shot out, grasped the bridle rein. "I give you one last chance," he ground out, "heed it. Or, by the Rood, back you go, with your gaggle of womenfolk. Help you can, but as hindrance I'll not have you round my neck."

"You need no help from me," I said, as mutinous as a stubborn child. Nor should he think to send me off as he might order a page do this, do that; I had given fair warning, too. He still held on motionless, his eyes their darkest gray, until I let my own gaze fall. Well, it was a cold response, not kindly given, no word of encouragement, God forgive me, no hope of success. A cold reply and as coldly taken. We rode forward, more sedately now, and came within the boundaries of the tourney field, side by side we rode, but might have been a mile apart.

Much has been written of the tourney at Boissert Field and all it meant. For me, who had not seen such things before, it overwhelmed. Ralph de Boissert had certainly had much practice in such affairs. Pavilions had been strung up for our use at the edge of a vast tract of land that stretched, as he had described, toward the hills. The hills themselves might have been scooped out to create such a gigantic hollow place, sloping slightly at either end, flat and level in the center part. At one side, wooden stands had been set up with a barricade to form two lanes, down which the jousters would ride. It was deserted now; everyone gathered to watch more humble sport, tilting at the quintain for the squires and younger lads. The rain had already blown away, the sun was coming out behind massed clouds. Had it been another day, another time, I should have been off my horse, or tumbled off myself more like, so eager to take in all the sights and sounds. By now, my ladies had revived, so many horses, so many knights, even those overweight and bleary-eyed more noble on horseback, so many ladies fine bedecked, to keep them amused.

Ralph de Boissert and his retinue advanced to welcome us; on foot they came, he in new byrnie of mail that shone and rippled as he moved, not too old then to take part in the tourney himself, bareheaded as mark of respect, I suppose. He had not been so polite at Sieux, and for a moment I feared he might remember me, although not much chance, I today in my green wedding gown, with my hair once more confined and smooth. Beside him came Jean de Vergay, more like a rabbit with twitching nose. He carried the white baton of his rank, a spectator he, no combatant. After him trailed his family, Lady de Vergay, portly fat as he was thin, his sons, two of them, both plump, the oldest Raoul's age, overstuffed in pale mauve. The de Vergay men muttered platitudes and bowed and scraped their heels like restive steeds. I did not think they had the breath to plan more than a dinner to feed themselves, and seeing them together, again I could not believe their father capable of mounting a surprise attack. Lord Raoul returned their greeting briefly, ignored their effusiveness, and, dismounting, came to lift me down, a sign of courtesy in him. But his hand about my waist was hard; I took it rather as a warning. My ladies clambered off with sighs of relief.

We strolled across the grass, sodden and muddy underfoot, to where great fire pits smoked, sending wafts of wood and roasting meat. Pages dressed in the de Boissert colors of black and white scurried with platters laden with food. There were roasts of every kind, from oxen whole to small birds, grilled and stuffed fowl, and sweetmeats for more delicate tastes, spun sugar swans, and honey cakes, and wine in flagons—such a display would have beggared us. Yet we did not look so impoverished; our horses were sleek and the red and gold pennons fluttered behind us. For once, Raoul looked his part, a noble lord, his mail coat slung over his squire's horse and his hair bound back under a golden band. Despite myself, I felt a glow of pride.

A shout went up to make us all spin around. The younger boys as I have explained were already tilting at the quintain, with a crowd of underlings to cheer them on. One of our squires had caught up a lance and ridden full gallop at the ring of steel that hung from its thick chain. He rode too fast, even I knew that, lance askew, and as we watched, the bag of sand that hung on the other end of the chain swung round and hit him squarely on the back, sending him headlong over his horse's neck. I knew his style. He was my impetuous Matt, more like to ride an enemy down than fight with him; but as he fell, with some strange twist, he pulled himself right way again. He grabbed the reins, sawed the horse round, feeling his way back over the high saddle, feeling too for the stirrup irons, weaving from side to side as if about to be tossed a second time. The horse was snorting with alarm, Matt breathless with effort and chagrin. Back he rode to snatch a new lance, rode as fast and fiercely as before. This pass, with more luck than skill, he hit fairly, rode on, reins flapping, wiping blood from his split lip. The peasants cheered; I cheered myself until I saw Raoul give his half salute that made Matt grin. He disappeared, still wildly lurching, and I caught Raoul's smile, the look he exchanged with his other men. That one will do, it said; aye, do for blood and war and death. I folded my arms firmly under each other, would not smile myself, and stalked on.

"Save you, Countess of Sieux," Lady de Vergay came panting after me. She had her daughter's voice, the same sharp tongue which flicked in and out as she licked her lips. "You and your ladies lie within." She pointed to where a large tent, striped red and yellow, stood to one side. "Your serving maids," she emphasized the word, "must direct your men to unpack your things. We have fair bedding, from our own geese plucked, and white, fresh laundered linen for your use." She gave a sniff as much as to say, You may need them. We know you are accustomed to sleeping on the ground. Perhaps she thought to hear me confess, as her daughter had, that we owned no bedding of our own. At my silence, she went on. "Count Raoul and his men sleep there, with the other contestant lords." She pointed again, out came her tongue. "My daughter, Alyse, whom you know, bid me tell you our maids are at your service if you so require. They are well-trained, too, no common sluts." Carefully were her words chosen, as if she had learned them by rote, as if her husband or her overlord had rehearsed her in what to say, but beneath them resentment lurked.

There was another commotion at our backs. I should have explained that all this while, other men had come riding in, each one of import making a circuit of where we stood, to see and be seen; it was still early in the day, no haste, plenty of opportunity to let themselves and their horsemanship be admired. Now a group of ladies came riding up. I knew the one at their head, although I had never seen her except in dreams. She sat sideways and bent her neck, letting a page in black and white lead her along. Not old, not young, her fair hair was bound into a kind of snood to free her profile of wisps and curls so that, as she passed, one could see the lofty tilt of her chin. She too was sumptuously dressed, in samite silk, pale cream and gold to bring out the color of her hair, her pale skin, and when her men lifted her down, she glided like a swan, her fur-trimmed gown barely touching the ground, her little feet in their violet silk swishing in and out. I heard Walter suck in his breath and could have hit him for a lout.

"Save you, Lord Raoul," she said, this paragon, this lily flower—whatever poet praises a woman whose hair is black, or red, whose eyes are brown and not sky blue, whose feet are not small and who always runs? "It is long since last we met," and she smiled, showing her small white teeth. Beside him, she was not tall, although taller I think than I, and her golden hair complemented his. "Too long," she said, and smiled up at him, "we should not have let so many years go by."

"So much for time," he said, and he too smiled, not his boyish grin but thoughtful, remembering perhaps days long past, "it outdistances us all in the end."

She tapped him on his shoulder with her painted nails. "Then we should make excuse to catch up with it," she said. "I would have news of you."

Well, I make no excuse for the way I felt. I had never liked her since I had heard of her, and although red hair may not grace a poet's verse, they say it is a sign of temper and of jealousy.

"My lady and the Count match together," broke in another remembered voice whose false sweetness I recalled, malicious-sweet with waspish bite. "When betrothed, all the world thought them well paired." Mistress Alyse had come to her mother's side, dressed in the pale blue she favored, her eyes like her mother's, flat and cold. She held a little lapdog in her arms that panted too, showing its pink pointed tongue. She smoothed its silken fur with bejewelled hands, the more it yapped and snarled. No greeting she gave to me, although her mother prodded her, asked only if I should attend the feast. "Then shall you see my Lady Isobelle dance," she emphasized those words, and nodded to where the lady stood, many lords of note crowding round, but she kept Raoul beside her, her little hand upon his arm. "No more graceful dancer than she," she went on, "the lightest in all of Normandy. She and Count Raoul danced at their betrothal feast without stint, all night long. And in the morning, his men claimed he said he had slept in Paradise."

And she smiled to herself to see the effect her words had on me. Now, I had not imagined Raoul had led a monkish life, and he himself had admitted once that in his youth when he first had known Isobelle she had attracted him. In his youth. Later, he had vowed he cared not for her, she was too much the older, had not been chaste. I said, "That betrothal was long ago, too many years perhaps for your lady to wish to dance. Dancing is for younger feet."

It was mistake to cross her; venomous, she struck back fast. "Since the tourney is in her honor," Mistress Alyse said, "and he is ranking guest, I think they'll dance. Unless he is too lame or halt. Or unless the damp air has made him stiff." And she smiled to think her barbs had caught.

Well, loyalty is to be admired, I suppose, among womenfolk as it is among men; it had not occurred to me that one of the reasons for her dislike was that she saw me as an interloper, usurper to the place her lady should have held. Despite the warnings, it had not dawned on me before that not only had she, Alyse de Vergay, been cheated out of her due as part of an earl's entourage, she felt her lady had been cheated too, and I the cause. Not to have understood until now the bond between these two women, so unlike, made me stupid, tongue-tied. And now she made me feel once more, as she meant, the contrast between what Lord Raoul had lost, what now had in its place.

"These will be French dances," she was saying, "hard to perform, intricate. I do not think anyone else could learn them. Dainty steps and delicate, not clodhopping through the mud in men's boots." And she stared openly at the hem of my gown where dirt had splattered from our ride.

"But Lady Ann is used to mud and dirt," her mother cried cheerfully, as if it were a game, "she is no fine lady to let a little rain worry her. You, my love, must wrap your mistress against the cold..."

Well, I give you but a glimpse of how they chattered on. I did not let them see again the misery they caused. But it is true, and now I will confess it, my other anxieties paled in comparison. I do not mean they vanished quite; but considered side by side, the one came always uppermost into my mind. Raoul had good cause to claim that women put domestic issues first. And so now, as if I did not already have enough difficulties to choke me with, that Raoul and I should be so at odds, I had the worry of this paragon flattering and pleasing him the more I nagged.

The women's tent was large. When we finally went there, many ladies moved in and out; my own women, close to the bed where I lay, pleaded weariness, whispering to each other this name or that, those ladies of whom Walter had such hope. The bed was soft, the pillows softer still; whence came such luxury save from an heiress able to afford it? The better then for our men to win. But perversely, if you will, it was no longer win or lose or even fight that filled my thoughts; and I missed, most perversely of all, not the hardness of our wooden bed, to be sure, but those strong firm arms that held me there, although I willed myself not to think of them. *Talk not to me of her*, Raoul once had said. *We were betrothed when we were young and she was not faithful to me long. Nor I to her.* When they were young and I still an orphaned brat, dragged up those early days far from Cambray. *All night long they danced. He said he slept in Paradise.* At Sedgemont, we had almost starved, no time for dancing, no paradise in those neglected far-off days. Judas, I thought almost savagely, the word fit for him, this is not an excuse I would have thought of, to avoid seeing her.

But think of it I did, all night long, no sleep for me. Nor do I think there would have been sleep in any event. The other ladies tripped in and out without restraint. At first I imagined they went to relieve themselves in the cesspits, they had seemed to drink as much as men; but soon I realized they had other needs, and, as was so often proved, Walter's information about them was correct. Where they went with their lovers I do not know; perhaps even privacy was no great thing, and whores in a camp can always find some place, so no doubt did they, the stable lines if not too particular, the backs of tents, under the benches for tomorrow's jousts, the distant tree clumps. For hours, it seemed, I heard their voices, teasing, high, and men's, urgent with desire. These be the Norman ladies they boast of, I thought, this is how men sleep in Paradise, flaunting sin for all the world. Well, I had not been chaste myself; I had lain

with a man and not been wed, I had hoped for—no—prayed
for a son by him. If sin it is to lie, to so desire, then damned
was I beyond redemption's hope. What hope then for those
who love for sport? But among those busy performers, I did
not distinguish any voice I knew. Lady Isobelle entertained in
another place, did not sleep where I did, and who her companions were that night—I did not let myself think of that.

The dawning could not come too soon for me, although
too soon perhaps for those knights who now must rise and
work, such a blare of horns as to wake the dead on Judgment
Day. Ralph de Boissert's men rode through the camp, shouting
that everyone should prepare, waking us with more vigor than
goodwill. The jousters, for this second day was given over to
them, were soon up. They were quartered apart from us, and
those who had been so active all night were no less forward
now that day was here. Their squires and pages, half-dressed,
were already saddling up their destriers, testing leather and
steel for weaknesses. As for the masters, some, like cats who
have spent all night upon the tiles, stretched and yawned,
allowed their squires to shave and wash them, buckle them
into their mail, prick up their spurs. Others, more devout
perhaps, or contrite after a round of pleasuring, attending Mass
and on their knees prayed for forgiveness or success or both.
Others, cautious to the last, checked each piece of equipment
themselves, paced on foot along the lists, noting its slight dips
and rises, marking the proper place for them to bear down on
their opponent, judging the firmness of the ground, if still soft
after yesterday's rains.

From first light, peasants had come crowding in, lining up
against the wooden palisades for better view, laying wagers on
this knight or that. Village lads, more shrewd, stationed themselves to be of service to a fallen knight, to catch his runaway
horse or drag the rider from the field. Meanwhile, the ladies
in our tent made their preparations, too. Mother of God, how
they elbowed each other for space, swearing worse than any
trooper does, letting curses fall from those dainty lips. Several
beat their serving maids for imagined faults, I saw one in tears

because a rival had used a looking glass before she could. I watched them pack out their wheaten hair with bits of straw tied underneath, color those pink cheeks with special rouge, blacken their lashes and eyebrows. At Sedgemont, we would have been whipped for such lack of common decency. And the clothes they wore, such displays of silk and fur, enough to cover an acre of ground. I could not help marvel how they would drag such finery through the mud, still deep in parts, or how they could bear to sit and stew in today's heat. But when the time came for them to depart, they were too lazy, or too great, to walk; rather, mounted on white mules saddled in gold brocade, they were led along by pages dressed in their own livery. I waited until most of them were gone, my own ladies fidgeting at the delay, and dressed myself to my own taste, looped up my skirts, bid them walk ahead. You would have thought I ordered them down a road to Hell, such faces they put on, and I could guess how they winked and nudged behind my back. Then too I had brought only spring flowers and leaves to bind into chaplets for our hair, no pearls and jewels such as the other ladies wore. Indeed, I had no jewels so could wear none except the queen's ring, which, by binding it about with a thread of wool, I made small enough to set on my right hand.

We had not far to walk, dear life, you would have thought it a monstrous chore, for during the night serfs had built long benches beside the palisades, and there most of the ladies were already bestowed with those lords who did not take part, seated under awnings which gave some shade. I found a place for us, low down, not over comfortable, to one side. Matt and Walter looked distressed, the more when Lady de Vergay sent word I should join her in a central box and I refused. "We are settled now," was the excuse I gave, "no need to upset everyone so late." In truth, I had no wish to sit beside these ladies and their noble lords and hear Mistress Alyse tell me how beautiful Lady Isobelle was. And, thanks be, the trumpets blew again; it seemed they blew all day long, to cut off argument. My ladies stopped their grumbling and craned out to see what would happen next.

Now, as you may recall, a tournament of this kind was not common in France even then, the third day's mêlée or open charge being more usual, and that I will explain in due course. Today the knights would joust, one by one, and jousting was a novelty, as was having women to watch and a crowning of a queen—all fripperies such as Ralph de Boissert had complained of, and Raoul too when he heard of them. All this was new to him since he had last been in France, and in England we did not yet know its name. Not so my womenfolk. I had guessed right that cracked heads or broken bones were counted among them as a kind of prize. And since Walter knew as little as I, we all watched and listened in amaze.

First, Sire de Boissert, as giver of the joust, rode out with six marshals all dressed in black and white, chief among them, Sir Jean. Behind them came the heralds, not yet out of breath, sufficient wind to shout out the name and quality of each man taking part. De Boissert made a commanding figure on his horse, a narrow-chested bay with strong legs. It pranced from side to side as the peasants cheered. He surveyed the field to see all was prepared, the spectators held firmly back, the lances ready, and the palings and barricade firm. Then he raised his white rod, and his marshals shouted that the jousters should prepare. They themselves, not being combatants today, scrambled off their horses into the stands.

Another blast of trumpets sent the birds flying in the distant trees. Then, two by two, the trumpeters stepped out, on foot, and after them the knights, also two by two, fighting to hold their horses back in line, their squires and pages straining on the leading ropes. Since only a knight could joust, I saw how my squires leaned forward, breathless with anticipation as these knights went by. The sun shone, the knights, still unhelmeted, waved to their friends; the serfs shouted and pointed and made their bets. Each lord seemed to wear a different color or device; some had strange closed helmets hanging from their saddle bows, with streamers flying from the crests, carved also into strange shapes of birds or beasts. But, strangest of all, as these knights passed the ladies rose to welcome them, and stripped off pieces from those fine clothes which they had just forced on their backs. Sleeves they tore away from their lacings, girdles, hair ribbons, even fur linings from their hems until you thought they would strip themselves down to their shifts. And, as strange, the knights leaned out, caught each fluttering piece of silk or stuff, tied it round their lances or their sleeves or tucked it inside their mail coats.

"Those are honor's gauges," my women explained, scandalized by my ignorance. "Each knight will wear a ribbon for a lady's sake. And he who fights and wins most times will be proclaimed champion of all who fight, and will have the right to crown his lady as the queen." They rolled their eyes at my questioning; better, I thought, they might have shown shock at those lewds who would have gone naked in broad daylight, as doubtless they had stripped themselves in the dark last night. I admit, though, to disappointment when the guard of Sieux rode by, resplendent in their red embroidered surcoats with gold hawks. Never a look they cast at us, but I was sure they stopped in turn at the central box, deftly caught the ribbons the ladies there tossed to them. And Raoul, riding his black stallion with his men, I was sure the ribbons he tied on his arm were black and white.

Now the jousters were ready to begin. They lined up in turn at either end of the lists. Some stayed in their saddles, testing one last time at girth and rein, balancing the weight of their lances. Others dismounted and let their squires walk their horses up and down to keep them calm. At the herald's blast, two knights rode forth, one from each side. Slowly they advanced at first, their faces hidden beneath those cruel helmets, with closed fronts and slits for eyes. Then, at the trumpet's sound, they urged their horses into a run. Down the lists they galloped, close to the central barricade, turf flying in clods.

Midway they met, each thrusting with his lance across the dividing rail. There was a crash, a splintering sound, both knights reeled in their saddles from the blow. Their horses, unchecked, galloped madly on. The knight closest to us had lost control; his head flopped back, he grasped his side, and slowly toppled to the ground. Too stunned to move, he lay there until his squires came rushing out to carry him away.

"One!" screamed the ladies in delight. They leapt to their feet and waved their hands, shouted until their faces grew red. That fallen knight must pay a price, in armor or horse or sword and shield to the knight who had unhorsed him. But no one thought of how he then should live without his gear, how endure the injuries that he sustained.

Again the trumpets blared. "In God's name, let the contestants ride forth." Again we saw two men meet, one to win, the other lose. Three more times I watched and felt my body jar as did theirs, felt each thud, each cry of pain, each howl of delight.

"These be the younger knights," my women now explained, their eyes bright, their voices quick, more vivacious than I had seen or heard them. They tasted blood as a hound scents it. One man had already broken his arm, another lay with a cracked rib. "Later will come the experienced knights. Then we shall see greater sport."

I began to count how often the victorious knight wore the black and white of the de Boissert house. She gives her favors to many men, I thought, and then, almost bitterly, Which one of them will crown her queen as she desires?

On an impulse I cannot explain, I slipped down from the wooden seat and made my way to the back of the stands. No one, not even my squires, saw me leave, nor did the serfs turn their heads. An old chained bear slept with his graying muzzle on the grass, dreaming, no doubt, how he too could rip his enemies with his claws. I walked rapidly away, the sun hot now, away from the noise and the crowds and the violence, until I came to one of those distant clumps of trees. The people, the jousts, seemed a long way off, the shade under these young oaks was cool and peaceful. The new foliage was not yet quite out, the sun filtered through a pale green haze, and the ground beneath was soft with a litter of last autumn's leaves. Finding a comfortable spot, I threw down my cloak, pulled off the chaplet that bound my hair, and put my head down wearily, upon my arms. The night had been long and sleepless; the day before fraught with care; today, who knew what perils faced my stubborn yet noble lord. And presently, I thought I was far from France, back at Sedgemont as once I had been with my friends: Cecile, my faithful companion, and her betrothed, and Giles, my beloved squire of those days. We sat upon the ground at the forest edge. Some of the castle guard had brought their horses to drink. The great beasts rolled and splashed; the men in their shirts laughed as they wiped them dry; the wildflowers grew pale pink and white; and where the hooves had crushed, wild mint made the air smell sweet.

"Shall you be wed, Lady Ann?" Cecile said. "He watches you, Lord Raoul, I mean. He must have a man to hold Cambray and many lords will bid for it. And he must wed, too, and be betrothed, to knit his lands with hers, an heiress in France to bring him joy."

"Love!" they laughed, "why, little lady, you dream of that. Marriage is not for love. He would be betrothed to have more lands; he will have you wed to save the ones he has. And you, if you wed, it will be for grief." Their laughter was not cruel, rather, sad; I could not see their faces, once so dear to me, my earliest, best-loved friends, and when I looked for them, they were gone. It was the Norman ladies who laughed in their stead. And when I woke, it was those Norman cries, those Norman shouts of triumph, that filled my ears. The sound of horses, however, was real, the drumming of hooves close to where I lay.

I sat up quickly and looked through the underbrush. A small group of men came galloping toward the trees on the side away from the jousts so they would not be seen. Their horses were lathered and their cloaks were white with dust, their mail coats blotched with it; they had an air of weariness that made me feel sorry for them. I pulled my skirts about me, made to rise, curious to know who it was who came so late. The one at their head suddenly reined in.

"Mark that one," he said over his shoulder to the men behind; there was something in the way he spoke, something peremptory, that made me ill at ease. I had heard that sort of command before. The men pulled in their horses at his sign.

"Maiden," one of them said, an unusual way of speaking he had, rolling his vowels, "our master would know your name."

I know not why, but some devil prompted me. "As first I should know his," I said. I began to brush the leaves from my skirt. Some rogue I thought, well, I knew how to deal with insolence; but his remark vexed, that he and his "master" should break upon my peace without a by-your-leave to question me. If his "master" wished to know my name, he could speak for himself, not have his underlings do it for him. They did not view it that way at all.

"Show courtesy when you answer," the man barked out, anger darkening his face. "In good time as he wills it. It is not your place to address him."

"Nor he me," I broke in. "Courtesy is due to everyone, I think, much more to women than to men."

He swore at that, leaned over his horse's side to grasp my arm. I backed under the low-lying branches in alarm. They were perhaps a dozen or so, all mounted men, and I alone. The little wood that at first had seemed a haven began to take on the appearance of a trap, too far off for anyone to see, too far off to cry for help. They could not ride within the wood, but that would not prevent them dismounting and coming on foot. I had a sudden vision of Raoul's face, taut with rage that I should bandy words with any group of raggle knights, not a mark of rank among them.

"Would you seek a maiden's name and fright her half to death?" It was their "master" who now spoke, who edged the other's horse out of the way, came crowding in after me. Like the other men, he was muffled in a cloak and talked through its folds to hide both face and voice, but I could tell it was a young man who spoke, and the ease with which he checked and spurred his horse, forcing it through the undergrowth, showed him to be trained in knightly skills. He put up his arm to drag the branches aside, and the cloak fell back. I saw his face. It was not a face I knew, and I had never seen its like before; but simply put, it was the most beautiful face I had ever seen, or hope to see again. Not beautiful as a man's face is, not like Raoul's with its faint scars, its emotions to etch lines and shadows on living flesh, its blood running beneath the skin, but beautiful as a statue carved in stone, such as since I have seen, with thick curled hair, smooth marble skin, dark eyes that too seemed shaped of stone. And a smile, as now he smiled, half human also, half something else; wild perhaps, pagan, like the men who carved those statues years ago. The only flaw was a slight chip on both front teeth, yet that flaw served a purpose, made his smile at least seem alive. And, when he spoke, the voice, by contrast, was warm and admiring.

My first reaction was sheer panic. I was poised to escape, as a rabbit bolts from fox or hound and then is mesmerized, unable to stir. I felt my breath come in gasps, as if I had run a great distance, and I leaned against the tree trunk as if the ground rocked beneath my heels. *Men will ride into your dreams.* That was how he rode into mine, to be my bane. My only hope seemed boldness and I showed him it.

"I am come, sir," I said, as evenly as I could, "to watch the tourney as you, I think, are come to take part."

"To sleep more like," he said, almost amused. "You expect someone I think?" His glance raked my hair, my crumpled dress. Yet perhaps when I moved, seeking, as he in turn moved his horse, to put a barrier between us, he caught a glimpse of silk beneath the cloak I had snatched up. His manner changed in subtle ways, more cautious perhaps. A man may take liberties with a serving wench that he would think twice about with a lady born. Or perhaps it made him more curious.

"With whom are you come?" he now asked, patting his horse to make it stand, thinking it alarmed me; a great brown horse it was, beneath the dust, its trapping rich and elaborate. He smiled again, that charming smile that never moved above his lips, his eyes cold, like marble carved. "Whom do you serve?"

I should have told him then who I was, but caution, yes,

and shame silenced me. I did not want it said that the Countess of Sieux lay on the ground, alone, to sleep, bad enough to have been mistaken once for a dairy maid. And to tell the truth, that half-wild smile made me more nervous than before. I said perhaps the worst thing of all, "With the Countess of Sieux whose squires will look for me."

A feeble attempt at threat, as quickly dismissed.

"So," he said, as if satisfied. "Now that *is* a chance we could have sought the world to find. Then you know the count? But you, you are not from Sieux. We know the way they speak."

It was the use of that "we" that alerted me, the arrogant Norman-French "we" that Raoul used when he was angry or spoke without thought, that "we" of a French lord. And I noticed too, although I should not, the admiring look he gave. Should not; but we are all human, and I have sworn to tell the truth. In a day of humiliation that look was to remain a comforting thought. Yet even then, some sixth sense warned me; danger came in gusts as a wind blows. I could smell it, almost taste, feel it, and instinctively I put my hand up to ward it off. The sun, reflecting off some piece of mail, a shield rim, glinted in my eyes and caught the ring upon my hand.

"By the Rood," he said, "where got you that?"

I looked at him, startled, not knowing at first what he meant. He took confusion perhaps for guilt. With a sudden movement, he forced the horse upon me, breaking down the branches with his arm and shield. Before I had taken two steps, he had caught me and dragged me back so I was pressed against his horse's side. Close to, his eyes were not as dark as I had thought, more gray than brown, and flecked now with an angry yellow light. I had seen eyes like that somewhere before. He seized my hand, crushing it in his grip, and pulled the fingers apart. The ring, too large, was merely tied with a thread that snapped, so slid easily off. He held it in his shield hand, fingering it, rolling it round, whilst with the other, he held me on my toes. I would not let him see the pain he caused, pulling thus on shoulder blade and hip.

I gritted my teeth, cried out, "Your manners are not overnice, nor your courtesy to a lady born. The ring is mine. Or rather," seeing the look of disbelief, "the countess lent it me."

"Then where did she, this countess, get it?"

I shook my head. "Ask her yourself."

"I shall," he said. "Tell her so. Tell her, whether you wish or not, that she look for me, else I shall inform her and her lord, the count, her servant women are thieves and harlots to boot."

That was too much. Despite the fact he held me, despite his men beyond the trees, I drew myself up and faced him out. "Both lies," I said. "Were I a man, I'd tear you apart for saying so."

"By God," he said, "red temper to match red hair. Are all the countess's maids red-haired and hot?"

A sudden thought seemed to strike him. He let me go, dropping me to the ground. He said, "I hear Count Raoul of Sieux has brought a Celtic wench to keep him company, from the wildest part of Wales, a Celtic wanton so they say..."

"A lie again," I spat out, "as honest a wife..."

"As you are virtuous maid?" he mocked, still playing with the ring. "Lying here in the sun, yearning for whom?"

"There be Celts," I said, telling him what I should have told them all, all those Normans who so belittled us, "as well born as any Norman alive. And once as great, holders of more lands than you'll ever claim. And respect due to them from wandering scum who think to pass the time of day. Take care, the count will not have me treated with less courtesy than is due his wife."

He looked at me carefully, a faint frown marring that marble forehead. "So," he said again, "we advance slowly as through a marsh. You are Celt yourself then, that you won't deny. You have their way of speaking French, a beast to be grabbed by the tail. And you have their way of answering, too; they none of them can answer a question straight. Ask any Welsh peasant or Breton serf what crops grow in his field, he will praise the weather, damn your eyes, offer to sell you his hut of thatch, anything but tell you what you ask. To find that out, you must wait until the crop is grown. Be not alarmed, lady," he mocked me with the use of the word, "we will not harm you. And indeed it is rather news of the count we seek. Is he here? They said he would not come. Can he ride?"

"Find him yourself," I said. "He is in the lists."

And I gestured toward the distant jousting field, where, faintly, came shouts and hurrahs.

His brow furrowed again. "So, horsed," he said, "able to fight. That too is news." He half-turned, his horse still blocking me, shouted something over his shoulder to his men, then turned back.

"And tell the countess," he emphasized the word, "we will speak with her. Let her expect us."

"How shall she know you?" I said, a feeble response to his aggressiveness.

He thrust out his hand. On it gleamed a ring, similar to the one the queen had given me. "So shall she know us," he said. "This for your pains." He bent down to return my ring with its green threads all snarled, and as I reached to catch it, took my chin between his fingers. Although the grip before had been so rough that I still could feel the marks, the touch of his fingers now was surprising soft, as a woman's hand. But his voice was hard, a threatening note to make the sun turn dark. "And were you a man," he said, "we'd not have lingered to have you put the lie on us."

He wheeled his horse, crashed his way out of the wood, his men gathered round him and turned to gallop back the way they had come. All save one who stopped to throw a purse of coins at my feet.

"Take that, too," he said, half contemptuous, "but my master bids you mark him well. Else he will to the count and tell him what he knows. Tonight at the feasting, look for him."

Then he too rode away. Soon nothing of their coming was left, faint dust clouds, the purse of gold, the red marks on my arm, the ring. I pushed the purse aside with my foot as if it were a sort of snake; buried it beneath the leaves. A Judas gift I thought, as if I should betray a mistress had I one. The ring I strung hidden about my neck again as I used to do. But the marks on my wrist I could not hide, they were burned into the skin. And after a while, I turned back myself.

So, pondering the effect he made, berating myself for stupidity, wondering where I had seen such eyes, heard such voice, worried what I should do if he came again, half believing that impossible, half suspecting that he might, I found my way toward the stands, hoping to slip in as unnoticed as I had left. But I had been absent longer than I knew. When I reached the lists, a great shout went up. I saw Raoul's horse come thundering down. I knew his style and, as I watched, saw what Matt had tried to show, what he had not yet mastered, how Raoul held the lance couched easily against his thigh, how the reins hung loose upon the horse's neck, and how, at the last moment before impact, he tightened them to urge it on, leaning outward in the saddle toward the blow. Most men instinctively lean away. Hooked from his seat, his opponent rose into the air, as if catapulted, and the riderless horse galloped on. At the end of the course, Raoul checked his own horse and came riding back, his lance tip raised in salute.

"So, Lady Ann, you have not deserted us after all?"

It was Mistress Alyse, who came swimming out from the crowds like some enormous fish, glistening with heat, damp with it under her silks. She smiled her malicious smile and sketched a curtsy so perfunctory as to show disrespect. "We thought you run home in fright. We thought you sent back to Sieux in disgrace. You did not hear Count Raoul's challenge to the other knights?"

I kept my back turned to the field, ignored the shouts. Challenge all, I thought, the more fool he. At least, I had the sense to keep the words unspoke, but I felt my flesh cringe as I tensed for the next round... I could anticipate the silence now, the pause as they waited for another knight to arm himself, the thudding hooves, the jarring crash.

Mistress Alyse smiled because she knew I would not look at Raoul, because not looking took as much effort as to look, because she had caught me thus unprepared. "Of course," she answered a question I had not asked, "he has that right. A king's champion has the choice to wait until the end." She paused delicately; the little lapdog still tucked under her arm flicked out its tongue and snarled. Behind her, there was the sound of galloping, a thud, another outbreak of cheers.

"The Countess of Sieux has forgot," the second voice was cold, the sort of silver-gold voice a paragon would have, a trill to it that readily could become too loud and shrill, a voice that could wound, if no one she wished to impress were near, "the countess has forgot that Count Raoul is not a lad, new-spurred."

Mistress Alyse rocked with laughter as her father had rocked with doubt. She swayed back and forth as if she had never heard such jest. Perhaps it was, for when she could speak, "And so she told him," she sputtered, "imagine, before his men, that he was a fool, as if he did not have the strength to master horse and lance, as if he had not only lost his arm but addled his wits." They both spoke as if I were not there, or at best, an inanimate thing beneath their contempt. "Why does she not turn and watch?" Mistress Alyse went on. "I hear she watched closely enough when he fought for her, her champion, rather than the king's, against the charge of witchcraft."

"And is that true?" Isobelle de Boissert wondered, as if amazed. "And did she cast a spell to make him lie with her? I hear, for that, Celtic witches are most powerful. . ."

"As she tries now perhaps to lie with other men," Alyse de Vergay spoke not to me, but she pointed at the leaves and grass that still clung to my cloak and gown, "to wait for them in broad daylight, like any whore."

That was the last jibe she would make at my expense. I advanced toward them, hands outstretched, voice hard. At the expression in my eyes, they cringed away. *Let men put the name of witch on you.*

"If I am Celtic witch," I cried, peppering my speech with Celtic words, most of them too vulgar to translate, "if I can put forth spells, do not cross me lest I put one on you. As you hope to marry, if you are not too old, or have children of your own, if not past childbearing age, do not tempt me to curse you."

The effect was gratifying. They both cowered, crossed themselves in alarm, each trying to hide behind the other's back. But Isobelle de Boissert was not done yet. She poked Alyse de Vergay forward, spoke around her, her fine white skin suddenly racked into a net of little lines that made her look her years, her cupid mouth distorted with spite. "God protect us," she cried. "She has no power over me. And God protect Count Raoul who needs it, tied to such a bawd. I shall have a marriage soon, greater than hers, who was betrothed and wedded within the hour. What was so done in haste can be undone and there are churchmen here in France to prove that truth. Let her not think to curse my marriage day, nor let her think that one so made as hers will last."

"Wedded and bedded, too," Alyse de Vergay piped up, "upon the altar, to have a child born so soon. Born they say with six fingers and toes, witch's get. How dare she play the prude. God will protect the innocent."

"Innocence," I said, "you mock the word. All here is false, double-faced. God has spoken once on my behalf, will speak for me now. Isobelle de Boissert's father broke faith with Lord Raoul, not Raoul with him. Faithless was her father, and faithless yours, to attack us. God has no liking for faithless men."

"You lie," Alyse de Vergay's face had flushed with fright. "My father is loyal to his overlord."

"Who is loyal to Henry, Duke and King," Isobelle put in as swiftly.

I seized upon their fears, remembering what was said of both men, remembering what I knew, wanting to turn the knife on these evil-tongued shrews. I should better have kept silent.

"Then tell de Boissert and de Vergay both," I said, "in Wales we have a word for traitors, and a curse. Let them twist to serve the world, one day the world will so twist them. And as their loyalty is held in such low repute, so will honest men hold you, their daughters. I am the Countess of Sieux, that my name, that my rank. Remember it."

There was silence. It merged into the silence behind our backs.

"Fool," Isobelle de Boissert spat out the word, "she will rue that speech one day." She suddenly spun round and began to clap. Alyse de Vergay followed suit; I was forced to turn myself. Raoul came thundering past, his last opponent tossed over the rail, still tumbling on the ground. The black horse shook itself, the white foam flew; Raoul's squires came running to catch it and take his helmet which he now threw off. The lance was shattered but he held it up and the black and white ribbons fluttered from the shaft. *See how I fight*. He had shown them very well.

"And see," Isobelle de Boissert said softly, and now she spoke to me direct, "how he will crown me as his queen."

To the victor then, the spoils. I turned on my heel and left.

7

E BURST INTO MY PAVILION AT day's end, sending the women running as from a thunder cloud. The worse for them. I expected him, had wound my courage up, waited for him, changed into my wedding dress, appropriate I thought for such an interview. I stood beside a storage chest where my women had been mending linen, and folded, unfolded it, to give my hands something to do. He himself had barely stripped off his mail coat, you could see the marks of it at neck and wrist, his hair was wet with sweat. He clanked into my presence, as dishevelled as a groom in stable yard, his pages running to catch his sword and gloves, his belt, as he let them fall, until he booted them out. I heard them cowering outside, muttering among themselves.

"What have you been doing, what saying, where have you been?" he rapped the questions forth.

"Nowhere, nothing," I said.

His hand came out, rough and callused with the riding he had done, and slapped mine flat upon the top of the storage chest.

"That nowhere, that nothing," he said, ominously slow, "has set the camp ahum. What bicker like a fishwife? Blurt out insults like a village idiot? God's wounds, bed down with anyone like a common tramp . . ."

Careful, I told myself, too proud to explain, too proud to contradict what they must have already told him, but it was too late to care. "I was bored," I said, "where else to sleep?"

"Then you never saw our triumph?" he said. He spoke as slowly but I marked the pulse of anger in his cheek, live flesh he had, and beneath the skin, choler, to make the blood run fast.

"Oh," I said, pretending to stifle a yawn, "I saw *your* triumph if you speak of that."

He swore, a soldier's oath. "Not mine alone," he emphasized. "I speak of the men of Sieux. They conquered all the field as I knew they could. Under a tree then, like a country wench. With whom?"

"Why not?" I retorted. "Although I was alone. Better so then watch your men tear themselves to bits at your command."

He said, "The men of Sieux are at our command, but without them, we would all be dead, you and I and our son. Some courtesy was due to them at least. Some courtesy to us as your lord, to gad abroad on foot like a country slut. Have you forgotten who we are?"

That "we," that "our," was the final touch.

"Forget," I cried. "*You* forget I am country bred. And slut if you would have it so, although who spoke that slander spoke it false. But I have two legs to walk upon, a mouth to speak when spoken to, eyes to see who plays the idiot. I put no shame upon your house, only what you put on me."

"By the Holy Cross," he said, "what do you mean?"

"Only this," hot rage to match his own, "I am loyal to my marriage vow." I nodded at the ribbons which someone had rebound about his shirt sleeves. "I thought," I said, "rather than watching me, all the world watched you and the lovely Isobelle."

"The devil," he said taken aback. "What do you know of her?"

"Enough," I said. "I can see beneath my nose. Unless there is more to tell." He released my hand, tugged at the ribbons to free them, threw them underfoot. "They were nothing," he said, "a woman's gewgaw."

"Then your nothing for mine," I said, "enough to make her queen."

"God's breath," he said, "you do me wrong again. I looked for you. Is it my fault you sulked apart? Nor had I time to go

crawling through the crowds searching for a wife. Was that all
that soured you thus? What would you have me do when one
of her maids, or she, threw them? Throw them back, say, 'I
cannot, my wife does not permit,' box her ears for impudence
as I could box yours? I took them in common courtesy."

I let him talk, the more he spoke, the more he damned
himself, but that word "courtesy" also should not pass.

"Courtesy," I said, "courtesy, that is all you Normans bleat
about, as if each thing you say or do has stock response.
Hypocrisy to hide the truth. Where I come from, for courtesy,
a husband does not flaunt his former loves, nor do they claim
what is not theirs."

"Careful what you claim, lady wife," he said. "Where I come
from, women do not claim to own men."

"That is not what I heard," I said. "I heard those Norman
ladies you admire so much flaunt their bodies to entrap, use
what charms they have, not many at that, to impress, put on
airs to make men think them saints. I have not tried their sort
of love."

"Nor shall not, while I am by."

"And you," I said, "what may you do when I am by or not?
Well, if you would act the part of Norman husband, I will act
the part of Norman wife. I can imitate their ways, go to their
feasting, smirk and flirt, bid other men serve me . . ."

"Try it," he snarled, "I'll break your neck."

"Why not," I said, "since violence and war are your first
loves."

He swore in earnest then, jerked me round the waist to face
him. I had to stand on tiptoe to look up. "Try those tricks,"
he said, "your dainty back will feel the mark of it. You'll smart
so sore you'll not outride me for a week as you tried to yesterday."

"Threats, threats," I hissed at him, "the more you rage, the
more to know."

I felt his anger flare like my own. "Tempt me not," he said.
"When you look like that, I could dare a hundred things. I
know how to stop your tongue." His mouth clamped down on

mine to cut off breath, he held me against him, skirts bunched up, legs apart, flank to flank, so that I was pressed to his body's length, his hands hard against my spine. "And I could ram you so full," he said when he paused to breathe, his voice too came in great gasps, "so full that it would be you that cries enough, no room for any other man."

His touch was fire; we were alone, my body ached for his. One move on my part, or his, and anger would have over-spilled, brought me beneath him to the ground. Yet I could not, must not, give way, not thus. I felt myself go limp, heard my voice say tonelessly, "As my lord desires."

He held me pressed a second more, then gradually let go. I felt his passion fade. "Nay," he said at last, "I have never yet brought woman unwilling to bed, least of all a wife. I did not think to have you cry rape at me." He suddenly turned away, leaned back against the chest, wiping his face. "Now there's a thing," he said, anger gone too, almost dispassionately he spoke, in his way of often hiding what he really felt, "a man, a husband, has all the rights he wants. By church law, your body's mine to take and use as I wish. Yet, although it might so pleasure me, I find I am not willing to have you by force. You'd only hold it against me the more, and still I would not have *you*. If that be one of your spells you speak of, you have caught me fast. But I'd not boast of it nor should you. Most men would not like to be so unmanned; I do not like it myself. You see, Ann, how it is. I told you we could fight ourselves one day into a space with no way out. And today, not time or place to try. But I'll send you back to Sieux. You have made too many enemies here, roused superstitions best forgot, caused too much talk; safer for you there, safer for me."

It was quiet in the tent then; outside, the movement of his men, the faint murmurs of their voices, the distant sound of all the camp, seemed lost to another time. He roused himself. I saw for an instant in the dimness the signs of fatigue, quickly dispelled as he heaved himself upright. He had fought today and won; tomorrow he must fight again, a harder fight. "At dawn," he said, "prepare to leave. Better so. I should not have brought you here, no place for women harpies, howling for blood."

I felt the sting: was it of chagrin or disappointment?

"Nor look for me at the feast this night," he said, "there is, are," he hesitated, "things to be done."

"Will they include de Boissert and his kin?" I said, still trembling, almost not daring to mention her name aloud.

He hesitated a second time. "What is done, not undone," he said, "will be arranged. That is all you need to know." He looked at me, blank-faced, pale now with weariness beneath the brown, the scar etched clear, his eyes green-gray like the sea. "Although you will not be here," he said, almost formally he spoke, "tomorrow, Countess, I fight for you." And he was gone.

Left in the tent, I might have wept, for foolishness, for grief, and for something else still not understood, some conflict between us that was not resolved. But presently, as I grew calmer, it began to seem that once again he had had the last word, and that, when I thought back over all that had been said, he had not explained anything at all, had sent me off for all the world to mock. Nor had he told me any more than he wished me to hear, what were these "things" that must be arranged, with whom? And so gradually out of pride, building up resentment to new height, I resolved I would not "sulk apart" as he had put it, would go to the feast, would watch Isobelle de Boissert queen it over us. Well, these things are all a foolishness, woman's whims, and I do not wish to dwell on pettiness. Yet, had I not quarreled with Raoul, had I not gone out of stubbornness to the feast, had I not looked for another man to taunt him with, our story would have ended here. So out of small griefs something good can grow.

I went early then to the feasting, my squires subdued at my heels. He probably had dealt with them as roughly. Matt looked to have another bruise on his cheek, to match the one he had won yesterday. But we never spoke nor asked about that. Nor did I loiter to look at all the sights and sounds of carnival, but went straight in; and although I found no pleasure, you would

not have known. I have been taught, too, to smile when grief
gnaws, and the man beside you bores to tears; I know how to
hide my thoughts. The feasting was more formal today; those
knights who had done well sat with their friends to celebrate.
Those who had fallen drowned their defeat in wine. I stayed
with the knights from Sieux at first, had them wait on me and
listened patiently as they re-enacted every bout. Since each in
turn had to explain how he had looked for me, I almost began
to believe it true, and since each in turn also praised Lord
Raoul, until I thought I would scream, my fault became most
obvious, to have turned my back on him. Then, as well, they
all expressed amusement at the way the women had thrown
ribbons at them.

"For it is new custom," they said, "Lord Raoul mocked it;
said we were like oxen hung for slaughtering. Once women
did not drape us in women's gear; tomorrow, we will not have
time for frills. Tomorrow the mêlée is serious work. But since
those eight of us who fight and win have right to chose a lady,
then we shall chose you."

I did not have the heart to say I would not be there, but
their enthusiasm, their confidence, gave me hope. I scarcely
noticed when the Lady Isobelle entered, all clad in gold again,
nor Raoul himself, although when I did, I saw he walked with
a slight limp, as if favoring his side. They rose to greet him,
stood with him; I thought them the youngest, the most alive
men there, handsome in their patched finery. And a surge of
pleasure, I suppose, filled me that these were our men, the
men of Sieux, although I tried to stifle it. Lord Raoul saluted
me but did not stop, although I still half-thought he might,
then went forward with Ralph de Boissert, Jean de Vergay, the
Lady Isobelle . . . So be it.

I turned to a man who sat on my right, who had been trying
to bore me with his talk, square and solid like the bench he
sat on. He grinned and perspired in his velvet gown, drew
pictures with his dagger point to show how he made this move,
then that. On his other side, his Norman wife scowled and
poked. Presently, the feasting began, such quantities of food

served on thick trenchers of fine white bread, the scraps alone would have fed us at Sieux for a month. Roast boar and venison and beef and lamb, capons dripping in their own fat, pheasant stuffed and pigeon and duck, pies of quail and eggs and hare, and saffron flavored pork and pike—even eels, jellied, and laced with some sort of fermented drink—all washed down with barrels of ale, and more and more casks of wine. My Norman partners ate as if their lives depended on it, spearing their food if they had time or remembered their manners, otherwise they used both hands. When they had the chance they offered me the choicest parts, but since I had no appetite, they settled down in earnest, juice dripping from their chins. Even at Henry's court, I had never seen such display of greed.

As I have said, most of the knights who had been in the jousts and who could still walk were there with their ladies, but when the cloths were drawn and the tables stacked, I noted that the older lords, Raoul himself, disappeared, no dancing for them; then what else? And since the Lady Isobelle and her maids had gone as well, I felt a jealous pang, sharp and cruel. Where were they, with whom? That turned my resolution up another notch; I began to laugh and jest with these Norman knights, and let my glance flutter from one red face to another to set them all at odds, began to think of the young knight I had met earlier on. If Raoul could dally, so should I, if only there were someone worth the risk. Two-Handed Raoul, I thought, he'll not find me pining for his other arm. Well, jealousy is a sin, as we all know, and the pain it gives deep as a sword thrust. I tell you, I could flirt with any man, and yet, the more I tried, the more apprehension grew. I sensed it as an animal does; the hairs rose at the nape, my palms grew damp. Yet nothing had changed, no one to look or spy on me, they had already done what they could for that; Raoul off with some other company, not even chance to say Godspeed, no good wish for tomorrow's success. But other, younger men, left behind, willing to dance and teach me the steps I did not know, lascivious enough to throw their partners in the air and let them slide against their chests, their thighs. There was one dance I did recall; we had danced it once at Sedgemont in happier days, the *tourdion*, where men must advance, women retreat, faster and faster as the music faster goes. The musicians with viols scraped and scratched; the sweat flew from them as it does from a horse; I thought they would saw the strings right through. My partner advanced to thrust me back, back and forth as on a marriage bed; a hand caught mine and drew me out.

There was a dark corner at one side where the tapers cast no light, and a stack of wine casks made an alcove. I could not see who it was, but remembered the touch of that soft white hand. And that voice with its strange accent. "So," it said, "sleep did you good. You have woken up."

I was hot and out of breath and, in truth, a good deal flushed with embarrassment. I fanned myself to hide my thoughts, tapped my feet to give myself time to respond.

"Do you always dance so vigorously?" he next asked, catching me to keep me still.

"Let me go," I said tartly, "it's not so dark that no one will notice us."

"Nor so dark," he said, "that your beauty does not glow, like candlelight." Another flatterer, I thought, yet nevertheless his words were not as displeasing as they might have been.

"And has 'your lord' let you out," I said, "to plague all the ladies with sweet tales?"

"Lord?" he said.

"Oh," I said, "I looked for you among the greater lords. I presume, of course, you were too young for them; bid your master, whoever he is, give you some years before you think to ape him, scarce old enough to grow a beard let alone have pretensions to high rank."

Too late, I saw his smile. "At least," he said, "you looked for me. I thought you would. I told you we would be here, Countess of Sieux."

I freed myself. "How do you know who I am?" I cried.

He shook his head, "Not difficult," he said. "Only one girl

we have heard of with red hair who has the spirit to outrank us. And the only one," he added, with another smile, "to lie asleep waiting , I've no doubt, for some knight to come riding up, waiting to be woken with a kiss."

"You would not dare." Again I spoke too soon, and almost blushed to have taken his meaning so plain. He laughed, showing his chipped teeth, a strange laugh he had, too, almost without mirth, as if he had not much practice with laughter. "When you are angry," he said, "the air sparks. I like my women with fire. But if you fear to be seen, here, hide beneath this."

He slid off the cloak he wore; it was plain but heavy, lined with fur and underneath I saw for the first time his surcoat, blue, gold embroidered, and the glimpse of mail.

"Who are you then?" I said, suddenly awed, and felt uneasiness stir near me, a wind's breath. "Who comes armed to a feast?" It was my turn to catch his arm, feel beneath the silk cloth the ripple of the supple mail, not like other hauberks I have known, but all of a piece, fitted low about the hips, small links riveted together in one shining sheet. I said again, "Who are you?"

We stood close together between the casks of wine. On foot, he was not tall, but strong made, broad, young. His eyes, as I had noticed before, close up, were more gray than black, and as I looked, it seemed to me I remembered that feline glance. There is only one other man I knew who outstared women in that way. Dear God, I thought, fear hot and rank. They were not alike in anything else—coloring, expression, stance—save that. And the same husky voice. I bit the question back but he knew what I had guessed.

"Aye," he said, "there is only one who resembles me, or, rather, whom I resemble, he being the older, the stronger, the wiser, the king, King Henry of England, Count of Anjou, Duke of Normandy and Aquitaine, my older brother and my curse."

"Then why are you here, Geoffrey Plantagenet?" I said, and could have cut off my tongue to have asked him so outright.

"You see," he said, almost good-naturedly, "you do know

me. Well, since you have accused me of so many lies, I could
lie again, tell you I was come to join in the mêlée, look for a
Celtic wife of my own, or, tell the truth, to find out for myself,
secretly, what these Normans plot and plan."

"Are you not afraid I shall give you away? I could scream..."

"No more," he said, "than you should be afraid of me. Look
here."

He moved slightly so that over his shoulder, some distance
away, I caught a glimpse of one of my guards, back discreetly
turned.

"The count has ordered you well watched," he said, "you
told me so. Shout to him if you will, I should warn you my
own men are nearby. Now, since neither of us would want to
sound the alarm to cause a greater scandal than we have already
caused, and since you would not have me tell the count you
lured me here with offers of your favors, as indeed I hope you
have..."

"He would not believe you," I cried.

"Yes, he would." He smiled again, and this time the smile
was all wild, the smile that a pagan god might have. "Now
you may be virtuous for all I know, but husbands always think
the worst of wives, and I have yet to meet a woman who is
chaste long. But if he would not believe, because of you, he
would because of me. I have a reputation to uphold if you do
not."

I suddenly remembered the stories told of him, and of his
father, Geoffrey le Bel, the greatest lover in all of France, whom
he so resembled in looks and name.

"Nor was Queen Eleanor so loath," he said, as if a second
time he guessed my thoughts, "despite what you may have
heard, to scorn my suit." He suddenly pulled at the chain about
my neck, brought up the ring from its hiding place. "Still
warm," he said. "I should not mind she gave it away to find
such resting spot. But I gave it her to plight my troth, duplicate
to the one I wear. My grandfather brought both back from the
holy wars, and when we parted, she took it from me as a

pledge. She promised me much in return." His voice had hardened as he spoke, grown bitter with an old and festering wound. "It lasted long, her pledge," he said, "scarce long enough to take her from King Louis's court to Aquitaine. Within the month of our rendezvous, she had wed with Henry, the king. And so another time does my older brother steal a march on me. But as she gave the ring to you, so I have restored it in good faith. I hope in turn you will befriend me."

"In what way, my lord?" I asked him cautiously.

"Niggard," he said, "weighing all, giving naught. As did she. And yet she likes me well enough, may count me better lover than my brother, better than my father who enjoyed her first to test her charms for his sons, or so he claimed. She helps me."

"You do not think highly of women," I said, almost frightened by the sudden anger that marred that attractive voice and twisted that perfect mouth out of shape. And frightened by his mention of the queen.

"And should I so?" he burst out. "Even a mother who played the whore. And the queen, no trust in her, to marry with my brother because he was the older. And you, Ann of Cambray, I have heard enough tales of you. You told me that I lied today. Were the stories about you lies, that Raoul of Sieux should have fallen prey to them? Although this, at least, is true, your beauty and your spirit, no man could deny you those."

"You should not say such things," I said, trying to slip around him. "I am a married woman, as you know."

He steadied the casks, so that his arm came across my waist. "Not happily wed, I think," he said. "Among the stories that too was told, that you were constrained to be man and wife. Well, Lord Raoul will not find you out tonight. Be comforted, you need not fear him.'"

"He would kill you if he caught you," I said.

"Perhaps," he said. "Rather, I heard he threatened to kill you. But he must catch us first. I know where he is, do you?"

When I shook my head, "There, you should trust me after

all. He is with those other Norman crows, croaking disaster and gloom, the Sire de Boissert and his ilk, in de Boissert's tent, to make their plot to attack the king."

A shudder ran down my spine. I felt myself shiver although I willed the words to form. "He will not join in conspiracy."

"Yes, he will," he said brutally. "And I will tell you why. And in so doing, reveal another reason for my private visit here: to learn what promises those Norman swine make. Tonight is the night they lay the plan and set the date to attack King Henry in my name. These are the real secrets of the jousts. And if your noble count," he jeered out the title as if it stung, "will not join with them, why, they will murder him."

I gasped at him, that last sentence loud enough to drown the music, laughter, all the sound of feast and merriment. When I recovered, "They would not," I cried. "And you, how can you stand there and talk of it, let them murder on your behalf? Treason, murder, have you no shame?"

He shrugged, "Conspiracy is not noted for its chivalry," he said. "Since fate has set you in my path, Lady Ann, I ask you to find out truly whose side Lord Raoul will join. Without his help, my fellow conspirators and I have little hope. And since I cannot think of any reason why Lord Raoul would support my brother, why not support us? Raoul is restored to strength and health—no man who watched him today could deny that— and Sieux rebuilt is a danger to all of France. He *must* choose one side, Henry's or mine. And, as I am young and do not look to die, I would prefer he took my part."

On one level, his words made sense, had not I said almost the same thing to Raoul? Had not Raoul himself weighed the balance as dispassionately? Yet on another level, the arguments were horror filled, the more Geoffrey spoke so coolly, without guilt, without surprise, to plot a man's death because he would not do as other men wished.

I forced the horror down, made my voice calm.

"What should I tell him?" I asked.

"Tell Raoul," he said, "that since Henry is here in France, we must march now, without more delay. Tell him we have the forces gathered here tonight, an army's core, lacking but his leadership. Henry cannot raise any troops unless he win through to Anjou. We can prevent his doing that if Raoul strikes first to get my castles back, those castles that Henry unlawfully took, Mirebeau, Chinon or Loudun, whichever Raoul thinks best. They guard the route to Poitou and the south, when we have them, Anjou will rise on my behalf. Henry took those castles from me a year ago or more and believes them loyal to him, but their seneschals are still in my pay and have promised to open the gates to us. But tell Raoul, most of all, not to trust de Boissert, or his lovely daughter, Isobelle."

His words brought back all my old fears, but I willed myself to listen to him.

"Why should I tell him any of this?" I asked, as coolly as I could. "Why should de Boissert wish him harm, or the Lady Isobelle?"

His answer was as calm as if he passed the time of day. "The Lady Isobelle plays for high stakes, too. Now, I do not mean to brag, and the lovely Isobelle once was fair enough, although rather old for me, but because her father offers help, I must take her to wife in exchange. As she has lost her chance of being Countess of Sieux (while you live), so now she hopes to win the title of Countess of Anjou, when her father makes me count. There are not so many counts in France for her to choose, nor, to be honest, much time left for her to bargain with. She, as much as I, needs Raoul to help us win, and tries to seduce him to our side. She will throw him to her father's men if he refuses. But tell Raoul also this: to be Count of Anjou is my right. Henry has stolen my inheritance, broken faith with me, ignored an oath sworn on my dead father's corpse. Not even a papal dispensation to undo that oath can remove the curse of it."

"And you, you would clamber to power over such a plan?"

His voice became hard, like stone, that beautiful face cold and cruel.

"As I am young, Lady Ann," he repeated, "I hoped one day to wed. I looked for better things, as do all men. But time is also running out for me. Should Henry have it all? Since I am but a scant fifteen months his younger, does that make me forever his slave? From earliest memory was he treated like a prince, and all the rest of our household ordered to bow down to him as god. Our grandfather, that first Henry, first to be England's king, taught the young Henry how to rule, and showed him how to trample the other grandsons underfoot. I play for high stakes myself, and marriage to Lady Isobelle will help me. And many powerful friends urge her claims, including the queen, who would, in this way, make amends for jilting me. But Ann," he turned his charm upon me full—oh, he had charm, to light up that beautiful face, those melancholy eyes, "Ann, as I am young, I would not wish for such a life. But think of yourself. Like me, you are caught up in their brawls. If Raoul should fall, who would then support you? The queen is far away, and you have angered her; you will be alone. These Normans are like the tide on their rough coast, as soon bid the waves hold back once the storm begins. Nor do I put much trust in them. When they are done with me, they will kill me, too, if it advantages them. And Henry is not so overfond that, if he dared, he could wish a death on me. We are but tossed adrift, you and I, at the mercy of other men; we could cling together to hope for calmer seas."

Now he had told me many things, and given many reasons for helping him, had named king and queen, so many names all churned together, to confuse and overwhelm; but despite myself, it was his last arguments that said the most. They touched some chord in me. It may be he knew the effect he made, for he smiled again, that half pagan smile. "And since I am young," he murmured, "and like not to die, God give me grace to enjoy what life is left." Before I could stop him, he had slipped both hands beneath his cloak, was kissing me, expertly and fast. I jerked my hand up, hit him hard, a second man to repulse in as many hours. He did not flinch, but caught my hand against his cheek.

"Now, Celtic witch," he whispered, and for a moment there was open menace, gone in a flash, "no woman smites me and escapes. But chance, that hitherto has not favored me, has given me you to use. I should be a fool to ignore it. Betray me not. Else my death, too, will be your guilt. And so will his. Look to see us again."

He released me, swung the cloak about his shoulders, and pushed past. I stood in the lighted tent once more. The music played, the torches reeked, pages ran with platters of food and wine.

"Where have you been this age, Countess?" Sir Martin, my table companion, wheezed into my path, wiping his nose upon his sleeve. I stared at him, unable to think. Colors, shapes, movement blurred; that men who danced and greeted friends, held knives to plunge into their backs; that women who flirted and preened, held death beneath their smiles; that king and queen used us as pawns. Titles, lands, power, put up for murder's hire, women to play at executioner for their own ends. *You will risk your life*, I had cried at Raoul. I did not know how close the truth. Dear God, I thought, wrenching myself free from Sir Martin's sticky embrace, does Raoul know? I must warn him.

It was not so easy to get away. Sir Martin followed complainingly, my squires uneasily followed him, my ladies trailed behind, again deprived of their share in the feasting. I had no idea if Geoffrey Plantagenet spoke the truth, nor where de Boissert and the other Norman lords were, but since I dared not blunder in upon them in the dark, better I thought to wait until I could catch Lord Raoul on his own. I did not know if he still lived, but, fighting panic down, I reasoned so. Not even these Normans would dare kill openly. Rather, sometime when he was off guard, they would strike, and soon, before Raoul and his men had won a victory over them. Before to-morrow's mêlée then, or during it. And the more I tossed and fretted in the dark, the more it seemed to me, were I murderer, I would choose the soonest, easiest way. Behind my closed eyelids a line of horsemen such as I had seen at Saint Purnace, seemed to wait, a massed black line, their cruel spears flashing in the sun, the thunder of their charge drowning out thought.

In the mêlée, then, that would be the time when Raoul must ride in front, and lead his side out. Someone behind his back, one of his own chosen side, would thrust him through. What better time when, in a general fight, any man might be killed and all men looked for blood, when murder could be called an accident. And when all of Sieux could be destroyed with that one thrust. It was a better plan than the one at Saint Purnace, and certainly easier to achieve. In a fever, I waited for dawn, until the trumpets sang out their early note. Then, taking the little hunting knife I always wore, I slit the back of the tent and crept out; no difficulty, I had done as much before. As I began to run, the dew beneath my feet so wet that I was drenched within twenty steps, I had a sudden memory of Cambray at this hour, the vast expanse of heather moors, the long stretch of open beach. Yet Cambray had not been so clean and fair that men had not sullied it; murder too had been done there, to kill my other loves long ago, and treachery planned as foul as here. Nowhere in this world is safe, unless you be willing to fight for it.

The morning had not yet truly come, the eastern sky was streaked with red, a half light on those empty fields; *les beaux prés de France*, now should I see them for what they were. At Raoul's tent, his guards would have barred the way but, seeing I meant to push aside their spears, they let me in, awkwardly knuckling salute. Inside, Raoul was partly dressed. He spun round and snatched for his sword. That quick gesture alone told me what I was sure was truth.

"My lord," I said. "I must talk."

He did not reply, one page already struggling with the straps of his mail, another burnishing up his spurs. In a moment, they would bind his hands to give him better grip. "Raoul," I said, anxiety making my voice break, "we must be alone. I have a thing to tell."

He eyed me, not suspiciously, not impatiently, but resigned, as if he thought I came to plead on my own behalf. I think his mind was already concentrated on the day's work and he wished me gone.

"It is too late," he said.

"Not for this," I said. Some urgency in my voice must have alerted him that this was more than a woman's whim. He gestured to his men to leave us alone, and went quietly forward with the preparations on his own. I had a sudden qualm that he would not believe me, or, at best, make light of it. But, guessing perhaps my hesitation, he smiled.

"Now speak," he said. When I was done, I found that I had clutched at him with both hands as if to shield him from harm. He did not argue or show surprise, not even when I told him how I thought his murderers would attempt to kill him, but quietly freed himself from my grasp. Nor did he question, then or ever, how or where I had heard the news, and I never mentioned Geoffrey Plantagenet's name. "Your ears have grown sharp," was all he said, "except in two instances are you mis-informed. The plan is to strike not south, but north against Henry's Norman hinterland, along King Louis's flank, a fool's attack, since the Vexin, at which the conspirators aim, is a tract of land both kings will fight to keep. As for those castles you name, why, they have already been promised me as bribe." He mused a while, fumbling with the lacings on his sleeve until I tried to tie them for him.

"Well, Ann," he said at last, as if resolved, "they have prom-ised us many things; since we have agreed to none of them, they have nothing to expect from us. But it cuts hard to think they would use me thus."

"Raoul," I cried, in my eagerness almost willing to drag him forth, "while there's time, let's escape. Ride out with me."

He disentangled himself from me a second time. "Ann," he said again, "there is no escape. I honor your concern. But think. I am come here for one purpose—to show our worth. If I leave now, what have I shown—only that I am not a match for them. If not now, then some other time, they will come after us. God's teeth, I cannot steal off like a thief. They are all here, one blow will finish them at once, rid us of their threat."

He turned and paced about. I watched the way his mail feet strode back and forth, the limp quite gone. *Touch what is mine,*

I'll smite body and soul. I knew before he spoke what his answer must be.

"We'll not run," he said. "By Christ, I've done with running in this life. Since I have been back in France, luck has favored them. Now it favors me." He paced and paced, that cat prowl I remembered, ready to pounce.

"How can you withstand them?" I whispered, "so many men, and you with eight?"

"Eight on the field," he said, "but off it, there are ways to have others standing by." He suddenly laughed. "When I was a lad and had a tutor to whip Latin verse into me, it seems I read the Roman cavalry ever stood 'waiting in the wings.' We shall try their tactics for ourselves."

"And what shall I do?" I said, although my voice still went wavering out of control. "You said one day I could lead a charge."

He spun round. "Now, by the Mass," he said, "there are times when you try me hard, yet I cannot fault your courage. I meant to send you away. But here's a truth: as companion, I'd prefer you at my back than almost anyone else I know. Most women would run at the thought, but if you'll offer help, by the Rood, I could use it. Not all the Norman barons are in de Boissert's camp, and I must have some way to distinguish friend from foe on the field. Walter is the man for that; he knows them all. You shall sit with the other ladies, if you will, and strew your favors on those contestants who are not yet committed to de Boissert's plans. Make no sign of anything untoward; show no fear; wait for me." He suddenly smiled, his wide, generous smile, so unlike that other one. "Little Ann," he said, "for all we rub each other awry, for all we fret and tear as waves beat against a rock, you see, I cannot manage without you. For wife, I have never known a woman before who could so bring me to anger's point and then show me that I am wrong. Trust you! You would carve my liver out if you could, but never let one breath of harm come near. And I, I could knock you head over heels and run to pick you up before you land. Together, then. We have been in such tight place before, and worse, and won through."

He suddenly took my hands, turned them over and kissed the palms. "Do not be afraid, *ma mie*. I cannot bear for you to be afraid. No one shall harm us today. Today, we shall not fail you."

He asked no other question, gave no excuse, no explanation more, nor did I have the chance to reply to his words. He strode out of the tent, already shouting his orders. Knights, squires, and groomsmen came running at his command. I had seen them run like that often enough. And, strange as it may seem, a sort of resignation came over me. I knew the nature of the attack on us and the danger entailed. I had fought Raoul to make him change and he had won. I had done my best to keep him safe and I had failed. And yet, suddenly, it was true; I was no longer afraid. He deserved to face his enemies as they should be faced. Let him go forth nobly and with honor high. That day, I think I realized what it meant to be the wife of a fighting man, a countess of an old and honorable line. Daughter of a soldier I was, wife to another, mother of a future one. I accepted fate. That day, for the first time, I understood what honor meant to him. And I felt, I cannot explain it otherwise, that his own resolution and courage had become part of me.

Two of the younger maids, steadier than the rest, I trusted to throw these favors with me; I marshalled the other women, marched them in good order to the spectator stands. I had them tear the red and gold flags of Sieux into strips, red for blood and gold for victory, that at Walter's whisper, we should tie our ribbons on men's arms as they rode by in the parade. And victory hung singing in the air . . .

A mêlée is what it sounds like, a mix, a mingling, when two sides meet as in real battle. The combatants pick sides, charge as in real battle, fight fiercely as in real battle, meet and thrust and charge again until, when only a few are left still horsed, they fight hand-to-hand with sword and shield. They do not seek to kill each other as in real battle (although men are killed) but today death was expected. When I saw those two distant lines, looming dark on the horizon, I knew at last I had found those menacing figures of my fears. Between the lines of horsemen the meadows were still mist encased, a sign of heat, the grass stretched green that, before the day was out, would be churned to mud. De Boissert led one side, Lord Raoul the other, eight men apiece, and all the other lords of Normandy, so attended, to fight against. Not all perhaps, for each time I rose at Walter's nod, I pushed my women up to shower our red and gold ribbons on as many men as we could, that Raoul could pick them out as friends. And when my lord passed, already helmeted so that his face was hid, I thought I heard that laughter in his voice to set his men at ease. "Decked out, by God," Raoul said, "a Yuletide log." And he dipped his lance in salute, then cantered on.

Beside me, Sir Jean squirmed. "Against the laws of chivalry," he cried, trying to prevent my standing up. "Favors are given only in the joust."

And what do you do against the laws of God, I thought, you, your daughter and that fair Isobelle? I let him whine who was scarce able to give the order to charge; and I outfaced the Lady Isobelle for a front seat, sat and watched that no man should say of me I turned aside today.

Charge the two sides did, in two great waves, meeting in the center with a shock that made the ground sway. Twice they met, parted, wheeled back. After each passage, men were hurtled into the air, horses ran on riderless, squires rushed to pull the fallen out of the way—dead men, if this had been a real fight; unhorsed knights do not live long. At the third charge, we heard the cry. Down they swooped, great dark birds, the sun full out to blind them, spears leveled like shafts of light. Loud the cry rang out, "To your left, lord Count, look left," above the din. There were many lords still on the field, many knights, and only one I think who was a count. I steeled myself to show no sign, so it has been said that without a look I watched Count Raoul ride to his death. But so did murderers sit beside me and smile while their hired assassin struck their coward's blow. I tell you it is no easy thing to watch for death. Down they swooped, those black uneasy lines; they met and broke; the dust clouds eddied like spray thrown against a cliff. Out of the mêlée, two figures emerged, one wearing de Vergay blue, the other that well-known black and white. The de Vergay man rode toward the stands where we sat, almost at his leisure, and as he approached you could see why. He had been wounded in the thigh and his saddle had slipped. Raoul's men had kept good watch for Raoul's assassin and had put their mark on him to brand him. The other man was de Boissert himself, and as we looked, two men in red and gold came hurtling after both. I knew each of the Sieux riders well. One, praise God, was Raoul, bareheaded, his helmet flung off, his black horse snorting as it came, although for a moment I had thought it riderless, the saddle empty, for Raoul had bent over the side to avoid the spearthrust that would have killed him. He rode fast after de Boissert, the faster when de Boissert urged his horse away off the field. But now, from various points behind the stands, from the tree clumps, other men of Sieux rode forth, both squires and knights, some to control the crowds, some circling round to hem the other contestants in. All save that other Sieux man, who rode helter-skelter as only Matt could ride, against Raoul's would-be murderer.

Beside me, Walter sucked in his cheeks, "Slow down, slow down," I heard him beg. On the other side, Sir Jean was on his feet.

"Squires on the field," he cried, "the order was not given to out swords; sound the retreat." The order, if such it was, was lost amid shouts of alarm and outrage. Almost beneath us, by the barricade, de Vergay's man stood his ground.

"Back, young master," we heard him shout. He beat at Matt with the flat of his sword. "I do not fight with unknighted boys." That rasping voice I had heard before, at Saint Purnace. And so had Matt.

His helmet gone too, his face twisted with rage, Matt reined up with difficulty. "Traitor," he snarled, "to strike my lord in the back. You owe me an arm. You did not mind to attack me once. I'll hack your spurs off to unknight you so we be quits. Stand you and fight."

He kicked his horse forward, it bounded on. He rode at the de Vergay man as if at a tilt. The older man had but to wait and thrust through as Matt plunged past. Yet even wounded, Matt still came on, blood pouring from his gashed side. He forced his horse forward again until another blow sent him crashing against the fence. But before the de Vergay man could escape, two more of our men rammed him and his horse and pinned them down. I closed my eyes. A murderer pays a brutal fee. And so does loyalty.

On the distant edge of the field, Ralph de Boissert still looked for escape, but as he fled we could tell now how Raoul out-circled him, forcing de Boissert to turn and run another way. You saw then what skill Raoul and the black horse had, to pivot and swerve, almost without thought, doing what Matt had tried to do, compelling the enemy to his will. So that, at last, unable to turn or run, de Boissert was forced to shelter beneath his long shield, which now shook under those relentless blows.

They want to see if I can fight. Proudly, arrogantly, Lord Raoul played de Boissert, although the black horse had lost half of its bridle and Raoul guided it more by voice than rein. And when Raoul bent, you saw the rip along the left side of his mail coat where a spear, thrown from behind, had glanced away. Soon all men watched them. At each blow, the crowd raised up a cheer. De Boissert's horse began to slip, the ground churned by its own hooves, buckling under that incessant onslaught. Its front legs gave way, it slid to its knees, tipping its rider gently off, feet first. Raoul leaned over and, with his sword point, snapped the other man's helmet up and slashed at the straps. The helmet fell and clattered in the dirt.

"Yield to me," Raoul cried, "lawful prisoners, you and your men."

De Boissert could not speak, his chest heaved as if with sobs. His gray hair was matted with sweat and his blank eye rolled desperately. But when he did not reply, I saw how Raoul's face tightened and his grasp on his sword hilt leveled it.

De Boissert turned to Raoul in suppressed rage. "Why should I yield?" he began, but Raoul interrupted him.

"Your hired man has paid his price, now shall you pay mine."

De Boissert cast a look around the field. Everywhere was confusion. Some of those in the plot, seeing their leader disarmed, had cried a halt, and had already thrown down their shields. Others, bewildered, had drawn aside, armed and ready, but most of these were marked with red and gold and had no part or agreement in de Boissert's schemes. A few fought on, but the Sieux knights were a match for them, striking indiscriminately. Even as he looked, de Boissert saw one of Sir Jean's sons unhorsed; another man's sword flew wide as he was crumpled beneath a slashing blow. Beside us in the stands, Sir Jean, still on his feet, danced with indecision, mouthed advice, too far away for it to be heard; but I could hear: "Say nothing, do not yield." To no avail. Before de Boissert could speak again, Raoul had reached over and yanked him hard; the surcoat tore but the sword belt held. Half-swung, half-dragged, he was forced to run as Raoul turned now toward the stands. He too stopped almost beside us and with another mighty heave cast de Boissert across the barricade. De Vergay licked his lips, all the women cowered away. How they screamed and moaned, even the Lady Isobelle, who so far had watched unmoved.

"By the laws of tourney..." Sir Jean began.

Raoul caught him next by the slack of his furred gown and held him as one might hold a rabbit or vermin to skin.

"Now hear me both," Raoul said, a trickle of blood still coursing down his face. I could see where his armor had been hacked from the rear, a coward's blow indeed. "I have been guest in your hall, toasted you, broken bread. Twice now have you plotted death for me and mine. What else shall you deserve of me? What you have begun, you shall end. Bid your carrion lay down arms, or I shall kill them and you."

Sir Jean knew a truth when it faced him. He dissolved like

wax, tore his gray hair, and begged for life. His wife beside him fell upon her knees, the other women started, horror-struck. Excuses fell from de Vergay like rain: Ralph de Boissert had acted on his own; he, Sir Jean, knew nothing of these plots; he was but a victim of them like the rest of us. De Boissert, struggling to his feet, smote Sir Jean across the mouth and took up a different tale: that de Vergay was a fool, to listen to his daughter's spite; that his wife was worse, (who recovering, added her pleas for *pitié*); that Sir Jean had planned it all.

"Not so," Sir Jean wept and wrung his hands. "We both do what we are told. We act for Geoffrey Plantagenet. And de Boissert has the ear of the queen..."

At those words de Boissert tried to strike Sir Jean again, berating him for a fool.

"But do you yield?" Raoul's voice cut like steel.

"Yield, yield," screamed Sir Jean, his face tallow white. There were the last words I ever heard him speak. Above our heads was a whistling sound, the sound most men dread. It made us all start back; arrows, shot from crossbows, their use forbidden by church decree, never found on tourney field. Heavy, vicious, they fell about us in the stands. One glanced, by God's great grace, off Lord Raoul's back where he had slung his shield; one thrummed in the wood between Sir Jean's legs, who fell down in fright; the third took de Boissert full in the throat.

I suppose we ladies screamed out. I suppose I closed my eyes and prayed. I suppose Isobelle de Boissert suffered, who this while, I grant her that, had scarce showed any emotion at all. I remember Raoul's hand to steady me; Raoul's voice, hoarse with weariness, bidding me be of good cheer. I remember asking if he were hurt. I remember his order to Walter to lead us away. I remember Matt's face, drained white; he still lived, but only just, and could not yet be moved. I suppose I heard the murmurs of the crowd, the women's wailing; already the death watch begun. I suppose I saw the grins, half hid, among the peasant folk—de Boissert was not a master well loved. I suppose I saw how even our pages and boys had taken men-at-arms by surprise, and disarmed them as they stood and gaped. I remember too the hot sun, the smell of blood, the black birds that swooped and cawed against the sky. But I recall nothing of the fast ride back, Walter at my side as if, like all our other ladies clinging close, I was not able to manage a horse. *Men will die.* But not my noble lord, thanks be to God, not our men. But that is how other men died, and that was how the tourney at Boissert Field came to an end, that was the sport they planned. I suppose men still talk of it. But it was not quite the end. Lord Raoul's vengeance has become a legend in its time, that men should use it as byword, as much to say, So it was at Boissert Field, or As they did at Boissert. You may have heard of it; many have been the songs, the jests, and many the women who wept for it. Since I had returned by then to Sieux, I can only repeat what I was told. But since it was Matt who told me, being there, I let him tell it in his own words.

He mended slowly, Matt, but he lived. And when he could creep into the summer sun, he would often sit for hours with my son Robert in his lap and speak of the mêlée slowly, with pain at times, for the sword that pierced his side had caught at something deep inside his chest so that ever after, although he could sometimes ride or hunt, he suffered from cruel short-ness of breath. It is his story then, although to tell the truth he was in such state, I doubt if he remembered much about it at first hand, but his, nevertheless, since it was the first and last time that he ever fought. Well, knighted he was, he won his spurs to good cause; and sometimes when I see his merry eyes repeated in his sons, I think it was better so, God's fortune, that he should live to wed and beget children to come after him.

"Well," he used to say, "the conspirators, both on the field and off, were not slow to surrender after that. For Lord Raoul had posted us at places where we could control them easiest, if and when an attack was made on him. Those who had no part, those you had marked with red and gold, we let them go. They galloped off, the devil at their heels, save one or two more sober lords who stayed to help. The rest we stripped down to their shirts. We heaped their helmets, their shields, their swords—Christ's bones, what stacks of stuff—and rounded them up at rope's end." He laughed and wheezed. "We might have made a better use of it. But, 'Nay,' says my lord. 'They thought to make a mock of us, play us along like fish on line; deal out life and death as if they played at dice. Tie up their horses, head to tail, we'll lead them home. Load up the gear. We've better use for rope than hanging them.'"

Matt laughed and coughed, still spitting blood. "As for them, conspirators whose plot was doomed even before they had it launched, 'Walk you home,' Count Raoul says to them, 'in your shirt tails and be damned.'"

At this point, even Robert used to laugh, not knowing why, and Matt would wipe the tears from his own eyes. "Since Jean de Vergay still lay in a swoon from which he never stirred again, we took one of his fat sons in his stead, tied him backward on an ass, nearly broke the poor creature's back, led him to the village pond, and dumped him in to make a wave. 'God's mercy,' called the village folk, 'spare us the rest, no water left for us.' But what an outcry made those unhorsed knights. You'd have thought we'd bid them march a road to Hell. 'Walk,' cries one, 'without sword belt and sword, that my father's father won on the crusades?' 'And where's my cap?' another complains, 'that I should go out bareheaded like a common man.' 'Better bareheaded without a cap,' answers Lord Raoul, 'than capped without a head.' He bid the serfs run him in front. Off down the road they trot, their chusses wrinkled about their hams, their knighthood reduced to dirty linens and wool. By the Mass, it made us laugh to see them go, and all the churls came out to point and jest. Lords and men, so they went on their two legs, who have not gone so far on foot since their mothers carried them. Nor had they traveled but half a league when the quarreling broke out afresh, each shouting blame against the rest, each accusing each until you'd think we had unearthed a thousand plots. Since we took all their gear, even that within their tents, it will be long before they can rearm, no danger now to us. But their ladies we sent forth decently, in wagons and carts. And they say that once out of sight, for we gave them fitting escort to the boundary of de Boissert land, well, out of sight, those proud Norman lords, whose blood would freeze for shame to be hauled in a cart like a common thief, by the day's end, were glad to clamber up with the women and ride the rest of the way.

"And so we returned to Sieux. If such is war's reward, we struck rich load. But my lord came up to me where they'd stacked me against a tree stump. 'Well, well,' says he, 'I never thought to see you ride to such good purpose, for all that grass sprouts between your knees and you bounce more out of saddle than in. My thanks to you for my life. You've won your spurs, in a good fight.'"

Matt smiled and wept at the thought, being weak, and Walter comforted him, promised to wait for him to heal so they should be knighted at the same time. Never word of complaint Walter let fall that Matt had fought while he had sat with me. So through those summer days they talked and planned, two friends, bound closer than before. But once when I asked what had befallen the ladies there, Matt spoke of Isobelle de Boissert.

"She left, too. They say, seeing her father dead, she turned without a word and rode away. And we let her go. They say, with Mistress Alyse de Vergay for company, she took refuge in a nunnery nearby, for fear of Henry, whose ward she now becomes. I could almost find it in my heart to pity her. With her father's death, so are her hopes, for Henry will not let her marry unless he choose." He hesitated for a moment, then went on. "They say too she hoped to wed with some great lord, Geoffrey Plantagenet, and boasted that, as she was a great lady, so a great lady helped her. A bitter bed to lie upon, for Geoffrey Plantagenet will not marry with her now. For afterwards, a villein came up to me, whispered he'd seen a group of horsemen watching from the hills. At the tourney's end, they rode away, heading south. They rode with helmets down, masked then, and fast, and he who led them was in a royal rage. Who they were, what wanted, why watched, the serf could not say, except he claimed they waited until the arrows' flight was loosed. And they wore sprigs of broom in their helmets' crests, *genet*, the word for broom, whence comes the meaning Plantagenet."

That was the end of conspiracy, then, the end of Boissert Field. But not the end for us. *As a stone is thrown into a lake, so the ripples spread.* Raoul lived, I lived, Sieux stood. Our enemies were scattered or dead. But there had been too many harsh things said between Raoul and myself, and too many things left unexplained. He had spoken of the bond between us. *Better you at my back than anyone,* he had said. (He had spoken those same words in jest many years ago at Sedgemont. He had not said them in jest at Boissert.) He had praised me, thanked me, shown me his esteem. He had not yet spoken of the Lady Isobelle, nor those mysterious archers, nor the horsemen riding south. Nor yet the king and queen on whose behalf, it now seemed, the games played at Boissert had been set afoot.

So, although there was peace at Sieux, all was not yet at peace between me and my noble lord. Nor was all at peace between him and himself. For I sensed a questing in him, a restlessness, which I remembered from his youth, a new air of resolution which seemed to make things move faster, and move forward, as if all that had gone before had brought us to this point. *I take the cares of the kingdom on my back.* So he had admitted, so now he did. For him, this day of triumph was but the start. It brought him to where he had been, to what he had been, before Henry's men had come for him at Sedgemont. Now were the evil days of inactivity and waiting over. Now would he strike against Henry and his men. So, although there was peace at Sieux, there was none for him who had earned it.

As for me, I had come to understand that even peace can be bought at too high a price. For what is peace worth if it brings no honor with it? And the consequences of that tourney were to reverberate down the years. As now shall be told.

8

HERE WERE OTHER CONSEQUENCES after the crushing of the conspiracy, so well remembered, that in future years learned men should debate them, each scholar arguing for this interpretation or that. Womanlike, I shall tell you first those that concerned us at Sieux, certainly those that affected me, and eventually so entwined with other larger ones that it would take a more skilled mind than mine to sort them through. I speak of matters of state, you understand, strategy and policy by which the great of the world rule and control; but since the main effect of Boissert Field was to bring fame and wealth to Sieux, that was what I noticed most. Sieux regained its rightful place of importance in France. Each day, it seemed men came to offer their services, soldiers of fortune, younger sons, vassals from Auterre and Chatille, looking for adventure and reward. The castle began to hum with life. Master Edward hastily hammered up a second floor to the gate tower, and hiring more men, began to raise up the outer walls and build on the foundations of the keep; a year ago, we could have prayed for half as much. Best of all, or worst, depending on the point of view, Raoul's triumph gave him freedom to act as he saw fit; and since Sieux's control of central France was assured, he could strike out on his own. And that I saw as most dangerous. But I rush ahead. For first of all, the things that took place before and after that mêlée had to be discussed, and as soon as Raoul returned to Sieux he surprised me into speech.

I had come hastily at noon that day into the new upper chamber of our tower. It was still damp and smelled of whitewash and lime, and I was laughing at something the men had said, a bunch of flowers swinging at my side, for in these peaceful times I used to dig in the herb gardens, once justly well-known that the ladies of Sieux had planted, overgrown these many years. Raoul was sitting there, long legs stretched out, boots on hearth, for even on a fine day like this he enjoyed a fire and was staring into it in his brooding way. I remembered how he used to sit in another world, in Sedgemont, long ago. It was seldom one found him indoors; he usually was with the men in stable or tilting field.

"Is aught wrong, my lord?" I asked him worriedly.

His boots crashed to the ground. "Nothing," he said, "unless the way your smile fades on seeing me."

"What, my lord?" I asked, puzzled by his tone.

He said, still in the same brooding way, "No cause for alarm. Merely a message from Louis of France. Oh, it seems he too has heard of Boissert Field and is beside himself with fear and rage, mostly that the conspirators thought to take that piece of land known as the Vexin away from him—a sorry place it is, too—along the border between Henry's lands and his and so coveted by both. And a sorry sort of man is that French king to froth and fret after an event which he had had within his power to prevent if he had but roused himself. Well, there's nothing new to that, but it seems he feels he owes me thanks, holds me in his gratitude, would repay one good turn with another and so on, and so on, each compliment more fulsome than the last. Compliments are his way of hiding what he truly wants. Which is my help in the west of France, in Brittany to be exact. Celts all, like your Welsh kin, the Brettons are about to overthrow *their* duke, a fashionable exercise this year. Louis, in turn, as he puts it, 'knowing full well my understanding of the western Celts' and 'mindful of the way the Welsh are poised for revolt' would like me to interfere on his behalf. Now, the French Celts or Brettons are no concern of mine, but the Celts in Wales are, and Louis's talk of unrest among them only confirms what Sir Renier spoke of last year. The Welsh princes dispute ownership of land among themselves and will set the border afire with their quarreling. I should go back. And Louis's

message has made me think of something else: what Henry
owes me for Boissert Field. True, it was my own skin I fought
to save, but in saving it, I saved his, too. Now, he may not
be as generous as the King of France (if Louis's way of thanks
can be called generous); but whether he will or no, Henry is
in my debt. I think to claim a payment of him. How would
you like a return to England as his fee?"

The thought took away my breath, I did not dare to con-
template it.

He said, "Cambray has ever been important in these border
disputes and will be again. I plan to keep its defense in my
own hands. Our return to Sedgemont and Cambray therefore
is of some concern, and Henry shall offer it, although it scald
his tongue." He sighed, "Henry cannot be everywhere at once,"
he said, "nor keep the peace without some help. He cannot
even control his wife. Nor can he deal with a rebellious brother
as he should." He hesitated. "The other news that Louis sent
is less kind. That little boy, Henry's firstborn that you spoke
about, that William, is dead, and between the inheritance and
Henry's brother, Geoffrey, stands but one small life, Henry's
second, and now his only, son. Louis fears Henry will give his
brother lands in Brittany to keep him quiet. I myself think it
a good idea."

I closed my eyes to pray for that young prince, ailing since
birth, set aside while he lived, or so it had seemed to me, in
favor of a younger, stronger son. Poor little boy, heir to so
much, yet never having the chance to savor any of it, God's
gifts his only inheritance after all—and when I looked up,
Raoul was watching me.

He said abruptly, as if the words were forced out, "What is
that man's life to you?"

I could not pretend I did not know what man he meant.
"We met by chance," I stammered out, "and then he told me
of their plans, how they would kill you if you would not join
with them. And he said they would kill him too if they knew
he spoke with me."

"Mischance more like," was all he said. "Well, you kept your word. I did not know he was there, not until afterward when he'd gone."

He mused for a while. Then, in the way of a man who speaks his thoughts aloud, as if we had been talking of it all this while, as if this conversation had been going on for a long time, as perhaps it had in his mind as in mine, "Afterward," he said, "we found out many things. Those archers who fired on us for one, well hid, well provisioned, well armed with cross-bows."

"Who set them there?" I cried. "Cannot they be questioned?"

He turned his eyes toward me, dark, unwavering. "They too were dead. Throats slit, bows piled underneath them, killed perhaps because they knew too much or because they misfired. There were three of them, since crossbow men can fire but once and must pause to reload. Three assigned: one to kill de Boissert, who is dead; one for de Vergay, who should thank his luck if he could speak, for he lives but as dead flesh; and the third for me. Who also then must give thanks to God." Even I could see what he meant.

"Aye," he said, "a second plot to kill me if the first one went awry, or if there were a change of plan that Geoffrey Plantagenet did not know about. For since he trusted his fellow conspirators as little as they trusted him, they must die too, who could have revealed the part he had played in their plot."

He suddenly stood up, strode back and forth. This little room, scarce space for chair and bed had seemed a palace when we saw it first; now it seemed to hem him in as if his energy would break apart the walls. He said, "Geoffrey Plantagenet knew what all these Normans planned; he was privy to all their secrets and he stayed to watch what would come of them. And, if their plan failed, he had one of his own."

"No," I cried, the words forced out, "he said he needed you." But even as I denied the charge, the thought crossed my mind that it would be possible. Had not even I felt that cold, dark wind?

He shrugged. "I have no proof," he said, "except three dead men, four if you count de Boissert, five with de Vergay. Five dead men, myself the sixth, would be small price to pay for Sieux. Six men to make him Count of Sieux in my stead, if he failed to become Count of Anjou. That was Geoffrey's intent. And you, I told you you would make a pretty widow, with a son too young himself to inherit yet." There was a note to his voice that I had seldom heard before. "And I told you too conspiracy is not nice," he was saying, repeating what other men had said. "I saw it in King Stephen's time, and now it shows again. Conspirators by nature are fearful men, afraid of shadows, suspicious, even of themselves that they reveal too much. A twisted coil is conspiracy, dragging down innocent as well as guilty men. And Geoffrey Plantagenet no better than the rest, except he expects other men to intrigue for him. What we speak of is but half of what he knows or has done."

He turned and turned about, then suddenly paused, gave the mantelpiece a thud as if to test its strength, as if to make up his mind. It was built of oak, a handsome gift, which Master Edward had had carved during the winter months, made to last, durable, a thing to rely on, where all else was shifting sand. He said, "When Henry comes south to Poitiers to claim the allegiance of his southern lords, which now he is free to do, I will make my claim of him. Let Henry create Geoffrey Plantagenet Duke of Brittany for all I care, as long as Geoffrey does not look to be Count of Sieux. But I'd rather my wife not see him again. I'd rather he stayed away from her. Is that too much to expect?"

"No," I said, subdued, shocked and, yes, still part disbelieving. "As long as you keep clear of *her*."

Nor did he ask who that *she* was.

"It was a nothing, too," he said. "To persuade me to their side, she used her wiles, as full of them as a honeypot entraps wasps. I remembered them from long ago; they had no hold on me."

Not even if she planned your death? I thought, but still I hesitated. *His* charms had been considerable, perhaps so had been hers. "And that attack on us at Saint Purnace—was Geoffrey behind that too? Or is there someone else behind him?"

He said, "De Vergay and de Boissert will plot no more. Forget Saint Purnace. Best put aside."

"And our marriage?" Again I hesitated. "They said your betrothal to her, coming first, counted more. And you, you said you regretted the yoke Henry put on you."

"And you," he countered, "'knock-kneed, fat-bellied,' I think were the words you used, a misshapen lout compared with that god of manly grace." He smiled, but I sensed a hint of anger, concealed, yet deep. I was surprised. I had not thought that jealousy might have gnawed on him, yet, had not I hoped at the start to make him feel jealous of me?

He suddenly smiled once more, his generous smile that lit his face. "Poor wench," he said. "I did not know they tormented you so. I see why you fought them as you did, although it was not wise. Witchcraft is a dangerous thought, better hidden in this land. But, despite everything, you were loyal to me. Was I worth that much to you?"

"Aye." My answer was simple and direct.

He gave the mantel shelf another decisive thud, came toward me. "There," he said, "you look at me as if to ask what can I mean, and I see a new expression in your eyes that was not there a year ago. Sometimes I think I have done you wrong to bring you here to mix with such rough company. I should have left you at Cambray. Do not you know that no one can hurt us two save only us, and that in striking you, I strike at my own heart? Come close, that I may prove the truth."

He put aside the flowers that I had been holding in my hands. "Ann," he said, "I owe my life to you. How many times has that been said? I have fought with you and bested you and yet not won. I do not know how other men manage their wives, but I cannot either do with, or do without you." He spread wide his hands as if he had no defense.

"I shall to Poitiers," he said, "and having dealt with this king, take my leave of France. Come with me then. I would please you, *ma mie*," he whispered. "I would please my Celtic witch."

And with each word, he kissed my breasts, slid my clothes off my back. "Open wide," he said, "and let me in. Let me love you as I ought."

Afterward, when his heartbeat had slowed to normal against my own and he lay tracing with one finger between my breasts, I heard the ripple of laughter in his voice.

"Not crown you?" he said. "I cry you pardon; I already thought you crowned of all I own, my lands, my name, my heart. Have not I given you a tower, nay two towers, fit for a queen? And a castle guard who would die for you? And a husband who will call this his wedding day, better, I swear, than the one we had?" He reached out his hand and took the flowers and idly dropped them one by one, tracing them down across my body, marking out each line and fold.

"Is not this better than our wedding night?" he asked again, and every flower was a caress. "And shall I admit what is not good for you to hear, that Henry had already given me the kingdom's prize when he gave me you."

"Not good, my lord?" I asked him, drugged myself with sun and love and expecting, I admit, other compliments.

The slap he gave was as brisk as his tone. "See," he said, "you purr for cream. Suppose I were to lie abed all day and whisper words like those southern lords, who lisp their time away in wantonness? Then would you, lady, lie idly in bed, too, and expect my praise, and Sieux would fall about us in ruins." He stretched himself, long like a cat, and his eyes grew blue-green like the sea. "But, by the Mass," he swore, and the flowers were crushed by his weight, "such a life might not be so bad. I might become used to it. I am not the man," he said, each word against my skin, "to mouth sweetness as you know. But I cherish it when given me. Let Henry dance to another tune. We are done with things in France. Let me ride you safely home."

But, even as he loved me then and there, why did his words ring out their warning note, things still not said, things not finished with, like a drowned bell echoing out the shiftings of the tide, like a fog horn rolling its alarms along a rocky coast?

After Boissert Field I thought the many threads of conspiracy were at last unwound, like that skein of wool which once Sir Renier had held. *Who knows how the ends start*, he had said, *or how they ravel out.* Why then did fright still startle me? For Jean de Vergay and Ralph de Boissert, who had begun that conspiracy, whose hatred of Henry had prompted them, who needed Sieux gold to buy support, death came for them. And one daughter, who for spite would have had her father's men kill me, she was cast aside; and another daughter, who would have made my husband her lover or climbed over his death to win rank and fame, she too now was shut away, both of them discredited to the world. *Beware the malice of womankind*, so had the lady of the moors warned and now so it seemed. (At least I thought that malice done with; not yet, as shall be told.) Those other Norman lords, nameless lords, who had come to Boissert Field to plan the date and place of attack on Henry's lands in northern France, who would have killed Raoul because he would not join in their schemes, they were disarmed, disgraced, and thrown to Henry's mercy, such as that was. And the man in whose name the conspiracy was begun, who had come to spy upon his fellow conspirators and had stayed to see them killed so they could not tell tales on him; he, whose archers had been placed to murder and then been murdered in their turn; he, who, if all else failed, would have killed Raoul to advance his own plan, which, God forgive us, was to marry me and become Count of Sieux in Raoul's stead; what next had he, Geoffrey Plantagenet, in mind, of all men in France the most fair and most treacherous? That thread which bore that Geoffrey's name was truly bitter in its unravelling.

There remained then one thread left, and it the most difficult of all for me to grasp, the part played by the queen. I should have left it well alone. As Raoul would have said, rather ignorance. Perhaps in this what he and other men felt was right; better their womenfolk bide at home, content themselves with women's work, and leave government to men. Yet now I believe, although then I could not bring myself to do so, that one thing was central to that twisted coil of conspiracy—the

wishes of the person who sponsored it. Not Geoffrey Plantagenet, not de Boissert, nor any Norman lord had that power.
Then who? For although the conspirators gave many excuses
for their actions, yet one reason seemed common to all of
them—each was tied to what the queen did. Now other men
had told me this, if I had but listened to them; and, on looking
back, I think Sir Renier had come, in part, to Sieux to warn
of it. But this now I also believe: de Boissert and his daughter
may have used the queen's friendship as license for what they
did, and even Geoffrey may have felt she owed him recompense
for failing to marry him, but none of their reasons affected *her*.
For there was another thing vital to that conspiracy, and it too
lay at the heart of it—the desire for land,. And in that the
queen felt more strongly than anyone.

She will protect her lands as fiercely as any vixen does her cubs. I
should have remembered that. For ownership of land, the keeping of it, the wresting away of it by force, the clinging to it
tenaciously, is the thing that motivates this world we live in.
For us, land equals power and wealth and fame, all those earthly
goods that God permits to humans in their earthly lives. And
in the end it is the only thing we keep, that little plot of ground
in which death gives us our graves. So then, for her, the desire
for her own land, and so also men had warned. I tell you this
so that you shall understand what at the time had escaped me,
that last strand in that knotted skein. For had I unravelled it I
would have never felt the need to go and find the queen. As
I did. This was the way of it.

When King Henry and his retinue came south to Poitiers,
as had been predicted, Raoul joined the king there. But Raoul
rode alone. That was something I had not bargained on. For
Queen Eleanor also had joined the king with her two children,
her son and new daughter, and came south with him. And
more than ever I felt compelled to see her again. What prompted
me to go in search of the queen, to brave the intrigues of her
court and think to settle all this rumor, these hints, these lies,
(for so I still thought them) concerning her role in the conspiracy? As you know I had not seen her since leaving England

and had only that news of her which Sir Renier had brought to Sieux. Yet I felt it only just to her to tell her in person what had happened at Sieux, at Saint Purnace, at Boissert Field, and hear her explanations in return. There were ties so strong between us I believed them capable of overcoming any misunderstanding. And I valued her friendship both for itself and for the help she had given me in the past. I could not accept that a queen who had sent me a ring as pledge of faith could withdraw that pledge and turn from me. I longed to hear her voice once more, retell old stories, share our joys and griefs as friends. I wanted, most of all I suppose, to have her help me put in order my own conflicting thoughts as she had done when I knew her first in England. I felt it only right for us both to meet. I explain all this so you will know with what mixture of fear and expectation I had hoped to see her. Deprived of that chance, I felt distraught, still caught up in all those snarls of plot and counterplot which only she could unwind.

Poitiers lies to the south of Sieux, a finger span on that map I once had seen, an easy ride, and easily Lord Raoul and his guard went south. Now it happened at this time that the king and queen were lodged apart, he within the city and she without, and learning of that fact in wifely wise (having sent messages after Lord Raoul to make sure he was safe and well), I too made a plan. Of all the things I have done in a long life, this was easily the worst, but I thought, since the queen kept court alone with her womenfolk, separate from the men, what harm should be if I joined her there, not so much in secret, since Lord Raoul had not forbidden it, but on a private visit such as one woman might make to a neighbor, having news to share or wanting company. Of course, one does not make private visits to a head of state without being asked, nor, to tell the truth, am I just to Raoul. He had not forbidden me to see her, it is true; but that was because it had not crossed his mind I would. But even he could not have estimated the harm. Well, taking Walter as my squire, and with three stout French men-at-arms, I rode south to meet the queen. An easy journey it was for us too, no haste, no great cause for alarm, my son bestowed once again in comfort with his village nurses, Sieux at peace. Then I saw for the first and only time the fair and rolling hills of Anjou, the neat roads lined with poplar trees, the many people traveling up and down, for the most part on pilgrimage to the famous sanctuaries in Spain and Italy. Every day we moved south under a pale sky like a robin's egg; and although it was the autumn of the year, the leaves had not yet fallen, the grapes hung in rich clusters in the vineyards. There were many smaller towns along the way, each throbbing like an anthill, each full of builders about their trade until you would have thought there was not one piece of earth that had not already been marked for a new tower or church. We lodged for the most part in quiet hostelries, peaceful too, for the counts of Anjou kept their lands safe, I grant them that, no robber bands, no thieves; and so we came at last to the banks of the Loire, the greatest river in all of France. We crossed it in a small flat-bottomed boat, propelled between the many islands and sand banks by brown-faced men who leaned on their long poles to steer us through. The poles dipped and glittered in the sun; flights of small white birds wheeled downstream; beyond the further bank, finally we came within the sight of the city of Poitiers, with its many walls and spires, as if suspended between the water and the sky. On clear days, they claim it can be seen like a forest of stone rising out of the plain. They say, too, if you dig beneath its ground but a foot or so, you come across the remains of stones and bricks, buried now a thousand years, left behind by the peoples who once lived there. And so I think it is with memories; dig beneath, you will find whole cities once inhabited, now empty, all who once laughed and played there, all those whom you loved, gone, vanished like dust. In this way then I came most of the way to the city gates but never entered in, turned aside, rode further on to find the queen.

To tell why Henry and his queen were lodged apart, I must again refer to the consequences of Boissert Field. (And since I learned this later, I will tell you it briefly as it was told to me.) What was intended by the king in Poitiers and what was achieved mainly resulted from the crushing of the rebellion, too. It gave him time and opportunity, which he otherwise would not have had, to secure what was claimed he long had planned: his hold upon the turbulent barons of the south. It seems that, when he had married with the queen in this same town of Poitiers, he was young, new come to titles on his father's death, and that far-off island kingdom promised him without importance to these southern lords. He was eighteen; Eleanor, some eleven or twelve years his senior, had already once been a queen. They say he was both overwhelmed and intrigued by her, and in his eagerness to please would do anything she asked. Queen Eleanor had, then as now, one main desire: to keep the lands she had inherited, to hold them in her own right as she had done since childhood, as she had done indeed throughout her first marriage to the King of France. An ardent bridegroom then, Henry let her do as she would, let her receive her southern lords alone, let her have homage from them for their lands. But afterward, he had resented having done so, the more because those lords had ignored him and honored her. For five years their arrogance had rankled him. Now he was come to Poitiers to put an end to it. Then, too, there was the question of what and whom the queen had supported in Normandy, and why. And rumors of what her life had once been, of her many "friends" both old and new, friends or lovers, who dared say, must have reached him. He may have heard stories of his brother's meeting with her, the promises each claimed the other had made, the support she may have promised *him*. These and other tales of this sort had made Henry less willing to please than he had been. Moreover, the death of his older son must have been a blow. The queen's next child had been a girl, and she had had only girl children with Louis of France. Henry needed heirs as much as Louis did to secure his inheritance; and, although in due course he was to get more than enough, the lack may have been a cause of alarm at this time. Finally, he was young and, like his father and brother both, amorous, desirous perhaps of "friends" himself—so many reasons then to cause a rift, if not an open breach, between the king and queen. And because of them he stayed at Poitiers with his men and received the southern lords in his name alone, entertained them without her, had them do allegiance to him for their lands. (For what that was worth. As I soon found out, they rather did him lip service and bided their time.)

As for the queen, the failure of Boissert Field had had effect on her, too. The Norman barons' defeat meant the failure of her plan, as I found out, to discomfort the king, although at that time I had no proof of what her plans had been. She stayed outside the town, housed in one of those religious buildings I had admired along the way, more like to an English country house, bigger than a house although not as strong as a castle, set about with many gardens, but fortified. They say she later shared King Henry's triumph and journeyed with him to meet each of her formal vassals; but first, seeing how he had triumphed in all things, she kept herself apart. And knowing what he guessed of her intrigues, she may have felt it wiser to stay away. They said she feared the spread of plague, the autumn being unusually hot; they said she preferred the country air, thought of her child's health—all lies. Poitiers was *her* city, where she had been brought up, where she had fled after leaving King Louis's court, where she had been wed to Henry; it was a city she dearly loved. Nothing would have kept her out of it save anger and pride. And these she nursed secretly, as she did her fear of her husband and her thought of revenge.

I arrived at Poitiers, full of hope, certain all misunderstandings would be put to rights, convinced one word from her would suffice; so sure of her, you see, that I thought at first it was merely ill timed that when we arrived at her court she was riding out, her falcon on her wrist, her falconer beside her, ladies swarming around. In the confusion of so many horses and riders I would have been jostled against the wall had not Walter thrust himself in front to take the strain. I caught but a glimpse of her, and she, I suppose, none of me; but I thought, When she hears I am here, she'll burst open the door in her impetuous way, and run in. Why little Ann, she'll say, her face alight with mischief as if she were but ten years old, why Ann, you've stolen a march on those stupid men who thought to keep us apart.

And so, not unduly alarmed, I left Walter to see our men housed and fed, and followed her stewards up the wide shallow stairs to wait her return. All day I waited; all day I expected her; and at night, after the feasting, after I convinced myself that she had some high ranking guest perhaps whom she had not been able to dismiss who kept her then at night, I was sure, she would come. *Kings and queens do not keep faith long.* So Raoul had warned me, but I had not believed it then, and now I found it to my cost (although that was but half of it). When old companions are out of sight, there are too many new ones overeager to fill an empty place, too many enemies waiting to whisper sly reports. By daybreak, confused, sleepless, I determined I would seek her out.

I knew enough of court etiquette of course to realize I broke the rules. It was not for me to approach her, nor should I address her out of turn. I should presume nothing unless she permitted it. Even to me, by then, it seemed that I had made a grave mistake to have come at all. I could not, perforce, ask Raoul for advice—there was no one else to ask—yet a year ago, she had begged for me, sent for me with many loving messages. I could not accept that she had changed, or, if so, understand what had caused such change. Only that I had refused to come to her? But that was a thing I must explain myself, and then, I thought, she would relent. I believed, you see, that she was as constant as I was, not realizing that constancy too can be judged in many ways and even my own was open to doubt.

The room where I was lodged was not large nor richly furnished, a fact which, if I had had any sense, should have alerted me. It had one advantage; it looked down into a corner of the outer yard where she and her courtiers went to and fro. When she returned from Mass next day, I watched the way she took through a narrow gate into the gardens, which were set into shapes and squares with grassy plots or turf meads in between, such as poets like to praise. Down among them, I was soon lost, wandering along one gravel walk to the next. The morning air was still, hot as an English summer day, the scent of flowers hanging like incense such as I had smelled at Saint Purnace Church, but fresher, unpicked. Despite the lateness of season, there were flowers in bloom, and herbs that I should have loved to study and learn about. Even in my haste, I noted how the flowerbeds were watered by streams that cut their way in channels across the grass. There was no sound, the queen and her court seemed melted away, only the splash of those little streams, the cooing of doves by the courtyard gate. I had despaired of finding her when a child's voice alerted me. It was the fretful cry a tired child makes, and in between the clipped hedges, he presently came stumbling along, not more than two years old, but dressed like a little man, in his lavish clothes, stiff jewel crusted gown, embroidered belt and dagger sheath, a small velvet cap set on his red hair. It tumbled off as he fell down. The gravel paths grazed his knees and he began to howl, the more when I ran to pick him up. I knew him at once, his paternity stamped on him from red hair to clear white skin to temper which made him pout and scream.

God's mercy, Prince, I thought, trying to set him on his feet, although he kicked and fought, such rage will stand you in good stead one day. He plumped down on the ground with a kind of mulish obstinacy which I had seen his father show, pulling at his Moorish boots with that look his father had when he wanted a thing and was not sure how to get it.

Queen Eleanor came after him through the hedge, his nurses scuttling in her wake, afraid to make a move unless she bid them. She was smiling, throwing some quick and clever remark over her shoulder to her companions to make them laugh. But when she turned from them, the smile died, a different expression crossed that fine-shaped face, she came toward the prince with the look of one who will not let anything hinder her and, seeing it, he began to scream louder than before. I had never seen her show interest in her children—a cool and distant mother had she ever been—and might have been amazed that she came to fetch him herself had not it occurred to me she had had him brought there for a purpose of her own, which his fit of childish anger did not suit. As soon was proved. But when she saw me, I forgot such thoughts, and all my hopes died on her look.

"You," was all she said, but with such contempt to make me cringe. No word of greeting, no surprise, no smile to light up those luminous eyes. She closed her mouth up tight, the arrogant tilt of her head more pronounced than usual. Neither childbearing nor child losing could dim that impetuous mind or still that quicksilver tongue.

I was still crouched over her son. Not knowing I did so, I stretched out my hands, a suppliant. "Lady Queen," I almost breathed the word, forgetting how she hated importuners—begging was a sign of weakness, a cry for mercy which might have roused pity in another, but angered her. "How have I offended you? Send me hence if you will, but do not ignore me, I beg."

She clapped her hands, sending the women scurrying to pick up the child. "Bear him off," she cried, "unruly brat. Lord Ademar came to see a prince, not have a baby spit at him."

To me, she said, "God's wounds, get up. We stand on no ceremony here, too far from court or courtly ways. I hear your husband, Count Raoul of Sieux, has come to make peace with the king. Are you come to make peace with me? After Boissert Field I doubted if either of you would dare." I knew better than to stem her anger. "Aye," she said, "I speak of Boissert, where you spoiled my plans, sent those Normans home like whipped curs. Who are you to be so bold? I knew you as a simple girl, I knew your count as a beggar himself."

I began to say, They were traitors all, but bit off the thought. If traitors then, what was she? It was against her husband they conspired.

"Fool," she said, angrier still, as if she guessed what I would have said. "They would never have won, no danger of that. Left to themselves, they would have pricked Henry's pride, no more. Louis would not have let them move against the Vexin, would have taken care of them. Why had you and your Raoul," she sneered the word, "to interfere? Should I thank you for it? Should Ralph de Boissert's death go unavenged? Should Isobelle de Boissert be cast aside?" The bitterness in her voice was as sharp as a knife blade. "I thought, since I had helped him, your lord might rather have helped me. Scorning Isobelle himself, is he so dog-in-manger to resent her betrothal to Geoffrey Plantagenet? It was a wedding I had arranged. Lord Raoul could have shown his thanks for his own marriage by leaving that one alone. Her lands would have contented Geoffrey Plantagenet, and now they are lost. What other lands shall he get in their place? Not mine I trust. I like him well but not enough to give him my lands."

Too miserable to answer (for what had I known of her plans?), I muttered, "I came to see you as a friend," a reply as obviously displeasing, for she stamped her feet, tore at the fringes of her sleeves until the threads broke and a line of pearls went cascading to the ground. Still on my knees, I began to search for them among the gravel stones.

"Let be," she cried. "More care for them than all the other treasures I gave you, strewn about for other men to gather up, as if gifts were worthless as straws. I never gave you jewels to rebuild Sieux to my despite. Do not add hypocrisy to ingratitude."

"No ingrate I," I said, almost angry in my turn at the thought. "Who accuses me speaks false. Ever have I counted you my benefactor and my friend." It was perhaps the repetition of the word "friend" or my show of anger—she did not like milksops—that made her pause, fingering the torn threads of her sleeve.

"Simpleton," she said. "You think, perhaps, having beauty still, your smiles will have all men running at your beck and call; you think the world owes you some joy, because you are young. Youth will not last long. Do you think Geoffrey Plantagenet cared for you? Why should you make him change his plans? Men are always greedy, wanting something new. Do not expect such attention to last."

I had seen her in moods like this, but certainly never directed against myself, and certainly, I think, never so fierce, so uncontrolled, although I sensed in part she spoke to turn the blade against her own breast. And certainly never so openly jealous of anyone. I was abashed. Jealousy I had known, but not like this.

"And do you think to flaunt your beauty here," she said, "to gloat on me?" She darted a look in the way she had, glancing out from those large almond-shaped eyes. "I am not yet powerless—men still serve me—for all that Henry woos them from my side. And as you have had a son, so shall I. Many more," and her face was twisted now with pain, with fear. "I am not too old for sons."

Behind her bitterness was a cry for help. Hearing it, how could I deny her? I got up, took her hand; cold it was, the long thin fingers shaking in my grasp. "Dear my Queen," I said, "there is no one in the world younger than you, no one more apt to win the hearts and devotion of men, no one more the king cherishes."

She made no reply, gripped my hand tight until the rings she wore bit into my flesh, stared off into the distance with unseeing eyes. And I think now, in my old age, although I would not have thought of it then, there are women, royal or not, who take the decline of beauty, the waning of their charms, harder than others do, the more perhaps the greater their beauty was. And there are those too who take grief, the death of a child, the loss of a husband's love, so hard that it becomes a cancer, hidden from the world, eating into their flesh to make them lash and rage. Yet, looking at her as I did then, no one would deny she was still beautiful; no one could have guessed how many cares, how many sadnesses she had endured. And I thought, Surely she who has known so much grief will not begrudge me my little part of happiness.

Presently, she stirred, as if remembering who and where she was, as if she remembered me. "So, Ann," she said, "you have come. Too late. I asked for you once and you refused when I most needed you. So now I presume you think to join my little court. I have done with state affairs; we talk of love. You should

know what that means, having a husband so new-wed," she
added waspishly, and before I could guess what she was about,
she took me by the hand, half-led, half-dragged me behind
the hedge.

A group of her companions were waiting there, most of
them men, although I had understood only women were with
her. Some were lying on the grass, their heads arranged on a
lady's lap, others were leaning against the trees in graceful
attitudes, hands on hips, as if posing like statues. I did not
know their names then, nor did she present them, but the way
they sprawled at ease in the warm October sun and the way
their equerries waited for them, holding their horses, richly
bridled and saddled for their pleasure, spoke of luxury and
power. They were dressed in hunting clothes but for the most
part unbuttoned, unbraced, and so languid in their movements,
their way of speaking, you wondered if they would ever have
the energy to hunt at all. But that was just their manner I think.

One of them, the most important one I presume, rose to
his feet as we appeared, led the queen back to where a sort of
throne had been made for her upon the turf, built up with furs
and cloaks, and when he had seated her there, he took up a
floral wreath that lay beside her and pinned it on her hair. I
must confess I had never seen her look so fair, as young and
gentle as a maid, the Queen of Flowers, such contrast to that
angry woman who, I hoped, was left on the other side of the
hedge. There is a song sung of her, that all men know I think,
and I remember it in part, but even now that I speak of her,
it seems to suit her, and conjures her up for me:

> Queen thou art and arbiter
> Of honor, wit and beauty
> Of largess and loyalty,
> Lady, thou wert born in fortune's hour...

Well, it was long ago and much has been done and said
since then, but I still remember the pride, yes, and the love I
felt for her, despite the wrong she did to me. *The great are ever*

fickle. Aye, so, but that does not mean we lesser folk can turn aside our affections as easily, do not suffer when we are cast aside.

"We spoke of different sorts of love just now," she said to her courtiers, "and I will put a conundrum to you. Suppose now, a lady loves a lord, and wants to be married to him, and he, high above her in rank, would not stoop to wed with her. Is love possible in such a case?"

I knew she spoke of Raoul and me, was vexed that she should discuss our lives and surprised and hurt that she should openly speak of something I felt best hid. The other lords there took her question seriously, began to debate as if in a Council of State, if love made public is love, if love based on shame can be so called, if marriage and love are contradictions in terms... Seriously they spoke and she heard them in all seriousness. If this be their courts of love, I thought, poor Walter is well out of them. And I thought too, as they argued on, how much nonsense they spoke. There are many types of loving and love, but I shut my lips tight upon my thoughts. Let them speak, I would be dumb. And this, I think, was wise, and perhaps, in time, she would have let me slip away, but something happened to rekindle her wrath.

One of the younger men, fair-haired and bold, had been watching me. "This lady is too quiet," he said. "As she is young and most beautiful, what says she to our discourse?" I saw the queen frown, but he went on, "Tell me lady, whose name is unknown to me, do you think men can be faithful to womenkind, or more to the point, they to men?" There was a burst of applause as if he had said a witty thing, but the queen was not pleased.

"Lord Thouars," she said, "as she is young, she has not the experience we other ladies have."

But he persisted, speaking to me. "And, lady," he now said, "like other maids are your thoughts filled with thoughts of us, how to make us your slaves?" And he smiled and rubbed his hand across his lips.

"As for making men her slaves," the queen snapped, "ask her to tell you the truth of Boissert Field. We heard she besotted my brother-in-law, that he preferred her to all women else."

They all laughed at that, but she had not meant to jest.

"And, Lord Ademar," she said, turning to the older lord, a tall dark-haired man he was, with hooded eyes and hawk-like nose, who came sauntering to her side as she spoke to him, "inform, if you please, the Count of Toulouse, that we have found that most rare prize, a virtuous wife."

A third time they laughed, as if all things were for laughing at, as if they mocked at ones which pain.

He said, and a strange way of speaking he had, new to me, which marked him, if nothing else did, as a man from the Spanish borderlands. "Then the lady is as virtuous as she seems gentle, her lord must be a lucky man."

Afterwards, I thought he spoke to be kind, to keep the peace, but again his words did not please the queen.

"Pooh," she said. "My grandsire used to say to his friend, the old Count of Toulouse, grandfather to the present count, that no woman's virtue was safe long. He told a story how a vassal boasted to him once of his wife's chastity. Chaste and fair is she, the poor fool bragged. Disguised as a beggar, deaf and dumb, Duke William came to her, found her with her ladies in their bower. They, amazed by his infirmities, let him in, tested him to see if he spoke the truth..."

She began to hum beneath her breath:

> How much I tupped them you shall hear
> A hundred eighty-eight times or near
> So that I almost stripped my gear...

And they all laughed, including Lord Ademar.

"The lady is not used to such bawdy songs," he maintained. "She blushes for our wantonness," and he smiled at me, a handsome amorous man himself.

"Pooh," said the Queen again, "I hear my brother-in-law charmed her as well. Is not Lord Geoffrey charming?" she asked, fixing her eyes above my head.

I had known before how clever she could be; she argued with learned men for sport, could quote Latin texts and debate church doctrine with cardinals, as she had done when she found reasons to annul her marriage with Louis of France. She would wind me up in words.

"Did not he tempt you? I heard he took back the ring I gave you once as pledge. He gave it first to me, you know. And how long did his vow to me last? As long as it took me to ride from there to here, so long it took him to find another woman to bed, so long shall his vow last to you. Sweet-tongued is my sweet brother-in-law, but double forked. And my ring," she said, when the laughter that followed had died down, "gave you it away as all things else I gave?"

"No," I said. "I have it here." And I pulled at the chain where it hung about my neck.

She looked at it, her expression by turns thoughtful and something else, malicious perhaps. "And would you swear on Holy Book," she insisted, "that you wear it in remembrance of me? Would you swear that loyalty, like love, is meant to last? I sent you it to keep your husband safe at home, not to let him go abroad to hinder me. Would you swear your loyalty to him? I hear he has found another woman and you have quarreled because of it."

I said, for I had grown mulish myself, determined not to be the butt of their foolish jibes, and disappointed that the meaning of her message that had puzzled me was so simple after all. (I had thought she meant to keep *him* safe, not to *save* her; it was *his* safety I had cared about.) I said the worst sort of thing, "I keep this ring, and wear it, in memory of past friends in the hope that they should also remember me. My womenfolk who guard my son know it as mine. I use it to send them word, I wear it about my neck, next to my heart, that all men should know whose gift it was. I never thought to see it lost or given away, nor did I look to have its value made a mockery of." An unwise speech, better to have kept silent, for they were reduced to silence after it, shifting uneasily, not looking at me. No one rebukes a royal queen, and I had spoken too much in my blunt

way. Even Lord Ademar looked grave. And too late I saw the
trap I made myself, made it for her to use.

"Fool," Queen Eleanor said for the third time, "give it here.
It was not meant for you. Better to have done with you at Saint
Purnace as de Boissert hoped." A silence followed, again too
long. In it were many things I had heard others say, but dared
not think myself. *Put no trust in royal promises, nor royal courts. Her
friends are powerful and she uses them... What her part is better you do
not know.* They hammered at my heart until I beat them down,
worse to me than the idea of treason.

She saw the way my thoughts ran and laughed at them, a
high laugh without mirth, that mocked at me and mocked
herself. You will never be sure, that laugh said, what I knew,
or if I had a part in that attack. But I have the power to order
men; men follow me, I command them to my will. And I shall
always have that power.

"Fool," she repeated the word, reached out and snatched
the chain. It caught about my neck and cut the skin before the
links broke. A trickle of blood started out, but she already had
the ring in her grasp. "And would you swear," she said, "your
women would obey you if you sent them this? Then are they
more loyal to you than you were to me. When my daughter
was born, did you come? Then is this bauble a symbol greater
than all the weight of those promises you once made. And
you, Lord Ademar, you are foresworn. You vowed to honor
me when I was wed. Now you swear as much to Henry in my
place." She swung the ring to and fro on its broken chain. She
said to her lords, who looked at her, consternation in their
eyes, "I shall keep my lands intact for my sons. You are my
vassals, whom Henry steals away. You think to make your peace
with him at my expense. One day you shall make your peace
with our heirs. That prince you saw just now is but the first
of many princes of my house. Deal with us as you would be
dealt with by him when he is grown."

The lords leapt to their feet, the air of repose, their lan-
guidness, quite gone. Lord Ademar stepped forward formally.

"Lady Queen," he said, "who first is Duchess of Aquitaine,

loyal are we, your vassals assembled here, who have honored our oath to you since you inherited, since you, a little maid, were carried off to Louis's court. And loyal to you throughout that time, and loyal now to you and your son."

Formally he spoke; they all muttered words to the same effect. Perhaps their protestations gave her strength, perhaps she needed their support to feel secure, perhaps, simply, she wanted to test her control over them, for she suddenly laughed, one moment to the next seeming to change, confusing them. But ever had she been willful, perverse; now there was a wildness to her as if she challenged fate, or God.

"Solemn-faced," she cried, "stiff-mouthed. This is no law court and far, thanks be, from Henry's court where such words are sworn."

They smiled at that, but nervously, shifting from foot to foot. Later, no doubt, they would be afraid that they had said too much, should Henry, in turn, hear of it. But, "This is a court of love," she next cried, "where we shall teach you how to love. As for this symbol that the Lady Ann so admires, well, take it who can, to keep in memory."

She was still dangling the ring by its chain, just above my head. I reached for it. She dropped the chain in my hand, threw the ring high into the air. It glittered and sparkled as it fell. Lords and ladies began to scrabble for it, pushing past. Upon the ground they crawled, the women rucking their clothes about their waists; their white legs stuck out, their skirts flew up; the men prodded and peered, mounted on them like so many dogs. Over they rolled, locked together, children playing on a grassy bank, and the queen rocked herself back and forth with mirth.

"Go to, go to," she said, noticing me, giving me a hard push, "it was yours once, make a bid for it. So much for fine words if you will not soil your dainty hands."

Now, I must have taken note of all here said and done, how else could I remember it? But I stood as if dazed. So I think a wounded man feels not the pain, only a numbness, cold as death.

When I was a child brought first to Sedgemont, I played with the other children there a game of blindman's buff; I had had hated it, the way they pushed and screamed, the way they pried. Now, in the same way, these many years afterward, the knowing faces stared, the same hard hands came out. Scarce knowing what I did or thought, I began to run along those gravel paths, between the high hedges, laughter welling up behind me as I fled. Without pause I ran, the gravel spurting beneath my feet, crisscrossing along those alleyways until, coming to a full stop, a stitch in my side, my breathing labored, my heart heavy with grief, I realized I was lost. I could not even have told you which direction I had gone, nor even cared, no buildings in sight, a maze of smaller paths on every side, and, in the distance, the outer walls. I made my way toward them for lack of anywhere else. They were tall, crenellated in the latest style, but deserted, too. I walked along them until I came to an iron gate, left ajar. There was a horse tied outside it in the open parkland beyond, tethered to a tree. Seeing it, I was reminded somehow of Saint Purnace, and once more overcome, I began to run back the way I had come. Blinded by the sun in this more open part, blinded more like by foolish tears, tears that only a broken illusion can cause, I ran headlong into someone on the path.

"Well met, Lady Ann," said Geoffrey Plantagenet. He caught me to steady me. "You run as if ten thousand devils were chasing you. See how your heart beats." He held his hand over mine, against my breast where indeed my heart pounded so I could scarcely speak. "And blood," he traced with one finger the line of splattered red where the chain had cut, across the neck-bone, along the shoulder of my gown. I snatched myself away, as if he stung. He said, "When you run, your skin glows, like a lamp which I once saw. The monks who own it in Le Mans swear it came from far away, further than the Holy Land, and when you light it, the flame burns through like a light in a crystal sphere. I am come this instant to see the queen, to visit with her and my nephew for a while. God smiles on me to find you here."

All this was flattery, openly given, yet even then I could not rebuke him as I should, even then, seeing him again, I could not accept what was said of him. He walked beside me, matching his paces to mine, keeping to the grass verge to deaden the sound of his spurs. In similar fashion to the other lords I had seen, he was dressed for hunting, but more exquisitely, aping his nephew with ermine for a royal house at neck and wrist and a velvet cap, same as the prince's smaller one, set at an angle above his curls. And when he took my hand to lead me along, the many rings he wore flashed like the one the queen had thrown into the air.

I said the first thing that came to mind. "I wish that you had kept that ring to mate it with the one you have; I wish that you had never given it to the queen, or she to me, ill fortune on it."

He stopped still, his eyes boring hard, and would not move until I told him all. Not all, I have never told all to anyone before this, so strange, so unnatural, so depraved a tale if those be not too strong words. Nor did I know if I saw too much, guessed too much. But even in telling what I did, I said more than I should. Much more. As a child, I had run from my tormentors and had Lord Raoul rescue me. Small thanks I gave him for his pains. But this was not Sedgemont, I not a child, and this man was the one whom all the world warned against. To show him weakness merely gave him room to move to his greater gain, as now he did.

"By all the saints in Christendom," he said, "who look after knights bachelor, I did not think it would be so easy to find you. They have been at their tricks, I see. They would not, were I near by."

"How did you know I was here?" I asked.

"Why your noble lord told me so," he said. Now that was an obvious lie, and somehow such a stupid, silly thing steadied me. He was angry when I told him so, angry to have given himself away, to have thrown aside an advantage which surprise and fright might have given him. But the mention of Raoul's name for me was a candle on a dark night.

Then Geoffrey laughed, pushed his cap to the back of his head, began to whistle beneath his breath. How easily they all laughed, I thought, at life, at death, dishonor, fear, ideas other men must weigh and think about.

"So, Ann of Cambray," he said, "what matter? I have found you again. There were too many things left unfinished when last we met. But the world has treated me well in the end. Henry has taken my castles as I said he would, but he pays me a fee for them, not what they're worth, but enough. And, as you see, I still have my head."

"Your loss of the castles seems of small concern," I said, looking pointedly at his furs, his jewels, "and you the little worse for it. Less, I suppose, than your friends' deaths. At least their silence assures your gain."

He flushed at that, his skin as delicate as a girl's, pulled the cap right off so the black curls came cascading out, as thick and glossy as a girl's, too. "Lady," he said, "how shall I swear, what oath shall I use that you Celts might accept, to prove my innocence of that charge. I know your husband brands me murderer. But since I do not blame you that he failed to help me, why should you repay me with such wickedness? Am I the man to dip my hands in another's blood?"

"No," I said. That at least was true, and others had hinted it of him. Sweet words were the weapons he used, not violence. But if not him, I told him, then his minions, his friends, at his command.

"Now by the Living Cross," he swore. "I mislike that word. 'Minions' has an ugly sound. They said your tongue was shrewd." He dropped my arm, rounded on me. "It is easily done," he said, "to lay blame at my door. Were you brother to a king, you would find there are always hangers-on who expect the worst. And there are always favors to be bought, monies to be lent in expectation of greater times. Is that my fault? You would not have me shuffle abroad in rags. Nor I think when you were down-at-heels at Sieux did your noble lord cavil to have dealings with the Jews."

I looked at him, a lack of propriety to put murder and vanity on a par, a selfishness that I had glimpsed in all these Angevins, from king to brother to little prince, that they must have their way at all costs.

He had a knack of guessing what I thought. His voice grew cold, cold to threaten with a flicker of fear. "You betrayed me," he cried, "I have not faulted you for that. And even if I did, I would treat you kindlier than the queen. Did she care if your enemies at Saint Purnace left you dead? All she wanted was for them to get her gold back. Did she want *you* in England or just your *skill*, to ensure she would have another son? She blames you now for her daughter's birth; she blames you that I wanted you. Indeed, I shall turn her to my enemy if I do not do what she would like. Wanting to protect her own estates, fearing Henry will give me lands of hers, she would have had me wed the lovely Isobelle and be satisfied with Boissert ones." He shrugged. "Henry has saved me from that fate. And there are other heiresses for the taking yet. They'll find me another, but I would have had you if I could."

His audacity overwhelmed me. His easy explanation of the queen's treachery overwhelmed me, that treachery which Raoul had tried to shield me from. But before I could speak, Geoffrey was continuing. "Why should we talk of unhappy times? De Boissert's death was no man's loss. I would not expect you to argue on his behalf who would have killed your husband first. The Lady Isobelle is no innocent, nor is the queen. But neither, Lady Ann, are you. I saw how you smiled and threw your favors at men as your husband bid. I remember how you aped a servant maid to lure me on. I saw how you looked for me at the feast. When my noble brother was still a count, at home in Anjou, before inheritance swelled his head, a man came to our court. From the west of England he came, a big dark-browed man, and many were the tales he told of you, to persuade Henry to give him your lands." His voice took on a slightly jeering note. "You grow pale, Lady Ann. His name was Guy of Maneth and I think you knew him well. I myself did not believe all that he said, nor have I permitted others in my hearing to call you witch, as Isobelle and her father claimed:

but if Raoul of Sedgemont was bewitched to marry you, does not that blame lie on you? I think I could be so bewitched myself. I have not lifted murderer's knife against anyone. I have not schemed against you. Marriage with Isobelle de Boissert was my only plan, that and my lawful inheritance, and Henry has taken both away. But seeing you, I willingly would have relinquished them. I do not think I have conspired against Henry, rather, he broke faith with me. If someone else has encouraged conspiracy, I give you leave to guess who it is."

When he spoke thus, his face flushed, I did not know what to think of him. He juggled words convincingly. Sometimes I heard an exaggeration that might hide a lie, sometimes a sincerity that seemed to argue truth. Conspiracy is twisted and dark, damning the guilty and the innocent. Even today I cannot decide. I only know this was a man, Geoffrey Plantagenet, like his father who swept down in the night and fired the vines for spite, like his brother who ordered the guard of Sieux hanged on a castle wall for vengeance's sake, a man who killed his own companions to free himself from complicity. I only know this was a queen whom I had loved, who would have had me killed to ensure her plans. I sit in no judgment on my fellow men— God does that—and God, I think, had judged me too, that even then I could not decide right from wrong, that even then, after hearing what the queen had done, I could not believe the worst of her, that even then, after my husband's life had been at stake, I could not completely fault the man who would have murdered him.

Geoffrey Plantagenet stood still and before I could stop him, ran his hand through my hair, as I have seen a woman feel a piece of silk. "I would not call it red," he said. "Guy of Maneth called it so, the red headed witch of Cambray was his name for you. It is more like to bronze new-coined. And your eyes like pools. I should have met you long ago. There could have been a time and place for us."

Strangely enough, those simple words touched me more than his other extravagances. True or not, there was a truth to them that made his own youth seem old, lost, damned before he had achieved his age, even though his skin was as unlined and fine as a child's, even though his melancholy smile hid the world's sins.

"I am not highborn," I told him, trying to conceal my grief beneath a brisker voice, "my lands are small, unknown. You'd never have thought of me without Sieux."

"Perhaps," he said, "perhaps not." He shrugged. "We cannot guess what may be, what is not. I would not have Isobelle de Boissert without her lands, yet could still think of you without yours."

All this while, paying little heed to where we had gone, he had drawn me into the center of those twisting paths, a place he must have known, for it was some sort of inner square, with a fountain, dry and overgrown with weed, and a stone bench, mossy in the shade of one large tree.

"Sit here," he said, "rest out of the sun. Frightened," he said, "like a captured dove. If I were to sit beside you thus," he said, "and hold you until your heart's fluttering has ceased, and if I were to put my arm about your waist, then no danger could creep up unawares. And if you were to lean, and put your troubled head against me thus, then should you feel at ease."

And as he spoke, he drew me back, carefully, gently, with such skill that soon my head was bent against his own, and both his hands were clasped in front. "And if," he said, softer still, a wind's whisper on the warm and sultry air, "and if I were to put my hands into your lap, then were I at the gates of Paradise." And he smoothed along the folds of my gown, ever lower where I sat. "And if you opened them," he said, and with his foot he stirred between my own, as his fingers began to move and fret, "a place of softest folds and pools where, if I trace their secrets out, then should you know Paradise as well."

His voice could have been a murmur lost, the afternoon drowsed away. I opened my eyes, not even knowing I had them closed, and as from a long way off, saw us sitting there, fitted together like two carved stones, two statues not yet locked into embrace, but on the verge. A moment more and it would be too late, sunk in on him as he on me. With an effort so strong it rocked me, I sat up, pushed away his hand.

His breath came ragged then, hot, in gasps. Sweat had matted his curls against his face. "I burn for you," he almost groaned, and pressed my hand to feel the hardening of his desire, "it is too late to stop."

"I cannot," I cried, more afraid than I have ever been, of myself as well as him. "I am married and have a child. It is sin."

His voice was sharp with lust, "Was it sin to lie with a man unwed? Did you preach so to Count Raoul then? What gives you the right to preach to me? Play not the coy, there is fire in your veins."

But the mention of Raoul's name again steadied me. I saw him as he had paced and paced about our little room. *No one to hurt us save we alone.* I would not be the one to bring the hurt. I said, my voice a long way off, deep dredged up, "I am no witch, no whore. Let me go. You keep me against my will." And I tried to fend him off.

He said, "You sought me at Boissert Field of your own choice, judge not that you yourself not be judged. Lie still. I shall not hurt you unless you make me to. We are alone, no one will know."

Then I began to struggle in earnest, but he was strong; the more I pushed, the more he smiled, his legs entangled now between my own, my body pressed against his. I always carry a little knife hidden in my sleeve, a trick I learned from childhood days; and now I sat still and let it slide point first into my hand, as Raoul had taught me. A woman has but one chance to strike—seldom is she given a second—and yet I hesitated. You see the effect he had on me.

"There is no hope for us," I said, "too late. Too many things done, not done. Let me go."

"First I shall love you," he said, "then you will talk of leaving me."

I drew the knife and thrust hard with it so it cut across his palm. He started back, releasing his hold, and I sprang to my feet. But even then I did not run.

"Devil's dam," he cried, sucking at the line of blood, "they said you were full of devil's tricks. Will you cross weapons with me as a man?"

"No," I said, "I will not fight you, Geoffrey Plantagenet. Nor will I lie with you."

"Then what they said of you is true," he said, "a devil's strumpet, to torture men, to make them lust while you turn to stone. We have a name for such in France." He stood up, followed me, the cut still welling red. Desire had faded from his face, all was smooth, unlined, and cold. He said, "I shall have you. And when I'm done, they shall drag you through the streets. When they plunge you in the river at Saint Purnace, think on what delights you've missed. 'Give us a witch to burn or drown,' they'll cry. Look for help from me then. As Raoul's widow, you'd have made a man a wife; as mistress, there are others where you come from." He made a half leap, I dodged away. He was not armed, but strong and quick. He thought one blow would knock the knife from my grasp, and yet he too hesitated. I think perhaps he still hoped I would surrender willingly, at least I could wish he did. Then he said, to end that hope, "Take what comes. What should be sweet, you have turned sour; what I would have, you've made me rip from you. Your loss. Let your devil comfort you."

And he came on again. I threw the knife instead of letting him run on it as I should, so lost my hope of escape. But God, they say, cares for the weak. He smiled, having won, and bent to pick the knife up. That was his mistake, my second chance, and only a man too sure of himself would have given it me. I took to my heels. And now those winding paths, those criss-cross ways, gave me a start. Looping up my skirts, I could twist and turn faster than he could; his spurs scraped upon the gravel, tripping him, his boots not made for running in, nor his clothes. I heard him slide and stumble after me, swearing most foul, and those hissed words gave me wings. I would not wish to meet him balked of his plans. Soon I had left him out of sight.

Then a new fear took me. For if still in the maze, how did the paths intersect, where did they lead? Did he stand in the shadows, with a smile upon his face, and wait for me to run into his grasp? Numbed by that thought, I now crept along, starting at every shift and sound, even a leaf's fall enough to startle me into a sweat. Sometimes the paths were long and straight, and those I learned to avoid, for if the end was blocked then I would be trapped between the rows of narrow trees. Sometimes they were short, cut by several other paths, each of these as dangerous, each to be manuevered round. I tried to walk on tiptoe, although my whole body ached to run; I tried to anticipate the openings, a flight worse than the one at Saint Purnace, for there Raoul had come to rescue me, and here the fault was all my own. When I saw again the outer walls, the open gate, the grazing horse, I thought it a mirage of my own imagining. I forced myself to creep those last few yards, scarce believing that he would not have doubled back, but no, all was quiet in the hot sun. I scrambled on the horse's back, stirrups too long, saddle too big, but it must do, unhitched its tethering rope, rode off. I dared not ride openly into the park, instead made a circuit of those outer walls and so returned after several miles to the main courtyard where I had first come in. Not wanting either to ride on a horse so richly bedecked, so known, that many men would recognize it, I slid off before I reached the yard, lopped up the reins, sent it galloping back the way we'd come. Nor did I think, knowing what I do of men, that he would admit to my having taken it so easily. Then, strolling past the queen's guard as if returning from some leisured walk, although how explain the state of my gown, my disordered look—let them seek an explanation for that—I summoned my own men and bid them prepare to leave at dawn.

9

O ANOTHER NIGHT HOVERING BE-
tween sleep and wake. But I have spent time in a
nunnery; I know how to tell the hours with prayer
and thought; I know how to mark time with rosary
beads. And I have lost loved ones before, but never quite like
this. *Do not sit in judgment on me.* How judge her who had abandoned me; how judge myself who with his would-be murderer
had almost betrayed my husband? And how judge love or
loyalty? *You were not loyal to me,* the queen had said. And laughed
to mock the words. I *had* failed her, but so today had she
betrayed me. Yet Raoul had kept faith with a king who had
not kept faith with him. Was loyalty, like love, more involved,
more difficult than learned men would have us believe? I
smoothed the laces of my gown with fingers that still trembled.
I remembered her hand that tore at my golden chain; I remember still his hand that caught my own, his melancholy
eyes, dark hair, white skin. And superimposed upon those images
my husband's came, tall, the scar on his face white, his eyes
rage-dark. How to explain to him, how tell him what had been
done?

When I was a child at Cambray, there was a stretch of beach
between rocks and cliff at low tide with finer sand than any
other part along our coast, always washed clean of weed and
shells. One year, a young man of my father's guard began to
ride across it. It was springtime of the year—he rode for wager,
-laughingly set his horse at a gallop close to the water's edge.
I heard my brother shout a warning as he rode. That young
knight had barely gone a score of strides when the horse was
sunk to fetlocks; and where the hoofbeats had been scored,

the surface closed behind him as a vise. Well, they saved the rider with ropes and nets, hauled him out, all laughter gone. His horse was lost and soon even the thrashing of its anguished feet, the mark of rope and wheels had sunk without a trace, only the unblemished sand. Here, I was the rider, heedless, careless had I been, and Eleanor, Queen of Flowers, and Geoffrey Plantagenet were like that sand, fair on the surface, unsullied, unmarred, beneath, who knows what depths and pits. And so I think was all at Poitiers; the more it showed its smiling face, the more was hid. Under its surface, then, not only the ruins of broken stones and memories, but things dark and treacherous. It was Sir Renier who told me what was to confirm those fears, and make what had passed before fade to nothingness.

I had not seen him among the queen's courtiers, and if I had, he might have spared me much anguish. I presume he had been in attendance on the king, and certainly that night he came in secret from the king's court at Poitiers with news for the queen. And perhaps he rode back and forth like this each night, bearing gossip and messages so she should keep abreast of all that the king did and said. In the middle hours of the night, then, came a scratching at my door. Half asleep, thinking it was morning and Walter summoning me, I ran to unlatch it. And in he came, Sir Renier I mean, in haste, as if fearful someone might see him. He snuffed out the taper flame, motioned me to silence, stood at the half-open door and listened for a long while. Nothing stirred along the passageway or by the stairs, although there were dark shadows caused by the fitful moonlight where a man could hide. And when he spoke, his voice came fitful too, in hurried gasps, as if he were out of breath, so unlike himself that, had not I seen his face before he doused the light, I'd not have thought he was who he claimed to be.

"Leave," was all he said, no graceful compliment this time, no courtier's phrase. "Today at Poitiers has Raoul outfaced King Henry, told him he's a fool, told him God knows what else, the devil to pay. And here is worse. God's wounds, why came you here at all? How came your husband to let you come?"

My silence must have revealed many things.

"Unknown to him? By the Living Cross, were you my wife, your back would feel my whip. Bad enough at Poitiers. But here, Isobelle de Boissert still has friends, they have noted your fall from grace and will make use of it."

"They will not harm me or my lord," I said, "not even Raoul knows where I am."

"He does now. Geoffrey Plantagenet told him so. And was bowled to the ground for saying so. A most unknightly blow." He gnawed his lip. I had never heard him so agitated, heard him speak with less guard, saw him so shaken from his usual aplomb. "Why put you the queen in such a rage? Why foolishly reveal your secrets to her? Get you home before greater wrong is done."

I noted how he fingered his sword, ever and anon glanced out the door. A slight man is Sir Renier, now he seemed to swell, not with rage, but tension, anxiety. "Why gave you your enemies a hold over you? Why came Raoul to this viper's nest? By the Mass, a fool's work, both of you."

He opened the door another crack. Still nothing, no sound, no movement. He gave me a shove. Luckily, I suppose, I was already dressed, an old gown on, high boots—there was no time for delay, and by his gestures, he clearly showed he meant me to follow him. He guided me down the stairs, soft-footed, hand on sword hilt (and as I have said I had never seen him go armed before), through a small side door leading to one of the inner cloisters. From there, we slipped through a long empty room, once a refectory perhaps, the window bars throwing dark lines on the cool tiled floors, the wooden chairs standing in stiff straight rows, a faint half-caught smell of wine and cooking oil. Then out through another yard, another wicker gate to cross, a barred gate next with the bolts flung wide (and it was only afterwards I realized what dangers he must have taken upon himself to have helped us in this way, what bribes given, what guards paid to turn blind eye, what risk encountered for our sakes). In the shadow of the park trees, Walter waited, and beyond him our three men with the horses already prepared. Sir Renier helped us mount, gave us more food from a sack beneath his cloak, every word, every movement suggesting haste. And, before he left, his one last whispered warning, his true message.

"I have just come from the queen," he said. "This forenoon, a group of de Boissert men rode north. They carry your ring." He stifled my cry with his own hand, a spate of curses in his southern tongue spilling out. "Why gave you them the chance to use it?" he burst out. "Why boasted you of loyal friends? Isobelle has loyal ones as well. Alyse de Vergay rides north with them."

He stepped back, hit the horse to make it run, released the reins. We rode at a gallop across the grass, the thick turf deadening the sound, the trees soon sheltering us from spying eyes. A harvest moon slipping behind clouds gave light enough for us to watch for pitfalls, and soon an open postern in the outer wall set us on the open road. But here again I must pause to marvel how a mind still numb with shock can interest itself in common things. I remember wondering at the care Sir Renier showed, for although Walter led us now along less frequented ways, it was Sir Renier who had advised him which to take, who arranged horses for our convenience, some signal given or sign exchanged that made those privileges of a royal courier available to us. I remember thinking there was no time to waste, no time to send explanation, nor plea for help to Raoul—I trusted Sir Renier would warn him. But as the long road stretched before us, that distance which had seemed a finger's span upon Raoul's chart suddenly translated into many wearisome miles, that journey which anticipation and happiness on coming here had made seem short gave me too much time to think. Since it was too late to change what had been, what was to come, you will know what a ride it was, running from catastrophe, trying to prevent a second one. Nor was I sure what Raoul had done, an angry husband confronting an angry king. We all felt the strain—Walter's young face was taut with it—and for the first time, I realized as well what a trap I had set him in, obeying me against his lord's commands. Our three French men stood us in good stead, they knew the route we took, could suggest short cuts. We hoped, you see, by riding fast and following these lesser roads, to get ahead of the de Boissert men, whatever their purpose, and warn Sieux. I presumed that Raoul would follow soon, but not sure when, and even he could not hope to ride more fast then we, perhaps slower, having a larger troop. *You'll not outride me.* Now he must hope for it. And remembering how Alyse de Vergay had ever grumbled at distances, needed men to lead her through difficult parts, I felt confident we would soon overtake her. But this, too, we misjudged. For, although Walter sent the French troopers ahead, turn and turn they took to search for news, nowhere was there sign of a large party riding north. Walter now began to worry that, in our haste, we might override them before we knew, or that they, hearing of us, would hide in wait to catch us. He had us therefore ride both day and night, for shorter stretches but faster, to enable our scouts to keep closer watch. But de Boissert's men, wherever or however they went, must have had horses waiting for them too, must have ridden as hard for a purpose of their own, and Alyse de Vergay must have kept up with them.

I cannot say I remember or wish to remember much else of that ride. There have to be thoughts, of course, or images to keep you awake. But occasionally, while sleeping in the saddle as I did, for seconds perhaps at a time, whole scenes came clearly to mind, so that on waking I would continue to speak of things that were so vivid as to seem real. Most of the time, I dreamed of Saint Purnace, what was attempted there and by whom, and why. And I dreamed, too, of the day my son was born, that little boy with the red-stockinged feet who played with his wolfhound and expected us. *I shall have sons*, the queen had cried. What of my son, who could have died? should have

been my reply. Sometimes I tried to guess what Lord Raoul
had done or said to King Henry to set those Angevin tempers
ablaze. And sometimes I thought that I was in London when
Lord Raoul had come riding in to Henry's court and Queen
Eleanor had smiled at me. Since for misery I'll not grieve you
with details more of that ride (save pray you never know its
like, save tell you I relive it often enough to have done penance
a thousand fold), I'll tell instead what Raoul *had* done, which,
although many years were to pass before I heard the full truth
of it, is a story that fits better here and should be told. And
of all people, Lord Ademar told me it, his hard laugh gone,
but not his watchful, hooded eyes. Nor his courteous voice,
both of which suggested what I had thought, that as a peacemaker, he had tried to turn the queen's mood, without success.

Lord Ademar knew the queen well and, as I had guessed,
was the leading noble at her court that day, or at least the one
she wanted most to impress. He came from Toulouse, the
furthest south of her lands (hence his Spanish way of speaking)
and the most important. The Count of Toulouse was Raymond,
whom the queen would have liked to have had under her spell,
and Lord Ademar was his spokesman to the king. Now, Henry
would have liked Count Raymond to have obeyed him and to
have been present for the oath swearing at Poitiers. Toulouse
is a large tract of land stretching from the western boundary
with Spain to the Alps, controlling many trade routes west and
south, almost separate from the rest of France, almost strong
enough to be independent. Lord Ademar claimed, as had Sir
Renier, that Henry was determined to bring all of Toulouse
under his complete control, and every day he questioned Lord
Ademar about the absence of his overlord, questions that became embarrassing as Ademar exhausted all the excuses he
could think of. But the Count of Toulouse was not the only
one to defy Henry, although the other lords, those present at
Poitiers I mean, tried in more subtle ways to challenge the
king. Henry, as you remember, loved to hunt, his Norman
passion with which he filled his days, and he often urged, nay,
commanded, these southern lords to attend him. They, the

night before, warm with wine and flushed with heat, for the season continued hot, they swore to obey, and at the evening feast raised their goblets in salute—the more that Henry, who was abstemious himself and seldom drank, watched their conviviality with jaundiced eye, especially when they drank at his expense. Come the dawn—for he rose at daybreak to ride all day, they lay abed, sent word that they were sick, blamed the weather, his good food and wine, his hospitality, for their indisposition. And since he could not, perforce, drag them all from bed, he was obliged to ride alone with his own knights.

Once he was gone, to break his neck for all they cared, in their own good time, they rode to visit Queen Eleanor as I had seen, to pay their respects to her and her son. They did this in private, of course, but as long as Henry had his spies in the queen's household, the lords' attendance there was known to him, did not endear them to him, and added to his grievance against her.

Well, then, that day we have been speaking of, Henry had returned to Poitiers after a full twelve hours of hunting in the scrub lands around the river Loire. He himself had scarcely left the saddle, had not paused for rest or food; his courtiers, who should have been used to him, were almost reeling for weariness. But the hunt had been successful, Henry himself had downed a stag with wide spreading antlers, and when he rode into the courtyard, he was in good mood. Soon dispelled.

"For," said Lord Ademar, and I let him tell the rest in his own words, "the yard was filled at that late hour with many of us nobles, returning from the queen, detained there by the events you have described. I was among them and I recognized the dark and angry look which crossed the king's face. 'So, my lords,' he says without ado, 'I have found you chasing other game. Be careful it does not spring a trap on you.' For once, he caught us off guard; we muttered among ourselves in our southern tongue which, it is true, we use to provoke the king because he knows it not, so all our jests and talk had to be translated for him. Henry was mounted on a fine horse, a gray which they say is bred in the western borders of England, rawboned and wild, hard to handle, being young. And on its back, this mighty king, lord I know not of how many lands, hunched forward more like huntsman than king, his clothes stained and bramble ripped, his face freckled with the sun. But where the sun had not reached at wrist and neck, the skin was white and fine as a child's. He has gray eyes, our king, and hot, and matted red hair, and a full and petulant mouth which he juts forward in a rage, as he did now, thinking again we would ignore him. We all stepped hastily back, myself among them, I confess, all those southern nobles whose names are, like themselves, rich, full-blooded; names to roll about the tongue like wine: Thouars, Châtellerault, Lusignan, hot-tongued, hot-tempered too, you met them; you should remember them; and Taillefer, Saintonge, and many other lords of note from the Auvergne and Gascony. But even they may have felt they had met their match in this king. They certainly had no desire to raise an issue with him at this time, nor bring a confrontation on their heads; they may have remembered nervously, as I know I did, what excess of enthusiasm they had let themselves show to the queen.

"At this crucial point, to our relief, although not to the king's, Henry's brother, Plantagenet, came sauntering into the yard. There are those who claimed afterwards that Geoffrey Plantagenet had been drinking too much red Bordeaux wine to know what he did or said, and it is true that ever since the king's arrival at Poitiers, Geoffrey had avoided him, (discretion on Geoffrey's part I'd say, since the northern rebellion could not have endeared him to the king). Now Geoffrey came on boldly, the more noticeable that we other lords had edged away, and swaggered as if he meant to give offense. His new and costly clothes seemed especially luxurious contrasted with Henry's plain and dirty ones, and in his velvet cap, he wore a sprig of broom, *genet*, that yellow flower of the Angevins. I myself, I would not have flaunted it, not to face an older brother I had offended twice. Nor would I have made a remark so doubly phrased, although, if drunk, he may have meant a simple thing (but drunkenness can serve as excuse for letting out many harmful and dangerous thoughts).

"'Well, brother,' he said, as if they spoke at ease alone, 'Off at your hunting again, I see.' Since his voice was slurred, he may have meant a simple thing; but there were those who, remembering how Henry had been hunting when his father died, wondered aloud that Geoffrey should remind him of that; and certainly Henry himself, sensitive upon an issue that had already caused him so much grief, Henry took the words amiss.

"Beginning to swing down from the gray horse, Henry paused, one foot in the stirrup which, as good horseman, he should never have done, threw his cloak back as if he felt too hot—another mistake—spoke angrily to his brother, which startled the horse.

"'And you, little brother,' he snarled, 'we have expected you to come crawling for your share.'

"'I have no land to do homage for,' Geoffrey said. 'My three castles are already yours, my bride shut up in a nunnery. Shall I lick your boots for fifteen hundred pounds?'

"Not a wise speech either, and again unlike him. I myself have never known Geoffrey to sound so wild. He has a ready tongue, but mostly coats it sweet, though beneath it is sharp enough. When I looked closely, I saw his fine clothes were dark with sweat and dust as if he had been walking or running a long way in the heat; and when he raised his hand, a red gash showed across its palm, an open cut that still leaked blood. Henry may have noticed this or not; in a rage, like a bull, he focuses only on one thing, but others of us there did, and commented on it loudly enough. But Henry, angry that Geoffrey chose such a public place to pick a quarrel, angry that Geoffrey should mention again his inheritance, angry that we southern lords were there to listen in, brought down his whip. He meant it for his brother's back, but at the last moment, Geoffrey jumped aside, a nimble leap for one so drunk. The lash caught the gray horse along the flank, making it thrash and squeal with pain; the cloak that the king had so carelessly tossed aside twisted and tangled in the reins. With one foot still caught in the stirrup as I have said, Henry was dragged backward, his spurred foot digging into the cobbled yard, his hand encumbered with the whip. That flash of anger, that whiplash had lasted but a second's space, it dragged Henry off his feet, like to trample him to death, sent Geoffrey cowering behind a horse trough, set us all off in a flurry of fear.

"Intent at first to take in every word, and make the most of a family quarrel, we all had crowded too close and were obliged to look to our own mounts to avoid being tossed off. I had already dismounted myself, so from a vantage point, saw how the king's men paled with fright. And saw how Geoffrey, although he shrank away, watched Henry avidly. It suddenly crossed my mind that Henry dead would give Geoffrey all he could want, but that thought, too, died on the instant.

"Although Henry was dragged along, he did not panic but rammed the whip butt into the horse's side, yanked down hard on the bit, and hauled himself up in the saddle. He certainly regained his composure first. 'In a nunnery, is it,' I heard him yell. 'We'll have you in a monastery yet, since you sniff under women's skirts like a monk.' Not a felicitous remark either. I saw several of the royal priests, on their knees praying for his life, cross themselves against such blasphemy. But Henry cares little for church laws, as you know, gives churchmen scant respect. And his anger was such that, although he did not ride his brother down, as for a moment I thought he might, he used the whip again and again against the horse.

"One of the other lords on foot, who had been watching the king's arrival, now came forward. Up to the king he strode, paid him no heed, bent down to examine the animal's weals and cuts. It still started and shook, but he paid that no heed either, smoothed its heaving sides, gentled it.

"'Those cuts need care,' was all he said, but when he straightened up, I saw the look he gave the king. He was not armed, of course—no man is, save the guard—and I had never seen the Count of Sieux before. They told me the last time he met the king he scarce could walk and had a price on his head. I know nothing of that but I tell you a brave man it was who dared cross that lord then. And the look Henry gave him back—I am not used to giving judgments out of hand, nor am I a betting man, but if I were, I would have wagered half my lands that one day, somewhere, sometime, these two would meet, not king and count, but man and man, and sword to sword, and God help him who tried to intervene. For there is a similarity, I think, between king and count, although both would run me through for saying so, something stubborn, untamed, which we men from the south have lost, if ever we had it, which perhaps we did not. We are an older breed and different, already lords of great lands while they were still pirates in the northern seas. But they have a look beyond arrogance, as unyielding as oak, a kind of strength that has already made them a master race, lords of the greater part of our known world—kings of England and Jerusalem, conquerors of all of southern Italy, holders of the island of Sicily, a Norman conquest stretching from north to south to east."

He sighed, "And they know it, more's our luck. Well, that too is the way of the world, as I told Count Raymond of Toulouse when he asked. 'Beware of Henry,' I told him. 'You avoid him now, he will seek you out.' And so that day, I thought too, 'Beware, Henry King, of Count Raoul.'

"'Greetings, Raoul,' Henry said. He was still panting to catch his breath, his scant red hair, for he loses it young, plastered across his skull, his pale skin mottled as with cold, the vivid bruises where he had been dragged showing on his arms and face. He managed the horse with knees and legs, a good horseman is he too, when not enraged, and the horse he bestrode was a noble one.

"Raoul gave him no such greetings—pride again—patted the horse one more time.

"They told me later it was one of the Cambray grays, and that I should have guessed. 'I know how to care for horseflesh,' Henry said, out of a silence that continued too long, making his face darken with chagrin.

"'Aye,' said Raoul. He wiped his hands along his sides. Like

Henry, he wears simple clothes, no elegance or style with either of them. 'As well, I suppose, as you do your lands.'

"'God's breath,' Henry swore, 'God's Holy Mass, what of my lands?'

"'Thus,' Raoul said. 'Give your brother land and title of his own that he stop envying you yours, and me mine. Give him a wife to keep him quiet—there are wives in Brittany for the taking— or geld him. But keep him away from Sieux.'

"'What of Brittany?' Henry now asked. He too is quick and to the point.

"'Nothing to me,' Raoul said. 'I keep only the Welsh in hand. But since the Brettons urge the Welsh princes to revolt, if you control the one, you control them both. I shall to England to patrol the border there, that is my concern. See you to the settling of Brittany here.'

"I had never heard a man address his overlord in such a way, much less a king, with such a lack of respect. And it is said Henry can reduce proud men to sniveling fools. I do not fault Lord Raoul, you understand—what Henry did at Sieux is well known, and what Raoul did at Boissert equally so. But to make a king look like a school boy with his breechcloth down— well, Henry got the worst of it this time. He beckoned to a page to bring him wine—Henry who never drinks, and who despises us because we do. (I count it no disgrace to wear silk or to like good wine, but if they prefer to ride in homespun like their grooms and drink watered beer, that is to their taste, not mine.)

"'By the Rood,' Henry spoke carefully, holding anger in check, 'you take much upon yourself, Count Raoul, to plan a progress along our border without our leave. You refused me last time I asked you to.'

"'"Ask" and "command" are two different words,' Lord Raoul drawled, 'but in any case, less of a progress than was spoken of at Boissert Field. It was a progress through a dukedom that your Normans planned, I speak of a stretch of bog and heath, not worth the fighting for, but mine I think. Mine by law and by holy oath to do with as I please. And that horse you so misuse but part the payment I gave for it.'

"'That's as we decide,' Henry said. Now, he may not look or dress like a king, but he has the tenacity of a bull, and when he lowers his head, he charges for the most vulnerable place. 'Your wife found Cambray worth biding much to get.'

"Raoul kept his hands clasped behind his back but I saw how he held them to keep them still. Henry had struck a shrewd blow with that remark.

"'But it is still ours,' Raoul said. 'And that's a lesson worth remembering. We cannot have one law for king and one for lord. Land done homage for is justly held, and that a feudal right your lawyers in England should take into account. Nor can any man, still less a king, quest back and forth across the sea to keep a peace. Better, great King,' and I think he spoke the word not to make a mock, but as if he wished Henry would merit it, 'better to give your vassals some credit for common sense. Leave the western border to our lordship as has been so these last three kings. Keep your queen out of our affairs. Give your brother charge of the west here, to quiet him. . .'

"From behind the horse trough, Geoffrey said, 'That's a gift I'd gladly take, and thank you for your lesson on loyalty. Ask all these gentlemen here arrayed where they heard so fine a talk, which the queen arranged for their delight. Poitiers is jammed with ladies these days, if you know where to look for them. Queen Eleanor keeps them under lock and key that we men must go there hunting for them, but we learned a goodly lesson of our own today, and the Countess of Sieux gave it us.'

"Raoul said evenly, without rancor, 'The Countess is left at home.'

"'Then I cry you pardon,' Geoffrey smiled. ' I thought she visited with the queen. I thought I met with her at Poitiers. She. . .'

"Whatever else he would have said was lost in a gust of wind. Count Raoul leapt across the trough, rammed his fist under Geoffrey's rib cage, laid him out into a midden heap.

Geoffrey hawked and spat, his silken tunic besmirched with slime and dung. Count Raoul a second time wiped off his hands.

"'One last thing,' he said. 'Touch not another's property lest your own be touched, a most important feudal law. And no man mouths my wife's name without my consent. That is a law of my own.'

"Without more ado, without a by-your-leave, Raoul left— the king still sitting on his horse, brother Geoffrey still on his face in the muck, we courtiers still with our ears pinned back.

"Long and many were the wagers made that day. I tell you, I am no wagering man, but those Angevins will not let him rest. Nor will he them. Bound together by some rule beyond my understanding, bound together by some code, they urge each other on. Lord Raoul left then; I did not see him again, Sir Renier's message from you, reaching him, I suppose, to speed his return, although not, I think, until many hours after your starting forth, for the man who bore it was delayed. And that delay too Geoffrey or the king or even the queen might have deliberately arranged." Ademar had paused then. "But if not now," he had said, "some other time Henry and Raoul will meet."

Well, the confrontation between Raoul and Henry was not now. Enough had been done now that there was no need for Henry to look for revenge, since others were already set on it for themselves. And what Lord Ademar foresaw, that final meeting between king and count, a wager that no man dared speak openly about, treason even to think of, yet one day Lord Ademar was to witness it. And when and how will be told by him in due course. Sufficient for the moment that Lord Raoul started after us, but too late to be of help. Had I known before the extent of Henry's newest quarrel with Raoul, would it have comforted me, made me change my plans? Was it worse not to know? Two men had done us grievous harm, a queen had done me as much, all three combined against us as Sir Renier had warned. And before us who knows what malice was poised to strike. So, with only imagination to feed my thoughts, no plans, no future but to reach Sieux before that malice did, we

crossed, unseeing, that fair and pleasant land, and on the fourth
day arrived at the Sieux River, close to our boundary.

We reached the river at an early hour, already tired, for we
had paused but seldom these past days and nights. We came
to a ford further west than usual, closer to the town of Saint
Purnace. Although I have never liked the place, and never
willingly have gone there since, even that day its name spelled
home, and its church spire, which can be seen for many miles,
took on a welcome look, floating from the autumn mist like a
building hung in space. The waters ran higher than usual, there
had been rains in the mountains and the coldness had a chill
like snow. All seemed familiar, safe, and for the first time,
Walter's frown of tension eased. He pushed back his mail coif
and ran his fingers through his hair. He had ridden us hard,
as hard as his master would, but, had we waited for Raoul's
command, we should perhaps have been too late, and that he
now acknowledged. Now he could admit we had done well to
have come so far alone, and since we were but a short ride
from Sieux—an hour or two—we must have outridden the de
Boissert men, all threat left behind. And Raoul, being warned,
would be in no danger with his much larger force. But the
French men-at-arms who had done us such good service un-
complainingly, they still swore it was a mystery.

"For, lady," the younger one explained, an argument we had
had many times before, "how is it possible that, in all of France,
not one peasant has seen a group of horsemen riding along,
not one child has waved at them, not one housewife tried to
cheat them of lodging fees?" He meant, of course, that they
too must have had support, fresh horses to exchange at need,
bribes given to keep mouths shut. Only great influence can do
that. They debated among themselves, an ongoing debate which
today had lost its urgency.

I sat with my eyes closed, letting the rising sun warm me.
We were not even unduly alarmed at the sound of hooves
coming from the east. Eastward lay Sieux, no one had gone
that way we should fear. And there was even less cause for
alarm when we saw who it was, a group of masons in their

monthly retreat, returning to Saint Purnace for supplies, among
them Master Edward, whose small horse and strong compact
frame were distinguishable from a long way off.

"Save you, good sirs," he shouted cheerily on seeing us.
"We did not expect you back so soon. And Godspeed to you
too, Squire Walter. Your companion Matt asks for you. When
return the Lady Ann and her lord?"

Walter jerked his thumb to indicate where I sat, the water
swirling green and cool about my horse's feet.

"Why, by the blessed Saint Purnace," he now cried, "greeting
then to you, Lady Ann. We thought you returned with Count
Raoul at a later date."

His words were pleasant, homely, kind. Why did a trickle
of fear begin to creep, a hint, a twinge?

"Why?" I said.

He stared at me as if I were daft. "Do I speak out of turn?"
he said. "I cry you mercy. I thought she said. . ."

"What she?" Walter shouted. He seized the mason by the
arm, "What one?"

But I knew. I knew at once what she had done and how and
why, and I had given her the weapon to do it with.

Master Edward and his men were already dismounting,
crowding round. They all spoke at once, but I already knew
what they said. A lady from the queen's court, they said, came
yesterday, a scant twelve hours ahead, bringing greetings and
good cheer from me, bringing messages from me to my child.
And I knew, I almost said the words aloud, carrying my ring
as sign of faith, to use it as entrance among my womenfolk,
to talk to the villagers as a great lady of the court, to give
them orders for my son.

One of the French troopers, already mounted, pounded off
to sound the warning, but he would be too late. I knew why
she had come and how she had achieved it. *Long will you rue
your tongue.* Many times had I flaunted that prophecy, and this
the last, that Alyse de Vergay and her mistress, Isobelle de
Boissert should fulfill it.

Walter questioned the masons over and over again; they too

were bemused, uncertain, grasped at straws. She was a friend, they thought, not knowing her, a neighbor's wife, they had seen no harm. She said I sent her in my name to play with my son whom I sorely missed—even Matt, who would remember her, had shrugged on seeing her—her reappearance in such friendly guise put down to women's ways. If they saw no wrong, how could the village women expect it, suspect treachery when I myself had shown my enemies how to trick them treacherously. Yet even when all hope is lost, you look for it; even then, you think it may not be so; even then, there still is hope.

A second trooper, moving downstream, brought back the confirmation we both sought and feared. A group of men, he said, a score perhaps, had made a crossing below the ford a day ago. They had swum the river, out of sight, away from the well-traveled path, a difficult crossing, for the banks on either side were churned to mud. And on the further, northern bank, they had paused, then turned back, away from any known place, certainly not east toward Sieux, nor west toward Saint Purnace. Walter and the second man now scouted the northern bank, the masons joined in the search. I heard them beating in the bushes, their cries, then their silence that discovery makes.

The evidence they brought back was grimmer still; Walter came up to me, his boyish smile wiped away, his face a mask. Beneath the cloak, across his saddle bow, he bore a dreadful thing, stiff and still. A village lad hung there, face down, an arrow through the shoulder blades. I knew who he was before they lowered him carefully to the ground, one of those urchins who, when Robert was born, used to guard us against the hens and goats, now promoted to man's watch at the outer region of our lands... Not much more than a child himself, some mother's son, set to guard the river bank, not my son, but someone's...

A second cry, a second thing, this, Robert's hound, dead too, stabbed many times, its golden fur stiff with blood, killed not more than an hour or so ago. It would never have come so far from Sieux unless there was someone to track; they would never have had need to kill unless it came after them to give them away.

"Lady Ann," it was Master Edward, his face creased with lines, heavily he spoke as a man loaded with care, "have heart. He still lives, else his dog would never have followed him. They would not have brought him here unless alive."

Walter said, "They must have waited for her to return, then moved on again. We can find their tracks, go after them. It is a two-hour ride to Sieux, two hours back, the men to arm and mount, we cannot wait for the guard at Sieux." He did not add what was obvious: We are but three.

Master Edward seized his shoulder and held it tight. "Courage, lad, they leave a trail like an army's path, but if you ride headlong upon them, they'll cut you down, or, hearing you, ambush you with the same result. I guess where they go, will come with you to show you a side road. We'll take them from the rear where they'll not look for pursuit."

He said, beckoning to his men, his nephew, last male child of his house, feeling for his knife to test its blade, "When I was an apprentice boy, my father sent me to the forest west of Saint Purnace to learn what a builder needs to know of timber and trees, the quality of wood, its grain, its age. Once, many years ago, a village stood beyond Saint Purnace, but empty, and empty has been for a hundred years or more since death struck down its inhabitants. The woodcutters used to go there in the summer; they claimed that heat dries off the fogs that breed up plague. But since my time, even they no longer use the place." He paused for breath. I had never heard him speak so fast or think so quick. He said, "That's where they'll go, I'll stake my life. Nowhere else is open to them. De Boissert lands are forfeit to the crown and the castle is barred. They will hide there until night before they move on, but we'll have gained on them before then. We'll leave word at the ford where we go and how, but we must ride without delay." Nor did he add the obvious: Otherwise we will be too late.

I took my place with them, reached for a dagger from Walter's belt, having lost my own. "I come with you," I said in answer to Walter's look, "he is my son."

We pushed our way through the brush, thick and matted, whatever path swallowed by neglect. There were many horsemen, those elusive horsemen we had been trailing all week, and suddenly I saw what the French men had claimed—no woman, shut into a nunnery, her father dead, his lands attainted for treason, could have mounted a troop that size without some help; and no troop that size without someone to back and shield it could have ridden so fast and left no clue. And that thought too was one to chill, but I beat it back. I would remember no smile, no cruel laugh. But sometimes when an iron hoof mark showed itself clearly in the mud, sometimes when we saw how bushes had been cut and slashed to make a track, the sense of evil began to take on substance, concentrate. And when once, silently, one of the stonecutters brought us something hidden in his hand, a scrap of silk, pale blue, found hanging from a bramble thorn, I had a sense, a feeling, that soon would come a reckoning.

The last few miles, we turned aside. Master Edward, riding in front, showed us the way, a longer route but secret. At his suggestion, we pulled tufts of grass to muffle clink of bridle or saddle iron, and those who wore mail, Walter, his two men, they hid it beneath their cloaks and rode bareheaded for fear, even in this underbrush, a flash of light should reveal us. I saw how Walter and his men turned to Master Edward willingly for advice, although he wore no spurs, carried only his sharp paring knife. *I live to serve you, I and my men.* So a third time for my sake they served. Praise God. At each turning Master Edward stopped, took note of tree or rock, ponderous and slow like a tree himself, yet his memory never failed, even after all these years he drew us on unerringly and led us ever deeper into this tangled wilderness.

The last hundred yards or so we came on foot, the horses left out of earshot with some apprentices to watch, three men having gone ahead to test the path. I would have thought us lost, nothing in front of us but a wall of trees, until suddenly we came out into what must have once been an orchard and, beyond it, a ruined clump of huts and a rutted village street. We crept forward then to the edge of the orchard grove. I noticed, in that strange way one has to notice unrelated things, how underneath the gnarled and mossy trees yellow apples lay rotting in the grass, covered with swarms of small wasps and flies, and I remember thinking how strange to see sweetness gone to waste and fruitfulness rotted away.

The village would have been a dismal place at best, now it was overgrown with vines and nettles rank and thick, its street or what had served as one, knee-deep in leaves. On one side of it, the remaining huts leaned together like a circle of stones, a blank wall facing out, no door or window well, the walls themselves almost overgrown. Once there would have been hives in the orchards here, and pigs and noise, children sitting in the dust, all the sounds of village life that we know at Sieux. And for a moment, I had a thought of how Sieux would be if transplanted here, and of how a little boy would have played with his friends. Today all was emptiness, only wind and bees, nothing else. But Master Edward had sent some of his men slithering round, they were good at that, used perhaps to burrowing underground or crawling into attic space. Walter went with them, all of them with weapons drawn, while we waited in the long grass. I noted how, for big men and broad, the masons moved most cleverly; and since talking was now impossible, they used hand signals among themselves, usual for them when the noise of their trade made communication otherwise impossible.

We watched the huts. The first two were almost caved in, the frame of wood sticking up like bones through the ruin of their mud walls, but the rest seemed sturdy enough. Then Master Edward tugged at my sleeve. From the central hut, a sort of gateway led to an inner court, built like that perhaps, or more like caused naturally now with the passing of years, a rough sort of passageway. A shadow moved against the wall, something stirred, and as we listened, we caught the strike of hoof against stone. The shadow crept back.

Master Edward sighed, wiped his forehead and smiled. "We have them," was all he said, but I noticed how he sat more comfortably and began to sharpen his knife.

Presently, there was a scuffle in the grass; it was Walter creeping on all fours. He had shed his mail coat and his spurs, and in shirtsleeves crept, his face darkened with dirt, his hair damp with heat.

"All of them," he reported, spitting out mouthfuls of sand, "their horses saddled in the yard, one a woman's. Ten men there on guard but drinking. Three more to watch the way they came, three on the other side, the rest within the biggest hut."

But to Master Edward's questioning look, the question I forced myself not to ask, he shook his head. No sight, no sound then of my son. But if he had been alive at the ford, he still must be alive. They would not carry him all the way if dead; they would not carry him this way to kill him here.

Master Edward had bent down, ungainly in his holiday robes. He and his men began to strip them off, their workaday tunics worn beneath. "Thrift," I heard him say, "our wives wash both at one time."

One of his companions wiped his lips. "Stonecutting is thirsty work," he said, "but soldiering is worse." He gave a grin on catching my eye. I felt a wave, not of relief, but of hope perhaps.

They were not soldiers, but they spoke and jested as soldiers do; they planned their attack efficiently; their knives were sharp. I thought, Thank God, that guildsmen are so quarrelsome. And for the first time since the ford, felt we had some chance.

Master Edward had already thought out the detail of what he would do, drew it in his precise way with his knife, as if planning a layer of stone. The six outer guards were to be removed silently, not difficult, needing younger men with knives (although knives against mail coats is hard, until two others hastily showed their bows, yew bows these, meant for hunting, yet good enough at close quarters). I thought of the archers at Boissert, who had misfired and died for it, but buried the thought. The guards dead first; next, one man alone at a signal prearranged was to burst into the yard where the horses were penned, to stampede them while the rest of us stormed past against the inside doors, such as they were, makeshift too, easily broken through. But that first charge must be a knightly one; Walter's then, with sword and shield, on horseback to give him speed and weight. And I must stand with the apprentices in the orchard here, to guard the path so no one might escape and to watch that our own horses did not stray.

"Take care, my lady," Walter said, his attention already fixed, assessing the best place to break through and take them unaware. His west country voice sounded suddenly very calm compared with all these French ones. "We'll have the little one soon," he said. I remember how he had held Robert in his arms and wished him joy. *I saw the day of your birth*, he had said. Pray God, I thought, not the day of his death. I tried to wish Walter luck in turn, but he had already gone, no time to strap his mail coat on; and by and by, I saw him and his horse disappear to the edge of the orchard behind us. Three other masons had already crept with our young French guard, left and right they went, to where, if they did their work well, the outposts would lie on the bloodstained earth.

Then we crept closer too, as close as we dared to the narrow road and, one by one, the men crossed, a handful of them, flitting over among the noonday shadows against the crumbling walls. Had there been door or window slits on that wall, our plan would have been nigh impossible, but those crafty peasants long ago had kept the outer walls blank so no one could look in and spy, so now no one could look out. The wait seemed long, almost as long as the whole ride back. Then suddenly there was a great cry.

Walter broke out from the bushes on the far side from us, charged his horse right into the yard, swinging with his sword. Master Edward and his men rose from their crouch, their cloaks and aprons wrapped about their arms as shields, and followed him. The de Boissert men were resting in the sun, their coats unbraced, their sword belts off. Some snatched for them, were cut down; others, fleeing from Walter's horse, ran upon the masons' knives. But already Master Edward was hammering at the door, two of his men tearing at the rotting frame. And I, unable to stand aside, had run across the road, last of all but my knife drawn, too. I saw how the terrified horses, cut free, went galloping off, reins dangling, saw the last of the de Boissert men fall back with three of our men to pen them in, but they were armed, these last of the de Boissert guard, and they were desperate. And I saw how the door to the inner room had splintered but had not given way.

Walter was already backing his horse against the southern wall. He lashed the beast's sides until it kicked and flailed, and its great hooves tore out clods of clay and dirt. Again and again he backed, using his shield rim to smash at the wooden doorframe, until at last he broke through, he and his horse, half in, half out. The wall was reduced to a shell against which Master Edward and his men, steady as veterans, thrust their shoulders. But inside the room were veterans too, four men who had been forewarned and had chance to take up their own weapons before the masons could rush in. And they, in turn, were desperate men. Even as I watched, a sword blade flicked out, caught Walter as he pushed himself off his horse.

From where I stood, I had but partial view and that was blocked by Master Edward and his men. Dodging through the yard took me but a second, but by then our men had broken down the wall into the little room. It was small, almost too small to draw a sword, and here the masons should have had an advantage, their knives being that much shorter and easier to hold. But swords wielded by skilled men could keep them back. Only Walter, on his own feet now, could match with the swordsmen there. And he, although he tried to cover our men, was more intent on moving to where the woman stood against the outside wall. It was Alyse de Vergay; I recognized first her pale eyes, now almost bulging with alarm. But she was desperate also, and in her hand, she held a knife. She stood between the door and a kind of alcove where my son lay asleep. Not asleep, I thought, desperate with fright myself, not with this noise, this confusion, breaking around him. But he did not move, lay on his back, motionless yet not dead. If dead, why would she threaten him with a knife, her own face a twisted mask, a thing to chill thought with?

Walter was on his feet, but his arms and legs were criss-crossed with blood where the men inside had hacked out at him, his face streaked red where her knife point had flicked his forehead.

"Stand back, squire," she said, "or give me safe conduct to leave with him."

Walter could stand, but only just, he swayed upon his feet, yet his voice was calm. He spoke to her almost soothingly. "Come, mistress," he said, "give me Lord Robert and go free. Why should you harm a child?"

"Lord, is it?" she sneered, watching his sword with unwavering eye; she was nimble on her feet for her size, the long ride seeming not to have daunted her. Except for her torn and stained dress, the knife, she might have been the Alyse de Vergay who outspoke me when first we came to France. Yet there was a wildness in her speech, as if it ran without her control. "Lord," she spat. "A guttersnipe, he was doomed before his birth. No," as Walter moved, step by cautious step, "he belongs to us; his name was writ that day at Saint Purnace. He should have never have escaped us there. He should have been another's child or not born at all."

Walter said, spitting blood, "Why have you tried to kill him before? Why try now? Your words make no sense." He attempted a smile. Behind his back, Master Edward had come between him and those de Boissert swords, was trying, with his fellow masons, to trap the swordsmen against some rickety stairs that led to a hayloft.

"Look, lady," Walter's voice was patient, a gleaner in the fields, a watcher by a cider press. "Lady," he repeated the word to gratify her pride, "your guards are overrun, your men outside dead or captured, you alone, what chance for you? What gain for you, what profit, why kill, to your own greater harm?"

"He lies," one of the de Boissert swordsmen cried, his voice the louder that Walter's was quiet, "what force backs him, only city scum." And with a soldier's dislike of city folk, he tried to drive past Master Edward's knife, and was beaten back.

But, "Liars all," she repeated, "they promised me much to come to Sieux. What did I get, sent off like a servant wench? The rightful mistress of Sieux would grant me more than that."

"Stand firm," the swordsman next encouraged her. "Do not yield. Remember what reward if we do what was asked..."

"Reward is not necessary for me," she said, edging round, she stood within a knife's edge of my son, "what I do, I do without reward. But I have friends, powerful friends, they'll help me. You lie, Sir Squire, like all at Sieux who put on airs to impress, jumped up like weeds."

Her men made another rush, but Walter did not even turn round, a trusting man was he to let a friend guard his back in such a place. To her, he made his next appeal. "Give up your knife, repent. My lord will be merciful."

"Merciful," she almost screamed the word, "what mercy then at Boissert Field? Overlord dead, my father in his death swoon, my brothers disarmed and disgraced." She made a feint with the knife to make my heart stand still, but still could not quite reach. "Rather," she said, "come you away with me. My friends will treat you handsomely. And take the child with us; dead or alive, Count Raoul shall pay. A ransom will cripple him, make me an heiress worth the marrying. That shall be my just reward. You are young, Sir Squire," and now she smiled a caricature of a smile, both arch and grotesque.

Perhaps she guessed what his reaction was, or, perhaps, in the clever way half-demented people have to guess at truths, she became more cunning, her speech slurred as if she spoke at random, to distract. But I sensed a deeper purpose underneath.

"You think me old. But, had my mistress been the lady here, then should I too have married to my rank. Lord Raoul owes me some recompense. This ensures I get it."

He said simply, "My loyalty is already sworn. I serve Count Raoul and his lady wife."

I think the mention of my name drove her on, or perhaps it was the coupling of both names, or even nothing that he said, simply the workings of her own mind.

"My loyalty is fixed longer than yours," she cried, "to her who should have had this place, to her who should have this as son. Shut in a nunnery, that living death, what hopes for her or me? I act for her, her mouthpiece, her right arm."

"Lady," Walter made one last attempt, he spoke to reason with her, "it was not she who was put aside; she and her father themselves broke the marriage vow. The Lady Ann is good and kind . . ."

"And should she have it all?" she cried, malice and envy breaking out, "let that Celtic whore who took my lady's place know what it is like to live with death. If our lives are done with, so be hers."

Quicker than seems possible for one so built, she jerked back the covers from my son, thrust down at him with her knife. There was no time to stop the blow, no other way. Walter leapt too, one great leap, threw himself across the child, thrusting up with his sword as she thrust down. There was a long intake of breath; they fell together, rolled upon the floor, a crash, a thud that reverberates in my ears until the world's end.

Master Edward ran to push her off, dead she was, her mouth agape upon those last cruel words. *Do not put a curse on me.*

Her curse is with me until my death.

Walter still lived, his eyes closed, a froth of red about those lips that smiled so readily. I wiped his face clean, pushed back his hair. I suppose about me swordsmen still raged, I suppose the last de Boissert men fought on and were killed. After a while, someone handed me the child, a bundle he seemed of fragile bones, yet alive. But he neither woke nor slept, his face as gray as unwashed wool, his eyes purple shadowed, his mouth stained blue from whatever drug she had given him. She had coaxed him to eat perhaps, that early hour while my village women slept, then took him forth, carried him to where a horse, and further on, other horsemen had waited her. His shallow breaths kept time with Walter's, a bitter smell upon his lips, a dose of some plant to quiet him. I held him on my lap, and Walter's head was in my arms, but I could not weep for them. And when they gave me back the ring, I strung it round my neck, a weight like lead.

Walter's eyes opened once, those warm west country eyes now lustreless. He tried to smile. "So am I cured of French women in the end," he said. A spasm caught him, he bit it back, never spoke to me again. I think he thought he was in his home, for he called for his brothers there, bid them saddle a horse. I held his hand, I willed him to think of it, to be in the western hills and smell the heather on the moors, and feel the western wind beating up the Channel coast. And I stayed with him, until his spirit rode away. And Master Edward came and pried my hand loose.

Well, he died, and all those de Boissert men, and she who died with them. Three masons were dead, one of our French guard, killed by a random blow as they stormed the hut, and Master Edward's nephew wounded in his arm which never grew straight again. And other wounded who had to be cared for. All dead, maimed, that my son should live... So we took up our dead and wounded, piled the other corpses, set the huts ablaze. They say the flames could be seen from Saint Purnace, and no man now dares go near that black and scorched patch of ground.

As for her, who had murdered twice, and poisoned, "Hang her body up," I said, "that she should have a murderer's end." Well, that too is something to regret, but it was so done. Yet sometimes I think of her and wonder what was loyalty to her, who claimed it as her excuse, and what was the bond between her and that Isobelle that she should sell her soul for her. We made a cradle for the child, his breathing still irregular, his flesh wracked with fever spells so that it seemed he would shiver his joints apart. We departed hence, silently, no joy in us. And the ring about my neck was worn for remembrance.

10

AT THE RIVER FORDS WE MET, LORD Raoul, his men, more men from Sieux, and we, with our sad and heavy load. Lord Raoul's face was weary, drawn, his men bone tired. He sat on his horse as if turned to ice. I do not think he knew what he said, his thoughts so fixed on this one thing that even I for a while was put aside.

"Save him. Ann, he must be saved." And he took his son into his arms, carried him before him to Sieux. I remembered the way Walter had held him, Walter of the gentle ways who had many younger brothers and a large and thriving family. And I remembered how Raoul had always been alone, mother and father dead before he could have known them, his grandfather far away in England. A lonely child he must have been, not used to children, not used to sons. He could not bear to lose this one, his firstborn.

At the castle gates, another sober group waited us, my women bathed in tears and our castle guard, the loyal Dillon and the men left in his charge, almost speechless for grief. As we passed into the courtyard, we trampled over the place where Robert had been born. The new walls were clearly visible. I remembered what Master Edward had promised: that before Robert was grown, they would stand to their full height. I almost thought now that promise would never be kept; I almost thought that the second Robert would follow the first, be lost before he could grow to boyhood. Yet I could not despair. We had already suffered too much to have despair destroy us. We took the child and laid him before the fire in the tower room. All night long my women waited with me. But we did not wait alone; Raoul joined us. He was wearier than I had ever seen him, plastered in mud. He had not changed his clothes for a week. I do not think he had slept or broken fast. He came in quietly for so large a man; he had not even removed his mail coat and his spurs grated over the wooden floors for all that he trod with care. He stood and watched us as we tried to bring the child's fever down, using damp cloths steeped in herbs. Presently, without a word, he went away, and I thought, if I thought anything, he could not bear to watch. But he returned; he and Dillon had been to the river's edge, in the dark, and hauled up buckets of water, cold and fresh, with its hint of ice. We scooped out the weed, Dillon and I, the day we had so scooped weed before forgotten then, although we laughed at it afterward, and I wetted the cloths and placed them on Robert's body that lay motionless, as if its vitality had burned away.

Raoul helped me. All night long, he worked with me, and sometimes our fingers crossed and touched over our child. *Flesh of my flesh.* So that night Raoul labored to give his child new life, so that night did Raoul woman's work.

And sometimes when I dozed, for moments perhaps at a time, so weary now myself I scarce could stand, Raoul kept vigil in my place. And when the child's fever at last began to break, and he tossed and cried, it was Raoul who held him. Raoul's broad hand with its long fingers could span the child's chest, and the skin was brown against the whiteness of the child's skin, but you saw the father in the child's face; you saw the child in his father's eyes. There are times when words get in the way. I knew without Raoul's telling me what his thoughts were that night. I knew what they must have been as he rode back; I knew, I had known them myself. He knew without my speaking of such things all of my guilt and regret at having gone to Poitiers. I sensed his, at having outfaced Henry in such fashion. Well, it is not only conspiracy that makes tangled nets, so do we live our lives, who knows how the ends ravel out. I think Lord Ademar had expressed it well: a sort of fate drives us on and holds us together despite ourselves. That night, without speech, without explanation, was the bond between Raoul and me tightened another notch. And when the dawn at last came and I knew the child was still alive, and the women dragged back the sacking that hid the window slits, we heard, faintly, that tap-tap-tapping of the masons on the castle walls. In their dour, uncompromising way, they too were already at their work. I looked at Raoul and thought, Thank God for you to back me this night.

He took my hands in his, those large strong hands, and turned mine over, as if examining them. Then he drew me to the window where he could see beyond the busy courtyard toward the cliff, the lake and the hills. He said, suddenly, abruptly. "Ann, I have seen you sitting on the ground, digging up the stones of Sieux to make its walls. I have seen you twice stand as firm as rock when our enemies would have overwhelmed us. And now, today, you have given me back my son. Look about you, *ma mie*. Here is Sieux spread before you, the Sieux you have helped rebuild. I told you you would be countess here one day in your own right. No lady more deserves that name." And he kissed me on the lips, the kiss of love, before all men.

Behind us, on his little bed, Robert suddenly called our names. He was awake, his blue-gray eyes conscious although they did not focus yet but gazed beyond us as if looking at something only he could find.

"See, young sir," Raoul's voice was as warm and comforting as his hand about my waist. "I have brought you a something from Poitiers." It was a little carved shield, with a gold hawk painted on the crimson wood. Robert held it in his hand until he slept. Well, he would live, and all the castle rejoiced, not such rejoicing in our time there, not such happiness since we first returned. And that night Raoul held me in his arms and plighted again his troth to me. *This is our wedding night.* Now had I what I long had dreamed of, then were those days at Cambray recalled, now did my lover lie with me without stint.

By Jesu, he had once said, *I shall love you until you it is calls cease.*
That night neither of us had reason to hold back, now did we
truly know what it meant to be man and wife. Warm flesh,
warm skin, to bury out the winter colds, we lay as one. "And
now," he said, his breath warm too against my throat, "now
shall I know what loves you promised me."

It is both meet and right that after sorrow pleasure comes,
that in our time we should know it. Thus was the sadness of
autumn turned to happiness. We nursed Robert back to health,
a slow business that. And sometimes I think, had he not possessed the power that children have to spring back from illness,
then swallowing that sleeping draught would have killed him
before Alyse de Vergay could have carried him to the forest
rendezvous, so unskilled was she. And she, so nervous in her
haste to steal him away from our village unobserved, she might
have killed him there, and brought away a dead child instead
of the live one she hoped to bargain with. But by the Yuletide,
Robert was well enough to sit by the fire and listen to Matt's
stories. Raoul gave him another dog, although he never loved
it like that first. And I think a caution grew in him from that
time, to make him more quiet than is natural in a child. He
never whined as sick children do, but watched, as if from a
distance, as if removed from us, as if suspicious of womankind.
As for Matt, the winter winds proving hard, he needed nursing
also, a shortness of breath still plaguing him. So he too sat by
the fire and by degrees became the new castle storyteller, taking
Walter's place, and his tales grew with the telling until who
knows what tremendous feats of arms he invented for my son.
And Robert lay in his father's lap and listened. At the Yuletide
too we had a knighting, long overdue, Matt wheezing through
the ceremony, unable to keep the night vigil, perhaps even
unwilling to without a companion by his side. We hung a pair
of golden spurs in Walter's name in an alcove of what would
be our chapel, and seldom a day passed but I went there to
pray for him. Yet I sometimes think he is not at peace whom
death took so cruelly in this foreign land, and God who knows
all things and sees all should find place in His mighty kingdom

for a man so far from home. In the spring we were to go back
to England. That was a thought to cheer the mind, lift the
soul, although by then we had many friends at Sieux, trusted
and kind, who it would be hard to part with and who had been
good to us. And remembering how we had sat in the rain on
that first day, grubbing in the ground for shards of stone, I
could scarcely believe in such a space of time Sieux could have
become alive again.

We were to leave in the middle of May month, and early
began to prepare for this. How the ladies chattered as they
sewed, how the young squires and pages bustled importantly
about, how at times I found myself skipping along. But with
the spring came other news: Henry's answer to Raoul. He was
clever, I tell you, Henry who was England's king; and his call
to arms was not what I had expected although I should have
done. No move is made without its counter one. Revenge is
never forgotten although it lags one step behind. Henry had
spent the winter in France, and went back to England a scant
month before we did, having made a peace with his wife.

The reasons for this truce are obvious when you think what
she most wanted was a son, and he too must have felt the need
for another heir to ensure his inheritance. And she must have
sensed she had gone too far, tried Henry too far; after all,
Henry was young, and other kings had put aside their wives.
I myself do not think she felt remorse. That concept was not
part of her personality, but she may have realized the quarrel
between them had to be mended sometime. What concessions
were made or what conditions laid down or how arranged we
did not know, but, as Sir Renier had said, in royal households
as with ordinary men, wives and husbands have to come to
terms if they are to live together at all. (And beget sons Eleanor
did, the next one born at Oxford in the autumn of that year,
a Richard who was to become king, and a brother to follow
him, another Geoffrey, and at the end, England's curse, John
Lackland.) I think, too, on considering it, the reason Sir Renier
had helped me, helped us, was not so much because he cared
for me and felt he owed us some recompense, (both of which

were true and so he may have felt) but because, loyal to the queen, he wished to save her from herself, wished to prevent her being embroiled in such an ugly episode. Yet how far she was involved or how much she knew, that I cannot say.

A truce then was somehow arranged between the royal pair, and a royal triumph planned through the southern lands. They were well-received. Great feasts and merriment attended them— even Count Raymond of Toulouse put on displays of loyalty— but it was also said that in order to rid the queen of a vassal she accused of treachery, Henry attacked and sacked the castle of the Viscount of Thouars, that young lord whom I had met. They say the queen called him troublesome, a nice euphemism to cover her displeasure; but the great are ever fickle in their choice of friends, and once the viscount had smiled at me!

In any event, the king attacked his lands; the queen appeared content, and harmony was restored. By what means she won Henry to her will I have said I cannot guess and still cannot, but two other points I should like to make. First, Henry did create his brother count, so was Geoffrey's ambition gratified, but not at the expense of Eleanor's lands. For, as has been mentioned several times, Brittany was uneasy, and among the restless cities there, one of the greatest, the port of Nantes, was in revolt. Nantes is a rich city, they say, a harbor on the west Atlantic coast, a city of ships and trade where the river Loire comes to the sea. The Loire is the lifeblood of Anjou, the artery down which all its goods and commerce flow, and to have the means to control its major port would delight the Angevins. The matter was simply arranged. Disliking their ruler, Count Hoel, the citizens of Nantes asked Henry to find them a new one, and he, encouraging them, gave them Geoffrey Plantagenet. Thus was every one pleased; and although neither Henry nor Geoffrey raised even a finger to take the prize, it fell easily into their hands, a bribe perhaps to keep a royal peace. I missed the sage comments Walter would have made when we first heard *that* news. The second point was something on which Walter had already said his say: Isobelle de Boissert's wardship to the king. Now it was openly proclaimed, her lands

and estates were held attainted in traitor's fee and she herself
banished for life to her nunnery on pain of death. Since it had
been obviously true that she could not have mounted such a
group of soldiers on her own or armed them after her father's
death, this public humiliation meant that Eleanor's support too
had been withdrawn. *I would be loyal to you.* So much for women's
loyalty, even that of a queen. And Isobelle's loss was Geoffrey's
gain.

As for us, we journeyed to the north coast in the spring, in
luxury, our entire household in state, a journey such as Alyse
de Vergay had coveted—turn memory back, stop thought. I
do not wish to speak of her, she lives where darkness dwells,
when in the night not even prayers can keep remorse or memory
at bay. We were to sail from Barfleur, and on our arrival there,
Robert and I came down to the quay to watch the loading of
our ships and admire the careful way the barrels and crates
were bestowed on deck, the bundles of gear without which no
noble household moves a step. I myself prefer, like snail, to
carry my goods upon my back. The mariners scrambled in the
riggings, barefoot, as nimble as Master Edward's apprentices,
and the master mariner, like a good general, supervised all their
maneuverings from the center of the deck. I thought, as I
watched the white sails furled, dripping wet with dew, how
from this selfsame port those years ago, a Prince of England
had set out. The only heir, his father's sole legitimate son, he
would have inherited England had he lived. His ship was the
fastest in the royal fleet, but since the weather had held calm,
he and his companions, sons of his father's lords, allowed the
other ships to leave without them, idled the hours away on
shore. When they hoisted canvas it was late, they had drunk
too much. The helmsman carelessly let the ship drift on the
rocks. And so was drowned that prince, that William, who if
he had lived, would have spared his country so much harm.
Thirty-seven years earlier had he been drowned, and yet his
death has overshadowed all our lives so that it could be said
our wrongs, our griefs, can be traced to him. Yet certainly he
and his friends had never thought of what awaited them when

they set sail that day . . . Nor did we. Fate had not done with us yet.

As I say, my son Robert and I were watching the loading of the ship, and had discovered a place in a sail loft with a view, out of harm's way. It smelled of tar and fish; there were bundles of rope and crab pots, things to keep a small boy amused while I sat at the door and listened to the sailor's songs. Lord Raoul eased his way toward us through the stacks of barrels that lined the wharf. He had been supervising the men-at-arms, who in tower-like structures, two wooden castles at either end of the ship, would guard our passage and keep watch for pirates lurking along the Channel coasts. He was gnawing on a scrap of bread, throwing the crumbs for the gulls. They swept downwind to snatch them from the air.

"So here you are, lady, tucked away," he said, "as snug as worm in sea biscuit." Not a felicitous comparison. Nor did I like to have those seagulls swoop so close, yellow-eyed and yellow-beaked, their hoarse cries reflecting their greedy selves.

They made me shiver, but Robert, suddenly seeing them, laughed and opened wide his arms. The gesture reminded me of the way his father had ridden along the shores of the lake when he knew his strength returned, and I took that as a sign, an omen of Robert's return to health. Raoul reached down to lift the child, holding him to let him throw out the rest of the bread.

"By the Mass," he said after a while, "I prefer the look of these ships better than the three tubs that brought us here, more like to drown than carry us, jammed to the rails. Remember how the women screamed . . ."

He choked back that unfortunate memory. "And remember how the mariners cursed? Women on board bring bad luck they say. Be assured. This time we've the best craft that sail this route; the king himself could not have better. The master mariner is worthy of his hire, and we've enough men to fight off all the world."

He was still throwing the bread to the gulls and had hoisted Robert on his shoulders. With one hand, the child clutched his father's hair, as once he held onto his wolfhound, and beat on his back with the other. I smiled to see their happiness.

"King Henry sailed in April," Raoul said; carefully he threw the bread, as carefully he threw the words, "in a goodly company. Queen and children, prince and princess, all his court. He goes west to Chester. I should join him there."

"Why the haste?" I asked.

He shrugged. "Oh, Henry knows the west of England well enough, I suppose," he said. "In his youth, he was under his uncle's tutelage, he who was Duke of Gloucester and spent time there. I should like to think he pays a visit for old time's sake, but in case not, I should be there when he is. Chester is not the best of meeting places."

"Meeting place?"

He said, quietly, "Henry has called his feudal army out. Not quite all, one third perhaps, and those who are not summoned must pay a tax, a scutage, so that with the revenue, he can hire more men if he must. Not a new tax, but one, having found, he will use to fill his coffers, I've no doubt."

"Army?" I asked.

"And for ships, to equip a fleet." He went on talking as if I had not spoken; afterwards I thought there was a sort of nervousness about him that I had never known in him before; but now I only heard the words that were to dim the brightness of the day. "Those Celtic princes of yours," he said, "not satisfied with quarreling among themselves, have let their quarrels spill abroad, as if civil war within their own territories was not enough. There has long been enmity between the rulers of central and northern Wales, both sides claiming land the other holds. Now a prince of the northern line has escaped to Henry's court, moaning for help, maintaining that his brother has robbed him of his estates. You might as well ask a lion which of two fat calves he'll swallow first. Henry has promised this Prince Cadwaladr, a mouthful of a name, to support him, and so attack the northern Celts."

"Support?" I asked, a drumming in my ears and brain, "Attack?"

"God's bones," he said, apprehension suddenly bursting out. He handed the child back to me, began to pace up and down, his head almost at a level where I sat on an upturned keg. His squire, who had been standing behind him, had to skip out of the way. "God's wounds, how can Henry hope to attack the Welsh? How can he march a feudal army through such a land? The Celts live on air, can run barefoot uphill and down if they have to, have skill to vanish when you think you've trapped them, like one of their highland mists. I know, I have sought them out myself often enough. They carry what they need like porters, food, weapons, especially their long Welsh bows which can put an arrow through a coat of mail. Henry's feudal knights need open fields, space to maneuver, level ground to charge, an enemy they can see to charge against. The likes of us are easy pickings for the Welsh."

I did not ask then the last question that trembled on my tongue, but later I did, that night, "And if Henry fights against the Celts, which side will you fight on?" It is a question that perhaps all women must ask who marry with their foes; perhaps my mother lived with it, who had wed an enemy to make a peace; but the thought tore me like a knife.

We were lodged in a simple place at Barfleur, close to the harbor for convenience, so that on still nights, we could hear the hiss of the waves as they washed against the pebbles and sand. The men were bedded down more noisily; some of them bivouacked along the pier, some sat and drank and sang those ribald songs that had amused us so at Sieux, and others stretched out upon their saddlebags while they played at dice, shook them, threw them to make a wager on the consequences of their king's plans, a king whose actions are but common soldier's jests. They were no jest to me.

"Ann," Raoul said softly when I had asked directly in my too blunt way that makes me afterwards almost blush, "I do not say that he *will* fight. He still speaks of treaty, negotiations, talks. But I sense his purpose. As warden, all the king's accounts must pass through me. I know the names, I keep the records, oversee his payments, by studying them, I can guess his intent. A third of England's knights is a goodly number of men. Not even in Stephen's time was such an army raised."

"An army has one purpose," I said, "to fight."

"Yes," he said, "but Henry has not commanded a feudal army in England before. He may not know its strength or its weaknesses. Yet I think myself that talk of parley is but a sop to appease the Welsh. No Angevin can parley without a spear to prick his enemy to heel."

"But Raoul," I cried, "the Celts are not *your* enemy."

He rolled over on his back, lay staring at the rafters. It was still light enough to see him and see his face. I was reminded suddenly of the way he looked that first night at Sieux, when we lay together in the ruins of his castle walls. A sad homecoming he had had then; I prayed that this would not be one.

He said, "I can choose not to go and be called a coward, forfeit my lands, and rightly so, I think. I can refuse to go and pay this scutage Henry asked in the place of military service, a tax so high it will beggar Sedgemont a second time. Or I can go as is my duty and try to protect the peace. And that too I am sworn to do. When I was last at Sedgemont," he said, and he spoke softer now, so that I had to strain to hear him. Our son slept near us on a small pallet bed, but that was not the reason why he spoke the way he did. "When I was last at Sedgemont," he said, "I was wounded, close to death, my lands and titles forfeit. I had reason enough for thought. It is not often that a man is given life back when he thinks it lost, nor time to consider what he might do if it were restored. It seemed to me that God has made us as we are for some purpose of His own. We may not know its cause but so it is, and we must abide the consequence. Some He has created high, some low, and why each is born to his place in life, no man either has power to judge. I was born to high estate, to lands, to rank, to duties which I willingly accept. I vowed if I lived, I should not let them go. For good or evil, God made me master over many men, and as their overlord I must do right by them. He also made me vassal to a king. I shall obey the king in this, if I can. A feudal oath is not easily sworn, easily undone, even to a king I do not trust or like."

He said, "I may not be able to hold Henry back. High King of Wales is a title that would suit him well; he may like to add that to his list of names. But I think to attack the Celts will be a disaster for us. I will prevent it if I can."

He said, "Do not turn from me, Ann. God's wounds, I would not have gone to Poitiers if I had anticipated Henry's plans. If wrong I did, it was to make a right. There has been enough of strain between us; I would not have added another burden to your load. I would not embroil you in their schemes."

He said, his voice husky now with desire, "Do not deny me, Ann. I return to where I was robbed of health and name; I would create new life to take the place of the one I lost."

He panted in my ear, "Thus, thus I spill my seed, thus I make our second heir." In the moonlight, naked we lay, his need as burning as my own; in haste, intent and in my womb, a fire spread. That was the parting we made, that was the making of our second son.

We sailed the next day with the tide. He went on board one ship with his guard, his horses; Robert and I on a second; the others filled with men and supplies. We waved to him as the helmsman bent his long oar to take us out of the bay. Beyond the headland, the waves blew dark, and white caps showed, the green rounded cliffs, like dolphins' backs, rose and fell, and the great white sails came tumbling down with a crack. We set straight passage toward the English coast. But the wind that had been blowing north to give us a quick crossing now veered, blew us back again; for three days it blew so hard, no thunder, no rain, only wind, to drive us off our course. The ships were scattered and my ship rode out the storm alone, tossed this way and that. I remember thinking, when I could think of anything, I knew we should not boast of safety in these ships, and I was used to sea and boats.

There was no danger of our foundering at first, I suppose,

as the White Ship had done, our vessel was stout-built and the
captain competent. But the waves were so high and the seas
so strong that even I thought every moment would be our last.
Not so my son. He exulted in the wind and waves, would have
capered about on deck if he could. I had a soldier tie him to
a leash like a little dog so that he could not escape from the
hold where we lay. So do we reveal our destinies I suppose, a
soldier's son, born to a soldier's world, adventure, danger far
away, his lot.

The third day out we sprang a leak, and then the mariners
jested no more, worked in shifts, sailors and soldiers too, (that
is, those who were able to work, for many lay prostrate with
sickness and fear) to bale the ship. It was an endless task, for
we were heavy-laden and the scuppers were awash. It would
have gone hard with us I think had there been any kind of
rain, but only that contrary wind that still drove us before it
east, then west, so that, at times, it seemed we had drifted
back where we started from. Even the elements conspired to
warn us if I had but read the signs. At last, taking down almost
all the sails, we crept forward with the currents and tide, and
after many days saw the English shore bob into view. Nor was
it easy coming to land through the surf, although Robert leapt
and jumped with joy. I myself, when finally we were tied beside
the jetty of the small English port, I scarcely could bear to
move, the houses and ground still heaved about me so, and
the very pier stones seemed as pliable as wax.

The first news on shore was cheerful. Having escaped the
worst of the wind, Raoul and his ships had already reached
safety, although blown off course as we had been. He had
landed with no mishap save the loss of several barrels of wine,
and as planned, had waited for me. A short wait only, for he
had been forced to go on, had left me messages and an escort.
The man who brought this news and led the escort was one
of my dearest friends, nothing else could have pleased me more.
His name was Geoffrey too—Sir Geoffrey of Sedgemont—
once Lord Raoul's squire, now his seneschal. His fair head, his

good-natured smile, were the first things I made out clearly when I could focus on anything. Now, Sedgemont is the place where I had grown to womanhood, and although I had never counted it my real home (that is at Cambray, where I was born), yet, as the years passed, I cannot deny Sedgemont and all it contained had become as dear to me. And Sir Geoffrey, then a squire of Lord Raoul's guard, and his wife had been my true and trusted companions. A good seneschal had Lord Raoul found in him, although so young, and he answered patiently while I questioned him about his life, his marriage, his children, two of them, a third expected, like to him, he swore, fair-haired, blue-eyed. And I questioned him too on how wagged the world and all our friends whom I longed to see at Sedgemont. Imagine then my surprise, dismay if you will, when I learned the rest of his message, namely that we were not to go there ourselves, but, sending Robert to the care of his wife, were to follow Lord Raoul directly to Cambray. For Raoul, having gone to Sedgemont from the coast, as he had planned, to call up his feudal vassals and their knights, had had to leave at once, disturbed by fresh tidings that took him fast toward the mustering grounds on the salt flats outside Chester, where in early July Henry was to meet his English army.

"For all of England is up in arms," Sir Geoffrey explained while I fretted at this sudden change of plans. "The king, they say, is like a child with a new toy. When he was Count of Anjou, and came fighting here in England, he had no such army at his beck and call, he had to hire his troops, his mercenaries. And they, as I well recall, are the most untrustworthy of men, harder to control than a runaway horse, wreaking damage if they fight or not, more damage truly when they do not fight. A feudal army is the king's own tool." By which outburst you gather how much he cared for his king. He smiled his young and sheepish grin. "And so," he said, "Lord Raoul should be at Chester to make sure the king gives the right orders at the right time. For Lord Raoul hopes Henry will forget that a feudal army serves only for so many days, then has the right to go back home." He grinned once more. "Though, for my part," he said, "I'd not mind seeing Wales again."

At the look I gave, "I remember it from former days," he said, "when I was at Cambray. You had some Celtic prisoners there; I used to like to speak with them. I learned their language and have longed to have the chance to practice it." He tried to recite the phrases he knew; dear life, what a jumble he made of them to make me laugh.

"But why Cambray?" I asked.

At first he said, "You should ask your noble lord that question, lady, I cannot tell." Then, relenting somewhat, for as I have said, he was good-natured, ever eager to please, one of the kindest men, "Lady Ann, the king has a need for border castles, so they say, and a liking for empty ones. Lord Raoul has asked that you and I together keep an eye on yours. This king has more tricks to him than a peddler at a fair, as well I know; his envoys are ever at Sedgemont's gates with this demand or that, this question to be answered, this right upheld. And lawyers they say in London town, clever enough to steal a man's head without his knowing, let alone his lands."

Behind his jesting, I sensed a real concern, which presently, as we rode along toward Cambray, a good week's ride away, I questioned him about. He answered readily enough.

It seems that, on arriving in England, Henry had called a royal council in the east, in Suffolk, without alerting Raoul that is; and taking advantage of a dispute between two lords he had claimed, and taken, all their castles in the eastern part. Now, when he had become king, he had exercised his prerogative to "dismantle" castles that he maintained had been illegally built. This royal order had already proved a cause of concern to many of the nobles, some of the greatest in the land. To claim castles now in his own right, to take them over as royal land, was a new and dangerous device. I could see Raoul's wisdom in having Cambray under close guard.

"As for this king," Geoffrey went on, "he is different from Stephen, there's no doubt. I am not the man to judge these things, but a king who thinks to govern of his own, make his own laws, turn his noble lords aside, he has taken on a thankless task. His lawyers argue he will rule by law, yet he tried to ruin Sedgemont out of spite. One day, I think there will be a reckoning between king's law and lord's law if he drives headlong against our feudal rights. And if he drives headlong into Wales, as Lord Raoul believes he will, we'll all come to grief."

He looked sideways in that west country way I had missed. "But there is a thing I'd like to see," he said. We were riding along through a forest track as he spoke, through that great forest that stretches almost to the borderlands, and he had taken his hawk upon his wrist, for there were many game birds in the open glades. It moved restlessly on his glove as if upon a perch, and spread its wings, although its eyes were still covered with a hood. Sir Geoffrey soothed it by blowing water in its mouth, and smoothed its ruffled plumage with his ungloved hand.

"Do you remember, Lady Ann," he said, "the hawk that Lord Raoul caught and tamed? She was a Welsh falcon, I swear. The mews at Sedgemont has been empty these many years, one blind gerfalcon, one half-blind falconer, the two pensioned off. I should like to restock it. They say that Welsh falcons are the best of their breed. My wish, if it were granted me, would be to ride into those high mountains I once caught a glimpse of and find out where those falcons nest. They say the king had a falcon once," almost shyly he spoke, for a man does not often reveal his inner thoughts, "he swore it could outfly any bird. He loosed it on a Welsh one, perched on a cliff, and it, untamed, rose higher than the king's, struck down and tore it all to bits. Such a hawk I should like to find and tame, if such a savage bird can be tamed."

I thought, God forbid that be an omen for these times. And I said, "Another thing to steal from us?"

"Not steal," he said, his round face crumpled into concern, "God's life, I meant not ill. By the Mass, I am no thief. But a wild thing is anyone's prey I think, nor does it belong to anyone, being free. It is not easy to climb into a wild bird's nest, easy enough if we had wings, but I should like to try. They say those rocky cliffs go into the clouds, but above the clouds there are still higher cliffs, and a man who climbs there feels one with the birds." He blushed to the roots of his fair hair.

"Now rot my tongue," he said. "I have no wish to war nor steal upon the Celts, but I would see their lands again."

"And if they fight," I said, "who will win?"

Again came that worried frown. "Lady Ann," he said, "I cannot speak treason. Yet I think, like their hawks, those Welsh will fight the fiercer being free. They love their freedom and will die for it. Even in those Celtic prisoners I spoke of, I noted that. But Lord Raoul will prevail against the king. And we, no more unpleasant talk, we'll hunt awhile and you can see how this bird flies." He loosed the lure, rode out merrily after her, as if we were hawking along the woodlands near Sedgemont. And so, presently, I rode after him, the June morning, for we were now well into June, like liquid gold, flowing round us in the sun. And so, with good cheer and company, he led the way toward Cambray.

These were the last days of my youth, so let me savor them in the company of my childhood friends. Now like a thundercloud, the pent up storm was about to break.

After a day or so, we left the forests to cross farmlands which still showed signs of civil war, were still in part unoccupied where battle had wrecked homes and fields. I could not help contrasting them with those fair and placid lands of Anjou, and felt anger in me rise that, keeping his own territories free from want, Henry should be at liberty to jeopardize again these English ones. *High King of Wales will fit him very well.* Ambition never is content, I thought, it feeds upon itself; not count nor duke nor king will satisfy him until the whole of the world is his. And I thought, too, what his brother had said, a god he had called him, that his grandfather would have all men bow down before, so as a child, so now a man. He has changed,

King Henry, Sir Renier said, he has grown to kingship; as soon expect the seasons to swing in reverse, as soon stop the turning of the tides.

We were come by now to a stretch of road that seemed familiar to me, bearing west, before turning south once more, toward Cambray. Sometimes the road, or track would be a more fitting word, was faintly visible when you scanned ahead; sometimes it dipped into a hollow where there should have been good grazing, had there been cattle or sheep; and sometimes, when it rose up to high ground, you could see the round whaleback foothills stretching ahead in undulating lines. They reminded me of those hills Raoul had shown me on his chart those months ago, almost unreal, round and soft and green. *Safely home.* Well, Cambray was my own true home I suppose, and I supposed safety waited for us there. Toward noon one day then, we clattered through a village, rare indeed to find one still intact though sparsely inhabited, more an intersection of several paths with a scatter of houses in between. We followed the more deeply rutted road which led to the well, and when we stopped to drink, we sensed rather than saw how anxious eyes watched us from behind locked doors. At length, guessing we meant no immediate harm, a young lad ventured out to ask what news. In his border way, he gave his tidings first, then his question, the one I think that gnawed at all men.

"Throughout this week," he said, "armed men have been on the move, going west. Banners flying, soldiers marching, provision trains. My sire says not since Stephen's time has he seen men so armed, so marching. There'll not be war here again, lords?"

"Nay, nay," Sir Geoffrey, ever kind, comforted him, "no fear of that. They go further west."

Catching my eye, he was silent, threw the lad some coins, bid the men mount up. War planned indeed, but not against these miserable souls, but yet a war to make other men miserable so that a king, great king, could add the name of Wales to his titles list, to balance nicely perhaps the dukedom of Brittany, when he got round to coveting it!

We mounted and rode on, Sir Geoffrey talking of this and that, as was his way, to put our minds at ease. Beyond the village, the path rose steeply between a hedge of hazel bushes. A narrow path it was, winding in and out until it came to the crest of a hill. And as we passed a battered hayrick, lying on its side these score of years, a group of armed men rode out behind us.

"'Ware, arms," Sir Geoffrey roared, he snapped his scabbard round, jerked free his sword, put spurs to horse. He snatched his shield from his squire and wheeled to face what danger threatened from our rear. His men, scrabbling for their shields, threw them up to make a wall, backed two by two to surround me. Between them, I peered out. This was certainly not a comfortable place for an ambush.

But I knew the leader of the men well, even before his soft voice cried out, "Hold. God save you masters, you start like fox before the hounds," he reassured my escort, "Your mistress recognizes me, if you do not."

He pushed back his coif with its sprig of broom, the black curls blew. Over his mail he wore the Angevin surcoat, embroidered in gold the Angevin lily for purity. And he smiled as if we had met but yesterday and met as friends. "Why, Lady Ann," he said boldly, riding up to us, his horse that one he had ridden once into my life at Boissert, thrusting its powerful way through our line, "you have failed to greet us, I am but a traveler like you through these deserted wastes. We go to join my brother's mustering. And you?"

He and that other Geoffrey, each so-called, as unalike as beer and wine, one plain and honest, dependable, the other fickle, capricious, treacherous, they stared at each other stony-faced as I named them both. Already the Angevins had flowed round us. They did not unsheath their weapons as we had done but came on empty-handed with arms outstretched as if in welcome, as if to say Godspeed, friend, or Good day, or any word that one kindly group would pass another with, meeting by chance like this on a lonely road. Yet this was no chance meeting and so I knew. Our men fidgeted, wiped their hands, looked foolish with their drawn swords, and turned to Sir Geoffrey for command.

He too was caught unprepared by this show of friendship. "Lady Ann," he tried to ask, "what are these men?"

I knew he asked, are they friend or foe—if foe, in a moment it would be too late, they would have surrounded us and our hope of a sudden breakthrough would be lost. They outnumbered us, looked well-armed, well-horsed but—friend or foe, how was that to be reckoned, how to know on which side anyone fought these days? Geoffrey Plantagenet had crowded past our ranks toward me. His blue cloak was tipped with fur, his squire close behind him carried sword and shield and bore his helmet with the Angevin crest. He looked himself a prince.

"So, Ann," he said, as easily as if we walked along the garden at Poitiers, "is this the way to meet after such a while? Hearing of your convoy hence, for at the coast there was talk of storm, delays, I thought to wait to offer you protection along the road. I thought you might have need of another horse, having taken mine last time."

I heard our men suck in their breath, his insolence offended them, there was a mutter at his insults. Geoffrey of Sedgemont tightened his hand upon his sword. To him, beside me, I said beneath my breath, "Forbear, no harm in him. Let me deal with him, stay calm."

Which was a lie; seeing him, I felt all my old apprehensions grow.

To the other, "My Lord Plantagenet," I said, as casually he spoke so should I, "or is it Count I should call you these days? My husband is not here. I am sure you look for him. He rides ahead to attend the king."

Geoffrey Plantagenet smiled his beautiful smile, but without warmth or mirth. "I also serve the king," he said, "see, I carry his coat of arms upon my back. But I was looking for you, Countess of Sieux. I guessed you must pass this way. It was not difficult to learn your husband's plans for you." He had noticed how my men eyed him, and for caution or courtesy, spoke low. I felt myself blush with chagrin. Looking at him with the wind blowing through his hair, blowing color into those fine-cut cheeks, you would have thought him the epitome of knighthood, like to charm a woman out of mind. Yet with what effrontery he spoke, and when he stretched out his hand, the scar upon it was still marked clear.

"You parted with me coldly," he was protesting, his voice full of reproach, "I looked for joy on seeing you. What harm, to ride as companions on this open road? Your face is as melancholy as your words. I told you you were niggardly. Well, I thought, since I'm to serve my life in Brittany, what better chance to find out all there is to know about the Celts than join the king in his Welsh campaign..."

Every other word a lie or half lie, yet also half a truth. As always, I did not know what to believe of him.

"Not likely to learn much," I said, "a land of mist and fog until a Welsh arrow takes you by the throat. Best for you to retreat now to southern parts, more to your taste and style than here. I thought fighting was not in your line. Besides," I hesitated, "when you speak of fighting, remember it is my kin you fight."

"God's life," he said, "the mist does not dampen your tongue. But who speaks of fight?" He looked at me, bold as brass. "The quickest way to get what you want," he said, "is to woo a woman to your bed. Most come willingly I admit. But then, not all are are beautiful as you are."

I shook my head to deaden the sense of what he said, tried to push my horse on. It was impossible—our men and his were already intertwined—there was no room to pass; we were all mingled together in the narrow path. As I have explained, on both sides hazel trees grew on a hedge, planted in west country style, first a wall, stone made, banked with turf and flowers and gorse, with a line of trees on top, making it impossible to break out of them. It was also impossible to ride more than two abreast, which he, taking my reins as if in friendship, now did. I felt Geoffrey of Sedgemont move in place behind. "Come, beautiful Lady Ann," Geoffrey Plantagenet whispered, "you welcomed me at Boissert. If I had won, I would have made you queen. Nor did you scorn me first at Poitiers."

"You had not then planned my husband's death," I said, "nor yet my son's."

"By the Rood," he swore, "always the same tune, each time another sin to curse me with. Isobelle de Boissert acted alone, she and her tiring woman. And the queen. I promised I would never harm you or yours. Did hurt come to you from me at Poitiers? I think rather you hurt me. Did I complain that you stole my horse? I could have kept you there had I wanted."

"And my husband knocked you down into the mud," I said, "where you belong."

He almost reined back then, with that sudden flash of more than anger distorting his face, but he kept his voice low. "Ever swift-tongued," he said. "I like women with fire, but not to burn. Ann, be reasonable. Why argue over old wrongs. I am made a count at last, my needs are well taken care of. I make no bones I admire you. No," he gestured for silence, "I do not deny that the lands and titles of Sieux became you well when I knew who you were. But it was not as a countess that you caught my eye. And although I admit I have no love for Count Raoul, is not all fair in love and war? As for war, if I told you I will join Henry in his campaign, would that endear me to you? I think not."

A shrewd remark, and again half true, half lie.

When I tried to speak, he warned me. "Be careful," he said, "my men are restless, so are yours. If we fight with words, they may with weapons. I'd not want more blood on my hands."

We rode on in silence for a while, and again I sensed that flicker of another life, another possibility, another way, behind those deep-set eyes, a loneliness, a regret perhaps. He knew what I had sensed. "It is no sin to love," he wheedled me, "I have never pretended otherwise than that I would have you if I could. Come away with me, Ann. I have horses waiting and men to attend us. We can be at a Cornish harbor within days. The Cornish sailors are rough and ready men, but they know the coast of Brittany like their own; they'll take us safely back to Nantes."

"I cannot," I said.

He said, "Your marriage is a forced one at best; there are French cardinals who would annul it if I so requested. Trust me. If a learned council could permit Eleanor so easily to leave the King of France; if yet another council let a King of France, years ago, steal a beautiful Countess of Anjou, my granddam, I suppose, why then, we'll make a third Council of Beaugency to end your marriage with Count Raoul, give you to me."

When I could speak, "No," I said. My lip jutted out as I know it does when my mind is set. "I'll not break oath."

"Then Heaven help us both," he said. "You did not think Henry or his queen would show me so much favor without some favor in return. You have had a chance to choose. Take me, and be saved. Unloved, we both are lost." He had almost reached the top of the hill, before us stretched the first range of the high mountains, some of them still snow-peaked. And immediately ahead lay the boundary ditch or dyke with its mound of earth, thrown up centuries ago to make the border between Celtic lands westward, non-Celtic east. South of it lies Cambray.

"I will not ride on with you," I told him stubbornly. "Our way parts here."

"No," his answer was equally abrupt. "We ride on together, north."

He repeated, as if it were the most natural thing in the world, "North, of course, to join my brother, who has planned on meeting you. He has come out hunting along the border here and expects me. I told him you would not disappoint us. He is not so particular as I am about receiving another man's wife. Especially a wife of Raoul of Sedgemont. He'll welcome you with open arms." He let go of my bridle, threw his hand out, the red scar was etched across one palm to remind him of me each time he looked at it.

"Henry is my brother, Lady Ann," he said; now the mask

was shut down, all thoughts were hidden and all hopes of what might have been put aside, "you do not think he would give away a title, a city, with its wharves and piers, without some recompense. Bringing you to him will more than pay my debt."

I sat back as if contemplating the choice. And even now, I am not sure he would have done what he said, take me to Henry, that is, although I think he might have tried abduction as an easier alternative. But I could not be sure, and not knowing forced me to act as if he would. At the hilltop, there would be open ground, space for the Sedgemont men to filter through and regroup where the narrow path ended and open moors began.

I leaned toward him, said as loudly as I could, "No choice then, why should I run? Take me with you. Come closer, love." I caught the scandalized look on Sir Geoffrey's face, the shocked look of disbelief; the Angevins heard me as well and, seeing their lord lean toward me with a smile, held back. And Geoffrey Plantagenet, God forgive me, in his complacency, for a moment he believed me, too. It gained us a second's respite. I took it. I rowelled my horse forward against his, jostling his out of line. It was bigger, stronger, yet I forced the pace in such a way he was pushed off balance down the facing hillside. "*A moi, Sedgemont,*" I screamed, again crowding him. I was on the uphill side so that, although his horse was more powerful, I had a slight advantage. With whip and spur I urged my horse on; I saw his look dissolve to astonishment and anger; I heard behind me the rasp of weapons as Sir Geoffrey gave the order to attack. The other Geoffrey, that dark Plantagenet, as dark as was my old friend fair, struggled to control his horse, tried to catch mine, curses breaking from that carved mouth, the more foul, he the more beautiful seemed. On the hilltop, a man cried out in pain, I heard the Angevin's battle cry, "*Vallée! Vallée!*" as his men rallied. *Men will die for you.* God forgive me again, but I let them die that day.

Pulling at my horse's head, I jerked it round, plunged on downhill; breakneck I went, letting the horse slide on its haunches when the ground became too steep. Another outcrop

of stone and hedge waited at the hill's end, I found a gap and
forced my way through, banking it as west country riders learn
to do on the moors, no hope of overleaping such walls. Then
on to level ground, at a gallop, thrashing through the undergrowth, over bush and rock until I broke into another open
field, no cover there, the dry earth thudding behind like following hooves. But when at last I dropped back to trot, to
walk, and I wiped the hair out of my eyes, I was alone, the
sight and sound of fighting far away, even the sky and sun had
clouded shut. And presently, as I plodded on, I saw that the
grayness surrounding me was not night come early, but one of
those border mists rolling down from the mountain peaks. That
mist now gave me the cover that I needed and, at first, I
welcomed it. Soon, however, I realized its blessing was mixed.
I lost my enemies, it is true; I also lost myself. For I had intended
to ride toward the dyke, tracing a path along the eastern rim,
keeping the sun on my right, that way eventually I must reach
Cambray. Now disoriented, as is the common fate of victims
of a moorland fog, I lost track of distances, direction, time.
My horse had almost foundered after such hard riding; I often
had to dismount to lead it over the rough stones, then struggle
to find a rock to climb up on its back. Once a mountain stream,
it must have come from those distant peaks the water ran so
cold, blocked our way so we were forced into a long detour.

By now, the evening chills had spread; it would be dark
soon tonight. Bitterly, I regretted having left my friends, to
have escaped and abandoned them. I put that thought aside,
stumbled on. I was cold, heartsick. And I will say now I think
that night on the open moors sapped my strength in such a
way that long afterward, I felt the effects of it. For it seemed
sometimes as if I floated through a cloud of wool, where objects
grew large, then small, or as if the ground beneath my feet
were not solid ground at all, or as if my feet had grown so
numb as not to have sensation in them. And when I heard a
noise, a sudden noise in the dim uncertainty ahead, it echoed
and echoed in my ears like the booming noise the sea makes
in a cave. But my horse had heard the noise, too; it pricked

its ears and began to step more quickly, anticipating food and warmth.

The mist appeared to brighten. I thought I saw a flare, a light perhaps from some isolated farm where I could hide. The thought of shelter lured me on; I seemed to ride in a kind of daze, yet even if I would, I could not stop. The track had narrowed again into a gorge, no hope to cut across it, no way to go back. So we rode on until at last a solid line of rock, like a wall, blocked the path.

The wall was made of stones, cut stones, dripping with wet, and from within them, or above them, came voices, Norman ones. I raised my own to answer them. Silence followed, as loud as noise; my heart throbbed; my body felt encased in ice. Now, there are places on the western moors which all men shun, that circle of stones near Cambray, for one. This was another such place. Evil had a taste, a smell, a feel, to make the hair rise; the stones I brushed against were cold and wet with the dampness of many years, as if, even on fine days, moisture collected there. The flares floated in midair as if the men who held them were peering down from some high place, and the sudden gusts of wind that blew down the gorge seemed to carry with them the sound of unspoken things, dark and terrible.

We rounded the last curve of the wall, came to a gateway I think, black and somber. There was a clatter, a scrape of chains. I heard my horse's footsteps suddenly ring out hollowly, as if we crossed a drawbridge.

And now I had come into an open space, where men were waiting to close the gate. "Jesu," I heard one man say and saw him cross himself. I would have laughed had my mouth not been frozen closed. The torches began to give a shape, a size, to this place, a courtyard revealed itself; the outer walls, castle walls such as Normans make. There is only one other Norman castle made of stone within reach of Cambray, built like it, close to the dyke. I thought Henry had destroyed it, one of those border castles he had sworn to raze, an unauthorized fortress made in Stephen's time, who had permitted it. A Norman castle, a border castle—where my enemies had lived and plotted the deaths of my brother and of my father and of me. And when the guards stepped hastily aside, glad to get out of my path, I was not even surprised to see the man who stood at the top of the stairs. Why should I have felt surprise or fear? It was all ordained long ago. The wheel had come full circle and I was here.

And, "You are welcome to Maneth Castle," Henry said.

11

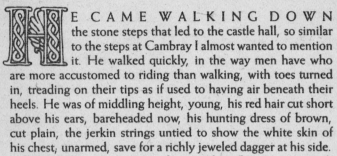E CAME WALKING DOWN
the stone steps that led to the castle hall, so similar
to the steps at Cambray I almost wanted to mention
it. He walked quickly, in the way men have who
are more accustomed to riding than walking, with toes turned
in, treading on their tips as if used to having air beneath their
heels. He was of middling height, young, his red hair cut short
above his ears, bareheaded now, his hunting dress of brown,
cut plain, the jerkin strings untied to show the white skin of
his chest, unarmed, save for a richly jeweled dagger at his side.

"No courtesy as is correct for your king?"

His voice was harsher than his brother's voice, plainer spoken, without guile or charm, although they claimed he could
be charming when he wanted something. His eyes were gray
and bold, that undressed each woman where she stood. The
white skin was mottled with the cold, the Angevin temper held
in check, that man, whose brother I had escaped, only to run
full tilt against the older, more dangerous king.

"By God," he repeated, "no smile, that men claim makes
their blood run hot, no kiss of peace? Not even a nod of your
head. Then I bid you good even, doubly spoke, for your lack
of it."

When I still sat motionless upon my horse, he snapped his
fingers in the way I remembered.

"Bring her," he said, spun round and strode up the stairs.
And I thought, Why struggle, why fight, the wheel is come
full circle and I am here.

I was too cold to stand on my feet; they crumpled under

me. I had not realized I could be so cold. His huntsmen, or
so they seemed by dress and speech, and the courtyard was
crowded with the evidence of a chase—hounds, horns, stretch-
ers of wood to drag the quarry, bowmen, spearmen, but no
knights of quality—his huntsmen helped me dismount, pulled
me up the steps. And when I came into the great hall, slowly,
dragging myself like an old woman, the king stood alone by
the fire, no courtiers in sight, alone then except for his huntsmen and squires. A table had been pushed before the hearth
and was set with food. It was a simple meal, a jug of ale, roast
game, some bread, thrust aside half-eaten. In one corner of
the room a heap of cloaks and furs made a makeshift bed, in
another his hunting gear, his sword, were jumbled in a heap.
A few torches gave a fitful light, the rest of the hall was dark,
disused these many years. There was a strong smell of mold
and damp.

"Sit you down," he said, showing no surprise at seeing me,
puzzled perhaps only that I rode unaccompanied, without escort, so sure his orders had been obeyed, so sure of his plans.
"Geoffrey said you would come with him; he could persuade
you, he said, when we heard you journeyed late and alone
toward Cambray . . ."

"He may be dead for all I know," I heard my own voice
reply, hoarse, as if it had rusted over from ill-use, "I left him
in a hurry, so did not stop to ensure it."

His expression clouded over. "Dead," he exclaimed, "and
you dare speak of that. You would not make a jest of my
brother's death?"

"Or perhaps he lives," I shrugged. "As a prisoner of him and
his men I stood on no ceremony, made good my escape while
I had a chance." I marveled at how my voice stayed cool and
level once I had got it to speak at all. It seemed I had learned
a lesson on how to deaden feelings and stifle them. But all
around me seemed numb, dead and cold.

He said, as if taken aback, "God's my life, what mean those
words, prisoner, escape? No violence, I looked for no violence.
Hearing from my brother that he would keep you company,

as pleased you, or so he claimed, I asked him to make a detour here so I could speak with you, in the absence of your noble lord, to ask a favor of you in his name. Nothing more. You see how I am come here to hunt, could have wished to show you better courtesy. We expected you and my brother as your escort, nothing else." But his smile, his knowing look, gave the lie to his words.

"To bring me here under guard? To force me and my men?" I challenged him.

"Not so, not so," he said. He eyed me, in the way he had.

"But you came of your own free will," he next told me, "alone. Lost, it was chance that brought you here..."

"Or the devil," I said.

He tried a smile, "Or God, perhaps. Many use God or His counterpart to justify whatever actions they take. God must have grown impervious, I think, to such overuse of His name."

"That is blasphemy," I told him, "and a sin. Are you not afraid of God to threaten me?"

He moved impatiently, almost nervously. "Let God stay in His own Heaven," he said. "I have seen enough of death, enough to last a lifetime; I've yet to meet man, or woman, who goes willingly to it, or God, who would not cling to life even for a few moments more. But you, lady, you are not afraid to ride alone, I think. You show your independence like a man. So came you to my queen at Poitiers, so came you to my court in London two years ago, although a suppliant then, to ask a favor of me. You owe me one." His words flicked out, a cat's quick pounce to make me retreat. "I have not forgotten what then you asked, what I should have refused, God's wounds. A maiden fair, the queen claimed, yet in truth, no maid, your maidenhead already lost, looking to be wed to hide your shame. God helped you then, I suppose?"

He went on talking to frighten me, to play with me like a cat, to stoke his anger. In the fire's heat, his scant red curls had ringed themselves as a bull's hair does and he fixed his gray eyes full on me. He said, as if a request so simple could not be refused, as if bluntness were excuse enough, "So it is now my turn to ask a favor of you, since I gave you one, since I gave you your desire, tricked into it. Thus will *your* debt be paid to me, so your husband had me pay him at Poitiers." He let that threat sink in. "You will not scorn our hospitality while we determine what payment is just. Our entertainment's scant enough, but yours to enjoy." He had no need to add, Provided you do what I want.

"I have lived roughly these past years," I too spoke directly, without pretense or denial. "Sieux has been in ruins above my head. I need no comforts. I have endured far worse than this."

As if I had not spoken, he went on. "Shall I call for wine, for meat? You have a peaked and famished look, not like your own."

I said, "Since morning, I have seen my companions, my friends, ambushed and betrayed. I believe them dead. Shall I eat or drink, forgetting them?"

And a sudden wave swept over me at the thought of my abandoned friends, their bodies tipped in some ditch, Sedgemont in mourning for them; Sir Geoffrey's wife and children weeping for a husband, father, who would not return, his kind heart stilled, he who would never see the Welsh mountains now, nor catch the hawk he longed to tame.

"I ask you, King, for restitution for their deaths, and for all the deaths you have so needlessly caused." My words came out the stronger for the pain that prompted them. "It is your royal prerogative to keep the peace. Then keep it, or on your conscience be its weight."

He gaped at me. "By God," he said, almost thoughtfully, "Geoffrey said there was fire beneath the cold. Come now, Ann of Cambray, who has tricked me once and thinks no doubt to try again, what will you give me in repayment?"

"What do you want?" I asked.

"Tell Raoul to do as I bid. He has already come to Chester before me, full of arguments, warnings, gloom. As warden of the marcher lands, he should obey me, not I him."

It was my turn almost to laugh at his boy's demand, asking for the moon.

"I need him," he was continuing. "God's teeth, without him, half the men I've gathered there will default, and he is the best cavalry leader I have. Aye, and one other thing I need," this time, the open flash of his lion claws, "that you give up Cambray."

"Cambray is not mine to give," I replied, "nor should I recommend its gift to you."

"I must have it," as if that were excuse. "I hold Maneth in the center, Chester in the north. Cambray to the south would complete a dam to keep those Celts from spilling out..."

"No," I said. "And rather than keep the Celts from spilling out, I'd rather prevent *you* from spilling in."

My obstinacy took away my own breath as it did his.

"Now, by the Mass," he shouted, his color beginning to mount, "I need not another woman to tell me what to do. I've wife for that. I require, must have, Cambray. Like Maneth, it was illegally built, for that alone it is forfeit."

"No," a second time I contradicted him. "My father, Falk, built it at the express command of Henry who was king at that time, your grandfather. Falk held it in vassalage from Earl Raymond who was then Earl of Sedgemont and Lord Raoul's grandsire. My father served Earl Raymond well, as did Earl Raymond serve his king. As will Lord Raoul serve you."

He had begun to pace back and forth with his springy stride, a Norman trait, I think, that they cannot long be still. In London, I had known Henry to take a thing, a piece of wood, a shard of metal, and bend and twist it out of shape, grind a lock apart, as if he must be forever doing something with his hands; so now, turn by turn, he marched about, as if his legs could not bear to be rooted to one place.

"One other thing," I told him, my last roll of the dice to match with his, "this castle here, this castle at Maneth, it belonged to my enemies, who killed my father and my brother and would have killed me. You received them at your court as friends, made much of them. I will not have them gloat from their graves that Cambray should be given away. I will not betray my house for them. They sought revenge and it killed them. Be careful you do not meet the same end."

"God's wounds, do you now threaten me?" he swore. "Call out my guard. We could ride to Cambray within the day. At its gate, see then what words you would shout out to make your men inside run to open it."

"It would not open," I said. "With my last breath, I'd bid my men keep it shut."

"Last breath," he was breathing heavily himself. "That's easily said. There are ways to make people talk. And Maneth Castle is full of them. Look here." He dragged me by the arm toward a wall on the further side of the fire. A chest stood aslant against a tapestry, and with a vicious kick, he scraped the chest aside and tore down the hangings in a shower of dust and moth. Behind them was a door, worm-eaten too, with rusted bolts that he snapped open with one hand. A cold and bitter smell gushed up from a dark stairwell, coated with green so that the very walls seemed wet, as if water seeped through them.

"Down there," he said, staring into the darkness himself, "are things you have not dreamed of."

He let me go and waited, legs braced, staring into that dark, cruel hole. Death and despair came from it, and the silent cries of tormented men.

I know I flinched; I know I drew back, danger heavy in me like lead, the blackness so overwhelming I could not think. This is what my enemies had threatened me with when they had captured me, the place where the lords of Maneth kept their power. Fear rose like vomit in my throat.

"The men who built and used that den were devils," I gasped, "not humans. Turn away. That is no place for you, not for anyone, much less a king." I saw indecision, yes, and fear in his own eyes, as anger struggled in them. I know few dared stand up to him, perhaps only Raoul and now myself. And perhaps his queen. I do not think many men said no to Henry of Anjou. Long ago I had been warned that granting favors, he would not forget. So now the payment must be made. So now, through me, he would have revenge. He paced and paced about. I saw how the sweat beaded his forehead under the scant fringe of hair and how he knotted his fingers so the joints cracked. I had seen his rage before, that Angevin rage which makes men work like maddened bulls, kneading their enemies into dust, grinding them. I had heard he would lie upon the ground and howl like a beast, eyes unfocused, reason gone. Such rage would take him now, so that he would not know what he did.

"I could put the name of witch on you," he panted heavily, "I could brand you witch and harlot. Geoffrey said you were hot beneath your skirts. Suppose we try, suppose we take Raoul's wife, spread her apart with whip and rod, would Cambray be too high a price?"

"You'd not dare," I whispered, "against your own law."

"God rot your tongue," he whispered back, "I'll rip it out. As king, I dare all things. Who would stop me, who would know?"

A thought struck him and he paused and smiled, not his brother's smile but one I remembered from court days, older, knowing, lewd. "Or beshrew me, perhaps Geoffrey tells the truth for once and you are already harlot hot. I have broken border wenches before, even they can be satisfied. Take off your clothes."

"No," I mouthed the word through dry lips.

"A third denial." His voice had slurred with lust, those gray eyes sparked. "On your knees before your king. Or is it," and again he smiled, "you prefer I take you in the Celtic way?"

Step-by-step, I drew back toward the wall as he advanced step-by-step. The blood beat in my head, no weapon at hand for defense, my little knife lost long ago at Poitiers; he unarmed, save for that ceremonial dagger; his great sword was propped beside the bed, but I had seen him rip things apart with his bare hands. Soon there was nothing behind me except the torch lights guttering in the draught from that open stairwell. The main stairs were guarded. There was no way out except down that fearful passageway. I had said I would not struggle, would not fight against fate, yet seeing it upon me, I knew I was wrong. To the end we must fight. So Raoul had fought when hope was lost, so now must I.

His feet scraped on the stone; in a moment, like a bull he would charge. I turned and fled down the steps. They were damp and slippery, thick with slime; headlong I went, fell against the side, rolled several feet, struggled up and fell again. I heard him behind me, cursing savagely as he tried to wrench a torch from the wall, tried to peer where I had gone. Battered, dazed, I came up on all fours, crept forward; the steps still went down and in the dark I followed them, step by painful step whilst now, above, he followed, equally cautiously. The room or cell where I came was small, or large—I could not tell—perhaps many rooms opening off each other or perhaps only this one. Darkness there had no shape, no sound, yet there were sounds everywhere. And evil, like a thickness you could touch, the evil of black and tortured minds working their fantasies upon other poor souls. I felt my way back until there was a wall behind me, a wall or corner or just an alcove, feeling with my fingertips along the stones as one might feel along a bloody wound, delicately, causing pain. For pain and terror dwelt here, too; I felt my flesh curdle with pity of it. And in my hand slid a thing, cold and hard and sharp. God put it there, and what it was I do not know, but with it, I was saved.

He had come clattering down the rest of the steps, still alone, and stood there blinking in the dark. I waited in my corner, hugging my weapon to my breast. Along my arms, my sides, the bruises burned and throbbed; there was blood upon my cheek running into my mouth, but all I felt was a sudden great surge of relief that I should have the means to be free of him.

"So there you are," he snarled and came toward me, "so anxious to meet old friends, you run to them. But I'll have you first before they do." He gestured around him where, in the torch shadows, all kinds of shapes, thick and heavy, loomed out of the blackness beyond. The light fell on my face, he saw me and saw what I held. It was a rusty kind of thing, twisted, black with soot, but the point was sharp.

It did not deter him.

"By God," he said, "you'll not threaten me with that. Although even to threaten a king is death, that'll not kill me, but will be just cause to end your life."

"Aye," I said, "so I mean it to. Stand back, Henry of Anjou. I have found means of escape that even you cannot take from me." And I held the point fixed below my heart.

"God's teeth, hell's fire," he cursed, saliva falling in a spray, "God's Holy Wounds, give it me."

On the stairs behind him, I heard men's feet running, men calling him. "Not one step closer," I cried, almost triumphantly, "but let them look. Talk your way out of this, great King, a scandal and shame you'll not live down."

I have never been so close to death I think, not by his hand, but by my own. Now, telling you, I wonder at myself to have had the strength, to have had the will, death in that way being God's greatest sin. Yet I felt then God would see and forgive, and so a peace came over me, the like I have not known before.

Not he. He stamped and swore, bid his men be gone, then called them back. They hovered like poor ghosts, half-dead themselves from fright, gaping about them.

"My death is in your hands," I cried, when once more he tried to draw close. "It matters little to me, only that I shall not be dishonored, or dishonor Raoul. You cannot touch him, great King, through me. What he will do is his own choice, but I will not give up Cambray, nor will I yield to you." And I shouted those words out loudly enough so that they all would hear.

Finally, he drove his men away, walked back and forth within the circle of the one light he'd brought, gnawed his knuckles as an animal gnaws on bones.

"And when you lie dying," I said, "let death stop your ears. All those men you have needlessly killed or hounded to their graves will be there before you, shouting out their wrongs at

God's feet. Cursed will you be. An icy Hell will make you regret the wrong you do to me and mine."

"No," he cried. I thought he would fling himself against me and braced myself. He shook like a man addled in all his wits, thwarted of his desire, in an agony of rage. "Put no curse on me," he cried. "Cursed am I in marriage to a woman who first was my father's concubine, who sucks me dry as a winter reed. Pithless am I with her, empty, and nightly forced to service her for her needs. Aye, sons enough to breed them up against me in hate. And cursed in my kingship, won by treachery so my sons will mock me that I was born but a count and they are born the sons of a king. And cursed in my birth, dear God, cursed there, most of all that men should point at me in scorn to say my father never fathered me. I need no more curses from anyone."

Presently, he grew calmer, hunkered down on that filthy ground, not too close, yet sitting where I could see him.

"I'll not harm you, Ann of Cambray," he said. "I'll not have Raoul of Sedgemont mock me too that his wife reduced me to the like of Guy of Maneth who lived here. Be done, for the sweet Virgin's sake. I am spent."

I watched him carefully. Such protestations must hide some trick, I thought, until it dawned on me that he spoke truth. Anger such as his, such angry lust, can not endure long; each feeds upon itself. Done with, they are done, no more force or will in them. *That Angevin temper is his curse.* Finished with anger, he became a normal man. And then too, I have heard since, Henry, like many hot-tempered men, was afflicted, or blessed, with a superstitious nature, which racked him with fears. In aftertimes, I have heard it said that when he took sick, like to die, he moaned and wept, promised half his kingdom to his priests if they would intercede with God to give him back his health. Spared, he forgot those fears, and certainly forgot his promises to the Holy Church. And so I think, although he might, in time, forget any promise to me, (and did, to my great harm) my words now had touched a chord, a nervousness in him; he shook with fatigue, his violent energy dispersed, as weak as a child he sat.

And then there was my position, too; a burst of energy had driven me also these last moments, hours even, since Sir Geoffrey's death. I could not stay long bound to such a pitch. The cold that had been seeping into my bones had almost crippled me. I must either use my weapon now while I had the will, or, hesitating, no longer would be capable. And in this Henry again spoke the truth; rare are men or women who, when faced with life or death, will not choose life if they can.

"Give me your word," I said, "swear on what you hold most dear."

"My sword," he said, "there is nothing else by which I have taken and kept all that I inherited, by which I keep all that I intend to get. On my sword, I swear." He sat back on his heels, as soldiers do, as if about to play a game of dice. I did the same, two veterans then, who had played at a game of wills, and gossiped as soldiers do. But I had still my weapon in my hand.

"And can it be true," he said, "that you cleave to Lord Raoul and he to you? They said it was not so, but I think it is. Then is he blessed among men."

"We did not look for love, great King," I said.

"Love." He almost spat. "Where is such a thing that does not leech the lifeblood away? See here."

He reached beneath the lacings of his dirty tunic, fumbled with his linen shirt. Under it, he had slung a leather bag tied with a thong; inside it was golden chaplet. "See this," he said. He put it on his head askew. "An ass's crown, the heavier grows the more it's worn. If I put it on, will men bow down to me? Yet I own more of the kingdom of France than the French king, I own all of England, and when I'm done, I'll be lord from the northern sea to the Mediterranean one, holder of an Angevin Empire larger than any in Christendom since the time of Charlemagne. Is one small castle too much to ask? It was not only to wreak a little vengeance or to make a little sport that I desired your presence here. I speak of lands and plans that will change our world and make or unmake it for generations to come.

"Your Raoul is a gracious man," he said. "There, I will admit, I could find in my heart to admire him, most of all his skills with men. They do not follow him for gain, are loyal to him because they will, not because they must. But there will be changes in this land, new ideas, new laws, new forms of government. We cannot bind ourselves to these feudal oaths, although I might like them better, too, better at least than the ones that will follow them. Although you have doubted my law, yet one day we shall rule by law, not faith. One day, men will have to decide between Lord Raoul and Henry the King and will judge us. I do not think I shall stand so ill, although my English lords look at me askance. To head an empire is not an easy task," he said, "I do not expect to win it easily. But win I shall in the end. And even Raoul must acknowledge that."

"He will acknowledge anything," I said, "save his dishonor."

"Then bid him march with me when I march. The mustering is called for the seventh of July, at the salting flats. A seventh day of a seventh month in a year that ends with seven, that should shake the Celtic mysteries. We meet at Chester but I'll cross higher north at Basingwerk and take the Celts in the rear, unexpecting us. Then will there be peace as you request, then they'll cease their raids across the border plaguing us, then shall I be High King of Wales as well."

Of all the things he said, these last words made a great impact. I felt them grow and fill my mind, like echoes of something heard long ago, like echoes in that tunnel underground, like a wind that blows...

I think he must have caught me as I swooned; I think perhaps he himself carried me up those stairs; I think I lay against his broad chest and heard his heart beat. I woke to find him rubbing my hands between his own. I lay upon the pile of cushions dragged before the fire and a little page with frightened face crept in with a cup of warm wine. And now I saw a Henry that I think few men have seen.

"Drink," he said, half kind, half gruff. He pushed the cup

into my hand. "I have known men take cold like that before,"
he said. "In the Scottish lands, where my knighting took place,
they said the winters are so cold a man can freeze as he walks.
I did not think England in the summer would be so bad. Here,
take off your cloak, it is wet through."

He helped me, almost gentle as a woman, and when the
laces snarled, he took his dagger and slit them loose himself.

"Harry," I cried, starting up, "do not march on Wales, I beg.
Do not. I cannot help you, nor can anyone."

He disentangled himself from my hands. "No one has called
me by that name in a long while," he said, almost wondering.
"There was a huntsman at my uncle's court, my uncle of
Gloucester that is, a border man. I cannot remember his name,
but he called me 'Harry' in a Saxon way. It is strange to hear
it on your lips, but I like it well enough. There is no one left
to call me by any sort of name."

As he spoke, he still chafed my hands; his own were rough
and bridle-worn as Raoul's are; and when he spoke, he stared
into the flame as if he were remembering from long ago. "Ann,"
he said, "I admit I have done you wrong, but not all the wrong
that you blame me for. Sieux I took in fair fight, my father
and I, before his death. That was our soldier's right, but not
to tear down its walls and hang its guard. Nor did I plot your
death, nor Raoul's; I am ill thought of among my peers, but
those are lies."

"You tremble still," he said, "lie down. Do not fear me. In
truth, I am not my brother who they say has slept with all the
women in France. He swore he had lain with you, but that
must be a lie. Is it a lie then," and he spoke almost beseechingly,
"is it a lie that he slept with my wife? Ann, you who know
them both, tell me the truth? And is it a lie that my father
slept with her to persuade her to marry me? Then am I cuckold
twice, to be the sport of all men, master of many lands and
nothing else."

There was suddenly such misery in his voice, I almost pitied
him.

"And my father, that handsome man, more beautiful than

his beautiful son, Geoffrey le Bel, are they both called, yet *he* was a man. The brother would have lands but without the danger, without effort. Not so my father. What he took, he earned. Yet to die as he did, so suddenly, in his prime. He never honored me as he should to leave a will so carelessly writ and to die without a word for me, only a curse, that he would not be buried until I agreed. I had done all and more that a son of his could do. Did I fail him in battle, did I lag behind? Did not I flesh my sword as a boy? And shall my mother's shame be on my head, that I am not even a count's son? Am I so ill formed, Lady Ann, that women would not look at me; am I so low bred that men should refuse my name and rank?"

He almost wept then, self-pity oozing from him like the damp in these walls. Yet I pitied him, poor wretch. "No," I said, although my voice still shivered—not even the fire's warmth could touch me—"a woman could like you, great King."

"Ann of Cambray," he said, "I will forgive you the trick you played on me. I regretted giving you away even as I ordered it. But I pledge you my word: I'll not harm you. I will lie beside you to share the warmth, for to tell truth, I, too, am half perished with the cold, and this floor is damp and hard. Here's my sword and my word." He unsheathed his great sword and placed it carefully in the middle of the bed. "I lie on one side," he told me. "Be satisfied. The blade is sharp; you have the right to pick it up if I misplease you. Which I will not, cannot. Eleanor has drained me dry, not able even to pleasure myself. There is something about you, Lady Ann, that I have not met in any woman I have known, not love, not lust, but soul to soul. I honor you. And I have told you things I have told no one." He suddenly gave a rueful laugh. It made him seem younger than he was. It made that other side of him seem unreal. "I have fought with many men, twice your size and strength, and never been bested yet. But you have bested me. So here's my hand. And here I give you the kiss of peace. I will not hurt you or yours, I vow. Do you not hurt me. So Harry of England bids you swear."

And so we swore, a promise that I have kept all these years, so I thought he would keep faith with me. And so we slept, that sleep exhaustion brings. And when I awoke, it was already day. Burnt out torches, dead ash, a dark void to a winding stair, a drifting light that filtered round the moth-eaten tapestries. If sin it is to lie beside a man, without love or lust, for comfort's sake, then God must count it sin, I cannot. We have not yet reached that stage, praise be, where today priests judge sins by magnitude, which one is worst, which one least, debate their niceties by the hour. Put simply thus, he did not spill his seed in me, he was not the father of my son. But I also know that when I woke, the sword was on the ground and we were in one bed.

He slept, that great king, who would have an empire, buried in the coverings above his head, his shirt, his clothes tumbled on the floor like a child's thrown this way and that, and on the chest, his golden crown where he had tossed it carelessly. Yet he would have an empire and would fight to conquer it. He had tested me and I had won. And I kept faith with him, have told no one what was done there, what was said, until now. But he did not keep faith with me—and that's to come.

I tried to stand, the room spun round, my body ached as if whipped with cords. I longed to sink back down again, but could not, knew I must go on. We have short nights, long days, in summer here, I judged it already past four of the clock. The birds had not yet begun to sing and the evening had left great fog patches on the moors. Silently, I put on my clothes, still damp, torn and stained, burnt about the edges from the fire and smelling of smoke. Then, taking shoes in hand, I felt my way down the main stairs to the stableyard.

There were guards of course, they turned to laugh or shrug as I passed. Who knows what the huntsmen, pages, thought of me, a king's paramour who leaves at dawn? They did not know me nor I them, but before the week was gone, they would not laugh again. Without their help, I reached the stables, found my horse, and saddled it, although, from time to

time, I was forced to lean against its side, the world swam
before my eyes much as it had done on shipboard, as if the
ground still heaved.

I took a saddle, any one, the closest at hand; with difficulty,
I swung it on, fastened it, climbed into it, a knight's high saddle,
well-worn and ill kept, but it would serve, and called to the
guards to open the sally port. Easy was it to ride into Maneth
Castle and easy to ride out, this place of nightmare where my
darkest fears had been. Every movement wrenched my head
loose, I felt it floated off; the slightest pressure jarred my spine
as if the bones were unstrung. Down the narrow causeway we
went, and at the curve, I leaned back and stared at that place
which had brought me so many years of sorrow. It was just a
gray shape after all, silhouetted against the morning sky. I
cannot say what I thought of it, not then, not now. Like many
things one dreads, dangers, even death itself, met up with they
do not seem as dreadful as we think, and come upon us with
the ease of familiar friends. As for Henry, who was great king,
I often think of him as I knew him that night, when he revealed
his inner secrets, when he had me in his power and I had him
in mine. Fate had caught him, too. He could no more escape
from what he was than could any other man. And at the very
end, he kept faith in his fashion, although he came to it late.
And that too in time shall be told.

The path soon degenerated into ruts and pits; I had to pick
my way carefully until I came on the open moors, similar to
those near Cambray but without the sea to give them added
depth. But the northern mountains were clearly visible as they
are not further south. I remember noticing that and thinking
it strange. I felt the sun's warmth upon my back and kept the
horse's head pointed away from it, west. I closed my eyes.
Although I was locked in the saddle by the high seat, I felt
giddiness and sickness in waves sweep over me. And somehow,
not knowing what I did, I turned north, not south when we
came to Offa's Dyke. I cannot explain how this happened. It
was against my will, plan, but fate perhaps overruled me. And

when I spotted a break leading to the bed of the dyke, I plunged down through the surrounding bank. The gulley was treacherous, rough with stones and flints, steep-sided and deep, but within the ditch the floor was wide enough for several men to ride abreast, or race their chariots up and down as I think they must have done in those far-off days. And I thought too of those legends which tell how a giant had plunged his hand into the earth and scooped it out in clods and turfs, tossing them aside to form our western hills. A small stream ran chuckling under the fern, except for that there was no sound, just a far-off bird cry, sharp and high like a lapwing's. After a while, when this open floor began to close in, I put my horse at the other bank and we scrambled up on the western side, the Celtic side of the boundary line. And so, beating down the bracken fronds that came almost to my waist, at last I came into my own people's land. I cannot explain, I tell you, what made me follow this unknown route; something deep, something unfathomed. So they say a salmon returns to its native stream. What makes it remember or know the way back from those far-off ocean depths, or what brings back a bird each year to the same nesting ground?

I suppose there was a watch at the crossing point. The path we now traveled was well marked. Although I saw no one, there were signs if I had had the sense to make them out: flattened earth, cattle and horse droppings, torn and scorched grass where someone had camped to make a fire. I might have guessed too that, hearing of Henry's approach as they must, the Celtic princes, suspicious as are all the Celts, knowing Henry and fearing him, they must have been on the alert. And, it is true, in places I came across great brush piles, watchfires they were, which, when lit, would warn the populace that the border had been crossed. So we journeyed northwest as I suppose and when this malaise, this daze, into which I had fallen, lifted, the morning sun had already dimmed, as often it does on the moors, sun in morning, rain by noon, and patches of fog began to roll about us, wet and thick so that there was

soon no telling where we were. And as the mists drifted in and
out, so did my thoughts.

As it later seems, I crossed their outposts more than once,
and my erratic wanderings, following first this path, then its
reverse, must have puzzled them, for I let my horse pick the
easiest way. Nor did I see them, although they had long kept
track of me. It was that thin bird's cry, cutting through the
fog, that alerted me. I heard it again, and thrice again, and
after that, rode more cautiously, not wanting to stumble upon
someone unawares. And sometimes now, as the mists closed
round, for they thinned and then grew dense again, it seemed
I heard other sounds, a clink of metal clipping stone or a rustle
an animal makes as it pushes its way through bushes and fern.
My own brain had cleared somewhat; I began to guess what
followed me. Tense with alarm, I continued cautiously to advance.

The fogs had lessened in the place where I finally came to
a halt, a kind of dell or grassy plot, surrounded by thick gorse
bushes whose yellow flowers seemed to give a yellowish tinge
to the air. More clearly than ever before, I sensed a presence.
Perhaps they had already gathered there, and hearing my approach had taken cover; more like, I think, they had been
tracking me these many miles, just outside my eye's gaze so
that, although I had caught glimpses of them, I did not know
what they were. Now on the rim of things, they began to put
on shape, become substantial, real; a horse or two moving
slowly in step, a foot soldier carrying his round shield and
throwing spear, and surrounding them, as I took in more,
archers, with their rough elm-carved Welsh bows. Finally, behind them, on a slope, a group of mounted men, their leaders
I presume, for they were better armed, better horsed. But
young, all young.

They were watching me intently as I them; but as they came
into view and the mist eddied past, some turned their faces
away so I should not look at them. And I remembered how
once my men had so turned away from the lady of the moors.

Yet many came crowding up to take in this strange sight, a
woman alone on a horse. I had not thought how it would look.
They were young as I have said, small-boned, wide-shouldered,
short and stocky like the ponies they rode. Their leaders, I
guessed that their rank, rode moorland horses with coats and
manes untrimmed. My own horse towered above theirs, yet if
I had tried to outrun them, theirs would soon have outpaced
me over the rough grass. The men were shaggy and ill kept,
too, not bearded as are most Norman men, but with long, fair
moustaches that grew low on their chins. Their hair was long,
bound back with thongs, little of a Norman man-of-arms with
them, no mail coats, no steel helmets, no Norman swords. I
saw all this clearly although afterward when the fever raged,
I wondered if in truth I had seen or merely thought I had.
Their armor was leather padded jerkins, coiled leather caps,
with little to choose between master and men save that the
archers wore leather bracelets on their arms to strengthen them.
Little to choose then between master and men, informality was
their style, except when the master gave an order it was obeyed.
They talked softly among themselves in their own tongue, but
when a spokesman questioned me, as he now did, he spoke in
Norman-French, haltingly, and his voice had that border lilt
that I had not heard for a long while. It made me think of
Walter and I almost smiled. But these questions were not for
smiling, and since I was not willing to speak of Cambray nor
to use my name, and since it even hurt to answer in mono-
syllables, they had little news from me. Nor was I inclined to
tell them I came from Maneth Castle; I had enough sense not
to mention a place which the Celts also abhorred. My answers,
then, not well thought out, hesitantly given, were almost worse
than giving none, nor could I make coherent reply to all the
other questions that they then hurled at me, almost drowned
in the hubbub as more and more men crowded round, questions
about the Norman troops, their strength, where Henry's army
was bestowed, who led it, military questions that, even if I
could have taken them in, I could not have replied to.

Meanwhile, one of the men was looking over the horse, testing its forefeet, fingering the bridle and saddle.

"A Norman warhorse, lords," he reported in his own tongue, having satisfied himself with thorough Celtic common sense, "ridden hard yesterday, see, the dried mud, and stabled in a Norman barn, although ill groomed. And Norman war gear, Norman saddle. As for the markings under the saddle flaps, I would judge both horse and rider have not come far, from Maneth by the look of it." They gave a hiss at that name, have not I just said it was ill omened among the Celts, many of whom had suffered there or had known of men who had; once brought there, they disappeared, and their lands and property fell forfeit to those lords. Of all the border castles Henry should have torn down, this was the one the Celts would have destroyed; this was the one that was an offense to them to let remain.

"A Norman warhorse," their leader repeated, a tall, slender man, young, although his heavy, reddish beard made him seem older. Since he was the only one with such a beard, I found myself wondering if he wore it to give the effect of age. But the questioner was straightening up, dusting off the grass and ferns from his knees, dusting his hands as if his mind was made up. "Norman horse, Norman saddle, Norman harlot sent to spy."

That judgment put a different aspect to the affair. I began to feel ill at ease, nervous. It suddenly occurred to me how I must look, how I might seem to them.

"No Norman spy," I said in his language, but the word that came out most clearly was still that "Norman"; remember I had not spoken in the Celtic tongue for many years, was but a child when I spoke it last, sometimes I think I got the rhythm of it wrong. And, understandably, what I said infuriated them.

"If not Norman," they sneered, "then Celt, more the shame, to traffic with our enemies. Or is it you hope to betray *us*, and have come here to seek news of us, where we are and what our ranks. You should know us better than to think as Norman decoy you'd find out our plans. A spy then, for some Norman lording, to whom you'll report back when you've lured us into betraying secrets."

"You have no right to think that of me," I began to argue, seriously alarmed, but the words came croaking out, and no one paid them any heed. The spokesman was already addressing his captain, this young bearded man who was listening intently to all he proposed, a veritable fantasy, such as Celts like to invent, yet it seemed possible, they, being on edge, over nervous, looking for scapegoats, might find one in me.

"Do I look a spy?" I now tried to ask the other men. "Why should Normans send a woman to do their work?"

For answer, one reached up, carefully, so as not to touch me in any way, and pulled back the cloak. They gave another hiss, of surprise or pleasure, or desire, I cannot tell, but it did not help me.

"No one thought the Normans such fools as to send a squint-eyed wench. But we've no time to dispute that with you today."

Their captain nodded, turned back to talking with his other officers; the spokesman came forward nimbly and seized the reins.

"Take this spy," he mocked the word, "hang her high, so her Norman masters will know what little she achieved for them."

Then I did begin to struggle as they tried to force me from my horse, kicking and scratching to tear myself free from their hard and sinewy arms.

"By God," said one, spitting a tooth I'd knocked loose, "a wildcat. What say we try her wares, pity to waste such charms."

In the end, my skirts hampered me and they threw me to the ground.

"Let's see if she's worth the struggle," another grinned. "Suppose the body matches the face?"

"If made like other women I've known," another said, "no matter what the face is like."

But all the same, in a single move, he snatched at my gown, tearing the fabric neckline to waist so that my bare flesh was exposed. They paused to stare as I tried to cover my nakedness, gave another hiss.

"God's Paradise," at last one breathed. "The pigs have sent a prize after all." Their voices were soft, those western men I had known as a child, I could not believe even then what they said could be meant so cruel; I did not even think they meant to threaten me, not until they tried to tie my hands and gag my mouth.

"I am no Norman." Then I did cry out, fear giving me back my voice. "I am kin to both Norman and Celt. I am Ann of Cambray."

They laughed at me, hands on hips, observing me. "And I the Lord of Maneth," one jeered, "who is dead, who thought to whip us with his Norman rods. I've marks on my back still that are his."

"And here's my rod," another made a crude gesture. "See how you dance to that."

"Stuff in the gag first," a third, more practiced, advised, "lest she tear it off with her fangs."

So they spoke, every word an obscenity to urge them on, dragging my hands behind my back with a strap, the leather biting into the flesh, trying to push a thong from their hair across my face. I bit the man who held the gag, struggled long enough to shriek out my name, again and again, until the air rang.

"Silence her." Their captain rode forward angrily. "Enough noise to rouse the entire Norman army. Who shouts the name of Cambray?"

He swung himself off his horse, came to stand above me, his booted feet planted on either side. I looked up. He was younger than I had thought, with long red-gold hair, like to the others in build and looks except for the beard which, now, seeing him close, I saw but partly covered the great gash that had seared his face from chin to ear, a sword cut or thrust along his left cheek.

"Who shouts Cambray?" he repeated impatiently; he poked me with his boot.

"Speak up. I know Cambray well. And have little love for it since it gave me this." And he fingered the side of his face as he spoke.

I looked up at him and despaired. Despite the years, the beard, I knew him, too. But would he remember me, a heap of rags thrown disjointed at his feet? When he had seen me last I had been the lady of Cambray. His father, a Celtic warlord, had taken my castle once and held it until Lord Raoul had won it back again.

I said, as steadily as my voice allowed, "Your wound was taken in fair fight. Lord Raoul fought with your father and his men, captured Cambray for me, who am the lady of all its lands. I know you, Dafydd, son of Howel. Do not you know me?"

He bent to look more closely, his eyes narrowing in thought. I knew what he was remembering and why.

At last, "Aye," he said, "aye, I remember Cambray," as if even that much stung his lips.

I bit my own, willing him to fairness. He had been cut down in a surprise assault, a young boy then, almost too young to bear arms; his father had died and we had tended him and his companions as best we could. But we had also kept them chained like dogs, in fetters, to make them work for us. I heard myself plead with him in a voice I hardly knew. "Lord Raoul dealt fairly with you. He bears as bad a scar himself, and the Lord of Maneth gave him it, whom he killed. He comes as warden of the marcher lands, to keep the peace as my father and Lord Raoul's grandfather did in their day . . ."

"Who does she say she is?" he next asked, never taking his eyes off me. I do not think he heard half I said, lost in his own thoughts.

They told him, cutting short their jesting as they saw his expression change. They pulled me up at his command, dragged back the hair from my eyes, wiped off the blood and dirt. I felt myself blush beneath the bruises, those of today added to yesterday's, and shook myself free. His eyes followed every move I made as, when a boy, he had fixed them on me, when, like a wolf cub on a chain, he had panted for liberty.

"By Saint David," he said at last. He whirled on his men, snarled at them to untie me, threw a wool cloth to cover my nakedness.

"I thought you hated all Norman swine," one grumbled beneath his breath.

Dafydd, son of Howel, rounded on him, his eyes black with remembering. "I do," he said, "but she, I owe her a life, mine, twice saved by her. She is who she says she is."

They worked faster then, although balked of their prize. And, in truth, Cambray is a word they all would know, and think of with liking as they thought of Maneth with hate.

When they were done, "I have no quarrel with you, Lady Ann," he told me. "Save wonder that you ride without escort among my border watch. Where is your noble husband, where his men?"

When I did not reply, he eyed me narrowly, sharply bid his men bring food and drink. He took my wrists to make the blood flow back, himself fed me water and their harsh brown bread. I was not hungry, although I had not broken fast for so long, the thought of food choked me, but I drank the peaty tasting water while he sat beside me, talking of old times, how Lord Raoul and I had ridden away from Cambray, and how, after we were both gone, he and the other prisoners had been given choice, either to stay at Cambray as part of its guard or go free, never to return.

"I chose freedom," he said, "who would not? They gave us food for our journey, gave us back our swords; we parted, I think, as friends. But I have never been back to Cambray since, never thought to hear word of you. By Saint David, who is my namesake, patron saint to me and my kin, to forget Cambray would be to forget part of myself. You saved my life when your men would have tossed us over the cliff at the battle's end, you saved it a second time when you tended me." And he fingered the scar on his face.

"Lady Ann," he said, "you claimed just now to be both Norman and Celt. So, I think, am I, not by birth but by what I learned of your Norman ways and the promptings of my own thoughts. There was much to admire at Cambray. So that, although it is true I hate all Normans in a general way, I also remember some good of them, although I do not tell my men that. Your squire, of the fair hair and merry smile, many were the hours we spent together; Jesu, how he struggled with our language as if a rope were tangled in his tongue."

Sorrow broke over me like a wave, I bowed under it. "He is dead, killed yesterday among my escort ambushed by a Norman lord."

He crossed himself, muttered prayer for the dead man's soul.

"God have him to His care," he said, "he was a brave and trusty man. But what manner of men would attack you, what Norman lord, without cause?"

That, too, was a grief better not spoken of. "He is not known to you," I said, "but his brother is, Henry, King of England."

"King Henry," he said, starting up, "but he has sent word he will meet us at Caer at July's end. He has bid the Princes of Northern Wales attend him there. They but wait his message to ride to his camp."

I did not recognize the place at first, for he gave Chester its Celtic name, Caer, which also means "camp" or "fort," in memory of the great Roman one that had once stood there.

"No," I said, "Henry is not there yet. He lodged last night at Maneth. He waits the mustering of his troops on the seventh of the month. And he will cross the river at Basingwerk..."

"Jesu," he swore again, "here be news."

He spun round on his heel, ready to shout an order to his men, then, recollecting, turned back to me.

"Lady Ann," he said loudly, and beckoned for them to pour him a horn of their fermented drink, mead, it is called, which the Celts prefer.

"Lady Ann," he said, "I drink to the honor of your house,

ever were they loved by us. You are welcome in their name, to ride among our company."

He drank to me formally, as a Norman would; his men raised up a cheer, then quickly scattered to whatever post they were assigned; the cooking fires were doused; we were ready to set off. A faster parting than a Norman army makes, no pack trains, no baggage carts, whatever Welshmen need they string over their shoulders. One of their small ponies was led up, I straddled its broad back, and we jogged off. Listening to the men chatter as they worked, listening to them whistle as we rode along, I might have been a child again, riding with my father's men above Cambray. But I had seen another side of them I had never seen before, cruel and angry, bitter against their enemies. *They love their freedom and will die for it.* So should Henry find to his cost if he attacked. And so we rode together over the moors, until the day had ended, and came by darkness to their Celtic camp high up in the mountain pass.

12

HEIR CAMP WAS SUCH AS MY FATHER had often talked about, like the one I think from which he had taken stones to build Cambray, an old place, made in Roman times. The outlines of gate towers, barracks, stables, were still clearly visible, and where the walls were intact, new roofs had been hastily thatched over with straw and great gates hung at the entrances, the whole laid out neatly in rectangles and lines. There was even a commander's house, brick-built originally, its marble facing long since disappeared, and only three columns of the ten that had once supported its front porch. The High Prince of Northern Wales was quartered there, and there we went after his guards had let us through. They were truculent, those guards, and my presence with Dafydd's men led to much dispute, it being considered lack of decorum to escort a lady into an armed camp. Dafydd was forced to pick a quarrel with them until, by dint of threat of fisticuffs and worse, he pushed his way past. He was quick-tempered, Dafydd, son of Howel, and proud. I do not think he liked not to be recognized, but that was a sign of his youth, although I have heard my father often say that Celts were vain, desirous more than most men not to lose face. And as he rode through the camp, I noticed how his men now ran beside him, one on either side, holding his stirrup irons as mark of respect.

"Look well at them," he shouted back at the discomforted guard, spoiling the effect, "You'll see their faces often enough."

I marveled again at the lack of formality between him and the common soldiers yet, on the whole, I do not think that was a handicap. When the time was ripe, they would fight, well, it was their land and their freedom they fought for. Preparations for war were going forward in every corner of that camp; archers, footmen, spearmen, the whole entourage of a high prince in movement, messengers riding constantly in and out of the gates, stacks of weapons sharpened, harnesses and leather coats restitched.

Sweet Jesu, I thought, if the Celts are so arming themselves, how will Raoul avoid a war, with Henry's men equally well prepared? Dafydd tried to explain who each man was, warlords all as his father had been, their names a jumble in my head, all sons of this prince, or that, as they style themselves, all famous men. Afterward, I thought I should have remembered some of those names from my father's time. But the highest prince of all, of the north, of Gwynedd, as the Welsh name is, Owain Gwynedd, his name I did recall. I had heard my father say that he was the most dangerous man he had ever fought, a stack of gold offered for his head, with little hope of ever catching him.

"Crafty as a mountain cat is Owain," Dafydd now explained, proud of him, "for twenty years or more, he has been a thorn in the Norman side. So strong is he that he took back Oswestry, used its castle for his own fort, won us land that has not been Celtic ruled for five hundred years. A just man, a peaceful man, but when aroused, their opposite." So I think my father had spoken of him. But for all that he called himself a prince, he was not yet a high king!

"When a boy," Dafydd was continuing, "he led that famous charge against the Normans, which caused their great defeat. They had crowded on a bridge, retreating from a Welsh force; the bridge broke, their weight of horse and armor snapping its wooden piles; the river was choked with drowning men and those who shed their armor to keep afloat our archers shot them down as they swam ashore." He relished the story, the Celtic side of him uppermost; it was what he hoped, they all hoped, would happen a second time. But his words had that same effect that Henry's had, approaching disaster, no way to stop it, a boulder hurtling down a hill, a tidal wave.

When I saw Owain, strangely enough it was of my father that he reminded me, a gray-haired old man, bent with age, yet powerful enough to pick up his Celtic sword in one hand, sing out his Celtic war cry as eagerly as a young man. And, like all the Celts I've ever known, he could still go uphill on foot or run a mile if he had to.

That night, he was sitting in this ancient hall, before a fire, sweet-scented of fruit wood, and as he talked, he bit into an apple with his strong white teeth. Or rather Dafydd talked, he listened, and I wondered how it was that suddenly words seemed to recede, then grow large, as if words could have shape and form. Much of what was said at that time escaped me; but as Prince Owain paid me little attention at first, I think no one noticed my distress as my fever ebbed and flowed. Owain greeted Dafydd with open arms, clasping him twice to his breast in Celtic style, in that strange offhand fashion I had come to accept as theirs. I noticed now, beneath his tunic, he wore a band of gold, or torc, around his neck, as our warriors of long ago used to wear, as I remember my brother, Talisin, had when he went to war. But when Owain heard my name, his old hooded eyes flicked in my direction; he nodded his large head with his shock of long hair, finished his apple with a decisive bite, threw the core into the flames.

"I knew your father," he said. His voice had a gritty sound, but he spoke more distinctly than his men, as if he were used to strangers and matched his speech with their understanding. "We often rode to hunt together, he and I. But before that we were enemies, rivals too who would have killed each other if we could. Yet when you fight a man like Falk you come to know his ways, he becomes your second self; his victories, defeats, are yours. He swore to me, as revenge once, that he would take that which we prized most. I thought he meant land or cattle or gold, the things I cared for in those days. It was your mother he stole from us."

He paused then, sat looking in the fire, seeing his past and theirs. "She was like you, lady, in looks," he said after a while, "and of all women, I cherished her. Yes, you are very like, and although I have not heard you speak, no doubt you have her voice; they say she sang like a lark, sweet and high."

"No, I fear not," I said regretfully, my words too sounding far off, oblique.

He raised his eyebrows, bushy white they were against his brown skin, twisted a gold bracelet about his arm, too courteous to contradict.

"Well, sharp or sweet," he said, "no matter if you brought us good news today."

"What news?" I had to force myself to ask.

"Why," he said, "where Henry will cross the river, where and when—a foolish move. The waters run fast this month, a season for high tides, and the estuary will back up and flood. To cross at all, he must go upstream to the nearest ford, where the river goes through a narrow gorge. Henry is young and reckless," he went on, "to think we'd let him cross unopposed. By Saint David, our patron saint, we'll make him rue the day he threatened us."

From the blocks of sound that his words made, I gradually began to pick out sense. "He means no harm, a peace treaty is all he asks," I tried to reply.

They started to laugh, the other lords in the room, Dafydd, Prince Owain. "Peace or war," the prince gasped, wheezing for breath, "Henry is caught if he crosses at Basingwerk. And you, my lady, daughter of Efa of the Celts, you have done us a service greater than you know, to put our enemy within our grasp." Then, at last, his words became real.

"I do no such service," I tried to cry, tried to deny. But Dafydd tightened his grip upon my arm, hustled me away. "They'll not attack the king as he crosses," I cried, my voice now far away and faint, as if I spoke through a gag, as if I spoke through echoes a tunnel makes, "they'll not ambush him."

"They must," Dafydd explained. "Against such an army we have no chance but to attack first. Thanks to you, we have that chance."

There was no way it could be unsaid. Owain still kept his place beside the fire, had laughed himself into a fit of coughing, but when it was done, he summoned each noble to his side and told each quickly what was his plan. One by one, they put down whatever they had been busy with, some with drinking, they left the cup of mead half-full, some with mending a sword or leather strap, work normally done by Norman squires, that too they left against their seats, quietly, without a word, they drifted off. In a moment or two the room was empty, and I heard feet stamping along the outside colonade, I heard a stack of shields clatter apart, I heard a clash of steel as men tested sword blades. There was a flurry of birdcalls, that high note I had been hearing all day long. Then silence, and in that silence came the realization of what I had done.

"Dafydd." In my distress, I took him by his jerkin front, and shook it, "tell him that I am mistaken, I do not know . . ."

He loosened my fingers, gently enough, "The order is given, Lady Ann. He would not go back on it if he could. Besides, it is common knowledge what Henry plans. We all know he comes to war with us. War has been brewing these twenty years. Your father's death put an end to peace."

"Henry may not bring war," I still tried to argue. "There are those who will counsel against it, there are those who will not follow him."

"Perhaps." He sounded dubious. He rubbed his hand across his face in the gesture I had seen Raoul make. "Since it is our only hope, we shall act on your advice. If proved wrong," he paused, "we go to our deaths in any event."

"And if proved right," I cried, "Lord Raoul will die by Henry's side."

He looked at me, pity contending with surprise. "Then are you too caught in a trap, Lady Ann," he said after a while, "but it cannot be stopped."

On whose side will you fight? I had asked Raoul that question, better, I think, that he had asked me. For that is how I betrayed him and his king.

Well, that is how the Welsh moved to prepare the ambush

for Henry at Basingwerk, and that is how I destroyed all I held
most dear for my Celtic kin. Bitter are the days I have lived
to regret it. *You shall do us a service.* Now was that prophecy
come true, and like all the others, two-edged. Owain's men
left before the day was an hour old, slipping away in the dark,
mounted on their swift border horses, whose hooves had already been muffled with straw. Owain's bodyguard, his family
retinue, more than a hundred strong, with Dafydd among them,
they went the fastest way north. The rest, on foot for the main
part, walked or ran down the long road we had come up,
carrying their spears and heavy Welsh bows. Since boyhood
are they trained to run like that; and within an hour or so of
my meeting with their prince, there was little sign of them,
only stray wisps of straw, a broken strap, their gear they had
left at their place, a young boy or two, the camp guards. And
their womenfolk—I had not even realized that the women were
there. They may have been waiting outside the camp for the
men to leave, for they had not shown themselves to bid them
good-bye or wish them Godspeed. First one of them, then
another, came out from wherever they had kept themselves,
and with the help of the boys, brought up saddlehorses for
them to ride. Some began to gather up the pieces strewn about
Prince Owain's hall; neatly and quickly they piled them as if
they must be accounted for. And when they were ready too,
to leave, one of them came up to me where I sat and bid me
follow her.

Where else, I thought, shall I go? And so I did. I mounted
as they ordered it, riding astride, no hardship for me although
I think they feared it, a heavy shawl of undyed wool, closely
woven against the damp, wrapped round my head. I thought
it was too late for warmth; I thought I should never know
warmth again; ice cold I was, and where my heart, my memories, all that I loved should have been, nothing but ice. And
so we also rode away.

We rode deeper into those northern mountains that Geoffrey
of Sedgemont had longed to see. (And, it seemed, already
word had come to Owain's camp of that attack, although no

word yet in Henry's. Many men dead, they claimed, Sir
Geoffrey dead, Geoffrey Plantagenet escaped, but so had I
already known that news, it too was dead to me.) It was
hard riding in the dark with only a few torches to light the
road, yet after many hours of zigzagging through small,
wooded ravines and under tumbled rocks, we came to Prince
Owain's dwelling place. It was not a castle in the Norman
style, although he owned those, but an old-style fortress,
hemmed round with deep ditches and earth ramparts, topped
by a wooden palisade with iron-studded gates. A battering
ram or a Norman siege machine would have made short work
of those ditches and walls, but how to get Norman army
there; we had ridden along trails so narrow, so twisted, our
ponies scarce could inch along, and the last climb had been
almost perpendicular from a valley floor into the clouds. A
Norman horse would have been too large to pass, would
have slid off in the precipice. I said little, thought little,
remember little of that ride. What was there worth remembering? It all had been told, long, long ago.

And the ladies of Owain's family, realizing there was no
harm in me, and sensing, in a way no man would, the sickness,
the darkness and the despair, they left me alone, although from
time to time, when I swayed in the saddle, I suppose like to
fall off, as in truth I thought I might, they sent someone to
ride beside me to catch me if need be. Most of the time they
chatted among themselves, a hardy breed these royal ladies,
wife, daughters and daughters-in-law, some of them red-haired,
some gold-red like Dafydd, some dark, all of them vivacious,
although in public they seldom spoke but that may have been
the nature of Prince Owain's household. I do not swear its truth
for all Celtic courts. The Lady of Gwynedd was a regal dame—
old, too—yet like other women of her race, her black hair
showed no sign of age, and her dark eyes were battle fierce.
She it was who noticed when I shook with chills and ordered
one of the younger boys, pages I suppose, to ride beside me,
had one of her daughters bring a blanket to put over my shoul-

ders. This was the youngest daughter, perhaps two years younger than I, red-cheeked, dark-haired, dark-eyed, one of the dark Celts, and she loved to laugh and talk, as by and by, I soon found out. For, although I could not or did not reply, she still chatted on, sometimes about simple homely things such as young maids like to discuss, but more often about her father and her brothers, all warlike men, and her sisters, aunts, the women of Owain's house, warlike all. And when we passed a certain place, she told how it reminded her of the story of a lady of great fame and bravery who had herself led out her men, in her husband's absence, against the Norman Lord of Kidwelly, far in the south. Alas for my boast to Lord Raoul, this lady and her sons were defeated, she was beheaded, her sons made prisoners; yet the site of the battle is still named after her, Maes Gwenllian. But I had not thought, when I hurled that boast, I should be the cause of a Norman defeat.

"And so am I named after her, called Gwenllian in her honor," the girl chattered on, "but my friends call me Lilian for short. As may you." And so she spoke, not disheartened by the lack of response on my part. And when, after many weary hours, we came to the gates of Owain Gwynedd's fort, she helped me inside, found me a place to lie down, tended me. But never once, not then or ever after, did she, her mother, or any of those women of Prince Owain's house, say anything of where their men had gone, how or why. And that silence was for courtesy.

For almost a week we waited, at least I think it was a week, time seemed to spin away, sometimes day, sometimes night, in no real order, indiscriminate. And on the last day, the seventh since our coming here or so it must have been, I rose from my bed. I could scarcely stand, yet I cannot explain otherwise, except some thought made me seek the open air; some awareness, some sense of things being done, of happenings, beyond our knowledge yet happening. There was a kind of watchtower, I suppose it would have been called in a Norman castle, and from its battlements there was a view over the mountainside.

There I crept and there I stayed. The sky was clear, which it seldom is in these parts, a land of mist and rain, and below us, sliced between the forest, green and secret valleys stretched toward the northern coast. Lilian had claimed more than once that this was the richest part of all of Wales, supplier of grain and food, having the best cattle grazing and best land for sheep. And it is true it had a graceful aspect that bespoke peace and harmony. But it was not harmony or peace I looked for that day.

Come the evening, for in these mountain regions the sun sank behind the peaks and brought twilight early, toward then the late of day, a cloud of black birds wheeling far below attracted me, and having watched them for a long while, I questioned a passing guard what they were. He answered in his Celtic way, not directly, but roundabout, first having looked at me carefully to know who I was and if what he said would offend. "There be two kinds of birds," he said, "those who know the place and those who know the hour. These be ravens, see how they swoop and cry. They tell the time. Keep watch yourself; if eagles join them, they will point the way, for eagles know the place but not the hour."

He continued on his march about the tower walk, but when he passed me again, he pointed with his spear. "Look," he said. Two birds of greater size came flying toward us from the south. They passed beneath the castle walls, their wingspan measured by the shadows they cast upon the trees, circled once or twice, then dipped into the valley, following the ravens north. I had never seen an eagle before and certainly not ravens flying in black clouds, and I stood and watched them for a long while until they disappeared into the shadow's line. Nor did I need to ask, nor did he tell, time and place for what—that I too had already known as did all men there.

And two days later, perhaps it was, perhaps more—time still had no meaning here—there was an outcry in the valley below, like the sound of falling trees, loud enough for us to hear in the inner hall.

"Harken." The Lady of Gwynedd suddenly stood up, tall and regal in her woolen shawl which she and all the women wore indoors and out to give them warmth. Her needlework rolled off her lap and fell unnoticed on the stone floor. "Open wide the gates," she cried; and as the guards ran to do her bidding, and the heavy gates creaked apart, she and her women moved toward them, stood waiting in the open court. It was dark now, and ever and ever from the pass we heard the sound, a crash, as if men struck their spears against their shields. Then the lady stretched out her arm for silence, and she and her youngest daughter, Lilian, drew me toward them and held my hands between their own. Hers were work-worn, and I could feel the hardness of the palm, the lines across it, the ridges on the thumb. But she held my hand for pity's sake.

And the other women, although their expression did not change, I saw how their eyes flickered for a second and I heard them whisper as a prayer, "Praise God, it is our gain."

They came riding in, doubled for the most part, their many wounded clinging each to a rider's back. And at their head rode Owain, his hooded eyes sunk with fatigue, his own horse almost lame; and he too had a wounded serf hanging on his waist. One by one the men came into the courtyard and as each entered in the gates, he clashed his spear and shield. The womenfolk led away those who needed aid; those who could walk went into the hall where already serviteurs had begun to heat up great cauldrons of meat and slice loaves of bread. There would be feasting without formality (no tablecloths, no fine linens, no gilded cups), but long, and with songs. And the Celtic bards, whose rank there stands as high as any lord's, would sing their victory chant. But I saw Dafydd, son of Howel, or rather, he seeing me where I leaned against the wall, he dismounted, looped the reins around a post, and came to stand beside me. His eyes were bloodshot and strained with watching, and he was weak with loss of blood, having taken a cut in the upper arm. I tended it as best I could, but the jagged edges had already been pulled together and the flesh was clean.

"You forget," he said, almost smiling, "you are among the Celts, who know more of living things and more of healing than anyone in our northern world."

But even he was silent when he heard their bards begin to sing:

> Fair western dragon, the best was theirs;
> Sword blade in hand, inviting death,
> Death bidden, ready, red-handed...

You, poet, I have heard you sing that song in quieter times at Cambray, you praise their skill who gave it words and tune. You do not know, I am sure, that I had heard them sing it first; you did not realize where I heard their victory song and stood listening when the harpers struck their Welsh harps and made the rafters of Prince Owain's hall ring with sound. But it was Dafydd who spoke the truth of it, carefully, thoughtfully, so I should know.

"That is Prince Owain's son who sings," Dafydd told me after listening for a while, "he is a fearless warrior who sings as he fights. Hark to him—The bright land of the north— that is how he thinks of us. And that is how it has been for us today.

"Well, Lady Ann, for all that I could sleep standing here, and may yet, I will tell you all I saw and heard, not so eloquent as our bardsman there, but the best I can. Prince Owain is old, but what he lacks in youth he makes up for in cunning. And King Henry underestimated us as Owain knew he would, for he set his whole force to cross the boundary, over the estuary flats at Basingwerk. The tide was high and it hampered him. Suddenly, on the western shores we appeared. Owain had kept us hidden until then; now we rose up from behind the sand dunes, clashed our spears and shouted until the very air rang. Many good horsemen were drowned; their horses, taking fright, dashed them down among the sandbars where they were trapped by the inrushing tide; and some of our bowmen, having secretly positioned themselves in midstream among the elder bushes that grow there on small isles, they too shot among the ranks to cause confusion and fright. And so that Norman army milled about on the eastern bank and could not contrive to cross."

"And Lord Raoul?" I scarce dared ask.

He said, "Lady, we had spies at the Norman camp, as they had sent their spies against us; Prince Owain's brother being there had many messengers going freely to and fro to him, and so our men slipped in among them. Until the very moment that the king ordered their march, your noble husband cautioned against it, steadfastly maintained the king should disband his troops, an army he could not long keep under control, advised (I use that word although some said command would be more like) that the king made good his offer to treat with us and meet with Owain's counselors as he had at first promised. They say he offered himself as emissary. But the king was in a strange humor. He had returned alone from hunting in a black and despondent mood, had shut himself up in his tent, would not speak to anyone, and gave the order to march even before some of his men were prepared.

"'Move out,' he is supposed to have said, riding up on his gray stallion and, without telling anyone of his council what he had done, sent dispatches to his fleet moored at Pembroke to sail round to meet him on the coast. A joint attack then, planned by land and sea, which would have gone hard for us, had it come without forewarning. Yet he kept sullen even on the march; they say his brother failed him, who did not come, although no word of the attack on you or your men had reached the camp. They thought you safely at Cambray. And the king did not enlighten them. I saw those Normans come, Lady Ann, a great and noble host; like a flood themselves, they rolled across the estuary sands. And among the many banners that flew, I saw the hawks of Sedgemont."

"And then?"

"Ah," he said. "I told you Owain was a crafty man. He guessed that Henry would not be stopped long, that failing to

cross the estuary, he would ford the river further inland, and
so, with that in mind, our leader had divided his troops in
three parts: one third had waited at the estuary, had stepped
out to make such a noise, both to frighten and to seem more
numerous than they were. The other two-thirds he had stationed on either side of the narrow track leading to the ford,
and hidden them among the woods of Coleshill, with his sons
in command. Their instructions were simple: to prevent Henry's
crossing the river there. The forest in that part is thick, one
of the oldest stretches of trees in the north, a perfect place for
an ambush. And Henry fell into our trap. He led his troops
himself, riding recklessly without his helmet on so that his men
might know and follow him. And those who saw his face say
it was white with rage to have been so thwarted by the wind
and tide and a handful of scarecrow men."

"Who rode with him, did you see who they were?"

"I did, lady." His voice was sad. "Your lord's red and gold
standard was ranged beside the Angevin one. Like showers of
gold, those flags blew in the sun. But in the shadows of the
wood, we waited for them, in the ditches where the path
funnels toward the river bank. Their van went through and we
let it go. I was there: I saw them, those proud Norman French
who rule your land and think to take ours. I heard your lord
shout out, 'Send scouts ahead, lord King, watch where you
go.' Henry would not wait, pressed on, shouted his reply over
his shoulder for those to catch as they could, 'He is coward
who lags behind.' Your lord's face grew grim. He drew his
sword, gave the word to his men. They held their place, not
one faltered out of line; Jesu, had they all been like that, an
iron blade slicing across the countryside, even an ambush might
not have halted them. And when the path narrowed, they
spaced themselves, kept a horselength between them, to swing
their swords. The king, seeing what Raoul had done, clapped
spurs, rode full tilt ahead, forcing his household guard and his
noble lords to accompany him. Courage has that English king,
but no sense. He willed a victory for himself, knowing it was
defeat.

"We waited until he was fairly in our grasp, then Prince Cynan, Owain's son, gave the signal for the archers to fire. They stood up on both sides, fitted arrow to their bows. How at that distance could they miss? The men around the king dropped like flies. I saw one man like a hedgehog pricked through. Henry himself was cut about the face and arms, although only one arrow hit him squarely, mainly because of the speed he rode. Even where the path had deepened, he still galloped like a madman to run us down. He shouted, 'Ride to the riverbank,' slammed on his helmet, plucked out his sword, flailed at air. Where were we, that enemy? Dropped again out of sight, slid back into ditch and bank that lined each side; all he had seen was that deadly hail of arrows.

"Lord Raoul caught up with him where our main force was hid—no, he was not hurt. He and his men, by holding to their pace, they had had time to throw up their shield wall above their heads, but he had to ride over the dead and dying to reach the king, his black horse nimble as a cat, leaping almost daintily. The king would have still forged on alone had not Raoul taken his bridle rein and forced him to stop.

"'Turn back,' he said, 'folly to ride on. Look about you, great King.' He made the king turn and look back. 'Half your nobles are hit or dead and the Celts lie in wait to strike again. You cannot reach the ford this way.' It was only when he had repeated himself twice that Henry seemed to hear. We saw him wheel his horse and turn about, as if searching for an escape. The grass beneath its hooves was splashed and torn, the sun filtering through the trees on red, not green, and at either side, we waited to send another rain of death.

"'Where is my standard-bearer?' Henry cried, 'where is my flag?'

"'Fallen,' Lord Raoul told him, but that was not the truth. They say the king's standard-bearer, the Earl of Essex, also had seen the trap, and when the first arrows began to fall, he had thrown the banner aside, forced his horse round, and had galloped out the way he'd come in. We found the flag, its Angevin blue strained and blotched, its gold lilies torn."

He stopped. Against my will, I had raised my hands as if
to fend off his words, as if, like that Norman army, its king
and its feudal lords, I hoped to protect myself from blows, as
if I hoped to protect my noble lord.

"Your lord is a seasoned warrior," Dafydd assured me, "he
has fought many times and lived; he knows us and our ways.
He took no hurt. Or rather, he took no hurt from us. I will
tell you it the way it was."

He said, "Lord Raoul also looked about him, one quick look
to assess the lie of the land, to see where we were most likely
hid, to see where the remnants of the mounted nobles were,
the rest having fallen or, like the Earl of Essex, turned tail. For
now there was scarcely any knight between the foot soldiers
in the rear and us, waiting to pounce on them. There was no
cavalry at all, save these few who remained with the king, Lord
Raoul and his men, either to protect the infantry as they ran
or to prevent us from picking them off, one by one. Seeing
this, Lord Raoul seized the king's bridle, spurred on his horse,
shouted out his battle cry so his men came on with him.
Athwart the path, straight at us they spurred, where we lay in
ditch and under hedge, straight across our line, broke through
the bank. I myself saw the bellies of their horses as they mowed
us down, as they leapt the gap in a flail of hooves and swords.
Although many of them were unhorsed, either by stumbling
at the banks or thrust through, our soldiers did not have chance
to stand up, our bowmen could not draw with them upon us.
Our line was broken and they rode past. Henry himself had
recovered enough to swing out on one side, Raoul on the other,
stirrup to stirrup they rode and hacked a path for the rest. But
those who could not ride through at that place, we cut them
down.

"So, swinging then in a half circle, they beat up the path
by which they had entered, driving their foot soldiers before
them like sheep, making a barrier against which we could not
pass. So was the rest of the army saved, but the king's courtiers
suffered grievous loss. And had not your noble lord rallied

them when he did, our victory would have been complete. They say one-third of England's knights were there; by Saint David, it was almost a massacre. And so the remnants of that army withdrew toward Chester. But this I will also tell you, as it was told to me.

"When Henry, faint from his wounds, would have fallen, Lord Raoul dragged him by the waist, carried Henry behind him on his own horse, through the outposts that we had set, and got the king back to the estuary flats. Even then, they were not completely safe; Owain could have caught them with the men he had stationed there, but the tide which earlier had hampered them, now hampered him. He could not get his troops across in time and so was forced to wait in turn, balked by the river which they say rises to give warning of Celtic victory.

"In full view of the Celtic host, Lord Raoul let the king drop to the ground, and waited for the surgeons to rush from cover to tend him. He pushed his helmet back, his Sedgemont guard, most of whom had followed him, stood beside him, few else.

"'Here is the flower of England, King,' he said, 'here we be at your command. The rest are gone or dead.'

"Henry looked up from where he lay, 'Gone,' he said, 'fled, wherefore?'

"'They cannot fight an unseen enemy,' your lord told him. They would follow you to the death if you command, but being sensible men, they would rather know what death and why. There can be no crossing of the river floods today.'

"Henry's face was mottled blue and white, the veins stood out on his neck. He tried to speak, choked and spat.

"'This is your doing, Earl of Sedgemont,' he said. 'We owe this day's defeat to you.'

"His nobles who were left, Raoul's men, gave a cry of outrage. In truth, even we, his foes, would take that lie amiss.

"Your lord said nothing, leaned forward on his horse's neck, smoothed its mane and spoke in its ear. They say it answers to his call, knows his mind before he speaks it; they say when he rides it, horse and rider think as one, and it too has killed many men.

"'If not you,' Henry cried next, as if in pain, for they were breaking the arrowhead from his arm, 'your Celtic wife has revealed our plans. Ask her, when you see her next, where she heard of them.'

"'She is at Cambray,' Lord Raoul said soberly.

"'Is she then? Then ask her how she escaped my brother Plantagenet, and what became of her escort? Ask her why she came to Maneth Castle and not Cambray. As she came to Poitiers perhaps. Ask her where she was a week ago. Ask her when she shared our bed...'

"In one bound, Lord Raoul leapt off his horse, took Henry by the throat. All smeared with blood, he pinned him to the sand.

"'You lie,' was all he said. 'Unsay that lie.'

"'My lord Earl.' Horrified, the king's men hurled themselves at him and tried to drag him off. But Henry lay upon the ground and smiled. Lord Raoul stood up—you know how tall he is, easily recognizable, and how he can look, his face implacable. He threw away his helmet, let it roll on the ground, unbuckled his sword belt with steady hands, took his sword and threw it so it soared in a great arc and fell with hardly a splash at the water's edge. He unstrapped his spurs and ripped them loose.

"'Here, boy,' he cried and with one hand wrestled with the straps of his mail coat. No one dared approach him. 'Here, boy,' he said again, and dropped coat and sword belt, shield, in a heap at Henry's feet. In shirt and jerkin, he vaulted back into the saddle, sat there looking at the king. His horse's hooves were within inches of the king's face.

"'One day, boy,' he said again, the contempt in his voice made men wince, 'one day we shall have the truth from your own lips, not here, not now, but one day.' The king's men had started back in alarm, terrified by that great horse; not so the king, I grant you that, he lay there without moving a muscle. But even he did not smile then.

"'Do what you will with our lands,' Lord Raoul said, 'there are other lands, and other wars. I hereby renounce all allegiance to you, a thing of straw. I dishonor you, who would seek to dishonor me. I spit on you.'

"He clapped his feet against his horse's back, bounded away, leaving Henry and the surviving lords staring after him. They say he rode southward without drawing rein, and two of his men, a knight and squire, secretly having gathered up his gear, followed him. But his guard wept for rage. And that is what they say, Lady Ann."

Daffyd said no more, and after a while, he too went away. Once, long ago, in a single moment I had lost all I loved. I remember how my father sat when they brought my brother's body back. *Drowned*, he had said. He slid from his horse and never spoke again, turned his face to the wall, so died himself. So turned now I to the wall, and hoped that death would take me too, having lost a second time all that I held most dear. Betraying, betrayed for vengeance's sake. *I had not thought Henry could do so much.* Now did he that much to me. Yet I lived, and a great sickness took me instead, welling up from my heart's core. I heard people around me, I knew when they brought me food, I must have heard them talk. Rumors of other battles reached my ears, but not my brain, how at Angelsey, an island in the north, Henry's troops again were overwhelmed, for he, recovering from the rout at Basingwerk, still fought on. I heard how Prince Owain finally made a truce, land for peace, and how the king disbanded his men, withdrew and returned to England, still in the mood of darkest gloom. Life in Prince Owain's castle went on as before. But of Lord Raoul no news, never news of Cambray or Sedgemont. The child in my womb quickened and grew, but never word of it either, until it seemed to suck my life away, a canker rather than a child, eating into the living flesh. And so I lay in a little side room which for kindness they gave to me, they themselves being more used to crowd together in some communal bed with only a stiff sheet to cover them. But I lay apart, a thing apart, as if never again to know life or warmth, and felt my loss complete.

Sometimes young Dafydd would visit me, bearing gifts as in the Celtic way, and I would lie for hours perhaps with the flowers he brought, not seeing them, only the blank stones. Sometimes the Princess Lilian would play her Welsh harp, or *crwth*, and the sound of her music too passed me by. And so time moved on and I lay there. Until one day, I sensed a difference. Had it been spring, I would have said it was the sense of living things, of sap rising, green grass, which in man as well as animals makes its presence felt. But this was the autumn of the year, when the first frosts covered the ground, and from the high windows of my chamber, a keen wind came whistling in. The room I think had been used for storing food, apples mostly, of which they eat vast amounts and drink as cider too, and although a bed filled most of the space, there were still some withered fruits lying forgotten on the rough wood shelves which lined the walls. A cool current of air streaming down brought into the room a cold white light, as if the frosts without were filtered through inside, and the scent of apples was suddenly strong and sweet.

I was lying, as I have said, my hair grown lank, uncombed. I felt someone take up a brush and begin to smooth out the snarls, begin to braid it with long cool hands. I turned my head painfully. Someone was sitting by my side, a woman cloaked against the cold. Her woolen hood was drawn over her head, and beneath, her tunic fell like silk. I thought she smiled at me.

"Ann of Cambray," I thought she said, "long has it been since I had word of you. Long since you promised me much and gave me naught. Now am I come to claim my due."

Perhaps I dreamt; perhaps I watched her for a while; perhaps she came a second time. She gave me food, a bowl of soup which I swallowed because I must. She held my head and I remember her fingers, how they smoothed the hair back from my face.

"Sa, sa," she said, and put the horn spoon into its bowl. "So, Ann of Cambray," I thought she said for a second time, "now do I ask you for my fee. What will you give me in place of it?"

And afterward or perhaps another day, or perhaps this was a continuing dream, she said, "Ann of Cambray, a third time have I called your name. I cannot call you again. What will you give me to make up the past? What will you give me for your future peace? We cannot undo what the gods have writ. Nor do we foretell your future, or anyone's, only what you yourself know in your heart. But give me my fee that I too may know peace."

Now, round my neck I still wore that linked chain which the queen had torn, and on it the great carved ring from which it seemed to me so many of my griefs were sprung. She must have guessed what was in my mind, for she pushed back the covers and drew it off. The white cold light from the window slit played on the stone, setting fires within its carved shape. She weighed it in her hand much as the queen had done.

"So," she said, "a bitter thing, but I will take it upon myself."

"I did not ask for bitterness," I thought I said. "I did not ask for men's lives. I would not live to have those guilts upon my soul."

"Then you should have stayed in your nunnery," she answered me, or I thought she did. "All who live will sin, and all must bear one another's guilt. Die if you wish, but grief is for bearing, not for turning aside."

"I remember all you said," I told her, struggling to sit up, "I remember your words and the shadow they have cast upon my life."

"Or have the shadows come and you have made them fit my words?" Her voice was shrewd as I too remembered. "The future is only the past made new. Like ripples in the lake, it flows on, not back. Have you sought me all your life to curse me or to have me take away a curse you think I laid on you? I bring you hope. A long life and hard will you have and men will die for you. Be comforted. Men will love you and you them, in the way of humankind, and love is worth the cherishing. Perhaps it is the only thing worth keeping in this world. Take pleasure in your happy days. Make peace with them and make peace with death. And if you have a son, cherish him. He most of all will need your love."

"And Raoul?" His name broke out at last, out of my silence and despair. I thought she watched me for a long while then, settling my golden chain with its heavy ring about her own neck. And I wept all those tears I had not wept since Walter's death, since Geoffrey of Sedgemont's death, since the end of my love for the queen and Geoffrey Plantagenet, since Henry had betrayed me to my lord, and since Raoul had ridden away and left me here. And it seemed to me, that where ice, numbness had been, a warmth began to grow again.

"I cannot tell you news of him," I thought she said, when I was done. "His life is his own, not mine. But he has never broken faith before. If not before, why should he break it with you? And if you have a son, which you must live to bear, will not Raoul claim him as he claimed his firstborn? Was it not a son he wanted when you parted with him?"

"How should you know that?" I cried.

"Nay," I thought she said, and almost a smile touched her lips, "I asked a question, you have answered it. But Ann, when I was young, I knew your mother very well, we were like two daughters born at one time, although she was younger and the fairer of the two. The seventh child of a seventh child was she, the fairest of her race. She lived to endure many griefs, they did not daunt her."

Her speaking of my mother was like balm upon an open wound, that lady I had never known, whose life I too had taken away. I yearned to hear of her. And, like a child, I listened to the story of Efa of the Celts. Perhaps I listened, perhaps she told it to me, or perhaps I dreamed it too, and some kind God sent it me to bring me hope and comfort. But I thought she told me it.

"Fairest of her race, she was," I thought the lady of the moors said. "A seventh born child of a seventh child is special

born, has special gifts, and so we treasured her. A child she
was, but scarcely grown to womanhood when your father saw
her first, a girl who ran free like a boy, and her father doted
on her and his sons did too, and all her family.

"In those days, the border was a wild and dangerous place,
the more the Normans, new-come to power, would try to take
lands from us and drive us back. Many were the raids we made
against the invading hordes, and many the attacks they made
on us. Your father soon won a name for himself, a strong, well-
made man, not young, not old, not tall, not short, a dour,
unsmiling man. But just. They say he had never held lands of
his own before, but with strength and determination he built
up Cambray, trained his castle guard, and followed his liege
lord, the Earl of Sedgemont, who in return gave him lordship
over these new lands. A self-made man then, but a valiant one,
a good swordsman and a leader of men. And one day, he led
them where no Norman had been before, on foot, which seldom Norman knights will do, to attack our fort. The way was
steep as it is here and the path slippery with rain. Our men
go barefoot on days like that, even leather too slippery for use,
but he made his men climb up in their Norman boots. They
lived like us on roots and leaves, carried their weapons in oiled
rags to keep them dry, and he forced them forward until they
broke through at the very foot of our walls. It was a rainy
dawn, no one looked for them; but they were weary, with
scarce strength to lift their weapons, and so were forced to
rest. The earth walls were stone faced in part, and the top was
bare save for one hooded figure who leaned out in amaze.

"'Kill me that guard, ho', your father, Lord Falk, shouts. A
man staggers up, draws his sword, begins to climb the wall. It
was faced as I have said with stone, rough-hewn and so gave
him purchase; he soon was hidden beneath an overlap where
no one could get at him. Your mother, for she it was upon the
wall, come there by chance, in the early light, restless as young
girls are, she, failing to see which way he went, leaned over
to look for him; then suddenly afraid he would pull her down

before she gave the alarm, sprang back, fitted an arrow to her hunting bow, and aimed it at your father's heart.

"'Get you gone,' she cried, 'I can kill a deer at twenty paces. I can kill you. Call your man off.'

"The other men of your father's guard having got their breath, began to laugh, one watchman and all the wall was clear. It would be an easy climb and the fortress would be open to attack. But your father held them back when they too would have scaled the wall, the sight of that one figure giving strength anew into their weary limbs.

"'Give up, boy,' your father said, 'we'll not hurt you. We do not war with boys.'

"Then she laughed as well, shook her hair free. 'If you cannot tell boys from maids,' she said, 'then you're no man to take this fort.'

"And she called out the battle cry of her house, and released her arrow, but it flew wide. I had never known her to miss before. Our sleeping warriors heard her cry, they struggled out of sleep and armed themselves. They say your father still had time to attack, one man was almost at the topmost ledge and the others were ready to follow him, but he called them down. Afterward, his men said he was like a man bemused or bewitched. And angry with a furious rage to have been so mocked. Well, we had warning to man the walls, but he still held the pass, no food went in or out, although water we had in plenty, for it rained every day. But neither had those Normans food, nor did they like sitting in the wet. On the sixth day, your father called a parley and the result was this: the Normans would withdraw down the pass, but as surety of good conduct on our part that we would not try to surround Cambray again, or steal from those herds of his which he was trying to build up, we must give a hostage of our word, else would the Normans cut a path through the woods and return with their siege machine to destroy us.

"'As for hostages,' your father said, 'we'll take but one. That maid who laughed scorn at us.'

"What an outcry then was made. What a moaning among the womenfolk, what a scandal among the men. But Efa of the Celts came to me. She had been weeping as you wept, but now her eyes were dry. Large eyes she had, as large as yours, and her hair flamed red.

"'I did not look to be wed,' she said wistfully, little more than a child and used to running free, as I have explained, and her father, loving her, had not thought to arrange a match, preferring to keep her with him, 'I had not thought to be a paramour to my enemy.'

"I smoothed her hair as I have smoothed yours. 'Do not go, my love,' I said. 'You will break your father's heart. And mine!'

"'And if not,' she said, 'they will break down our walls. So they have sworn and so will do. Wish me well, sister of my soul. If I wed, I shall bring peace. And joy to him who would wed with me although that joy may not last long. I shall never see you again. But remember me.'

"Next morning, they led her out; her father had aged twenty years in that night, her brothers came sadly to bid her good-bye, her sisters cried out for her to stay.

"'Nay,' she said, 'it is writ.' She was dressed simply as she had been that other day, her hair knotted back, her tunic as short as a boy's. They did not tie her feet, but as hostage had bound her hands behind her back and led up a horse which she rode astride.

"Lord Falk scowled down at her, for he had had his horses too brought up and the path beaten down so they could ride.

"'Come you as maid or boy?' he asked.

"'In my father's name,' she said, 'I come as boy. But for you I come as maid.' And for the first time, she smiled.

"Well, that was years and years ago. Your father escaped that iron-tipped arrow she aimed at him, but not the one that now pierced him. He cut the ropes that tied her hands, himself led her horse down the path. And when it stumbled, he set her before him against his heart. She never came back again, nor did he. But peace was made between his kin and ours.

Bound was he to her by bonds of steel, that when she died, his heart died, too. And so I think, Ann, is love like that for you, so strong it cannot bend nor break without tearing you apart with it. So perhaps it is for your lord, rare in men. If you would see him again, remember him. You lord is not dead. I cannot swear he will return, but when your son is born, go back to Cambray and wait for him. No man will harm you here or there. Keep Raoul of Sedgemont in your thoughts to draw him back to you. You have the skill, you have the power."

She paused, "And if it is a girl sometime you bear," I thought she said, "give her your mother's name that we may have a princess of our race again, as fair as mother and mother's child, to grace our halls. Do not forget me, Lady Ann, as I do not forget your mother, sister of my soul, as I have not forgotten you."

I did not see her again. Was she a dream or not, or fever's shape, culled from memories and wishes that I had deep buried? Or was she formed from my own heart's needs? Even when she was there no more, I felt her presence still, as real as the bitter wind, the scent of ripening fruit. And certainly too, from the start of those first winter days, I began to mend; the sickness abated and the nightmares; and although the frost was so thick that year that it coated trees, low growing shrubs, and plants as white as if with snow, the cold weather suddenly saw me revive. And one other thing: when I felt for the chain, it was gone and with it that royal gift that had seemed such a heavy weight about my neck.

Never since have I sought from king or queen a royal favor; their friendship comes with too high price, although it was a man's life that time I bought. Nor ever since have I trusted royal word, although it has been asked of me. And one other thing: although I did not speak what was in my mind, ever in my secret thoughts I remembered Raoul and willed him to come back to me. They say, chuchmen say, that the prayers they make rise up in columns to God, unendingly. And in this way are all men blessed and are kept safe by holy rituals. So went my thoughts. In all my waking moments, even when I did something else, I never ceased to think of him until, at times, he seemed more real than the world where I found myself. And so I lived and waited in Prince Owain's court until the birth of my second son.

13

SHALL NOT DENY THAT, AS THE months went on, I achieved a sort of tranquility in Prince Owain's court. For the first time in my life, I suppose, I became part of a family, loving to its members, giving support and comfort in time of need, cherishing each other in happy days. Prince Owain was a loving man himself, considerate to his wife and womenfolk, and a good friend to his sons and followers. The word prince in the Celtic tongue means "one who leads," and so he did, a most exemplary man. And for this reason his brother's treachery was deemed that more treacherous and was more deeply felt. And when his daughter Lilian told me the truth of that quarrel, I grieved for him, as did all honorable men. For his brother, that Prince Cadwaladr, who had been the cause of Henry's campaign, was a schemer, fickle, inconsistent, and cruel. Although he had inherited lands of his own, he was one of those Celtic lords who had hoped to profit by the civil wars in England, so had supported first one faction, then the other, and on returning to Wales, had tried the same tactics there. Finally, in some minor boundary dispute over some minor boundary right, he had fought and killed Owain's nephew and son-in-law, a death that Owain had taken hard, for his nephew was a young man, beloved son of a beloved sister, and a youth upon whom he had pinned his hopes. That murder had plunged Owain's house into deepest mourning. Lilian herself did not well remember the dead man except as a tall and laughing presence on the fringes of her memory, but all of Wales had been shocked by such a wanton killing. For that reason then had Prince Cadwaladr been driven from Wales and had been forced to ask help from the English king. Such was the evil man that Henry had befriended as he had other evil men. Lilian told me many things during this time, and showed me many more so that, as from a sister, I learned the ways of my Celtic kin. She taught me how to bind my hair under the white veil they wore, crimped up in folds or pleats like a crown, it never looked as well on me as it did on her, for her hair was short and curled about her ears and cheeks. She showed me how she took care of her teeth, brushing them with the green shoots of hazel twigs, and explained how she never ate food too hot or cold since that would darken the whiteness she admired— a practice which may have explained the state of the kitchens. For although the food was copious, it was badly served. It could have disgraced a Norman hall—Celts seem to eat but once a day and dine without benefit of tables, linen, or table napkins, plunking the food down on a bed of rushes or fresh grass, and letting you pick at a trencher of bread, three to a slice. Yet Welsh hospitality is proverbial, and if a guest of rank came to stay, Prince Owain himself and his lady wife would serve the visitor first, and if need be, go without food themselves.

Lilian even tried to teach me how to make the Welsh oaten cakes which she rolled out thin and sliced, but I was so bad at that, she dissolved into gales of laughter as she often did when something amused her. She told me once that she would wed only with a man who knew how to make her laugh. She herself was a laughing, joyous girl, who would make a man happy one day, although when I looked carefully around Owain's court, I saw there were few enough men of marrying age. They were either old, or boys, all the rest in between were dead, I think, dead for honor or for liberty. But best of all, I liked to hear her sing. Poet, you would know those songs of heroes long ago and valorous deeds, songs you sing now and we still enjoy. And sometimes, when Dafydd had the time, we would walk together, and he would tell us of his adventures since he had left Cambray those years ago. These were simple pleasures, simple ways such as I prefer to pomp and ceremony. But always, underneath them were my silent, constant thoughts that made Raoul appear to me as clearly as Lilian and Dafydd did, sometimes so real I felt, if I stretched out my hand, I could touch him and bring him back.

What of Lord Raoul? This I know. He tore off the trappings of an earl and repudiated a title which since it had been bestowed on him had brought him nothing but rancor and sorrow. He disavowed those oaths that he had in honor made to a king without honor, and sluffed off those cares of faith and loyalty which had marred his life. *I bear the weight of the kingdom on my back*—now he rode alone without thoughts, without plans, unencumbered by them. I do not know what words to use to tell of a man choked with rage and pride, perhaps no woman does. But even as dying horsemen keep in the saddle until their last breath is gone, by instinct only they ride, so I think did he. South he went, across that land that at the best of times takes eight days to cover coast to coast; he and his horse, tireless, beat down those miles, gone beyond all normal needs of food or rest. I cannot tell you what drove him thus, except the pain and the numbing cold of grief, those I can share with you and him.

At the southern coast he turned west and shortly came to the Cornish ports where Geoffrey Plantagenet had hoped to lure me. The harbors there are small and quiet, havens for fugitives and exiles seeking a quick passage to France, and the fishermen, although rough and loud-voiced, are good-natured at heart, and for a fee in ready gold will take you where you will, no questions asked. Good sailors are they in their tiny boats, who know the Channel and where to find a quiet cove or inlet for a secret landing. Where Raoul meant to go and what he meant to do on getting there was still not clear, and perhaps he himself did not know. But, praise God, he did not really ride alone. One of his knights and a squire secretly followed him. So in the past had other men for love shared his exile, so now did these two.

His squire I never saw, lost to fever at some time in some dank and sordid hut, but the knight I did, Sir Piers, a comrade since they first had fought in Stephen's war. Having no kith nor kin of his own, this knight took it upon himself to accompany his lord, keeping a distance behind, not too far to be unable to come to his aid if he needed it, not too close for him to notice. But Raoul might not have noticed in any case, lost to the world in his own thoughts. Sir Piers brought his armor, his sword and belt, for Lord Raoul rode in tunic, uncloaked, unarmed, a mad fool he must have seemed to ride so heedlessly through so many wild and lawless parts. Yet those who, on seeing him, might have been tempted to attack, were frightened off, either because they sensed that madness, that carelessness in him, more threatening than a drawn sword, or because they saw behind him a more tangible threat, those two menacing figures of his guard.

Well, at the Cornish coast Raoul never paused, passed without hesitation down those narrow winding lanes between high banks of fern and flowers, came to the nearest port. Often in my own dreams I followed him there, a place I have never seen except I could describe it to you: a small village smelling of pilchards and crab with rocky gray cliffs and granite walls. Raoul paid no heed to anyone, not even to the women who ran after him, the most handsome man ever to ride their way. He dismounted by the harbor wall, stormed on board the nearest ship, threw himself upon the deck and slept in an instant with his cloak wrapped about his head, the sleep of the weary or the damned, after those days and nights without rest.

Sir Piers, spurring after him, found the black horse cropping along the cliff edge, Lord Raoul on board, and the Cornish fishermen whispering like housewives among themselves. Since Raoul had never left a horse uncared for, certainly never that black horse that was his second self, it showed more than anything how deep his distaste for himself had gone, that, if he could, he would have flayed off his skin to be rid of all that he had been and all that Henry had taunted him with. Sir Piers then, on his lord's behalf, made peace with these suspicious sailors, and having persuaded them to jettison whatever cargo they had in their stinking hold, went on board. To pay for the passage, he was forced to use those monies which Raoul had left in his charge for largesse to the public when he rode out on the king's business in the marcher lands. (And for this reason, too, it had been decided hastily among Raoul's friends, that Sir Piers was the most fitting of Lord Raoul's knights to accompany him. For Sir Piers was the keeper of this wealth, which all agreed should now be most justly used to succor the warden of those lands in his own need, rather, that is, than be returned to King Henry to squander in a useless war.)

This embezzlement Henry might well have levelled charges against, but never did—all the other rolls and accounts having been most carefully and accurately kept by Sir Piers's scribes as Lord Raoul had instructed. But strangest thing of all, that black horse, which in ordinary times would never let anyone come near it, walked of its own accord up the plankway to the ship as if it too could tell there was something amiss. So for pity and loyalty and for some unnamed thing that I think is between men, Sir Piers and Raoul's squire followed him. They did not speak or interrupt his sleep, and bedded down near him upon the open deck and slept too. At first, that is.

For hardly had they sailed a day away, knowing nothing of their destination for Raoul said no word to anyone, a storm blew up that drove them to the Irish coast. Heavy seas swept the decks and even the horse stalls below were awash. Stripped to the waist, Raoul's men were forced to tie themselves and their lord to a mast to avoid being swept overboard, so did the sailors, all hope lost. But when the storm blew itself away, as quickly as it had blown up, Raoul at last roused himself, drank rainwater, broke his fast on whatever waterlogged food was at hand, seemed come back to life, although changed. And this I could understand, having experienced something of the same myself at Prince Owain's court.

Sir Piers explained it thus, in more soldier-like terms. "When a boy," he said, "I was wounded in the leg, a scratch that, turning septic, was like to have been my death, for the arrowhead had buried beneath the skin. It was a small campaign to kill me, a night skirmish only, and my companions tried at first to bear me on their backs. They had to wade around a cliff face in a cold stream, the current so swift it seemed like to run the cold into their bones if the water's race did not carry them all away. Believing I was done for, certain sure of drowning if they stayed, they left me on the bank, tied to a tree bole, thinking never to see me again. All night long the water rose, I sat there to my knees in it. When they returned next day, I credit them that they came to bury me, they found me new-born, weak but alive, the fever gone, the poisons in the wound washed clean. Yet even now when the weather changes or I am tired, that scar I bear throbs and burns. So I think it was with my lord, a wound washed clean yet beneath the scar, it was still raw. His eyes were clear, although he spoke only little, his voice was normal, he looked and lived like any man—but beneath, hidden, there was some deep and dreadful wound."

So Raoul and his two men came at last to the coast of France, south of the region called Brittany, and there they took horse, rode on, as companions, not earl and lord, or knight and squire, but three men, buying their way by feats of arms, sometimes biding in one place, sometimes journeying on, sometimes going on pilgrimage to one holy shrine only to hear of another one more holy still.

A good man was that Sir Piers who lived to see happier days, and good and true that faithful squire who saw the world end for him far from home; but death did not come for Lord Raoul, although there were those who said he sought it.

By now, a Yuletide had come and gone, and I remained at Prince Owain's court, cut off from Cambray, from Sedgemont, from Sieux, and all that was done in Henry's England. I cannot say I did not think of that time nor these places I had known and loved, nor of all my friends left there, most of all of my husband and my son. But I had learned to build a barricade around those thoughts and only let them out when I was alone.

And so it was in the New Year, in a week of snow and ice that brought the wolves howling round our gates, that blocked the mountain passes and froze birds as they flew through the air, then was my second son born. An easy birth and I cherished

him, son of my grief, born out of time and place. And they
called him Hue, spelt in the Celtic way, although a Norman
name, which means "thought." And so he was, a child thought
about, although in no way an easy or thoughtful child. He was
as loud as Robert had been quiet. Sometimes Lilian stopped
her ears and claimed she had believed the devil driven out of
Wales until he now seemed come back again in this strange
guise. And a greedy child, who drained me dry, so full of
vitality he seemed to have taken mine as well. His hair was
red, like my own, red hair, red temper, that one day men
should notice him. But his eyes were gray. And often when
Dafydd came and sat with us and dangled the baby in a way
that reminded me of Walter at Sieux, he and Lilian would plan
the future of this little prince, or so they called him, to make
me smile. Well, for all of us is the future begun the day of our
birth, we make it as we move through life, so for him.

Thus was born my second son, a scant few months after
the queen gave birth to him who in time should be a king. But
my son Hue would be befriended by a king's son, who never
became a king himself, and who would bring woe and death
to his friends. And sometimes, when we were alone, I held the
child so that my mouth was close to his ear, shell-shaped and
perfect, so that I could whisper in it. Then I told him who his
father was, a great and noble lord, and what high hopes Lord
Raoul had had for his son, even if he did not yet know he was
born.

"But he will return," I told the child, not that a baby under-
stands the words, but he does the sense. Hue knew everything
I said to him, he drew it in like the air he breathed. "Your
father has gone far away because he has something he must
do. No one knows in truth what he seeks, perhaps not even
he himself, but he will when it faces him. Those who ride with
him, and I myself, we believe he will never rest until his quest
is finished. You would not want him here with us, incomplete,
a man who feels his honor has been tarnished?"

Sometimes, when I spoke those thoughts aloud, a great
sadness would overwhelm me that, unwittingly, I had been the

cause of so much woe. The baby uncomprehendingly watched the tears fall. Grief was not his to know. But when I told him how his father rode with his men and how the fame of their progress spread until, sometimes, there was never a joust or tourney that, on learning Raoul was there, knights wouldn't come flocking for many miles to run a pass with him, when I spoke of these things I thought my son listened more intently than before.

"And so your father and his men wander," I told Hue, "like migrating birds, now here, now there, until there is no famous place, no holy shrine they have not visited, no pilgrimage they have not made. I do not know if they think of us. But I promise you, Hue of the Celts, your father will come for you one day. He will set you on his black horse and ride with you over the hills. Then shall you see beyond these lands, all of England, and France, all the world with him."

"And you, my son, are heir to a great name," I told him another day, when another long day was drawing to a close. "You are a Celt. You were born a Celtic prince. That is your true name. For Wales and Welsh are foreign words, Saxon words, not Celtic ones. Cymry are we called, and the land sometimes Cambria, from a Latin name." Solemnly I spoke and solemnly he listened, as if he had to memorize what I said, and Lilian, passing by, smiled to hear me recount all I had learned about this country which I had only recently come to know myself. She did not know why or to whom I really spoke. Hue did.

So when I told him on a certain day it was time to return to Cambray, I did not have to explain to him why that day more than any other one, or why Cambray. I knew it to be so, and so did Hue, a feeling, a sensation hung in the air like the sound a harp makes before it is completely strung, a yearning far away, like the wind that blows across the moors.

"Raoul needs us there," I told Hue as I wrapped him in his lace shawl, woven so fine like cobwebs, "now is the day he will wish to come home himself." And Hue felt it too, that bond as strong and irresistible as the sea tides.

It was not easy to leave this Celtic court. Prince Owain tried to dissuade me, and my friends wept. I did not wish to seem ungrateful for their kindnesses—I had never known such kind people before—but I had to go. So with many protestations of sadness then on their part and mine, with their wishes for my happiness, with auguries of good fortune, I took Hue, and in a cavalcade, we came down the mountain pass and turned south. Dafydd and Lilian came with me. Before we reached the castle at Cambray, Dafydd drew me aside. He was riding his moorland horse, its long tail and mane blowing in the wind, and the bright March sun glinted on his hair.

"Lady Ann," he said, after many starts, "it is not too late to change your mind, turn back with me. Or, having come to Cambray, stay but a while, then come again to Owain's fort. You are as welcome there as flowers in spring. I should be waiting for you at the border pass."

He put out his hand to cover mine, a small fine-boned hand he had for a warrior, strong and supple like steel. "I should wait for you," he repeated. "If I feel myself part Norman, as well as Celt, you alone made me so, nothing else. If I had thoughts of staying at Cambray, it was because of you. I left Cambray for freedom but I also left because you were gone. Now I think God has given you back to me, lost in the mist that day." He hesitated. "Your husband has gone," he said, "and where, who knows. You cannot wear your youth away waiting for a shadow that may never become flesh."

How should I explain that that shadow world was always real for me?

When I did not reply, "Wait then, for the summer's end. I will send again in the autumn time," he said. "But if you need me, summon me. My men and I will come, although I swore never to trespass on Cambray lands."

He hesitated longer before he said, "And if, in God's time, you should think of another man, remember Dafydd, son of Howel, to whom you gave life back long ago; give me chance of it again."

A gentle man was Dafydd, too. But I could not give him what he wanted, and he could not give me my heart's wish. We made a parting there, for he would not be foresworn and come within the boundaries of my father's lands. He turned back to the high mountains, and Lilian and I rode southward toward the sea.

I had not seen Cambray since the day I had left it to plead for Raoul's life, knowing then I was with child, knowing that Raoul was marked for death by Henry's men. Little had changed at Cambray in these past years, the walls more gray, and the outer battlements battered by heavy storms. But the moors behind them were undisturbed, and the sea below the castle was as permanent as the sky above. Once I had wanted nothing more than to return to this small and simple castle at the far end of the Norman world, until that Norman world wanted it. But Henry, it seemed, had made no move against us after all, and tranquil had been the castle all this while. And tranquil came I back to live there and wait. In time, they brought young Robert to me from Sedgemont. Then had I both my sons in my care to my content. At each season, Dafydd sent messages, or sometimes I would ride out to the edge of the moors and meet him there.

But these were the outward things of my life. In my mind's eye I lived in Raoul's world, and what we waited for was the same. For I waited for love and so, I think, in the end did he. His love of me, his hatred of Henry were different sides of the same coin. *You will never know if he loves you.* Now far away, he avenged that love; he avenged that hate. And in my thoughts, I shared both with him. Well, this too is a tale that must be told and I not the one to do all the telling of it, a man's story this; of war and death as well as love. Let Lord Ademar speak of it, as he once told it me, Lord Ademar, who came to Poitiers to be with the king and tried to spare me the queen's wrath, and who lived to see his wager come true and to be a witness of it. It was a wager no man dared breathe aloud, that one day, Raoul would challenge Henry to combat. And still today

no men talk of it; you will not find it written in the chronicles;
silent they are upon such a thing, beyond their understanding.
But so it was done, and so foretold.

Now, there are two other points which must also be said
before we come to the last part of our tale. One is what King
Henry did not do, the other what King Henry did. After Raoul
had left in such a fashion as to send waves of scandal through
the English court, Henry made no move against him. He never
tried to take Sedgement; he certainly never tried to take Cambray, although he had wanted it so badly, and his lawyers, ever
greedy for more lands, tried to persuade him that now he had
the right to seize both within the process of the law. Why he
did not is not clear. But, as if to make the distinction plain,
his standard-bearer, that other earl, Henry of Essex—who,
you remember, had thrown down the king's flag and run away—
for six years, Henry pursued him. At the end of that time,
when the Earl of Essex might well have thought himself safe,
Henry's wrath caught up with him. He was hauled before one
of Henry's new courts on charge of cowardice and forced to
answer for his treachery. He was defeated in a duel by a champion chosen by the king, left for dead, immured in a monastery,
his lands forfeit. A monk he lived the rest of his days, in Reading
Abbey, no slight thing to give up the world for honor's shame,
yet never word of blame or complaint Henry dared let fall
against Earl Raoul; and whether that was for guilt, having
broken oath with me in such shameful wise, or whether for
justice to the earl himself, I do not know. In any case, Lord
Raoul's lands were not touched; he could have come back
without constraint. And never Henry spoke of Basingwerk or
his defeat, and all men avoided reference to it.

As to what Henry did, a restless wanderer too was he, crisscrossing the Channel like a man possessed. Having recovered
of his wounds, having given up the Welsh campaign, seeming
to have lost interest in it, he went back to France, tried to
make peace with King Louis at last, tried to capture all of
Brittany and veered from one place to the next as if pacing
about a room, not a continent. Finally, he turned the full blaze

of his attention on Toulouse. He had another score to settle there, an old one too, with Count Raymond, Lord Ademar's overlord. And it was there, now, that the two wanderers met. Henry had long held a grudge against Count Raymond of Toulouse, incensed by his failure to pay court at Poitiers. He chose now to move against Toulouse because, since he had not succeeded in having Count Raymond do fealty for his lands, he feared that the Count would try to make them independent of the Duchy of Aquitaine. Cleverly, Henry justified his attack by declaring, not that Count Raymond held lands without swearing homage, but rather that he had no right to them at all. Toulouse, he said, in fact, belonged to Queen Eleanor! Naturally enough, Count Raymond laughed this idea to scorn, so Henry began to raise a second army, a mighty one, bigger, they claimed, than any army raised in France since the holy wars, to use against him.

Lord Ademar described Henry's army thus: "A mighty dust train, a serpent's trail, writhing its way along those hot and dusty roads, such a gathering of all of Henry's feudal host, packed out with mercenaries where he could squeeze them in, that the whole from head to start stretched many miles, not counting the baggage train. Lord Raoul spoke true when he said that Henry had found a new toy, a feudal army that, at his command, would march or stop, attack or besiege, as he gave the word. I was with Count Raymond in Toulouse itself, and the city teemed with rumor: how many miles the army marched each day, how many castles they took along the way, how many lords they forced to submit, how they skirmished through Perigord, seized Cahors, with its great Roman bridge, until, by and by, they were expected at our very gates.

"Count Raymond was a brave and stubborn man. 'Let him come,' I heard him say. 'I can outface a Count of Anjou, a trumped up title and a jumped up man, not half the size of my estates.' Bravado he had, to refuse to call Henry a king, to ignore such a danger coming at him; and in truth, things might have gone ill for us (I was in that city too and knew how ill-prepared we were to hold off such a besieging force), had not two things conspired to help us. One was the arrival of King Louis of France. Now Henry claimed King Louis had blessed his plans, knew of them, and welcomed them. Certainly, Louis knew of them—Henry had told all the world—but whether he agreed to them was another thing. For Louis's sister was married to Count Raymond, and although Louis had little liking for the Count, he did not want to see his sister and her sons dispossessed. Besides, he more than anyone else in France had had enough of Henry's whittling away at his lands. Seldom does Louis decided anything (they say he spends all day determining what shirt to wear); but in this, for once he took the initiative, came quickly to the city before Henry reached it, and undertook to help us with our defense. The second source of help was Lord Raoul himself."

Among King Louis's soldiers came the man Lord Ademar had seen but once, but had never forgotten, Lord Raoul, who was claimed to be the greatest knight in all of France. He did not answer to any title, not even that of Count of Sieux; he wore the plainest clothes, who had been plain to excess before, but his armor, his shield, his gear, were as well cared for as any man's. And his great horse that no one dared approach, they say he handled it like a hound. Two men followed him, both as taciturn and dour, and since all three by then counted as one man, fought, warred and rode as one, Count Raymond was glad to welcome them. Ademar remembered when he had seen Lord Raoul that one time at Poitiers and had judged Raoul as impulsive, arrogant, and proud. Now Raoul seemed, reserved perhaps is a good word, turned in upon himself, like a man with some secret cause that drove him on. Nor did Raoul take anyone into his confidence, but everyday came up upon the north facing ramparts of the city wall and waited there until the sun set. And when at last, in the July month, that telltale dust cloud finally appeared, to make the citizens cry out and wring their hands, he never showed any outward sign, but sat resting there with his chin upon his hands. But his hands were clasped about his sword hilt. All night long he sat, and after dark the little pinpoints of flame where Henry's men had made camp seemed to hold his gaze, as if by turning his head away or blinking even one eye they might disappear. Lord Ademar marveled that a sight which caused so many men's hearts to sink, even the most courageous ones, should so gladden this man that, for the first time since Raoul had come to Toulouse, he almost smiled.

"A siege army is an awesome thing at best," Lord Ademar later was to explain, "and few men watch its approach without some sense of foreboding. I confess, when I saw the numbers of men Henry had brought, and the great siege machines that can hurl stones and torches to shatter a wall and burn down a house, and battering rams, and siege towers made of rawhide and wood, I felt a sensation close to fear. And since there was nothing else to be done, for our preparations were as complete as we could achieve, I watched from the ramparts beside Lord Raoul. I did not stand where he could see me, and I am not sure he would have cared if he could. He did not know me then, and there was that about him, that fixed purpose that I had only seen in religious men before. His silence and his immobility, like a bird of prey, a cat that stalks at night, fascinated me. And at dawn, he rose, strapped on his sword, and ran down the stone steps two by two as lightly as a boy. In the courtyard of Count Raymond's castle, Sir Piers had already saddled his lord's black horse and had slung upon its back the trappings that I had never seen Raoul use, scarlet and gold, and over his work-worn mail was slipped his surcoat, gold and red. His squire broke out his flag, and on his shield the golden hawks of Sedgement flared. They clattered out of the yard, and men made way for them; down the empty cobbled streets they went, the morning not yet come to the city depths, shadows deep in alleyway and court. Toulouse in peace is a gracious town, full of flowering vines and pretty maids. The three men paid no heed, although I myself could have paused to let the sun catch the red petaled flowers, to listen to the girls singing in the morning cool as they washed themselves. I followed Lord Raoul. Call it curiosity or fate, what you will. I, too, looked for my horse and rode behind him until he came to the city gates. They were locked and trebly guarded, and no man could pass in and out. Then I spurred up to him where the guard had challenged him.

"'Where are you going, Lord Raoul?' I asked, without word of greeting as if I expected him to know why I was there. He did not ask who questioned him. He may or may not have known my name, but his answer did not surprise me.

"'I go,' he said, 'to honor a vow. The time of fulfillment is here.'

"At my nod, the guards clashed to arms and drew back the bolts, his horse clattered through, already pulling at the bit, tossing its head. Before it reached the open road, it had broken into a canter. And his men let him ride alone.

"'Will you let him go into Henry's camp without escort?' I cried, 'They will cut him down.'

"But Sir Piers looked out through the half-opened gate, and watched his lord gallop toward the north. 'This is the end for us,' he said, 'he goes with God and is in His hands.' Then he and his squire turned their horses and plodded back the way they had come. The guards began to close the gates.

"'Wait,' I cried. They looked at me in amaze. I am no gambler as you know, a cautious man, considering things many times. I never act on impulse, but I did then. Call it stupidity, curiosity or call it fate, I rode out after him."

(And that day was the day, I, Ann, went back to Cambray. What made me go? What force bound me to my lord, like a sea tide? Let other men explain it as they can. I can only tell you in my thoughts I knew it to be so. And in my thoughts I rode with him.)

Afterward, in the city, they said it was the hand of God that saved them from the siege. For three days there was no news. Henry's army ringed them round; the machines and the sappers' mines were brought into place. The wooden towers that would be wheeled against the walls were half-built. The third night the campfires sparked as they had each night before. But by dawn, the army had gone, their tents dismantled, their machines abandoned, only the retreating dust clouds showed where they went. Many are the reasons given for this sudden withdrawal, sickness, plague, lack of food, change of plans, dislike of fighting against an overlord, since King Louis was still in the town. The chroniclers list many such reasons, all conflicting ones, until it seems clear they but guess at things they do not know. And they do not know because the truth was such that no man dare speak it, much less write it down. So now that truth should be told. Let Lord Ademar tell it also, that lord from Toulouse, who was in the city and destined to be the witness of such strange happenings. And although this be a man's tale, yet I, Ann of Cambray, and all women, may share in it.

He used to pause, as he spoke, Lord Ademar, in his age, and stare, as if seeing, after all these years, the white baked city walls, the white dust trail, the burning sun that glittered on the vast encampment, the two horsemen riding one by one. And as if he saw too, himself, for once all caution thrown aside, as if he sensed the shadow figure of myself, riding with them to make a third.

For Lord Raoul rode ahead, not fast but fast enough, a man with a mission to achieve, and little chance of accomplishing it, and death waiting him before the day's end. And honor shone clear about him like a lamp. The main camp was farther off than it had seemed from the city walls, and they had to ride through a stretch of woodland, more like scrub bush and thorn, with many paths winding in and out. Lord Ademar let his horse pick its own way, always keeping that distant figure in sight. An hour or so they rode through this wasteland, not even birds left, all fled before the storm, so that it was close to noon before they came to the first lines.

"Raoul's horse suddenly reared back, as if stung, and so I too drew rein," Lord Ademar explained. "One of the king's outposts was stationed there and rose from their hiding place to challenge us.

"'In the king's name,' the captain began, then backed, seeing such a knight, so armed, in front of him almost alone. The word of alarm died on his lips.

"'Let me pass,' Lord Raoul said, moved forward as if the fellow did not exist. For a moment I thought the captain would call his men to arms, but perhaps, seeing me, seeing the splendor of Raoul's accoutrements, he hesitated, thinking this was some emissary from the town, or even, if God should be so kind, a peace offer from the Count of Toulouse, since sieges are as little popular with troops outside as they are with those trapped within. But, 'Let me pass,' Lord Raoul repeated until the captain fell back, his men with him. So Raoul rode on through, and I, Lord Ademar of Toulouse, rode after him.

"All the world, the world of men and soldiers and knights that is, knows of Raoul's meeting with the king," said Ademar. "There is almost no need to tell it again. Only the chroniclers try to hide it, an event so contrary to their political theories they do not know what to make of it. Word of Lord Raoul's coming had leaped ahead, like wildfire spread, so that even before he came to the big pavillion where Henry lodged, men had begun to gather, at first furtively in small groups, then more openly as their numbers grew. Some of them, remembering the Welsh campaign and knowing they owed their lives to the Earl of Sedgemont, came to thank him and to wish him well; others, having heard of Boissert Field, came to look at the man responsible for it; and some, not knowing anything in particular, came to see a warrior whose reputation they admired. And they say that, afterward, there were men, younger men, who took him for their model, a knight errant, or wandering knight, who roamed the world on a quest. But never quest like this.

"In front of the king's tent then, Raoul stopped again and sat with that same hard, intent look that made men afraid. There was no sound, strange in so large and mixed a gathering, and the hot air closed round them like a fog; even the king's standard fell in limp folds.

"'Henry of Anjou.' Raoul's voice was low, yet it carried to

those waiting men, a tone to make many shiver for all the heat. Some crossed themselves and muttered prayers beneath their breath.

"'Henry of Anjou, I am come.'

"That was all, no name, no explanation of why or how. No one dared move, either forward or back. The stillness, the heat, was like the wait before a cloudburst. But Lord Raoul was calm and still, and his lean form was as beautiful as a coiled up snake, and as deadly. But his face, without expression, with that thin white scar across the cheekbone, was a death mask.

"Suddenly, the fastenings of the king's tent were torn apart and the king strode through the flaps. He was on foot, of course, but already in his mail coat and his coif, and he carried his helmet with the sprig of yellow broom. Behind him, a frightened squire struggled with his shield, while another bore his battle axe and sword. He said nothing, looked nowhere, merely pushed through his councilors, who wrung their hands, although afterward it was marveled that he came forth so speedily armed, as if (could it have been so?) he already sat there expecting Raoul. No word, no sign either, from him; he simply snapped his fingers, thus, as he does, to send his guard scrabbling for their mounts, and the grooms running with his. It was the great gray stallion from Cambray he rode; he did not even bother with the reins, but vaulted on its back and spurred after Raoul, who before the king was fairly in the saddle, had already turned and moved off, cantering easily along the track he had come in, without a backward look. In silence too the crowd made way, parting in front of them on either side as a field of wheat is cut by a scythe. And the king followed him, riding like a man mesmerized, as if some tethering rope kept him in line, as if some bond attached him to the rider ahead. His face was mottled blue and white, though not for fear, and he kept his hand so hard clamped on the bridle rein that, where the bit cut into his horse's mouth, the foam was tinged with red. And that was for impatience.

"Behind Lord Raoul and the king followed the king's guard,

and I, Ademar, and so, keeping to our place, we came to a path that led away from both city and camp. But it is said that after we were gone, every man who could walk or run, every boy and scullion, scurried to find some conveyance, some of them even begging to be taken up behind a mounted man. Thus, in the rear a motley group followed us. (And, in my thoughts, I, Ann of Cambray also followed after them.)

"The countryside around Toulouse is wild and rocky but where a river cuts its way from the north, beyond that first stretch of woodland, there is a wide flood plain mostly bone-dry at this time of the year, although in places trickles of water still pool into hollows among the sandbars. Wild iris grows there and sorrel, and there are stands of tall flowering weeds along the dried-up waterbeds, a breeding ground for snakes and other vermin so that few local men go there, no use in summer even for hunting.

"The afternoon was now well advanced, the air as thick and still as dawn; there was no breath of wind to bring relief, even the shadows in this arid soil were stark and hot. The men were sweating in their leather coats; to ride in full armor under that sun would have daunted many knights. Nor was it easy riding across this coarse and gritty sand, but Raoul kept up his steady pace, not deviating for rock or bush until he came to a place where a large meander of the main river had cut out a long level stretch between its banks. His horse forged on through the rank marsh grass, then stopped and turned. Raoul had been riding bareheaded all this while, and after he had drawn his sword and clapped his shield over his left arm, we saw how he unbuckled his sword belt, threw it and scabbard to the ground. No quarter then, to the death. He urged his horse toward the king. (And perhaps, in my thoughts, I, Ann of Cambray, saw him ride.)

"King Henry had paused when Raoul did and was already fidgeting for his shield and sword. Now he too stood up in the stirrups, as if eager to begin, and spurred his horse forward. Young and fresh, it bounded over the flinty soil, and as Henry rode, he closed his helmet down. The sand spurted beneath his hooves; no one could hear the cry the king gave, but Raoul's was clear, a clarion, the first time his battle cry had been heard for many weary months.

"'A moi, Sedgemont, a moi, Sieux,' and he raised his sword and leveled it like a lance. Henry met him head on, swerved at the last moment before impact; shields clashed rim to rim, and when they turned, Raoul's swordtip was red. Back they wheeled, slash and thrust. Never in this life shall men see again such a fight; the dust swirled in clouds; the thunder of their hooves beat up and down the sand. At each turn the gray horse bore its master in, bore him safely away; each time, when the dust had settled, Lord Raoul, standing firm, had let Henry beat upon him, had thrust Henry back, advanced a pace or two himself. They were well matched as swordsmen; such men could fight all day until one tired. They were well matched with horse and horsemanship, again until one tired, or made a mistake. And like a flame that leaps between two fires, they sparked each other on, until it seemed an energy, a rage, flared back and forth between them both.

"I wish," Lord Ademar used to say, "it had been given to me once to know such courage, such strength, such grace. No fighting man could wish for more, or to make a better end. So they say the Vikings fought, beloved of their gods. Happy the man who dies in such company. But they fought on, not gods, not heroes, two weary men, each hammering at the other through to human flesh. The sun sank lower to give them coolness but they heeded it not. And we waited there, the scatterings of any army, at an arena rim and watched."

(And in my mind's eye, I, Ann of Cambray, waited, too.)

"King Henry sat in his saddle as if immoveable, locked into place. That gray horse had a heart of steel; time and time again it bore him in, carried him out of reach. But Raoul and his horse moved as one, a single being, neither man nor horse. Tireless Raoul seemed, a man so coiled in upon himself you could not reach the depths of him.

"And so they fought to day's end. We could hear both men sobbing for breath; they panted as they heaved their mighty swords; their horses were glassy-eyed, lathered with foam, having in them strength for one more charge. Henry pushed his helmet up, wiped a bloody hand across his face, slammed the visor shut. But I heard him shout first, 'Rot you in Hell, Raoul of Sieux.' He set his gray stallion in one final sweep. Down that scuffed and stained stretch of sand it came, panting now, its breath short and rasping, almost stumbling for weariness, but he pulled it up.

"And Raoul too rode out at Henry. His shield rim caught Henry's so that the buckles snapped, ripped it off, almost unseating the king. We heard the rasp of it, edge to edge, then the clatter as it fell to the ground. Sword to sword, right arm to arm, until Henry's arm began to bend. And then we saw how Henry reached behind his back, reached with his left arm, empty shield arm, and plucked the battleaxe from his belt, and threw it in one fast move. He could not miss at such close range, nor could Raoul move to deflect its path. It struck high on the black horse's side, cutting through the scarlet saddlecloths, cutting through Raoul's mail coat, cutting through to the bone. The force of that blow shook both men apart. Raoul's face had paled with shock and loss of blood, yet he gave no cry of pain, simply wheeled his horse back.

"'Then this, Henry, great king,' he said. And straight at Henry, jubilant, he rode. The black horse bounded forward, although with each step the scarlet of the cloth ran deeper red; up on its haunches it rose, those murderous front hooves slashed through air, and down upon the Cambray gray that reeled under them.

"Down crashed Raoul's shield to break through Henry's guard; down sliced that deadly sword blade to slash and thrust. Both men were reeling now, reins gone, hold gone, only instinct kept then horsed. And with one last effort, with his last strength, Raoul thrust at the king's horse to make it run. Neck to neck, and man to man, they galloped away, and were lost in the growing dark. Only the drumming of their hooves was heard, until that, too, faded away."

Then Ademar fell silent and sat as if he too had lost breath, as if in his thoughts he saw and heard again that bloodstained charge. There was a far-off look upon his face as if he were one who, in ancient times, had seen heroes do battle before the gods. (And I, Ann of Cambray, in my thoughts, had seen them fight.) After a while, Lord Ademar roused himself.

"Almost immediately," he said, "came the quick southern night. No moon, later it would rise, no path, no man who dared follow where they went. Down on our haunches we squatted, one by one, trapped there ourselves until the dawn. But I, I dismounted and went on foot, step-by-step, carefully threading out the way they had gone. And in the end, I found them," he said. "Side by side, as if for comfort's sake in this desolate place, and what said or done in the aftermath of that dark and dreadful day no man should know. Yet I know it. I heard it from Lord Raoul himself, panted out in a fever fit, cried out in his delirious dreams. His secret then, no man else's, and so I have told no man else. But since he lived to speak of it, in broken phrases, mumbled words, like a man whose voice is not used to speech, it should be told. Thus, from those fractured pieces I round it out as his testament.

"'We galloped on,' Lord Raoul said, 'Jesu, I do not look for a fight like that again. Henry was better armed, better horsed, better disciplined than I thought.' And he almost gave his mocking grin. 'Better than he promised as a boy when he modeled himself on me. All was dark. I remember little of that ride—pain perhaps, you grow used to that, weakness, a sense of calm. I expected death, only hoped to meet it with due honor. And that I too had known before. When I became aware of where I was, I was still in the saddle, dripping wet, my horse still heaving under me.'

"'We had blundered into one of those penned in pools and there the horse had paused, the water at least to give it comfort, every step it took opening its wound. The axehead was still buried in my leg, but for me the blade acted as a kind of pad, if the pain could be endured. The cool of the water rose like mist, I was parched with thirst, no way to get down to it, no way, unhorsed, to mount again. So, after a while, we inched back to land, limped along the water's edge. I saw the gray horse first, a blur in the dark, where it had fallen on its side, its great heart burst. God knows it was a noble beast. The king lay where he had been tossed as it fell, spread-eagled on his back, not three paces further on. His helmet had fallen off, his face was bloodless white. I thought him dead when we came up, and I sat looking down at him for a long time. His surcoat was hacked and torn, his mail ripped through, there was another dark smear across his head. I cannot say if I was glad, was sorry—I felt nothing at all, thought nothing, too weary for anything except to sit and watch. And presently, after a while, or perhaps after a long while, for in the meantime the moon had begun to rise, I saw his eyes were open and he was watching me.'

""Not yet," he croaked as if he guessed my thoughts, "I still breathe." He struggled to sit up, one arm crooked from the fall, the other he kept tight pressed against his side to stem the blood.'

""Get off your horse," he said. "I can fight on foot. Can you?" And he nodded to where the axe shaft was still clearly visible. "Where is my horse?" he asked then, but he saw it before I could reply."

""Then is your earl's fee in part forfeit," he said in gasps, "that was one-eighth of your land's worth." He leaned back and, for a moment, closed his eyes. "Then you have won," he said, "so take your revenge. Or sit there and wait. This wound will kill me just as well. God's head, why do you look like a statue watching for death? Which shall it be, yours first or mine? Where are my men? How have we come so far from them?"'

""One last lesson in horsemanship," I croaked in reply. "All hope lost, let your horse run with you, better that than fall for your enemies to hack to bits." The moon was half-full but I could see clearly the continuing stain down my horse's side, the spreading stain where Henry lay.'

"'"You always hated me," he was muttering. "Rot you, Raoul, you never once gave way to me. What made you hate me so? I never did you harm before. And she, she never gave way either, your wife. You tricked me to marry her or she tricked me, to make me look a fool."'

"'He whispered, suddenly afraid in the still and lonely air, "Do not let me die thus, a stuck pig, to bleed to death. As you are a huntsman, Raoul, let the kill be quick." Then, after a long pause, as if he swooned in between, "I thirst," as simple as a child.'

"'I had no belt. With sword and teeth, I wrestled a strap loose, cut it free, wrapped it round my upper thigh, pulled it tight, pulled out the axe. Sweet Virgin, that was not easy done. When I could see again, pain red-hot, golden-dark, consciousness returning in sickening sweeps, I tried to pry myself out of the saddle; how to do that a greater engineering feat than building up a castle wall, each move a year's duration worth. I did not know I had gnawed through my lip. My horse, that I have ridden since manhood, in tearing loose myself, I tore at him, no way to strap his wounds, at every breath, blood poured to the ground. But it was only when his legs buckled too that I could free myself. And down he went most gallantly, on my good side and his, so then I could drag myself off his back... God have mercy on both men and beast. I could have wept for him... Inch by inch then, like swimming in a current, one moment head up, the next drowned, head beneath, the ground firm, yet groundless, too, no feel to it, a sinking through.'

"'Henry was still conscious but barely so. I came up to him. "What of my wife?" I said.'

"'He panted out, "Come, Raoul, be generous. A clean kill. You always do the gracious thing, in the gracious way. I could never hope to match your style."'

"'"What of my wife?" I said.'

"'He gave a laugh, half laugh, half groan. "To the death then, you with but one leg, I with no arms, what shall we fight with, words?" I drew him up as best I could, loosened his mail, the rings had driven into his side, the wound gaped black. I tore off strips of his shirt and mine to plug it, made a pad under his ribcage. My sword had ripped his flesh, why did I try to put it back in place?'

"'After a long silence, he looked at me, his eyes dark in the moonlight. "You always were too generous, Raoul," he said. "Was that what you admired in King Stephen so much? He was no more faithful than I have been."'

"'He tried to grasp me with his one good hand, sense fading from him fast. "Come back to England, Raoul," he said. "I give it to you back, all of it. I beg you. Take your earldom and your wife. I have needed you, nothing goes as it should. Come back to her. Only you and she to outface me, yet that is all the harm you did. Yet I never did her harm I swear, nor she you. I lied, to catch you where you are vulnerable. I lied. She is both chaste and fair. And she loves you."'

"'When I could think or move, I crawled down the beach, brought water in his helmet back. Jesu, water never tasted so good, part for him, part for me. I took his head in my arms, waited until dawn. What else? I did not hate him, Henry, great king, only wished that he might be something else. I did not wish for death, only expected it . . . And a great calm, as if at last I was content.'"

But Raoul was still alive, barely so, he and the king, when Lord Ademar found them both and brought them both back to their men. Henry's guard carried him away, took him in a litter to Poitiers. He lived to fight and war again and seek revenge; he did not, could not, change. But never again crossed he swords with Raoul, never again broke faith with him. Raoul they took back to Toulouse, his life despaired of more than once. But he was strong, a body honed like steel, and Count Raymond had surgeons justly famed, the greatest in all of France, trained by men from the East. Another man would have bled to death, but he lived, although he walked lame on that side all his life. And when he could understand what was said to him, Lord Ademar told him what he had heard, of all that had been done at Poitiers that day, when the queen had betrayed me, and of the ambush Geoffrey made when I was on my way back to Cambray. Then, like a man lightened of a load, Raoul lay in Toulouse, in one of those pleasant inner courts with the flowering vines, and willed himself to live.

And I, Ann of Cambray, knowing all, knowing naught of this, in my little castle at the far end of the Norman world, time passed for me. And on a day in early autumn, what year, I forget the year, what matters in a world that time has forgot, I came up on the moors. It had been a wet and windy summer, but this day was fine as spring, and it drove me out-of-doors. Restless for some reason not clear to me, I had ridden out with my men and my sons, Robert on a little pony as I used to do, to jump over the rabbit holes. Hue and I had come mainly on foot; but I could not stop, went on again, farther than I meant.

The air was fresh and clear after so much rain; it seemed each leaf, each blade of grass was etched out fine; there was a sparkle to the world. Already the heather was turning blue and mauve, and little Hue's mouth was stained with whortleberries he had found among the furze. From time to time, when he shouted loud enough, his brother let him pat his pony, scarce bigger than a dog, with a long blonde tail. The child who once had ridden on his wolfhound with stockinged feet now beat like a man with his spurs and boots. The castle guard at Cambray watched his every move. Already they had made him his first wooden sword and shield, and he practiced with them every day. I did not try to stop him nor take the toys away—he was his father's son and I could not change his destiny either. And presently, as the afternoon wore on, I saw we had come high up on the moors. There was no mist today. Looking back down the path we had come, you could see the castle with its walls and keep, set at the cliff's edge, the thriving village in its shadow, and beyond it, the vast and open sea, shimmering in the heat. To north and west stretched the undulating hills, but where the mountains were, my Celtic homeland, there was a great rack of cloud. And in front of us, at the hill's crest, stood the circle of old gray stones. For one heart stopping moment, I thought I was a child again, and held Hue back, as the captain of the guard had held me.

The circle was clear today, the stones old and leaning together in the sun. Taking Hue by the hand, I passed inside. It was damp and cool within the shelter of those stones, and I walked from one to one until I had made the complete round, feeling their rough texture with my hand, noting the moss and lichen on the northern side, running my fingers as a mason would, over the marks where men had hammered them into shape and set them up, in this place where never man nor beast now entered in. *You will not come up here again*, she had said, but there was nothing to fear here, only old stones sunning themselves. I sat down and leaned back, and felt the warmth against my skin. A lark was singing somewhere, so far-off it was lost in the pale sky. I think I closed my eyes; I think, perhaps, I slept. And when I opened them, Hue was looking at me with a puzzled frown. He tried to tell me what he saw, shivering a little in the sun; I think he tried to say the word for man. And I sensed a presence there. I took him, and went to the circle's edge.

A score of paces down the hill, the guard were lazing along, laughing among themselves while Robert tried to jump a gorse bush. I could hear them whistling as they rode. I beckoned to Robert to come close, and when he did, put Hue before him on the saddle of the little horse, clasping the older brother's hands about the younger's waist. They rode together, laughing down the hill toward the men. I turned and looked across the open moors, eastward.

Far away, a horse and rider were coming over the purple hills, slowly at first, then, as I watched, moving effortlessly into a gallop. It was a knight, in mail coat and armed, his shield slung on his back and his sword hilt ready to hand. In one day I had lost all I loved and never thought to have it given back to me. Why did my heart beat so fast, why did the sky swim above my head, why did I feel the sun and yet be cold? The man looked up. I could not see his eyes, blue-gray like the sea, or his mocking smile, or the faint white scar across the high cheekbone, and the horse he rode was brown, not black, but the hair was silver-gold and blew in the wind. And I ran down the hill to him.

EPILOGUE

SO THAT WAS HOW THE EARL OF Sedgemont, Count Raoul of Sieux, came back to Cambray, begged to return by a king, peace made between them at last, faith kept by him who to all others was not a faithful man. Returned, the husband of the fair Ann, longed for by his lady wife. Down the hill she ran, they say, her skirts gathered up as a girl, her hair breaking free of its braids; they found her shoes kicked under the bracken fronds. He slowed to watch her come, and when she was by his side, they say, he leaned to push her long hair back.

"So, *ma mie*," he said, "I am here. Will you take me in? I swear never to leave you again; will you forgive me if I so swear? But I must have all of you, great heart, I cannot share the smallest part."

They say she never answered, but smiled at him.

"Jesu," he said, "and so my wedded wife runs to greet me in her bare feet. See how you have cut them on the thorns. Well, then, Ann of Cambray, shall I come home and have you keep me safe? Here then I make my peace with God and you." He leaned down and swept her before him on his horse, put his arms about her, rode down to Cambray, and entered in its gates. They say he left the great world behind, exchanged it for our small and simple one, found happiness at last, content forever and a day. So it is told, although happiness is as each man must find, and forever is too long for mortal men.

Thus then the story of their lives and loves, their joys, their griefs. Honor had they known and loyalty, treachery and dark revenge. Should not, free of them, they live out their lives, and should not they be happy in Cambray, that border castle that had cost them so much pain?

I, Urien the Scribe, write this, that it should be known. Praise God for life, praise God for the child of his homecoming, yet to be born, a blessing on her and on our Celtic race. But since it is given to no man to see ahead, nor should anyone seek God's place to judge the future what shall be done, not done, let it be enough to wish this: that as they hoped to live and prosper so may all men.

Ora pro nobis.

The Best Of
Warner Romances